A Stand-Up Guy

Also by Michael Snyder

My Name Is Russell Fink

Return Policy

A Stand-Up Guy

a novel

Michael Snyder

ZONDERVAN.com/
AUTHORTRACKER
follow your favorite authors

ZONDERVAN

A Stand-Up Guy

This title is also available as a Zondervan ebook. Visit www.zondervan.com/ebooks.

This title is also available in a Zondervan audio edition. Visit www.zondervan.fm.

Requests for information should be addressed to:

Zondervan, *Grand Rapids, Michigan 49530*

Library of Congress Cataloging-in-Publication Data

Snyder, Michael, 1965-
A stand-up guy : a novel / Michael Snyder.
p. cm.
ISBN 978-0-310-32193-4 (pbk.)
1. Comedians—Fiction. 2. Nashville (Tenn.)—Fiction. I. Title.
PS3619.N938S73 2011
813'.6—dc22 2010052130

Cover design: John Hamilton Design
Cover photography: iStockphoto®
Interior design: Matthew Van Zomeren

Printed in the United States of America

---

11 12 13 14 15 /DCI/ 22 21 20 19 18 17 16 15 14 13 12 11 10 9 8 7 6 5 4 3 2 1

If one tells the truth, one is sure,
sooner or later, to be found out.
Oscar Wilde

And ye shall know the truth,
and the truth shall make you free.
John 8:32

Oops ...
Unknown

Part One

Emcee / ʻem-ʼsē / also known as the opening act, host, master of ceremonies; typically the first person on stage during a show who will then introduce the following acts.

Chapter One

OLIVER MILES PACED BACKSTAGE, sporadically wetting his lips while trying not to wet his pants. He peered around the thick drapes, but all he could see was blackness where the crowd was supposed to be.

He closed his eyes, intent on mentally rehearsing a new bit about reality TV shows, but all he could think about was his mother, wishing she could be here to see him perform. Maybe then he'd know whether to thank her for the inspiration ... or blame her.

According to Delores Miles, her son was born funny. Her simple declaration had planted itself in the fertile soil of his nine-year-old brain then sprouted like Jack's proverbial beanstalk. And it was this weird alchemy of language and inspiration that transformed a needling boyhood curiosity into his lifelong obsession with making people laugh. So for more than a decade, Oliver honed his blossoming sense of humor into kind of a sixth sense, perfecting his mother's uncanny ability to "find the funny" in any situation, no matter how mundane, morbid, or even tragic. Creating laughter became Oliver's calling card, his shield, sword, and escape hatch. It was his alter ego, his imaginary friend, his security blanket. It was not, however, such a great way to make a living.

Oliver paged through his notebook a final time as if cramming for a test, then squinted into the blackness once more, trying in vain to make out the actual faces in the gloom. Finally his gaze drifted to the exact center of the stage where the spotlight had painted a lopsided moon, silhouetting a skinny microphone stand. The padded barstool, which now served as an oversized coaster for his sweating tumbler of ice water, remained in the shadows.

His mission was simple enough. Walk out onstage—no, scratch that—*command* the stage, and deliver a ten-minute set of stand-up comedy. This gig would neither make nor break his career. *That* particular gig was still more than two months away, provided he survived the audition.

Still, when the emcee's voice echoed in his head, panic struck him like a pebble in a pond, rippling outward in small, strutting waves until the rest of him shook as badly as his hands.

It was show time.

Oliver closed his eyes and mouthed the words of the emcee's scripted introduction. He never allowed himself to imagine wild ovations; that way he would never be disappointed. After wetting his now-chapped lips a final time, Oliver Miles strode out from the wings and across the familiar stage. The wooden planks creaked and groaned under his feet.

He snatched the microphone from the stand, fixed his gaze on some random spot in the crowd, and delivered his trademark opening.

"Let us pray," he said, bowing his head somberly. He paused for effect, popped one eye open for a quick, nervous scan of the crowd, then mumble-whispered a litany of heartfelt syllables that culminated in a breathless *Amen*.

"There," he said, as if something had actually been settled. "If you people don't have a good time tonight, it's not *my* fault."

Oliver ignored the abject lack of crowd response and forged ahead. Years of practicing in front of his bedroom mirror had taught him more than a few ways to cope with uninspiring feedback from uninspired crowds. He'd learned to simply invent laughter as needed, then have his brain insert it like a laugh track on a sitcom. After all, didn't he know his own material better than a roomful of strangers? Was he not the expert on his own jokes? For the most part, audiences merely confirmed what Oliver already knew.

This flimsy bit of self-deception almost always worked too. Like WD-40, it displaced his sagging confidence and greased the rusty hinges of his vocal cords. In fact, it was working tonight. He was a machine, setting up one joke, punching it just right, tagging it a time or two, then slipping in and out of segues like a runway model swapping outfits backstage.

Oliver used the glow of the spotlight to check his watch. He'd timed his set perfectly so far. Just two more jokes to go, then hit the closer, say goodnight, and go back to work.

But the laughter building inside his head ceased when the house lights came on, temporarily blinding the newly befuddled comedian midsentence and filling his head with deafening silence.

As his eyes recalibrated, so did his brain. The tables scattered around the ballroom were empty, just like they were twenty minutes ago when he'd set up the microphone stand, placed his water glass on the barstool, and killed the house lights in favor of the spot. Vacant chairs, all sporting the garish hotel insignia, were still piled high on dollies. And the spotlight, now rendered impotent, mocked Oliver and just made his eyes hurt.

His mystified gaze finally landed on the only other sign of life in the room, a shadowy female form in full Harrington Hotel regalia—a unisex ensemble of dark slacks, white dress shirt, and a maroon vest. Her brassy nametag glinted in the glow of the sparkling chandelier. She looked familiar, but in a distant, impersonal way. Like an extra in a really old movie or a headshot from his grandmother's yearbook.

Oliver clipped the microphone back on the stand, retrieved his notebook from the wings, and descended the steps with all the nonchalance he could muster. As he made his way across the ballroom, he glanced under tables and behind curtains or wherever else imaginary villains might be lurking. He stopped a few feet in front of the intruder and leaned casually on the back of a chair. They exchanged bewildered expressions as the silence loomed between them, vacuum packed, coiled like a spring.

"I was just, you know ..." Oliver's voice sounded shrill, lilting with unintended question marks. "... making my rounds. I am the security guard, after all."

"You're Oscar, right?"

"It's Oliver."

"Right," she said. "Sorry."

It was obviously Oliver's turn to speak. But every time he opened his mouth the sluicing roar of adrenaline made it impossible to focus on forming words. His addled brain peppered him with unanswerable questions: When had she come in? How much did she hear? What had she thought of his material? What must she think of *him*? Not to mention his idiotic uniform. The question he finally settled on was *So, how may I help you?* But it came out like: "So, what are you doing here anyway?"

"Working," she said. "Same as you."

"Oh." Oliver braced himself for the undertow of sarcasm in her tone. But there was no subtext, no irony, no ridicule or disappointment or threat of sanction. As far as he could tell she was wholly earnest.

"We met at my orientation last week."

"Right," he said as a vague memory of a quick introduction a few days ago began to emerge. All he could recall was that she had a little boy's name, a little girl's haircut, and a seeming inability to break eye contact. But that version of this girl had been a throwback to another era, something mid-sixties, pre-hippie, a mash-up of chiffon and velvet and patent leather. All that remained now was her lazy bouffant flip.

Oliver tried not to be too obvious as he allowed his gaze to migrate to her nametag. That's when it finally dawned on him that he was staring at the hotel's new night auditor, the only other person he would see or talk to for the countless hours that comprised the graveyard shift.

He was mid-squint when she said, "It's Matilda. They misspelled it on my nametag."

"Right, nice to see you again, Matilda. I thought—"

"Please," she said, "call me Mattie."

"Got it. But I thought you didn't start till next week, Mattie."

"That was the plan," she said. "But I think the last girl eloped or something. So Mr. Sherman called and asked if I could start a little early."

So much for having the hotel to himself for an entire week.

"Anyhow," she continued. "I had to work late at my other job. So I told Mr. Sherman I'd be a little tardy tonight. Turns out, it was later than I thought."

"It'll be our little secret," he said, shocked at how creepy it sounded and wishing he could take it back.

"Are you okay?"

"Sure," he said, although her unrelenting eye contact was making him a bit dizzy. "Why do you ask?"

"Because ever since I flipped the lights on, you look like you swallowed a curling iron."

"How does that look exactly?"

"Bug-eyed, sweaty, short of breath, and blushing in too many places at once."

Oliver chuckled. Her obvious attempt at humor sanded the edge off his humiliation. But she never smiled back. She simply stared. And blinked.

"Anyhow," she continued, "I'm just glad I finally found you."

Finally? he thought, then said, "You are?"

"Yeah, you got a phone message."

"I did?"

"I think her name was Lindsey. Said she'd call back later."

In the three years Oliver had worked security for the Harrington Hotel, he'd never once received a phone message. And as far as he knew he'd never met a Lindsey before. He was about to indulge a few morbid thoughts about his mother when Mattie spoke up again.

"And I'm pretty sure we were just robbed."

Chapter Two

INVESTIGATING ALLEGED CRIME SCENES was not Oliver's forte. Unfortunately, talking to drunk people in the middle of the night was. So he was feeling at least partially qualified when he knocked on the door.

While he waited, he reviewed Mattie's version of the events so far. She had parked her car, punched her time clock, and fielded the phone call from someone named Lindsey Whitaker, whoever that was. Then before Mattie could plug in her own personal adding machine, the phone rang again. It was the Johnsons from Room 218. According to Mattie, Mister Johnson sounded cryptic and vague, maybe even a little sleepy. Apparently his wife could be heard shouting details in the background.

Mattie had suspected they were both high on something. Now, after only a few minutes with the Johnsons, Oliver suspected she was right.

Their story unfolded in a series of inebriated corroborations. The husband handled the bulk of the narrative while his wife added unnecessary punctuation. She managed to correct, cajole, and threaten without adding a single helpful detail. They allegedly left the hotel around noon to attend an afternoon wedding followed by what was described as a drunk and disorderly reception. They returned a little after one a.m., noticed some "valuables" were missing, and eventually called the front desk.

"What exactly is missing?" Oliver asked.

Mr. Johnson started to speak but was interrupted by a series of obnoxious throat clearings. They shared an unreadable expression, then he said, "Um, just some cash."

"How much?" Oliver asked, pen poised over a spiral notepad.

The Johnsons exchanged another round of pointed glances. Their dilated pupils made them look constantly surprised to see each other.

"A lot," the husband finally said. He scratched at a scab on his forearm.

"Could you be a little more specific?"

"We'd rather not," Mr. Johnson said.

"Speak for yourself," said his wife, absently fingering the patch of fiery acne on her chin.

Oliver pretended to make another note, then pretended not to watch their soundless altercation: fists balled, fingers pointed, jaws clenched, but no actual words exchanged, reducing the couple to a pair of belligerent mimes in a silent film. The subtitles were not that hard to imagine …

Mrs. Johnson: *Don't just stand there.* Tell *him.*

Mr. Johnson: *Are you nuts? How are we supposed to explain that kind of cash missing?*

Mrs. Johnson*: Don't be such a wuss. Either you tell him or I will.*

Mr. Johnson*: Yeah? Over my dead body …*

(Mrs. Johnson cuts her eyes suspiciously to the security guard.)

Mrs. Johnson: *Or maybe his.*

When Oliver cleared his throat, it had the same effect as a referee's whistle. The couple turned their glares on him, both breathing hard. When he asked if there was anything else missing, Mrs. Johnson said, "Not yet."

Oliver watched the unhappy couple glare at each other some more, waiting for one of them to expound upon her cryptic answer. Instead, she wheeled around and locked herself in the bathroom.

"So, what's next?" the husband said, attempting a weak smile, one meant to convey apology or embarrassment or both.

"I'll file my report with the hotel. Then I'm sure the police will show up and want to fill out one of their own."

Mr. Johnson then announced, loud enough for his wife to hear through the closed door, that, on second thought, they were actually too tired to deal with the *police* at three a.m. He added, "Right, honey?" To which she suggested he go to that fiery place filled with demons and pitchforks and politicians.

Oliver's interrogation ended with a final halfhearted threat from Mr. Johnson about pressing charges and making the hotel pay—but only *after* they got some sleep. That left a few short hours for Oliver to fill out his report and dread telling his boss about the alleged burglary.

But that too would have to wait. The front-desk manager arrived at 6:30 a.m. and promptly informed Oliver that Mr. Sherman had been called to Memphis for an emergency meeting with Claude Sherman (Mr. Sherman's father, aka the owner of the Harrington) and the Shermanettes (Gladys, Montel, Morty, and the rest of the Sherman family) and wouldn't be back on property until Monday. Oliver found some solace in this news, but not much. As much as he hated delivering bad news, he still preferred getting it over with. The only consolation was that it afforded him a couple of days to coordinate stories with Mattie.

He intercepted her just as she was coming out of the ladies' room. She looked bleary-eyed and exhausted, just like he felt.

"Hey, Mattie. Got a second?"

"Actually, I'm supposed to meet the controller in a few minutes to review my first audit."

"Okay, I'll be quick. I just wanted to compare notes one more time, while everything's fresh in our memories. You know, before we talk to Mr. Sherman."

"You make it sound like we have something to hide."

"Oh, no. Nothing like that. It's just that Mr. Sherman likes details." Oliver held up his notebook as some kind of tangible proof. "*Lots* of details."

She stared at him again, a human polygraph machine. "Didn't we already have this conversation?"

Oliver wished now that he'd brought the official incident report he'd typed up. That way he could stare at it thoughtfully instead of avoiding the penetrating eyes of Mattie Holmgren.

"Sorry," he said. "You don't know Sherman."

Mattie's gaze ricocheted from her watch to the hallway leading to the executive offices and then back to Oliver. "Alright, let's see. I clocked in, got the call where the guy basically just repeated whatever his wife was yelling at him in the background. I hung up, went looking for you, and eventually found you in the ballroom. That's pretty much the end of it."

"So that's all you can remember? No other details or peculiarities worth mentioning? Nothing else you saw or heard that Mr. Sherman needs to know about?"

"Look, I really don't know what else to tell you, Oliver."

He knew he should leave well enough alone. But Oliver was suddenly consumed with the desire to explain himself—that he wasn't just some hack or wannabe comedian indulging pathetic fantasies, that he'd been working out new material for a big audition he'd been hearing rumors about, that he routinely performed actual stand-up comedy in actual comedy clubs, that sometimes he even got paid for it (if by payment, you could include chicken wings, fries, and all-you-can-drink coffee), that he wasn't just goofing off or shirking his responsibilities, that he was actually working on his *real* career. But he'd already asked her the same series of questions and she'd never once mentioned anything about the ballroom, the quality of his jokes, or his stupid uniform. Chances are, she didn't notice. Or didn't care.

Still, before his brain could convince his mouth to shut up, he said, "Well, it's just, you never really said where you were before you found me. You know, between the time you clocked in and when you took the call."

"Well, I didn't stop by Room 218, if that's what you're getting at."

"No, Mattie. That's not what I meant, not at all. I was just trying to—"

Actually, he was trying to apologize, but it wouldn't come out right. He could feel the regret thrumming inside him; he just couldn't seem to form it into a coherent sentence.

"Sorry," Mattie said. Oliver followed her gaze to the grim-faced controller. "I have to go."

But she didn't sound sorry; she sounded accused.

. . .

When his shift was over, Oliver stopped by the hotel's "Business Center" (an elaborate cubbyhole with a Formica table, a chintzy computer, and even chintzier printer) to check his email. Of the dozen or so new subject lines, Oliver only saw one: "Downers audition, invitation only." He was amazed how the opportunity to fulfill a lifelong dream could be reduced to a four-word sentence fragment. Still, exhilaration sparked inside him like a lit fuse, and Oliver had to make himself wait for the printer to finish before he dared read the actual email. Afterward he folded it neatly and slid it into the breast pocket of his uniform, trying to ignore the sensation of his stuttering heart through the thin layer of polyester.

He was so preoccupied that he made it all the way up to his car, down the winding ramp, and finally to the mouth of the parking garage before he realized he was still in uniform. He flicked his blinker in the other direction, U-turned back into the gloom of the garage, and reparked his car. Head down, he jogged back through the side entrance and locked the security closet door behind him. His Adidas gym bag was right where he'd left it. Minutes later he emerged again, this time in blue jeans and a T-shirt, his uniform folded neatly into a duffel bag. He supposed it was possible that he may someday get "caught dead" in his security guard costume. But he vowed never to get caught wearing it in public.

Too wired to sleep, Oliver decided to go see his mother.

Chapter Three

THE GROUNDS OF SHADY GROVE were neither shady nor grove-like. The building was bordered by parking spaces on three sides with a fenced-in backyard featuring a pathway that meandered around a smattering of park benches and scrawny shrubs. All the shade-producing wildlife (mostly fake plastic) was in the lobby, a room that never failed to evoke the sensation that Oliver had stepped out of a parking lot and onto the set of a TV preacher. The fireplace never went out, the books lining the shelves remained unread, and the steady trickle of the cascading fountain always made Oliver's bladder cramp.

He signed the faux-leather guest book and rested his elbows on the counter, a thick slab of some expensive wood. He then waited for Betsy to finish her phone call while avoiding eye contact with the muscular security guard strategically positioned between the receptionist's desk and the state-of-the-art security door that led to the patient rooms. Shady Grove always employed imposing specimens with big scary muscles and all the more modern gizmos that Oliver lacked—glittering handcuffs, billy clubs, tasers, mace, and boots fashioned out of bulldozer tires. This all seemed like overkill to Oliver, especially in light of the condition of most tenants. The security detail seemed like everything else in the lobby, overblown for effect.

As he listened to Betsy wind down her phone call, Oliver wondered again if he'd ever work up the nerve to ask her out, but knew he never would. She ended the call and grinned up at him. "If I'm not mistaken, I believe your mom is up on three."

"Healing bodies?" he said. "Or saving souls?"

"In her case, I'm not sure there's a lot of difference."

Oliver found his mother in Room 321, squinting at a thermometer and lecturing Mrs. Tompkins, ironically enough, about taking her vitamins. Mrs. Tompkins didn't respond. She never responded. She was mostly blind, completely deaf, and borderline catatonic.

"Mom?" Oliver said. "Does Dr. Strahan know you're up here?"

Delores Miles plucked the yellow plastic thermometer from her patient's gaping mouth, wrinkled her brow at the readout—a frowny "sick face"—then wiped it with the tail of her T-shirt before tucking it into her green Fisher-Price tote bag. Ever the consummate professional, she acknowledged his question only after she'd secured the Velcro tabs on a blood pressure cuff and started pumping. She had to supply her own sound effects.

"Why of course the doctor knows where your mother is." Delores motioned with her chin toward the old woman tucked neatly into bed. Her voice was airy, compassionate, the best kind of patronizing, the tone of a stranger comforting a lost toddler in a grocery aisle. It had the opposite effect on Oliver. "She's been right here for the better part of a decade."

He didn't feel like arguing. So he watched his mother work, her lips making a silent count of Mrs. Tompkins's pulse. Satisfied that her patient would live through lunch, Delores compressed the plastic ball again and held it. She made a hissing sound to replicate the release of pressure, then peeled away the armband and placed the apparatus neatly into her tote bag alongside the bright blue stethoscope, a thick yellow otoscope, and a bulky toy syringe.

"Mom? I think we need to get you back downstairs."

"That's a splendid idea." Dr. Strahan had somehow materialized out of the ether. He treated Oliver's shoulder to a paternal squeeze as he eased into the room. Both men watched patiently as Delores Miles recorded her patient's vital signs on a clipboard. After pretending to consider her work, the doctor guided her by the arm to where Oliver was standing and said, "Delores, your son is here to see you."

Oliver watched his mother turn and appraise him. And for one sliver of one second, her addled brain flirted with recognition. Her shoulders dipped, her head tilted, and the corners of her thin lips lifted. And in that one fleeting instant, although he knew better, Oliver allowed himself to hope. But then it was gone, and the woman he loved more than any other extended her hand in greeting.

"Good morning," she said in her sweetest phone voice. "My name is Delores Miles and it's a pleasure to meet you."

Oliver hesitated, then took her hand in his. It was too cold and impossibly thin. Nothing like the hand that checked his brow for fevers or tucked love notes into his Spiderman lunchbox or held his chubby little hand on countless walks to countless new schools.

"I'm Oliver."

"So you must be the new physical therapist we've heard all those rumors about?"

Oliver looked past his mother. The real doctor stood at the foot of Mrs. Tompkins's bed, smiling at the last few entries from her chart when his gaze rose to meet Oliver's. Strahan's shrug was helpless, sympathetic, a silent reminder that they were doing all they could, that Oliver just needed to be patient and maybe one day soon his mother would snap out of it and recognize her only begotten son.

Oliver extended his arm and she took it. Although he craved his mother's lost affection, he couldn't shake the feeling that, at least in her mind, she was flirting with the nursing home's new physical therapist, who just so happened to share the same name as the son she didn't realize she had. He escorted her to the elevator, trying to convince himself that misguided affection was better than none at all.

• • •

As a kid, Oliver was fascinated with the philosophical dilemma: If a tree falls in the forest and no one is around to hear it, does it actually make a sound?

He pondered this as he drifted off to sleep at night, while daydreaming in class, and on those odd Sundays when his mom dragged him to church. The mystery eventually solved itself, quite by accident. Or maybe it was divine providence? Someone somewhere had said that coincidence was merely God's way of remaining anonymous.

Oliver received a handheld tape recorder for his eleventh birthday. At first he went around taping everything—TV commercials, conversations between strangers, and whatever random thoughts he dared speak into the built-in microphone. Eventually, he began recording himself mimicking routines, verbatim, from his favorite stand-up comedy albums. Of course there were no laughing crowds, and he replaced all the nasty words with their G-rated cousins.

Being a chronically shy kid, Oliver made these recordings in an abandoned tree fort he'd discovered the previous summer on the outskirts of his neighborhood. One April afternoon, as he was perfecting a Steve Martin bit that compared smoking to flatulence, a pleasant breeze escalated into a violent wind. Nashville may not be Kansas, but she did have to endure the occasional tornado. Somewhere in the middle of scrambling down out of the tree fort and sprinting home, he dropped the recorder. Even more than losing his prized birthday gift, Oliver was mortified at the thought of some neighborhood kid finding it, recognizing his voice on the tape, and playing it for the entire fifth grade.

It took hours of pleading to talk his mom into finding a flashlight and helping him search the woods. Amazingly, they found the blocky plastic machine facedown and unharmed, sheltered under the massive trunk of a felled oak tree. Oliver snuck the flashlight and the recorder under his covers that night. After replacing the soggy batteries, he was more than a little dismayed to learn that his Steve Martin routine was gone, erased forever. But what he did hear was the wind whipping itself into a frenzy, a series of splintering creaks, then a violent cracking sound, followed by the impossibly long, impossibly loud whoosh of thousands of wet leaves thrashing against thousands of others as they attacked the ground.

Mystery solved.

That first playback was nothing short of thrilling ... and a little disappointing too. Because that's when he realized that the point of all his philosophical pondering was not discovering the actual solution. That part proved anticlimactic. No, the point was to wrestle with the question. There had been dozens of others through the years, but none more nagging or unanswerable than this: If a son is born to a mother who no longer recognizes him, does that then make him an orphan?

. . .

As he led his mother back to her room, Oliver had to ignore urge after urge to brag about the Downers audition email burning a hole in his back pocket. Whether she could help it or not, Delores Miles didn't really seem to care much about his stand-up career. Which always made Oliver feel like he cared too much.

Once inside, he noticed the dusty outlines on the bookshelf that marked the exact locations where Oliver persisted in setting up framed photos of the younger, happier versions of his mother and himself, and that she then methodically took back down again and hid facedown in a drawer.

The tape recorder was right where he'd left it.

It seemed that although she could no longer bear to look at her only son, she couldn't seem to get enough of his preadolescent voice.

She climbed dutifully onto her bed and pulled the covers up over her knees. When Delores was up and roaming the halls, she moved with the clinical precision of an accredited medical professional. When she wasn't nursing patients she was preaching at them. Delores had been unabashed about proselytizing in line at the grocery store, during parent/teacher meetings at school, and *apparently* upon waking up with men she was not married to. After the move from prison to Shady Grove, Delores limited her revival tactics to impromptu sermons in the TV room and baptizing patients against their will. But once ensconced in her own room, she reverted seamlessly back into the role of patient. Her real biography, however, remained complicated and unreliable, a moving target with no discernable bull's-eye.

She said, "Would you mind storing my medical bag there on the shelf?"

Oliver took the colorful doctor kit and placed it alongside the row of first-edition John Irving novels he'd given her two Christmases ago. He'd learned to cope with the fact that he'd paid a few thousand dollars more than what the volumes were actually worth, but not with the sad realization that she'd taken the personalized inscriptions to heart (delusions of grandeur was just one of her many symptoms) and dreamed up an imaginary love affair with the master storyteller from New England.

Oliver sat in his mother's old recliner and watched her stare at the ceiling. He remained grateful that Shady Grove allowed the more ambulatory patients to furnish their rooms with relics from their past. The theory was that it made the residents feel more secure. It calmed them. In his mother's case, the hope was that it might trigger some contagious memory. Oliver had crammed her room full of familiar furniture and knickknacks, but they had no noticeable effect on her. He tried not to let it hurt his feelings.

His mother began to show symptoms during his junior year in high school, even when she was sober. It started in her eyes. They would track along, smooth and normal, then just stop and shake erratically, sometimes refusing to move at all. Other times one pupil would dilate while the other remained tiny and unfocused. A friend from school said it made her look like a cartoon character after a blow to the head. Oliver stopped bringing friends home after that.

When Delores Miles was officially diagnosed eight years ago, Oliver was more relieved than dismayed. His mom was finally going to get the help she needed. Or so he thought.

Wernicke-Korsakoff sounded more like a European law firm than a mere vitamin deficiency. The doctors eventually crammed Oliver's brain with one technical explanation after another about his mother's disease. But it really boiled down to the fact that she refused to eat and never stopped drinking. It was no secret that Delores Miles was an alcoholic. But by the time her particular condition had a name, it was too late to do anything about it. She persisted in trading food for alcohol, starving her body and eventually her brain. In an attempt to simplify the diagnosis, her primary physician kept insisting the alcohol had depleted her supply of "essential vitamins and nutrients," making it sound like the remedy could be found in a box of Pop-Tarts or breakfast cereal.

"So far," Dr. Strahan had said, "there is no cure, only coping."

"And how do we do that?"

"Treat her normally, or as normally as she will allow. Talk to her like she's your mother, no matter how she talks to you. Tell her stories from her past, help her retain her dignity, and if you're a religious man, pray."

So Oliver coped and talked and prayed. Or at least he tried.

She cleared her throat, a deliberately awkward gesture to bring her visitor back to reality, or at least her version of it. The crook of Oliver's arm was still warm from her touch. It radiated a fading intimacy that made him want to crawl into her bed and snuggle up to her like he did when he was ten. But the one time he actually attempted it, she'd hit the Nurse Call button and tried to get him arrested. Instead, he swiveled her old recliner around and rested his feet on the lowest rung of her bed rail.

When she met his gaze again, she looked self-conscious and even a little frightened. "I'm sorry," she said. "Tell me your name again?"

"Oliver. Oliver Miles."

Chapter Four

HE WAS GOING TO HAVE TO DO SOMETHING about that refrigerator. The hulking Kenmore that came with the house suffered from a mechanical form of croup. It would cough and splutter through its various cycles for a few days and then get better, sometimes with Oliver's help, most times not. Under the cyber-tutelage of Google, he had learned a few troubleshooting skills. Things like defrosting the freezer section, cleaning the condenser coils, oiling the compressor, and replacing faulty door gaskets—most of which were way easier than they sounded. It seemed now though that the coughing had turned chronic, tubercular, inoperable. Oliver would either have to replace it or learn to live without it. Or maybe there was another one buried under all the junk in the garage.

Obviously, his ailing refrigerator wasn't his only problem. It wasn't even the biggest. It was just the one that had elbowed its way to the front of his brain and gave him something to worry about as he stirred his soup. Others included the recent robbery at the Harrington, Sherman's reaction to said robbery, and Oliver's unintentionally accusing Mattie Holmgren of committing it.

But he did his best to ignore those things, focusing instead on things he could control—a warm meal, a hot shower, seven uninterrupted hours of sleep, and finding an open-mic night he could hit on his way to work. If he wanted to survive the Downers audition, he would need to hone his material. Although there were only a handful of actual comedy clubs in Nashville, it seemed open-mic nights had sprouted up all over town in restaurants, bars, hotels, and coffee shops.

Oliver turned the burner off and brought the entire pot to the table. He placed it on a potholder on the table next to a half-sleeve of crackers and a chilly jug of apple juice. He paged through his spiral notebook until he found the folded printout of the audition email and flattened it out on the table. The message began with an entire line of capital S's and H's and exclamation points, imploring its readers to keep quiet about what followed, basically this: that on Saturday, June 19, 2010, the owners of Jesters Comedy Club would be holding tryouts for an upcoming benefit concert for the legendary Roscoe Downs. The auditions were by invitation only and slots would be limited, since the promoter expected "numerous national acts" to commit in the coming weeks. The email ended with a telephone number and instructions for the invitees to call for an audition time.

Oliver wanted this gig more than was probably healthy. And he had exactly ten weeks to prepare for it, or more accurately, to obsess over it.

The simple truth was that while most comics dreamed of landing a spot on *The Tonight Show*, Oliver's overriding ambition was to finally finish one decent set of stand-up comedy at Downers. He could worry about Leno and Letterman later.

After crumbling a fistful of Saltines into the thick tomato broth, Oliver ferried a spoonful to his mouth and burnt the tip of his tongue. He tipped the bottle of apple juice back to cool his tongue and noticed movement on the other side of the opaque pane in his front door. A second later he heard a knock. Two seconds after that the door swung open.

"Knock-knock. Anybody home?"

Joey reminded Oliver of a furry snowman — a round head perched atop an equally round middle, long reddish nose, and dark eyes that did indeed appear buttonlike behind thick eyeglasses. Only his stubby legs threatened the illusion, but not much. His body seemed to compensate for the lack of hair on his head by sprouting billowy tufts of prematurely gray hair from his ears, nose, forearms, and neck. He waddled to where Oliver was sitting and thrust out a beefy paw.

"My name's Joey."

He greeted everyone this way, no matter how many times they'd actually met. Which, in Oliver's case, was about twice a week. Joey was his mother's handyman. She'd apparently hired him after she moved into this house. Joey took care of leaky faucets, cleared out gutters, mowed the lawn, sprayed for bugs, and did a variety of other chores. Whenever Oliver attempted to butt in and fix things, Joey got his feelings hurt.

Not that hurting Joey's feelings was hard to do. He was a little boy in a big man's body, mentally challenged and physically imposing. So Joey fixed things and Oliver paid him out of his mother's checkbook. There would likely come a day when the account ran dry and Oliver would have to turn Joey away. But he would worry about that when the time came.

"You got any jobs for me?" Joey said, smoothing his T-shirt over his belly.

"Not at the moment." This felt like a lie. The refrigerator obviously needed attention. But Oliver craved privacy right now more than cold food.

"Looks like you do got a message though."

Oliver followed Joey's gaze to the indicator on his mother's old-fashioned answering machine that was winking at him. He had a love/hate relationship with the clunky device. He loved that his mother's voice was captured on the tiny cassette tape, accessible at the push of a button. He hated everything else about it though, a conditioned response to its potential for bad news. So he kept it out of sight, tucked between the toaster oven and breadbox.

"Thanks," Oliver said.

"Aren't you gonna thisten to lem?"

"I'll get to it eventually."

"I won't mind if you do."

Joey wasn't that hard to follow if you had the patience to actually listen. It was mostly a matter of juxtaposing consonants and confusing his verbs. But Oliver wasn't feeling particularly patient this morning. And he didn't want to hurt Joey's feelings. The big man stared blankly at the floor and finally said, "I sure miss your mom, Oliver."

"She's not dead, you know."

"She's kinda dead in the head though." Joey's grin was wet and rubbery. "I know all about dead in the head."

"You should go see her," Oliver said.

Joey looked horrified. He began rocking in place and finally said, "Mind if I root around in the garage?"

"Help yourself, Joey."

For some reason Joey loved to forage through the piles of junk in the garage. According to Oliver's mother, most of the stuff was there when she moved in and she just never got around to moving it out. To Joey's muddled brain, the garage was a sanctuary. He seemed to revere rummaging through things, sorting them into piles, then coming back and resorting them again. More than once Oliver suspected that Joey was pilfering stuff. But he couldn't make himself care that much. He'd sifted through it all himself in search of clues about the house and how his mother came to live there, apparently rent-free. But there was nothing personal—no old phone bills or receipts or photo albums. The only things of any real value or interest to Oliver were his mother's boxes of vintage clothing, a few old-fashioned mannequins, and a trunk full of camping gear (although he knew he'd never use it). Regardless, there were much worse hobbies Joey could indulge in than some harmless petty thieving. Maybe it was therapeutic. Either way, it got him out of the house.

"Guess I'll run along then," Joey said. On his way to the garage he turned and said, "You really ought to unpack and stay a while."

This was Joey's favorite joke in the world. And although Oliver understood its intrinsic humorous value—the truth is funny, after all—he was not amused.

. . .

The first message was from Simon Childress, the emcee and organizer of Rank Amateurs, a weekly open-mic night held at various Holiday Inns. Apparently, he had "come down with the flu," which was Simon's standing excuse for bailing out on his responsibilities. This meant he was either nursing a nasty hangover or that his overbearing flight attendant girlfriend was in town, demanding they do something "special." Apparently every minute they spent together had to be special. Simon worked up a killer routine about their ability to turn codependency into an art form. But he was too chicken to perform it onstage.

The good news for Oliver was that he could host tonight, which entitled him to at least thirty minutes of stage time, albeit in small increments. Even better, a guaranteed spot meant he wouldn't have to endure the first-come-first-served sign-up sheets with the rest of the wannabes. It didn't hurt that he'd be sandwiched between several hacks and first-timers, always a nice boost for any middling comedian's esteem. The best news of all was that this would afford him an extra hour of sleep.

He jotted a reminder to call Simon onto a blank page of his notebook and jammed an entire cracker into his mouth. Oliver always ate his crackers whole to prevent Saltine shrapnel.

The second message began with a one-and-a-half-second delay of bustling office chatter, followed closely by the cheery stench of a telemarketer. He aimed his finger at the delete button and was just about to press it when a female voice said, "Hey, Oliver … or at least I hope this is Oliver. Anyway, not sure if you got the message I left you at the hotel the other night, but my name is Lindsey Whittaker, a reporter with *City Rhythm* … if you call me back I'll buy lunch …"

Instead of deleting the message, he turned the volume up. It seemed Lindsey wanted to talk to him about a story she was working on. He transcribed her number down next to Simon's, then listened to the entire message again to make sure he got the number right, then a third time just because he liked the way she said his name.

If a reporter from *City Rhythm* was calling, then she was obviously doing a follow-up article on the local stand-up comics. There'd been quite a bit of grousing among the real locals that the original cover story focused on a trio of comedians that had either moved on from Nashville to New York or LA, or had never really put down any roots in Nashville in the first place. The subtext was that any comic with any amount of talent had the good sense to move on to greener comedic pastures. It made the locals seem like unmotivated hacks by comparison. If the paper wanted to make good on their original story, Oliver would be all too happy to oblige. With the Downers audition looming, the publicity couldn't hurt.

He could feel the dopey grin on his face but seemed unable to stop it. Hearing his name was one thing, but seeing it in print had to be better.

But the first syllable of the third message flatlined his grin. Every syllable after that chipped away at his earlier aspirations of seven uninterrupted hours of blissful slumber.

It was Mr. Sherman, the general manager of the historic Harrington Hotel and signer of Oliver's paychecks.

"Good morning, Oliver. I hope I didn't wake you. I just needed to make you aware of an emergency staff meeting at four o'clock this afternoon. It's obviously mandatory. And your punctuality is appreciated."

The word "emergency" didn't sound good. Nor did the sound of Sherman's voice. Apparently he was back in town and ready to sniff out details about the robbery of Room 218.

Oliver ignored all things Harrington, dialed Lindsey's number, and left her a message.

Next he called the number listed on the Downers email. A squeaky-voiced man answered, "Harry McNabb's office."

"Yeah, I'm calling about the Downers audition. It says on the notice to call for an appoint— "

"Name?"

"Oliver," he said, a little too proudly. "Oliver Miles."

He listened to the sound of heavy breathing until he realized it was his own. Oliver was already nervous. And this was just the phone call to set up the audition for the gig that he may or may not even get. He covered the mouthpiece and took a long, calming breath, and waited.

"Sorry, no Miles."

"Excuse me?"

"No Oliver Miles on the list. No Miles Oliver either."

"Could you check it again?"

"I just did."

"But there must be some kind of mistake," Oliver said.

"Apparently."

"But I have the email. It says 'by invitation only.' And it clearly has my name on it."

"Maybe *that* was the mistake."

Oliver resisted several urges at once, then finally said, "Could I speak to Mr. McNabb then?"

"Nope," the man said. "But you can speak to his voice mail."

Oliver's heavy breathing returned as he listened to the outgoing message on Harry's voice mail. By the time the machine beeped, Oliver's voice was as squeaky as Harry's unhelpful assistant. He stumbled and stuttered and whined and eventually left his own phone number. Then he vowed not to think about it until he heard back from Harry.

Instead, he consulted the digital clock on the stove. A four o'clock meeting would split his sleeping time in half. This meant he would have to scarf his soup and try to force himself to sleep in a hurry. Since he wasn't that sleepy yet, he would lie there and obsess over not falling asleep fast enough, which would make him more anxious and even less sleepy. After much pillow fluffing and body repositioning, his brain would finally give in to slumber, but only until the UPS truck roared by his window or one of the neighborhood dogs decided to chat up a squirrel. Still clinging to those last tendrils of grogginess, Oliver would then will his body and brain to *not* wake all the way up. And it would almost work. But inevitably, one eyelid would betray him with a glance at the alarm clock.

He was tempted to raid his mother's medicine cabinet for sleeping pills. But his body had virtually no tolerance for barbiturates of any kind. The last time he chugged a legitimate dose of Nyquil, he woke up thirty-six hours later in the emergency room.

On the way to the shower he stopped in his mother's room. Little had changed since the fateful day the ambulance carted her to the ER. No one ever mentioned overdose. And Oliver was convinced she hadn't done it on purpose. But the combination of his mother's weakened physical state, her declining mental faculties, and the fact that she'd chased a handful of sleeping pills with several snifters of gin convinced her team of doctors that she would need constant care. Back when he still believed his mother would get better and come home, Oliver splurged on a new queen-size mattress. It was his way of helping her get a clean start. Now it just sat there, shrouded in its plastic wrapper, looking as ridiculous as Oliver felt about buying it.

As he moved from room to room he couldn't help noticing the house had lost his mother's scent, but not her personality. Every time they moved, she would throw herself into the task of appliquéing her personality on every wall of every room of whatever they were renting at the time. She ate more, drank very little, and fantasized about being featured on one of those home improvement shows where the voiceover would praise her originality and style as "playfully chic." Then she would inevitably mime filming Oliver's room, pitching her voice lower and saying, "The décor here is a bit more stoic, angular and minimalist. Kind of a serial killer meets boy-next-door motif—a very *boring* boy, I might add." And it was true; he gave up ever trying to hang a poster or pennant or personalize his room in any way. Because every time he got settled in his new room, they moved again. At some point he stopped unpacking his clothes.

Oliver emptied his duffel bag directly into the washer and punched all the right buttons. Back in his old room he dropped his keys, watch, and wallet on the laminated surface of his empty dresser, wincing again at the chunky hollow sound. Then he rummaged through an open suitcase at the foot of his bed for clean underwear and socks. He shaved, showered, brushed, and dressed in jeans and a T-shirt. In the living room, he put a James Taylor record on his mother's turntable and tried to sleep.

It wasn't working.

Oliver gave up hope long ago that his body would ever get used to working third shift. Naps helped, but God's best recipe for human existence included waking with the sun and sleeping with the moon.

He must have nodded off a few times. Because he startled himself awake more times than he could count, then had to repeat the entire process. His last waking thought was, *This isn't working. Might as well get up and work on some new material.*

Oliver might have dreamed of missing his staff meeting, of performing stand-up on TV in his underwear, or of getting chased by a gorilla trying to force-feed him yogurt. He couldn't be sure.

Because by the time he woke up, he was already late for the staff meeting.

Chapter Five

By the time Oliver arrived, the staff had assembled itself into a crude semicircle in the hotel ballroom, what he now considered the scene of his most recent crime. Managers and supervisors congregated on Sherman's left while the bellman, valets, and chambermaids fanned out in loose clusters around unclothed banquet tables. This organic segregation between the haves and the have-nots, between salaried-with-benefits and wage earners, was the hospitality equivalent of the caste system.

Mr. Sherman did not discriminate however. He faced his staff, not so much berating as sermonizing, careful to make deliberate eye contact and temper his voice with the proper balance of authority and sincerity.

Oliver eased the door closed behind him, but was betrayed by the metallic clank of the latch snapping into the strike plate. Sherman paused midsentence, then glared at Oliver over the rims of his bifocals. The only thing Sherman hated more than negative publicity was tardiness. A quick scan of the room did provide a small measure of consolation, however. Barry Sherman—Mr. Sherman's nephew, part-time front-desk clerk, and eventual heir to the Harrington Hotel empire—was nowhere in sight. Oliver may have been late, but at least he'd made an appearance.

The staff exchanged conspiratorial glances as he made his way down front to one of the two empty seats in the room.

"Mr. Miles," Sherman said. "So good of you to join us. We were just discussing the, um ..." He coughed, as if it actually pained him to dislodge the next word. "... *incident* that occurred in my absence."

He seemed more offended than angry, as if his own privacy had been violated. Sherman had begun his career in the hospitality industry when he was eleven, toiling away in the laundry room of his grandfather's Memphis hotel. Years of ladder climbing had taught him that appearances trumped all else. He was not in the business of acquiring customers, but of serving guests. Anyone could furnish crisp linens, hot meals, and miniature bottles of conditioner. Sherman provided an experience, an escape. And part of the façade was never letting them see you sweat. Over time, he'd developed a serene exoskeleton of wool suits and half-smiles that made him impossible to read. He'd also developed the unconscious, if not catastrophically unfortunate, habit of picking his nose when he thought no one was looking.

"Ms. Holmgren was just giving us her version of the events from the other night."

So much for apologizing to Mattie *before* she talked to Sherman. Oliver imagined her regaling her new colleagues with a blow-by-blow description of discovering the hotel security guard rehearsing his painfully unfunny stand-up routine instead of patrolling the grounds and protecting the guests. He risked a sideways glance, noticing she looked as drowsy and discombobulated as he felt. But her expression was unreadable.

"Where were we, Ms. Holmgren? Oh, yes. You were about to remind us what time you clocked in?"

"I thought I just did," she said.

"Humor me."

"Twelve forty-eight."

"And your shift was to begin at what time?"

"I believe your exact words were, 'as soon as you can get here.'" Mattie paused, then added a rather blatant, "Sir."

The room grew agonizingly still. Sherman's staff meetings adhered to strict protocol—he talked, everyone else listened. But this new Mattie person was talking *back*.

"I don't mean to accuse you, Ms. Holmgren. I'm simply trying to clarify." Of course, this sounded exactly like an accusation to anyone who worked for Sherman for more than a few hours. "Is there anything else you'd like to add to your account?"

It seemed to take Mattie a few moments to realize it was her turn to speak again.

"Like I said before, I didn't notice anything out of the ordinary, no funny business." She cut her eyes at Oliver, a hint of a grin in her expression as she stared into her lap.

"So how about you, Mr. Miles? Anything you'd like to add? Did you notice any peculiarities? Shenanigans? Funny business?"

He wished now he'd hit the snooze button a few times, or maybe slept in altogether. The extra rest would come in handy when he started looking for another job later that evening. Eventually, he said, "No, sir. I'm sure whatever Mattie saw is exactly what I saw too."

Sherman made a funny face, even for him.

Against his better judgment, Oliver kept talking. "I mean, I don't think we'll make the papers, if that's what you mean."

Sherman seemed to recoil. Then one of the valets faked a cough to cover his laughter. Although Oliver wasn't really trying to be funny, he did find himself savoring the familiar swell of pride in his chest.

Simply put, Sherman revered the written word—at least as it pertained to his career and his hotel. What he craved more than anything was landing a feature in some glossy magazine. His biggest fear seemed to be "making the papers," which was Sherman-speak for bad press. But just like ghosts or haunted hotel rooms, his staff was forbidden to talk about it.

"This is only the third robbery since the Harrington opened in 1918." Sherman took the time to make excruciatingly deliberate eye contact with each of his subordinates. "I fully expect it to be the last."

Sherman then adjusted the links in his already immaculate cuffs and turned the meeting over to Gordon, the very large and savagely infantile front-desk manager. A collective sigh gathered in Sherman's wake, then released when the ballroom door clicked shut behind him.

As rumor and innuendo filled the void, Gordon played moderator to the rampant speculation bandied about by the mostly ignorant, gossip-mongering hotel staff. Everyone had their own version and they all spoke with eyewitness authority, although none of them was actually there when the robbery occurred. Apparently the Johnsons were rude guests, bad tippers, and towel thieves. Somehow they also managed to be gracious, generous, and may have saved a toddler who was about to step in front of a city bus. There was talk of public drunkenness and gang activity. But when the conjecture veered into mafia connections and possible terrorist plots, Gordon recommandeered the meeting with a thunderous throat clearing, followed by a steely glare.

"Let's get down to business, people." From there he launched a detailed review of the hotel's event calendar, sought a few volunteers to work a banquet the following evening, then ranted about too much overtime before sending everyone back to work.

No one hurried out. Instead, the staff mostly lingered and loitered and eventually meandered toward the exit. The valets made creepy ghost noises, which prompted two of the ladies from housekeeping to cross themselves. The first-shift employees fanned out toward their respective posts, while the second- and third-shifters filed down a narrow hallway toward the time clock.

Oliver fell in beside Mattie, who was bringing up the rear, and tried to think of a clever way to segue into an apology.

"Something on your mind, Oliver?"

"I just wanted to say thanks."

"Thanks?" Her features crinkled into a question mark. "What did I do?"

"Apparently, you didn't rat me out to Sherman?"

"And what would I have told him?" she said. "Or do I even want to know?"

Oliver tried to slow his pace in hopes she would match. The idea was to create a discreet distance from their co-workers. But she either missed his cue or ignored it. And Oliver had to work to keep up.

"Just that, you know ... like how you found me, um, goofing off in the ballroom."

"You *said* you were making your rounds."

"Yeah, well— "

"I mean, if you were up to no good in there, we're going to have a major problem. I can't really afford to lose another job."

Another job? "Oh, no. It's nothing like that. I was just sort of acting silly on my way out of the ballroom. That's all."

"I just figured all that talking to yourself was to keep you from getting spooked. I do that sometimes too, especially when I'm all alone in strange places. Nothing to be ashamed of."

"Oh, right."

"Of course, I don't usually tell jokes though."

"..."

"Or use a dead microphone." Mattie seemed to be biting back a lopsided grin.

"..."

"And I prefer a disco ball to a spotlight." Mattie's smile bloomed in stages. The left side of her mouth arced, forming a small dimple as it made its ascent. A millisecond later, the right side followed suit. It was a good smile, delightful, one of the best. Even if it was at his expense.

Oliver forgot about segues. He was about to blurt out his apology when Mattie tilted her chin toward the ceiling, gulped a mouthful of air, then another. Then she sneezed. Compared to the buildup, it was mostly a muted *Shhh!* sound, followed by a little squeal that trailed off like cartoon gunfire.

Oliver joined a friendly chorus of *Bless you*'s and *Gesundheit*'s while trying not to smile and wondering if he'd ever heard such a cute sneeze before.

"Oliver?" It was Barry Sherman. He'd somehow materialized by the time clock. "*There* you are. General Sherman wants to see you in his office. Like, *now*."

Heads swiveled, first toward Barry and his audacious use of Sherman's nickname, then toward Oliver. Their collective gaze seemed to whisper, *Better him than me.* Barry loomed in the narrow hallway, exerting undeserved authority and ushering everyone out the door with a fake smile. Mattie was the only one who seemed unfazed as she clocked out and disappeared through the parking garage.

"Man, she's something," Barry said when they were alone.

"What do you mean?" Oliver knew exactly what he meant, but it didn't seem appropriate to admit it.

"Mattie. She's totally hot. You know, in like an old-school, Mary Tyler Moore sort of way."

"Huh, I hadn't noticed."

As Oliver contemplated this inadvertent fib, Barry grabbed his right hand and attempted to press it against his own forearm.

"You feel that?"

Oliver yanked his hand back before making contact with Barry's hairy, and now deformed, arm. "What? No, no way. What is it?"

"It's a knot. And I think it's moving around under my skin. Do you think that's normal?"

"No, I think it's creepy."

"But you haven't even felt it yet."

"It's creepy enough that you actually *want* me to feel it."

Barry looked hurt as he continued to fondle what looked like a giant marble trapped under his skin.

"So," Oliver said. "What's up with Mr. Sherman? Did he sound upset?"

"Does he ever sound upset?"

"Good point," Oliver conceded. "But what do you suppose he wants?"

Barry nudged the lump on his arm a half inch in either direction. "Man, I hope this isn't terminal."

"Everything is terminal if you give it enough time."

Barry ignored him. "Look, Oliver. I could really use your help."

"What is it, Barry?"

"Don't you have another job? Some kind of performance art thing?"

"It's more like a glorified hobby."

"But you do gigs, right?"

"Yeah, I guess you could say I dabble in comedy." Oliver knew better than to admit this, especially to Barry. Most of the comics Oliver knew were shameless self-promoters. They dragged family members to their shows. They hassled co-workers, accosted strangers, and emailed every former classmate or distant relative in their vast social network. They put up flyers in coffee shops, on college campuses, and stapled them to telephone poles. Oliver did none of these things. Since the death of his mother's computer (a viral infection), his social network had been limited to actual people that he actually spoke to. His relatives were not just distant; they were remote. And whenever he stepped onto a college campus he tried to remain invisible. As far as work was concerned, the thought of strong-arming valets or bellhops or front-deskers was as creepy as the knot Barry was still fondling on his hairy forearm.

"Perfect," Barry said. "A stand-up comedian."

"How is that perfect? Thought you said you needed help, not a comedian."

"Actually, what I need is a job, Oliver."

"What's wrong with the job you have? Other than the fact that you show up late? Or that you don't really work that hard? Or seem to care that much about the hotel business?"

Barry shrugged, sheepish but not ashamed.

"Never mind," Oliver said. "I withdraw the question."

"Look, we both know why I'm working at the hotel."

"We do?"

"What's my last name, Oliver?"

"Yeah, I know. Sherman. Speaking of which, why do you think he wants to see me?"

"See, most people mistakenly think my dad owns all thirty-two hotels. But it's really Gramps. In fact, he was looking at purchasing a couple of small chains to add to his empire when he got sick."

"What's wrong with him?"

"Not sure what caused it, probably another stroke. But now he's in a coma. And it doesn't look good."

"I'm sorry, Barry. I hope he's okay."

"So," Barry said, having moved from ignoring Oliver's questions to ignoring his grandfather's health. "About that job?"

"Why do you need a job? Aren't you supposed to be an heir?"

"It's complicated. The sons are first in line to inherit everything. Which means I'd have to work for my stupid uncle for a couple of decades before I can even sniff at any kind of ownership. The only way to accelerate that process is for me to show some initiative, some entrepreneurial spirit. So, what I need more than real-world business experience is for someone to vouch for me, Oliver. Which is where you come in."

Vouching for Barry was the last thing Oliver wanted to do. However, since the Shermans seemed to thrive on nepotism, humoring Barry a while just might provide some needed job security, at least until this robbery business blew over.

"So what are you proposing exactly? You want to be my manager?"

"Exactly." Barry snapped his fingers, then winced at the pain in his knotty forearm.

"But there's nothing to manage," Oliver said. "I make very little money and I really have no prospects. Even my act is in disarray, or at least in a bit of a transitional phase."

"Maybe that's why you need a manager."

"I really think this is a bad idea. You'd be wasting your time."

"Perfect. So what do you say, Oliver?"

"I'll think about it." Oliver pointed toward Sherman's closed door, now a mere fifteen feet away. "In the meantime, would you please tell me what your uncle wants to see me about?"

"Oh, I see how this works. You want *my* help with Sherman. But you're not willing to reciprocate?"

"Okay, fine, whatever. You can be my manager. Just tell me what he said."

"Cool," Barry said, then added, "And nothing."

"What do you mean *nothing*?"

"He didn't really tell me to find you. I just made it up."

"And why, pray tell, did you do that?"

"I needed your undivided attention. You know, to ask about the managerial gig."

"So why make the big announcement in front of all my co-workers then?"

"To give them a thrill. You know how they all thrive on gossip. We just did them a favor, shortened their shifts by giving them something to talk about all day."

"Didn't do much for me though."

"It's show business, Oliver. It's what we do."

"Speaking of things *we* do ... any chance you could work a shift or two this week?"

In theory, Oliver was supposed to work five days a week with Barry covering the other two shifts. However, Barry seemed bent on disproving this theory. Since the last part-time security guard quit six months ago, Barry had worked exactly one half of one graveyard shift.

"I'd love to help you out, Oliver. I really would."

"Does that mean I can count on you for a couple of nights this week?"

"No way, it just means I'd love to."

Barry clapped Oliver on the shoulder, pushed his way through the glass lobby doors, and sauntered off, still massaging his forearm. Oliver was about to follow suit when Sherman's office door opened and he said, "Oliver, might I have a word?"

It just *sounded* like a request.

Oliver stepped into his boss's office and was struck again by how immaculate everything was. It made him wonder whether Sherman was the most organized man on earth, or if he just sat around his office all day posing for imaginary pictures. Oliver couldn't decide whether to start with an apology for being late for the staff meeting or for the wisecrack about not making the papers. But Sherman spoke first. "I wonder if you might give me your impressions of Mattie?"

"The new girl?" Oliver's mind scrambled to find whatever it was Sherman was hinting at. "Well, you know, she seems nice. And obviously very good at math."

"I was thinking more about her character, her work ethic, who she is on the inside."

"I've only really ever noticed her outside."

Sherman grinned at this, not quite lascivious, but not quite his benign hotel grin either. Oliver had never seen him look more like his nephew before. "Now that you mention it, she is quite pretty. However, need I remind you that office romances are strictly verboten here at the Harrington?" Then Sherman winked, confusing Oliver all the more.

"Well I've only known her for like a weekend. We just say hello when we pass each other in the lobby and stuff. So I really don't know her much at all. "

"I see," Sherman said, but in a way that made Oliver wonder what his boss was actually seeing, or if he really saw anything at all. "Well then, we need to see to it you do."

"Do what exactly, sir?"

"Get to know her. Or at least keep an eye on her for me."

"Am I looking for anything in particular?"

"I'm sorry. I don't mean to cause alarm or cast undue aspersions. It's just that she's new. And I do have my hotel to protect." His use of the personal pronoun was not lost on Oliver. The Shermans seemed to be a territorial bunch. "Besides, you said yourself that we don't really know her all that well. Not yet."

"I see," Oliver said. But he really didn't.

"Just remember," Sherman said. "My door is always open."

Then he stood, promptly ushered Oliver out, and closed it.

Chapter Six

Oliver expected to find his mother in the cafeteria pushing scrambled eggs and sausage around her plate between sips of coffee. But according to one of the orderlies, she'd skipped yet another breakfast. He eventually found her in the backyard of Shady Grove, sitting alone on a decorative park bench and staring off at nothing in particular, either reliving distant memories or imagining new ones. He approached quietly from behind and said, "Hey, Mom."

Delores Miles turned slowly, her eyes registering only a flash of confusion before her mind could concoct a workable scenario. "You're the new therapist, right?"

"Sure, Mom." At least part of her memory was working.

Oliver had two choices when talking to his mother. Either he could turn every sentence into a pathetic segue in an attempt to get her to remember him. Or, he could just play along with whatever she said, using equally pathetic and leading questions to get his mother to remember him. Sometimes, when he was feeling especially desperate, he resorted to trying to trick her into saying his name. He wasn't feeling especially desperate this morning. Mostly, he felt sleepy.

"So," he said, just to have something to say, "how are you this morning?"

"Better than Thomas."

Oliver followed his mother's gaze to the back corner of the yard where a severely palsied man in a tattered bathrobe and black knee-high socks crouched by a chain-link gate that was overgrown with thick, weedy vines. He kept sneaking glances over his shoulder before attempting to pick the fat, rusted lock with limp dandelion stalks.

She shook her head and said, "Poor man. But if he ever does open the gate, it'll be a mass exodus."

Oliver bit back a grin as he imagined a slow-motion prison break, with tottering old folks ramming walkers into wheelchairs as they elbowed their way through the rusted back gate, across a busy intersection, and into the promised land of a shared parking lot between a Chinese restaurant and a State Farm agent.

His mother often compared the conditions at Shady Grove to prison. And she would obviously know better than he—her rap sheet included public intoxication, driving under the influence, and numerous accounts of domestic violence—most of which found her in the role of aggressor, exacting vengeance on one of her worthless boyfriends. She'd only been busted for child abuse once. But it was enough.

"Frankly," she said, "I hope he makes it out someday. We all do."

"Really? Why do you think everyone wants out of here?"

For one split second, she morphed into one of her old selves—the incredulous mother regarding her imbecilic offspring as he laid in the yard, wiping his tears with his homemade cape and cradling his newly splintered forearm after a not-so-super-heroic flight out of a second-story window. But her troubled expression disappeared as quickly as it came.

"I'm sure it's the drugs."

"Thomas is on drugs?"

"Sure," she said. "We all are."

"Does that include you, Mom?"

She blinked once, then again. Finally, she said, "So how much schooling does that take?"

"Does what take?"

"Physical therapy," she said. "You know I'm thinking of going back to school myself. I've always been a strong proponent of continuing education."

"Yeah, I know, Mom."

"I'm still leaning toward becoming a pharmacist."

"But I hear you make a fine nurse."

"Thanks, anyway," she said. "But I'm retiring."

"Why would you want to do that?"

"They don't appreciate the work I do around here." She stood then and brushed her backside with hands that looked like they belonged to a woman twice her age. "I think I need to go lie down."

As she walked toward the building, Oliver grabbed her nursing kit and followed her inside. This was not a good sign. Ever since she'd gotten sick, she'd occupied the healthy parts of her mind with various hobbies. For a while, she assumed the role of resident hairdresser, until visiting family members complained about the crew-cutted mothers and mohawked grandpas. She had spurts of interest in jigsaw puzzles and Sudoku and crosswords, but those never lasted more than a month or two. Her happiest times had been while leading Bible studies and preaching Sunday morning sermonettes. But that too ended when Dr. Strahan revoked her baptizing privileges. If she gave up nursing, she'd be hobbyless once again. And when she didn't have a hobby, she sat and stared at the television and napped a lot. That's when it felt like a race to see which would deteriorate faster—her body or her brain.

Oliver placed her colorful nurse's kit prominently atop her bookshelf, exactly where her framed mother/son photographs were supposed to be. His hope was that she would wake tomorrow morning and see it there, causing her selective memory to forget about taking early retirement.

As if on cue, she climbed into her bed and thumbed the remote control until she found a talk show with a panel of teary women discussing the difficulties of child rearing. Oliver didn't realize he'd slipped into a TV coma along with his mother until he heard the sound of hushed voices and scuffling feet in the hallway. He knew better than to suggest she turn off the TV. So he motioned to the weepy woman on screen and said, "So … do you have any children of your own?"

She shook her head, fondled the frayed edge of her quilt, and sighed longingly at her bookshelf. "No, I never married."

That was true. She never did marry, though she did sleep around a lot. Oliver decided to honor his mother by keeping that particular thought to himself.

He sat opposite her, watching her eyelids sag and droop and eventually close altogether. That's when he sat up straighter, listening for his three favorite syllables. The last time he'd heard his own name cross his mother's lips was just moments after she'd nodded off, her voice tender and dreamy and reducing him to a blubbering idiot. His irrational obsession with hearing his name worried him. But what actually frightened Oliver beyond words was the thought of ending up like his mother.

She fidgeted for a moment, as if she could hear his thoughts, then nestled further down under a thick quilt.

That's when the commotion started on the other side of his mother's door. Oliver followed the sound into the hallway and was nearly decapitated by an orderly sprinting toward the stairwell.

Eventually, he followed the bustling sounds up to the third floor where he found Betsy at the nurse's station in an intense conversation with a police officer. Her practiced lilting voice had given way to tremors. Oliver leaned against the counter, pretending to search for something in his wallet, and listened. Apparently the body of Mrs. Tompkins—Oliver's mother's most recent "patient"—had just been discovered in her bed, her soul having already departed.

The cop brushed past Oliver and into the dead woman's room. He emerged moments later engaged in a serious dialog with the beefy security guard, treating him like an equal.

Betsy approached Oliver, clearly in shock.

"So," he said, "she's really … you know … like, no longer with us?"

Betsy nodded gravely, a single tear spilling down over the slope of her pink cheek.

"Wow," was all he could manage as his head swiveled toward the open door.

"But listen, Oliver." She put her hand on his arm and squeezed gently, letting it linger there as she glanced toward the uniformed men outside Mrs. Tompkins's room. "Trust me on this. You have nothing to worry about, okay? Nothing at all."

"Then why am I suddenly so worried?"

"Just because your mother was the last person to see Mrs. Tompkins alive ... Well, I'm sure she had nothing to do with ... you know ... her untimely *passing*. Nothing at all."

• • •

The police eventually made an appearance. They asked Delores Miles a battery of questions about her last few moments with Mrs. Tompkins. But either she didn't remember, or she didn't want to.

"What about you?" one of the cops asked Oliver. "You know anything about all this?"

Oliver shook his head, blissfully ignorant. Some things are better left unknown. The frustrated policemen dropped business cards on the nightstand and left. Oliver stayed with his mother until she started nodding off. He stretched out in the recliner and watched her until she fell asleep. He was tempted to close his eyes and take his own morning nap. But he'd made his mother a promise years ago and he intended to make good on it—even though it felt like an orphaned promise that, like so many falling trees in remote forests, would splinter and crack and eventually tumble to earth, impotent and unheeded.

He got up, kissed her on the forehead, and set off to finish his education.

• • •

Oliver checked his watch, not to see if he was going to be late for class, but rather to see *which* class he'd be attending this morning. And where.

He decided to let his stomach be his guide. *American Lit.* was closer, by about thirty miles. But the road to *Intro. to the American Legal System* was paved with donut shops. At the Krispy Kreme drive-thru Oliver swapped a faded green portrait of Abraham Lincoln for two blueberry cake donuts, a large coffee, and a handful of coins. Then he pointed his asthmatic Integra toward the big state school in Murfreesboro.

The only decent parking spot he found was in the Humanities

lot. So he nosed in and kept his car idling while he thumbed through a stack of parking decals—all from various universities—that he kept rubber-banded together in his glove compartment. He reminded himself that this was not stealing. Oliver had actually purchased these preowned decals on eBay and had the receipts to prove it. (He realized most universities would take a more narrow view of this rationale, so he silently renewed his vow to someday repay this vehicular debt to society by endowing a few of his favorite colleges with a Parking Scholarship—anonymously of course, and only after the check cleared for his first HBO special.) Two strips of Scotch tape later, he abandoned his now-authorized vehicle and fell in step with a horde of overly serious students. After consulting a threadbare note card to make sure he had the room number right, Oliver checked his watch again and slowed his pace.

Timing his arrival was critical—too early led to unwanted attention and actual conversations, whereas arriving late might arouse suspicion. So his goal became to show up inconspicuously on time, careful to keep his head down and avoid sitting in either the front or last rows. It also helped to hide behind sunglasses or under headphones while pretending to cram for some upcoming, nonexistent test.

But the gods of academia conspired against him that morning. First, he'd forgotten his earbuds, remembering too late that he'd left them in the security closet at the hotel. Plus, the professor was running late, which rendered Oliver's timely arrival early by comparison. And the only empty seat in one of the middle rows was directly behind a conversationally needy redhead he remembered from a previous unauthorized visit. So Oliver was forced to sit in the back. To avoid any unwanted conversation, he leaned his head against the block wall behind him, closed his eyes, and pretended to nap.

The next sound he heard—or would remember hearing anyway—was the sound of shuffling feet and backpacks. He'd managed to sleep through yet another class.

Oliver kept his eyes on his shoes and fell in line amid a gaggle of students making lunch plans. He was three short steps from the open doorway when he heard his name.

"Mr. Miles? Could I have a word?"

Oliver ignored his first impulse, which was to bolt into the hallway and sprint toward his illegally parked Integra. But if the professor already knew his name, then how hard would it be to track him down and have Oliver arrested or kicked out or dragged off to the collegiate equivalent of detention hall?

In the end, it was simple curiosity that made Oliver pause in the doorway.

He turned, his steps plodding and rueful. But his teacher didn't appear angry or offended or even perturbed. If anything, he looked kind of nervous, probably more so than Oliver. And why not? The man was a trained educator, not a bouncer. There was probably no handbook on how to confront students caught illegally auditing classes.

"I don't think we've been formally introduced," the teacher said. But Oliver was suddenly convinced that they had. And it was more than a nagging familiarity in the man's kind eyes and prematurely graying beard. Something intimate, paternal. "I'm Professor Laramy. Daniel."

"So," Oliver said. "Am I in trouble?"

"Funny, I was about to ask you the same thing."

Oliver studied the man's face for any trace of irony, but he looked utterly sincere. "I realize this looks kind of bad, but I promised my mother I'd get a good college education. She never really specified the parts about enrollment and meal tickets and graduation and such."

Laramy laughed through his nose, a nostalgic sound.

"That sounds like Dot." Then the man who was not really his professor looked him in the eye and said, "Tell me, Oliver. How is your mother?"

Images from some distant past clicked through Oliver's memory like frames in a View-Master. He saw Laramy again — beardless, paunchless, his skin flushed and pasty from postcoital exertion, eyes brimming with equal parts panic and shame. The younger version looked anything but professorial as he beat a hasty retreat from Delores Miles's bedroom. He was obviously surprised to see the bed-headed youngster perched on the sofa, spooning Lucky Charms into his little mouth. The younger version of Laramy paused at the door, thinking. The lingering image was that of Laramy's wedding ring glinting in the glow of the television set as he turned the knob and left.

All at once, the idea of getting busted by his teacher, and quite possibly getting kicked out of school (or at least *this* school) didn't seem like such a big deal anymore. Oliver had had these conversations before. Ones where some middle-aged guy, all blushed and sweating and unsure what to do with his hands, would accost Oliver about the welfare of Delores Miles. They all had one thing in common—at some indiscriminate point in their past, they'd gotten drunk, then eventually gotten naked with his mother. She had been a conquest, a proverbial notch in their literal belts, a trophy they didn't earn and couldn't keep. Or didn't want to.

Oliver never questioned their sincerity when these random men asked how she was doing, only their tact. A few had no doubt loved her, or at least thought they did. Some were convinced they could reform her, but she turned out to be unreformable. Most simply used her. But without exception, they all felt sorry for her. And there was nothing Delores Miles hated more than pity.

Oliver studied Professor Laramy's beleaguered expression, trying to figure out which of these categories he belonged in. He decided it didn't matter. He was simply too tired to care.

"My mother is sick."

"Oh? I'm really sorry to hear that. Is there anything … I don't know … something I can do?"

"I'm guessing you've done enough already."

Laramy stopped fidgeting and eased past Oliver to close the classroom door. He returned, looking pensive, and said, "Look, that was a long time ago, Oliver. It was a different era; we were different people back then."

"No, not different." Oliver didn't speak the words so much as mouth them, as if having to solve each one as it occurred to him. "Just younger."

"Pardon?"

"Weren't you about my age when you decided to fool around with my mother?"

"I suppose so, yes." Laramy sighed his sentences now, obviously weary of this conversation and where it was headed.

"So I take it you were already married when you guys hooked up?" Laramy nodded, shame personified. Oliver resisted the urge to feel sorry for him. "Tell me this, Professor. Do you have any kids?"

"I'm not sure what that has to do— "

"Humor me."

"Okay, yes, I have a daughter. She was married last year, in fact."

"Perfect. So based on your logic, it would be totally cool for me to get your daughter drunk, have casual, meaningless sex with her this week, so long as I eventually grow up and acknowledge years later how *different* I've become."

Laramy must have locked the door when he shut it. Someone jiggled the handle, then knocked. But Laramy ignored whoever it was.

"Look, I didn't mean to upset you, Oliver. I just wanted to know how your mother was doing."

"Okay then, why?"

"I don't know. Why does anyone ask after someone else? I care about her."

"Just like that? After all these years you magically start caring again?"

"Frankly ..." Laramy's voice quavered. "I've never really stopped."

"Which is why you sent her all those birthday cards, right?" Oliver hated the way sarcasm made his voice go shrill. "And why you were always around to help us load up moving vans? Or why you called so often just to check in and see how she was doing? To tell her how much you care?"

"It's not what you think, Oliver."

"What I think is that you somehow recognized me in class this morning and it reminded you of some passionate tryst with Delores Miles. I'm sure it's all very titillating for you. You get to relive it, picture it all over again in excruciating detail. But guess what, Professor Laramy ... so do I."

The second hand of the battery-operated wall clock ticked away the seconds. Voices filtered in under the closed door. Students would begin lining up outside the door soon.

"For the record," Laramy said, lowering his voice, "it was not some one-night stand. We were together for months. We were in love."

"I doubt that."

"Pardon me for saying so, but how could you possibly know if your mother was in love with me or not?"

"Because," Oliver said. "I don't think she's capable."

"Why on earth not?"

"Mostly because of guys like you."

Oliver could see that he'd gone too far, and he almost felt bad about it. At least Laramy seemed sincere. This wasn't his fault, not entirely. In all likelihood, Delores Miles was already broken when this guy found her. Like so many others, he probably thought he could fix her. Besides, to acknowledge his mother's culpability was to admit his own. A better son would have done a better job protecting her from herself. So it was more convenient to blame the nameless string of guys. It made him feel better, or at least a little less culpable.

"I'm sorry, Oliver. I really am. About everything."

"It's fine." Oliver mimed his own weak surrender. He was afraid Laramy's apologies might turn sloppy. Or worse, that he might ask for forgiveness. And if he didn't ask, Oliver wouldn't have to deny him.

"And for what it's worth, I recognized you months ago. But your attendance is rather sporadic. You confirmed it today with all that snoring."

"You recognized my snore?"

"No, but I did make my way to your desk and gave your shoulder a hearty shake. You didn't wake, but you did quit snoring. Your notebook was open on your desk with the heading 'Jokes.'"

"How did that help?"

"Your mom always bragged about your sense of humor."

"She did?"

"But she worried all those comedy records were going to rot your brain. By the way, what did you think of the Steven Wright album?"

"That was you?" It was called *I Have a Pony*, and Oliver had found it leaning against the screen door the Friday before his twelfth birthday. There was a red bow in the corner and a note that said *Happy Birthday, Oliver!* He wasn't about to admit it now, but that collection of cerebral one-liners had changed his life, or at least drastically altered its comedic course.

Laramy nodded, pleased with himself. "Anyway, after I recognized you in class, it still took me awhile to work up the nerve to ask you about your mother. Since I didn't see your name on the roll, I checked with the registrar's office. But it seems they've *misplaced* your enrollment records."

Oliver recognized the metaphorical olive branch being offered, even without the customary wink. It felt more like a Get Out of Jail Free card. They both knew he was freeloading. All he could muster was a grateful nod.

Laramy said, "Actually, I've always been a fan of auditing classes. And I do hope you'll keep studying with us."

"We'll see," Oliver said.

"And I meant what I said. If there's anything at all I can do for you or your mother, just let me know."

"Thanks," Oliver said. "I'll keep that in mind."

"Anyway, would you at least tell your mother hello for me?"

"Here," Oliver said, patting his pockets for something to write on. He pulled a scrap of paper from his notebook and snatched a pen off Laramy's desk, then scribbled the address and handed it to his teacher.

"Why don't you tell her yourself?"

Chapter Seven

The sign on the door posted a discreet warning that "authorized personnel only" were allowed beyond that point. Oliver Miles certainly qualified. He even had the uniform to prove it, along with a badge and the five-digit security code. Despite all that, he still felt compelled to knock as he punched the required buttons and swung the door open. Seeing her there behind the desk embarrassed Oliver for some reason. He realized he didn't really want to apologize for accidentally accusing Mattie. What he wanted was to get it over with.

But she didn't look up. Instead, she stared at the long ribbon of adding machine tape in disbelief. The only sound came from the pencil she drummed between her teeth. The resulting echo wafted up through the open-air ceiling and repeated softly overhead like gossip. Oliver was about to clear his throat when Mattie blinked once, clamped her teeth around the pencil, and went back to work.

The sound registered before the image.

In perfect synchronicity, Mattie's hands—*both* of them—assaulted the keys of two different adding machines. The fingers of her left hand mirrored those on her right as the machines coughed up a steady stream of tickertape. Mattie's gaze remained fixed on a handwritten ledger propped between the dueling calculators. When the clattering finally subsided, her eyes flitted between the last line of the ledger and the printouts on either side. She blinked again and grinned at her handiwork. That's when she noticed Oliver standing by her desk and screamed.

"Hey, sorry," he said. "I'm sorry. Didn't mean to scare you."

"Startled, not scared." Mattie gripped the edge of the desk with both hands, then took two measured breaths before speaking again. "Ever hear of knocking?"

"I *did* knock."

"Oh ..." Mattie's expression blanked, as if she was rewinding a videotape of Oliver's entrance. "I suppose you did. Sorry, didn't mean to yell at you."

"It's okay. I'll try to remember to knock louder next time."

"Thanks," she said. "And you can put your arms down now."

Oliver was surprised to discover his hands suspended in front of him, palms out, as if feeling his way in the dark. He motioned toward the adding machines as he lowered his arms. "That's some trick."

"Oh, that? It's nothing." A pink stain bloomed along her neckline, then migrated north until her cheeks filled with color. "Just something I learned to do on a dare. I'm actually out of practice."

"Could have fooled me."

Mattie nodded. Or maybe she shrugged; it was hard to tell. Finally, she said, "Didn't your mother teach you not to stare?"

"I'm sure she tried. But somewhere between potty training and running with scissors, I was diagnosed with Attention Surplus Disorder. After months of physical therapy and countless vials of designer drugs, I was pronounced incurable."

Mattie tilted her head and chewed on her bottom lip, causing Oliver's affable grin to wilt, then trail off altogether. She stared back at him, adamantly not blinking.

Finally he said, "That was a joke."

"Yeah, I know."

"But you forgot to laugh."

"Some jokes are not quite as funny as they sound."

"But ... you admit it was a little funny, right?"

"If it will make you feel better, sure."

"But you're still not laughing."

"Neither are you," she said. "But you are still staring."

Oliver tried again to avert his eyes, but they kept roaming back to the keys on the adding machines, replaying the image in his mind.

"And please don't ask me to do it again. It's not some carnival act."

"What do you call it then?"

"A simple system of checks and balances. It's standard practice to keep adding columns until you come up with the same answer twice. I just figured it would be faster if I used both hands."

"The last auditor used this cool new device. I think it's called a computer."

"That was another joke, right?"

"Yeah, but I will admit it lacked some of the more humorous elements typically found in a lot of other jokes."

"You seem to really like jokes," she said.

"I'm kind of a comedian," he said. "At least when I'm not here serving and protecting."

"I gathered that. And you know, there's nothing to be ashamed of."

"Who said I was ashamed?"

"Never mind," she said, allowing her eyes to drift back to her work. "Anyhow, I'll eventually log all this into Excel and email it to the comptroller. There's just something gratifying about doing it the old-fashioned way. Besides, what else am I supposed to do all night?"

"You could help me catch robbers."

"Is that what this is all about?"

"What what's about?"

"Well, you finally stopped staring. But now you're just standing there, trying way too hard to look casual."

"Okay, well I did want to give you a heads-up about Mr. Sherman. You may have noticed he has a bit of a paranoid streak when it comes to the hotel."

"More like a mental disorder."

Oliver met her eyes, prepared to share a conspiratorial laugh at their boss's expense. But apparently she wasn't kidding.

"Anyway," he said, "you can expect an onslaught of questions about the other night. He's grilled me three times already. And if he detects any lack of consistency in our stories he'll turn it into an inquisition."

"You actually think he'll suspect one of us of doing something wrong?"

"It's not personal. He suspects everybody."

"So is that what happened to the last girl?"

"Not exactly. Gretchen was fired for sleeping."

"That's ridiculous. All night auditors nod off occasionally. It's impossible not to. It's in the job description."

"But not every night auditor changes into silky jammies and makes a pallet on the floor."

"No way."

Mattie did finally relinquish a guarded smile, but she kept it hidden behind a loose fist. And that's when Oliver realized he'd been comparing Mattie to the last night auditor, unfairly it seemed. Gretchen was an open book, and very likely the moodiest person Oliver had ever met, including his mother. She was petty, vindictive, and a ruthless small talker, which primarily focused in mind-numbing detail on her boyfriend whom she seemed to despise. Mattie was none of these things. She seemed smart, deceptively witty. But somehow reserved too, like an unposed question.

"Every night about two a.m. Gretchen plugged in her white-noise maker and bedded down with her hypoallergenic pillow, Wonder Woman sleeping bag, and stuffed monkey."

"And you actually witnessed all this?"

"I was her alarm clock," Oliver said. "Which is kind of what I wanted to talk to you about."

"You want to be my alarm clock?"

"What I had in mind was establishing a routine of some sort. Since there's just the two of us here and all."

"Along with eight floors full of hotel guests," she said. "Not to mention the ghost of Old Man Harrington."

"Which, as you know, you're not supposed to talk about."

"Sherman does," Mattie said "He mentions it every chance he gets."

"Yeah, but he's the boss."

"So was that part of your routine with Gretchen?" Mattie said. "*Not* talking about ghosts?"

"Well, she was sort of fired for that too."

"Too?"

"Gretchen was fired a lot. It just took awhile to make it stick. Rumor has it that when Sherman refused to give her a raise, Gretchen threatened to sell her own version of the story to the tabloids. She claimed the gho — um, spirit of Old Man Harrington got her pregnant."

"You're not joking now, are you?"

"I wish," Oliver said. "Anyway, we will need some kind of system covering each other's posts, you know, for when nature calls — potty breaks, midnight raids on the hotel kitchen, smoke breaks if you need them. Especially after what happened in 218."

Mattie pursed her lips and squinted. "Did you just say 'potty breaks'?"

"I guess I did. But that's Gretchen's fault. It's what she always called them."

Mattie smiled again, less guarded this time.

"Anyway," he said. "The quickest way to find me if you need me is the walkie-talkie. You don't even have to talk into it. Just press the send button a couple of times — it makes this awful static — and I'll come watch the desk for you."

"Sounds simple enough. Anything else?"

"No, I don't think so."

"Are you sure?"

"I thought I was."

Mattie did that smile again, the one that unfolded in stages. "I forgive you, Oliver."

It took a few seconds for the sound to register, as if Mattie had suddenly started speaking in Chinese. "Oh, right. That's kind of what I came in here for, to apologize, you know, for the other night."

"I know."

Oliver wanted to ask how she could possibly know that. Instead he simply said, "Well, I am sorry if it sounded like I was accusing you."

"Oh, please. Don't worry about that. I'm sure it won't be the last time."

Chapter Eight

SOMETIMES, BREATHING THE AIR inside Downers made Oliver feel small, inadequate, like an eleven-year-old in a boardroom full of suits. More times than not though, it felt like home. As he scanned the room for Roscoe's stooped silhouette he wasn't sure how to feel.

Downers wasn't the biggest comedy club in Nashville. Neither was it the hippest or most celebrated. By strict definition, it really wasn't even a comedy club at all. The building's eleven thousand square feet moonlighted as a deli by day, a family-style bistro in the evenings, and a showcase for stand-up comics after dark. Locally, it was known for strong coffee, rude waitresses, and an ageless club owner named Roscoe who was notorious for turning comics' microphones off in the middle of subpar sets, no matter how many times he or she had been on *Letterman*. Among touring stand-ups, Downers had a cultlike reputation that spanned both coasts. It was the place to test one's comedic mettle, to separate the artists from the posers and hacks. In the subculture of stand-ups, Roscoe was not unlike a mafia don—once you received his blessing, you were a made man. There were dozens of obscure professional comedians roaming the country that would never grace a network sitcom or write for *The Tonight Show*, but they carried the knowledge that Roscoe Downs approved of their work. And they knew the other comics knew it too.

The protocol went something like this: Famous comedian finishes his high-paying gig at Jesters, cabs over to Downers, and is eventually ushered into Roscoe's cramped office. After exchanging pleasantries and some obligatory industry gossip, the famous comedian then agrees, via handshake, to perform a single set of new material for the lofty sum of one Roscoe Burger Platter—an artery-choking basket consisting of a fiery, high-fat burger, fries, and a malted shake. Most nights, Roscoe moonlighted as the club's bouncer and short-order cook, as well as the owner.

None of Oliver's fellow comics ever believed him when he tried to explain that Roscoe's mission in life was to create the perfect burger, *not* to christen new comic sensations. That he was way more interested in The Food Network than Comedy Central.

On one such night when Oliver was twelve, a slightly tipsy Eddie Murphy showed up in Roscoe's office, negotiating hard. He wanted to do a set but was politely refusing to eat the Roscoe Burger Platter.

Apparently, he had just been cast in a romantic comedy and was under contract to shed fifteen pounds. He glanced at Roscoe's blank desktop and realized that he'd barged in on a game of paper football. Murphy raised one eyebrow in supplication and a deal was struck. If Eddie wanted to forego Roscoe's fat-filled entrée, all he had to do was win a game of paper football—*against Oliver.* The game was close for the first few minutes, then Oliver began drubbing the good humor right out of the renowned funny man. That's when Murphy began surreptitiously flashing money. Once, as he fashioned a goal post out of his long brown fingers, Oliver noticed a five-dollar bill peeking out between his knuckles. Oliver split the uprights. On his next extra-point attempt, Murphy flashed a ten and Oliver aimed the triangular projectile to the left. The point was good, but he'd sent the signal that Eddie Murphy was getting close. When the ante rose all the way to twenty dollars, Oliver began to shank kicks and leave touchdown attempts a hair shy of the tabletop's edge. Eventually, Eddie Murphy defeated Oliver Miles in paper football by a score of 91–90. Murphy lit up the office with his signature grin and accompanying horselaugh. He shook Oliver's hand on his way out, transferring the damp bill.

When the door closed, Roscoe met Oliver's gaze and said, "I woulda paid double that to see you beat him."

As proof, he flashed a palmed fifty-dollar bill, just like Mr. Murphy had done. Oliver's face grew hot and he began spluttering apologies, more for his new friend Eddie than for himself.

"Don't sweat it, kid. The first time he drops an F-bomb I'm killing his microphone."

When it came to crude material, Roscoe had a zero-tolerance policy. It was an unwritten (but widely known) rule that any comic spewing overtly racist, sexist, homophobic, or crass material was promptly uninvited to the Downers' stage. It wasn't the filthy talk that bothered Roscoe as much as the abject lack of creativity it implied. To his way of thinking, any junior high school kid with a decent command of the English language could wield a microphone, talk nasty, and make drunk people laugh.

Eddie Murphy had a really short set that night.

No amount of begging ever helped Oliver land a gig at Downers. Still, as far as he knew, he was the only comic in America who could claim to have grown up there.

Upon graduating high school, Delores Miles piled into her boyfriend's VW camper and spent several delirious months camping in Daytona. When her savings ran out, the boyfriend ran off, and she moved back home and went to work for Roscoe. Somewhere along the way she got pregnant.

On average, she worked six nights a week and filled in at lunch when money got tight. Whenever she couldn't find a babysitter—because frankly, she never really looked that hard—Delores Miles brought her son to work with her. She would exaggerate a few obligatory apologies and make Oliver promise to stay out of trouble. Roscoe would then exaggerate his frustration before inviting the boy to his office where they would play gin rummy or paper football until the comedians started up. That's when Oliver would follow Roscoe to his customary booth in the back where he'd be treated to burgers and fries and all the pie he could eat. Sometimes they would even critique comics together. Roscoe not only liked having Dot's kid around; he preferred it.

Now they sat in the exact same booth, eating the same burger, same fries, same pie. A trail of hamburger grease snaked its way down Roscoe's stubbled chin. He dabbed at it with the back of his hand. And that's when Oliver noticed the slight quaver in the man's fingers, the brown-spotted skin, the way his slight frame seemed to be hollowing. It was subtle, but very real. Not quite into his sixth decade, Oliver's oldest friend was getting old before his time.

Neither one spoke until the comedian onstage worked through his opening. The guy was a prop comic, much too loud and too zany for Roscoe's tastes.

"How's your burger?"

"Perfect," Oliver said. "Just like always."

Roscoe frowned at his plate. "I don't know. I think it could use a touch more garlic. And a little less blood on the plate."

"Speaking of bloodletting, isn't it about time you had a change of heart and offered me a headlining weekend spot?"

Roscoe ignored him and craned his neck to meet his bartender's eye. He held up his index finger for a long moment before drawing it across his own throat like a blade. Then he swallowed hard and said, "You already had your shot." Roscoe took another large bite and chewed faster, no doubt to mask his grin. "And you sort of blew it."

"I was only sixteen years old."

Roscoe nodded as if he couldn't agree more. "If you remember, that's what I kept telling you when you kept begging to take the stage. Told your mother the same thing. But she wouldn't listen either."

"Wait," Oliver said, "Are you telling me that Mom *knew*?"

Roscoe opened his mouth then closed it again. A cluster of french fries hovered just inches away.

"Well since you asked, it was kinda her idea. Thought it might help get it out of your system."

"How so?"

"She knew you had talent. Dot was your biggest fan, actually. But she'd met a slew of touring stand-ups and wanted a better life for you. She was afraid my stage would stoke your obsession and keep you out of college."

Roscoe and his mother were obviously close, maybe even intimate. But he never suspected them of anything this underhanded. Maybe he was more naïve than he realized. And their scheme almost worked too.

Almost.

After months of relentless begging for stage time, Roscoe finally relented—sort of. He had called Oliver into his office and closed the door. "You want to work for me, you work your way up first."

So Oliver cleaned toilets and hauled garbage and washed dishes every day for a month. When he complained, Roscoe would say, "You want the gig or don't you?"

"I don't see Seinfeld cleaning latrines."

"Seinfeld don't need a backup plan."

A week later an up-and-coming comic named Ray Romano finished two shows at Jesters, then cabbed over to Downers for an obligatory burger platter and a short set of all-new material. His final joke ended with a whiny punch line about having just opened for an underaged, rookie comedian. Oliver had shoved another rack of glasses into the steamy Hobart when he heard Romano whine, "Please put your hands together for Olivia Mills."

The crowd cheered gamely and waited for this new comedy sensation to arrive. And Oliver cheered right along with them, craning his neck in the dark, and anxious to glimpse this new upstart comedienne. That's when he heard Roscoe's familiar growl from the back of the room.

"It's *Miles*, you imbecile, not Mills."

And that's how Oliver was introduced to the professional world of stand-up comedy—sweaty, reeking of dirty dishes, thoroughly unprepared, and way over his head. It did not go well. In fact, his set was shorter than Mr. Murphy's. But it had nothing to do with profanity. In a word, he was terrible. Oliver didn't realize until he moped offstage that he was still wearing his apron.

He'd wanted to surprise his mother. It appears now that she was trying to surprise him. Despite their scheming, Delores and Roscoe didn't quite manage to scare the comedy out of him. There were days however when he wished they had.

Oliver's reverie finally broke when the voice of the zany prop comic died in midsentence. Oliver alternated his gaze between the bemused comedian and the top of Roscoe's head. When he finally looked up, his gaze was defiant, unapologetic. "I'm trying to eat here."

An awkward murmur rippled through the crowd as the emcee barged out of the men's room, stumbled through the maze of tables, and clumsily introduced the next comedian on the docket.

Roscoe seemed unfazed by it all.

"You know," Oliver said. "You could have at least warned me."

"Good comics are always prepared. Kind of like Boy Scouts."

"I wasn't a good comic, not back then. I was a kid washing dishes. Anyway, how about another chance?"

"Sorry kid."

"Come on, Roscoe. You don't have any work for me at all?"

"Well, now that you mention it. One of our better cooks just moved to Miami."

"What I had in mind was something, you know, a bit funnier."

"We've already got a dishwasher. Although you'd have to admit, that'd be pretty funny."

"You leave me no choice then. I'll just have to go to Jesters."

The truly big names played Jesters, Nashville's premier comedy club. These were the guys with HBO specials, sitcoms in development, regular spots on Comedy Central, and stints on *Saturday Night Live*. They hawked T-shirts and CDs at their routinely sold-out shows. Jesters was a franchise deal, quite literally, with showcase clubs dotting the map in Boston, LA, Vegas, Chicago, New York, and a dozen other major metropolises. Agents booked their comics at wholesale prices in exchange for steady work, prodigious exposure, and pedigree enhancement. If you were not already famous, then landing a touring gig with Jesters was one of the fastest ways to become so. It guaranteed a steady paycheck, countless radio interviews, and ample opportunity to rub elbows with industry insiders. If you wanted to headline on the Jesters circuit, it was not enough to be known—you had to know somebody. The only opportunity for local talent at Jesters was reserved for open-mic nights, showcases, and the occasional chance to emcee for bona fide headliners. Prestige aside, it didn't matter how famous the Jesters comics were because the real comedians—those serious about plying their craft, the true artisans, the comedian's comedians—always made their way to Downners when their paying gig was over.

Roscoe didn't take the bait, mainly because he didn't see Jesters as competition. Instead, he drained his coffee and said, "Got a call from an old acquaintance of your mom's this afternoon. Said he bumped into you recently."

"Who's that?"

"Lawyer named Laramy."

"I thought he was a teacher?"

"Apparently, he's both," Roscoe said. "And since he was sort of, you know, dating your mother when she was incarcerated, he was the attorney of record. His name's all over the paperwork."

"So, why'd he call you?"

"Well it wouldn't make sense to call your mother."

"No, but he could call me."

"Would you actually talk to him if he did?"

"Probably not."

"And when you do talk to your mother's old boyfriends, don't you tend to get a bit ... how do I say this ... unreasonable?"

"How would you know that?"

"When it comes to your mother, you're not the most rational person in the world."

"And I could say the same thing about you."

Roscoe's thinning shoulders dipped, as if the air had gone out of him. Back when she was of sound mind, Delores would get fed up with something or someone at Downers and quit. Roscoe would let her cool off for a day or two, then allow her to resume her normal shifts as if nothing happened. More often than not, he paid her for the work she missed anyway, referring to it as her dental plan. Despite the obvious age difference, Oliver always suspected their relationship ran much deeper than that of a typical boss and capricious underling.

Roscoe dragged a french fry through a puddle of ketchup and made aimless circles on the plate.

"So what did Professor Laramy have to say?"

"That Tompkins lady's family is threatening legal action."

"Against Mom?"

"It will start with the facility. But Laramy says to be prepared for anything. Says the kids seem pretty greedy."

Oliver had already heard some of this from Betsy—that the bulk of Mrs. Tompkins's savings had been depleted by the monthly fees at Shady Grove and that her heirs were bent on recouping their inheritance by suing anyone who had anything to do with Shady Grove, from the board of directors all the way down to the janitors.

"But it makes no sense," Oliver said. "She's got nothing, no money, no assets."

"Don't really matter," Roscoe said. "Anyway, if they can prove Dot had anything at all to do with her untimely passing, it'll bolster their case against the nursing home chain."

"What's the good professor going to charge for his legal help?"

"It's on the house," Roscoe said.

"His or yours?"

"Not your concern, son."

"So," Oliver said, "should I be worried?"

"You'll worry no matter what. Just thought you should know."

They sat together, each nursing his own thoughts. During finals week of Oliver's only semester in college, he'd received a midnight call from Roscoe. His mother had been arrested for public intoxication, disturbing the peace, destruction of public property, simple assault, and resisting arrest, apparently the result of another nasty breakup with another loser boyfriend. According to Roscoe, Oliver's mother snapped the antenna off an unmarked cop car and proceeded to whip her ex-boyfriend as well as the wide-eyed arresting officers. The incident prompted a battery of state-mandated psychiatric evaluations and her eventual incarceration in the Tennessee Mental Health Institute, a minimum-security facility that housed the state's criminally unbalanced. The court kept adding to her eighteen-month sentence for persistently bad behavior. Through it all, Roscoe was always around to bail her out, offering rides to the courthouse and checks for the lawyers. Her official diagnosis wasn't made until she was already a ward of the state. Due to overcrowding, she was eventually moved to Shady Grove. And of course Oliver never went back to college, at least not officially.

Eventually, Roscoe asked, "How's Dot doing?"

That was basically the same question Laramy asked, and so many men before him. But it was different with Roscoe. Although Oliver had no idea just *how* intimate they'd been, it didn't really matter. Roscoe had earned the right. He took care of her—and not just financially—even if he did refuse to visit her at Shady Grove. Oliver considered asking Roscoe if he was in love with his least reliable employee. Or if he ever had been. Instead, he just answered the question.

"About the same."

"She need anything?"

"No, she's good."

"What about you?"

"You know any good jokes?"

"Nope," Roscoe said, allowing his eyes to drift toward the comic onstage. "And apparently, neither does he."

"You should go see her," Oliver said.

"You're right, I should."

"But you won't."

"Right again."

Chapter Nine

INSTEAD OF RUSHING HOME from work and getting into bed, Oliver showered and changed and walked eight blocks to the nondenominational gathering with the hip music and semifamous preacher, and eventually found an aisle seat near the back. On principle, he avoided the last row.

His mission that particular morning was a specific one. He was there to pray for his mother. It seemed like every time he closed his eyes the last few days, the fresh corpse of Mrs. Tompkins would shimmy and saunter into his dreams and repeat Betsy's admonition to not worry. It was time to exorcise that demon.

Oliver rarely missed church, at least physically. Mentally and emotionally however, it was a crapshoot. Not that he didn't want to pay attention, but it was usually a struggle to stay awake after guarding the Harrington all night. His faithful attendance wasn't just to make God like him better or to earn some spiritual perfect attendance award. Oliver liked church. He was especially fond of being part of a crowd instead of trying to manipulate one (that said, he made sure to laugh out loud every time the preacher made a joke, as a professional courtesy).

Everything Oliver knew about mercy and grace and forgiveness, he learned through osmosis. Whenever Delores Miles was feeling particularly guilty about her life spiraling out of control and the rotten influence she was imparting on her only son, she would wake him up and drag him to church. They would dress nice, arrive late, and find a spot on the last pew.

He wasn't sure about the rules. But as soon as the preacher would give the cue to bow their heads and pray, Oliver would drop his chin to his chest and rush to get God's attention by starting his prayer first. He didn't mean to confuse God by adding a competing voice. And he certainly felt bad about butting in line in front of the preacher. But that guy had access to God all week; Oliver had to seize his opportunity when it arose. So his strategy never changed—to intercept God's attention, then try to hold it with frantic supplication, mostly on his mother's behalf. He would compliment God on his big house and the good turnout that morning. He even prayed for "big and bountiful" offerings. But mostly he prayed for his mother. When the preacher started winding down, Oliver would thank God for listening, promise to be good, and apologize again for cutting in the prayer line.

After the final amen, Oliver would usually have to elbow his mother awake.

Ironically enough, it was one of his mother's "steady" boyfriends that had introduced her to the reparative, guilt-assuaging properties of church. His name was Chris. He drove a red Mustang, smiled a lot, and always smelled like gum. Oliver remembered him as an earnest listener and perfect gentleman. He didn't drink or swear or yell at his mother. His particular weaknesses were Roscoe's Burger Platters and sex with Oliver's mother, but not in that order.

Oliver had learned early to become an expert fake sleeper—slow, steady breathing with his mouth open in a slightly unnatural position. He considered it more art than skill. When Chris came over, Oliver sat vigil in his bedroom as he did with all his mom's "dates." Sometimes the sex noises scared him, but most times they just grossed him out. The moaning normally gave way to whispers and cooing and eventually snoring. On rare occasions things got ugly and Oliver would sit paralyzed, a lame and impotent protector. Chris never hit his mother. He was the weepy type, apologetic, a pleader. Sex seemed to trigger immense and immediate guilt. He rarely slept over. Instead he would ask forgiveness—from God, from Delores, from Oliver—and flee the house. But then he'd show up early in his Mustang, wake the Miles family with the smell of sizzling bacon, and coerce them into going to church with him.

One Sunday morning he didn't show up. So Oliver woke his mother, prepared a less fancy breakfast (Eggos and milk), and talked her into going to church with him. He didn't realize until the sermon was almost over that they were sitting directly behind Mustang Chris and another woman. When the service was over, his face was as red as his car when he introduced Oliver and Delores to his wife (clumsily avoiding his mother's name, referring to her as "a waitress I know"). The wife was prettier than Oliver's mother, a thought that filled him with his own immense and immediate guilt.

To her credit, Delores Miles elected not to make a scene. She was overly sweet and kept the conversation going longer than anyone was comfortable with. On a typical ride home from church she would ask Oliver all about the sermon and how they could apply it to their lives. He eventually learned not to get his hopes up, however. That day though she took Oliver through the McDonald's drive-thru, then gave him a ten-dollar bill and turned him loose in a convenience store. After that, she went home and drank herself into a three-day oblivion.

Oliver realized he was nodding off in the pew, just like his mother, when he heard what sounded like a familiar sneeze. So he sat up straighter and unwrapped a fresh piece of cinnamon gum. The guy making the announcements had the hiccups, which sparked titters of good-natured laughter. The worship band launched into a lively set. The players were about Oliver's age, all sporting cool haircuts and expensive jeans. He sang along with the songs he recognized and scanned the church bulletin during the ones he didn't. Oliver was more than a little pleased to see the morning's sermon title: *Sifting the Ruins to Find Your Purpose.*

As the final song wound down, Oliver couldn't help wishing his mother were with him in the pew.

The worship band milked the last somber chord as the preacher took his position behind the pulpit. Before the words *Let us pray* reached the back of the room, Oliver had leaned forward, planted his elbows on his knees, and buried his face in his hands. As silly as it was, he was still trying to capture his share of God's attention by getting a small head start. Oliver's prayers still lacked formality or even the use of complete sentences. Instead he conjured an image of his mother, then lobbed a series of blessings and entreaties and requests toward heaven, all on her behalf.

Oliver didn't wake up until the drummer clicked off the final, benedictory song. Everyone stood in unison. Oliver looked at his pew mates, but no one would meet his eyes. He stared at the simple wooden cross above the pulpit and offered two more prayers—one to assuage his guilt for sleeping through church and another, more desperate plea for God to not let him turn out like his mother.

Neither felt very effective and Oliver slipped out of the pew and into the sunshine. He nodded and smiled at the familiar faces but kept his head down to avoid making small talk. When he heard the familiar sneeze again he looked up and thought he saw Mattie ambling down the sidewalk. He quickened his pace and eventually caught up with her as she was unlocking a silver Honda Civic.

She looked startled when he said hello.

"Oh, hey there, Oliver."

"So," he said. "Do you go to this church too?"

She looked confused, as if contemplating a much harder question than the one he asked. Finally she said, "No, not really."

He wasn't sure what to say next, so he pointed to her purse and said the first thing that popped into his head. "That's one green banana."

Mattie lifted the severely under-ripe banana, ran her thumb along its contour, then dropped it back into her purse.

"Yes," she said. "I suppose it is."

"Do you really eat it that way?"

"Oh, no. I hate bananas."

"Then why are you carrying one around?"

"I just like the way it looks."

"Oh, okay. Well I guess I'll see you at work then."

Chapter Ten

Although they'd come a long way in one short week, the new girl was definitely going to cramp his style. According to Sherman, Oliver's job description now included keeping a wtchful eye on Mattie. And the more he watched her, the more he *liked* watching her.

Oliver paused outside Mattie's door, arranged his features into a serious security guard expression, dialed in the access code, then opened the door.

"Just finishing up my rounds," he said, his voice pitched lower than necessary. But it made him sound ridiculous, not masculine or casual or even very sane. "And I brought coffee."

"My hero," Mattie said, then ran another quick two-handed calculation on her adding machines.

Oliver poured a cup, scooped a handful of creams and sugars, and said, "So how do you take it?"

"Surprise me," she said.

Oliver laughed politely. "Seriously, just let me know and I'll fix it any way you like."

"I am serious; just stir something in there. I like to be surprised."

So he dumped in one sugar and two creams and set it on her desk. He poured himself a cup as she worked, then finally said, "Okay, then. You need anything else?"

Mattie hit Enter on her computer, swiveled her chair to face him, and said, "I don't suppose you play drums?"

"I used to be pretty good with a pair of Lincoln Logs and toy bongos."

"I like that, very alternative." Mattie sipped her coffee and nodded her approval. "You interested in auditioning?"

"Maybe," he said. "What's it pay?"

"At this point, we're still a nonprofit organization."

"Not by design, I take it?"

"You can't make money doing original music in this town." Mattie squinted at something on her computer screen, tapped a series of keys, then hit Enter. By the time the screen went blank, Mattie had pulled a huge wad of dark blue yarn into her lap and began clicking a pair of long needles together. "Besides, our band is too gimmicky."

"So why do you do it?"

"Do what?" Mattie counted a series of tiny loops and frowned. She unwound several inches and began again. "The knitting or the band?"

"Both," Oliver said.

"Knitting relaxes me. It allows my mind to wander, fosters creativity. But I only know how to make scarves and shawls." She inspected what was left of her work, then unraveled the entire thing and started over. "As far as the band goes, I'm the glue. I write the lyrics and break up all the fights. Keeping the band together keeps my kid brother married, in school, and off drugs."

"I don't think I've ever met anyone that played in a band against her will."

"It's a bit complicated, like a soap opera plot."

"Try me," Oliver said. "I used to watch *The Young and the Restless* with my mom."

"The drummer's about to go on maternity leave. She's also about to marry my brother, who's a recovering addict and claims music is the only thing that curbs his craving for meth. So I plan to hang around until he gets his diploma, then I'm gone. Of course he doesn't know that. But by then, he'll be employable. Not to mention, a husband and a father."

"So what will you do then?"

"Finish a few more semesters of college, then move to New York to chase my own improbable dream."

"Which is?"

"To write and record my own songs." Mattie tugged on the line of yarn that fed her giant aluminum chopsticks. "And hopefully make a million dollars in the process. But first I need to find a roommate willing to take over my lease. I can't really afford to pay rent in two places."

"Pardon me for saying so, but you just don't seem like the band type."

Mattie reached into her bag and retrieved a tattered piece of cardboard that looked to Oliver like instructions. She compared the illustration on the card to the wad of yarn in her lap. "So what 'type' do I seem to you?"

The deceptively pretty type, Oliver thought. *And a really bad knitter.*

"I didn't mean anything by it," he said. "Actually, you should be flattered."

"And why is that?"

"Because everyone else I know who plays in bands needs to bathe more."

Oliver watched Mattie wage her own small-scale sword fight. Clearly, she was coordinated. And quick. But she seemed to be sacrificing accuracy for speed. As if on cue, she seemed to spear the yarn when she should have looped it. Or maybe it was the other way around. But instead of correcting her error, she tried to knit through it and ended up making a thick knot.

"I wish you'd stop watching and say something."

"Oh, right. Okay, so what's the name of your band?"

"Trust me, you don't want to know that."

"Or maybe you just don't want me to know?"

"It's a totally dorky name, even more so at three a.m."

"Hey, it can't be as a bad as Elvis Hitler or Cat Butt."

"You'd be surprised."

"Why don't you just change it if it's so embarrassing?"

"It's not my band. I'm just the lowly bass player."

"Like the Talking Heads, right? Didn't they have a girl bass player?"

"Tina Weymouth, yes. But a less sexist way to think about it might be that she's just a tremendously talented musician. Her ability to mass-produce estrogen really had nothing to do with her bass-playing skills."

"Sorry, I didn't mean anything by it."

"You keep saying that. That you don't actually mean what you're saying. If you keep that up, I'm not going to know what to believe. Anyway," she continued. "I'm not offended. I'd just hate to see you get beaten up by another girl."

"That was no girl," Oliver said, much louder than necessary. "It was a man, *dressed* as a woman."

Mattie knitted and purled and said, "Looked like a woman to me."

One thing Oliver had learned during his third-shift tenure is that the freaks do indeed come out at night. On their third night working together, Mattie was on break when Oliver had smelled cigarette smoke and heard heels clacking on the marble floor. He peered out from behind the front desk and saw a mannish figure wearing a minidress enter the women's room. His plan was to wait for the guy to come out and politely remind him of the hotel's no-smoking policy. But fifteen minutes later, Mattie still wasn't back at her desk, the drag queen was still in the restroom, and the smell of smoke was getting stronger. So Oliver approached the ladies' room and knocked.

He eased the door open and offered a flimsy, "Hello?" The only sound was his own voice, cracking and wobbling like puberty, echoing back unanswered.

A red leather purse sat perched on the sink, along with a disposable razor and a few tubes of makeup. The basin was still wet, littered with stubble mites. When Oliver knocked on the stall door it breezed open a few inches, but enough to see the muscle-bound guy in a pink leotard dabbing blood from his knee with a wad of toilet paper.

That's when he screamed at Oliver. It was a shrill falsetto, riddled with words that would get his microphone turned off at Downers.

When he threw the bloody tissue, Oliver ducked. Then the guy came storming out of the stall, grabbed his purse, and started swinging. His shouts grew increasingly less feminine. And there was something hard in the purse. Oliver assumed it was a gun so he just backed away, through the door and out into the lobby.

He was still fending off painful blows when he tripped over his own feet and sprawled in front of the elevator doors. The freakish man-thing loomed over him, kicking and raining down blows with his purse.

That's when the elevator had dinged open. Mattie had rushed out and body-blocked the man in the dress, who then kicked Oliver in the face as he scrambled back to his feet and disappeared around the corner. Mattie had tried not to laugh as she helped pull Oliver up off the floor.

But now she wasn't even trying. She just worked her needles and bit back an adorable grin.

"Please tell me you saw the Adam's apple," Oliver said.

"I remember she had a long and lovely neck, the kind us girls would kill for."

"Look at this." Oliver pointed to his cheek, pleading now. "His scruffy calf gave me razor burn when he kicked me."

Mattie looked and shrugged, maddeningly noncommittal.

"And I caught him peeing *standing up*."

"Lots of girls do that in public restrooms," Mattie said. "Germs, you know?"

"Facing forward?"

"That's none of your business."

"And what about all those muscles?"

"I don't know. She—I mean *he*—went down pretty easy when I hit her—sorry, I mean *him*."

"It was a guy," Oliver said.

"Okay, if it makes you feel better."

"So do you think he was our robber?"

"I seriously doubt it," Mattie said. "She—pardon me, *he*—was a crackhead and a brute. Probably too stupid in the head to do much more than snatch a purse or steal some kid's lunch money."

"Speaking of hotel security, there is something I wanted to warn you about."

"You really need to work on your segues."

"That's what I've heard," Oliver said. "Anyway, it's about Sherman."

"What about him?"

Mattie paused and inspected her work, apparently pleased. Oliver could see what the pattern was supposed to look like, but only if he strained his imagination. Mostly, it looked like she was knitting a rag. But he wisely kept that to himself.

"I get the idea that he doesn't, um, *trust* you."

"What makes you think that?"

"He sat me down in his office and said, 'I don't trust her.' "

"Did he give a reason?"

"No, he didn't really say anything else about it at all. And for what it's worth, I told him you were a great worker."

"Thanks, Oliver. But how do you really know that?"

"Know what?"

"That I'm a great worker. For all you know, I could be making all these numbers up. Or selling crack to muscular girls out of the ladies' room. Or sneaking into rooms and taking people's stuff."

"Guess I'll have to keep an eye on you then." Oliver was shocked at how easily this came out. It was flirty and fun and improvised right on the spot.

"Please do," she said. But she didn't look flirty at all. She looked sad.

Chapter Eleven

IF IT'S POSSIBLE to actually recognize someone you've never seen before, Oliver certainly did. Wendy looked just like she sounded over the phone—earthy and uneventfully pretty, the girl you wished lived next door. She wore threadbare jeans, a faded Wilco T-shirt, and thick braids that bounced in rhythm with the slap of her Birkenstocks.

He'd gotten her name off a corkboard during a reconnaissance mission at Vanderbilt University. Sneaking into a classroom at Vandy was the holy grail of Oliver's educational larceny, but so far he hadn't worked up the nerve. So he'd sipped lukewarm coffee from a recycled cup, tried to blend in with chatty coeds, and pretended to study a nearby bulletin board. His mind had been busy fantasizing about adding pre-med from such a prestigious institution to his fake transcript when he spotted her pink construction-paper note:

> Need money for textbooks, Xmas gifts, cat food. Will do most anything if it's legal. Call Wendy.

A series of perforations dangled along the bottom of the ad. Oliver had peeled off one of the strips with Wendy's phone number and dialed as soon as he got home.

"Yeah, my name is Oliver Miles and I'm calling about your ad."

"If it's about the futon I sold it already." Her voice was stilted, preoccupied. Probably with the game show blaring in the background.

"Actually, I was wanting to hire you."

"You need a Spanish tutor or clarinet lessons?"

"Um, neither?"

"Sorry, I place a lot of ads. You're going to have to be more specific."

"It was the 'will work for cat food' one."

"Oh yeah, my desperation ad. What kind of work are we talking about?"

"Good question." Oliver realized he should have rehearsed this part. "I guess you'd call it performance art."

"Not sure I like the sound of that."

"Don't worry. It's totally legal."

"And we'll be in public, right? With plenty of witnesses?"

Oliver faked a laugh, hoping it sounded more casual than he felt. "You'll be totally safe. I promise."

"I wasn't worried about *my* safety." A buzzer went off in the background, followed by strange synthesizer noises and raucous applause. "I'm a black belt."

"Oh, good to know."

"I give karate lessons too, if you're interested."

A little late, Oliver thought as he remembered Mattie having to rescue him from the drugged-out she-man. They spent another ten minutes swapping particulars and negotiating terms. Once Wendy Tatlinger bullied Oliver into paying her twenty dollars more than he intended, she said, "Just so you know, I'm a terrible actress. I don't sing. Or dance. And microphones make me nauseous."

"Perfect."

Now here she was, less than twenty-four hours later, scanning the room for her mystery employer. The longer she searched, the more her second thoughts seemed to multiply. Which was okay with Oliver. This was only going to work if she were sufficiently nervous. Just when it looked like she was ready to give up and go home, he waved her over. She responded with a severe frown and a wary glance at the entrance.

"Are you Wendy?" Oliver said.

She hugged her hemp purse, nodded once, then extended her hand in greeting. "Oliver, right?"

"Thanks for coming," he said.

"What's this gig pay again?"

"Sixty. Just like we agreed."

"And what exactly am I supposed to do?"

"Just repeat after me. And try to speak clearly."

Wendy motioned toward the stage with her chin. "From up there?"

"Yep. Right up there."

"And where will you be?"

"Right behind you. Feeding you lines."

"I don't know about this."

"Trust me, the more nervous you are the better."

"Maybe you'd better pay me half up front."

"You mind if I ask why?"

"In case I vomit onstage."

"You'll do fine," he said. "Trust me."

Wendy sat at a table near the stage, nursing some colorful cocktail while Oliver scribbled additional notes on the cheat sheet he'd prepared.

The format was open mic, and Simon Childress, a self-pronounced "redneck humorist" in the vein of Jeff Foxworthy and Larry the Cable Guy, was the emcee. He was predictable but funny enough to warm up the overly cool crowd.

The first two comics were painfully amateurish. The first was so nervous he kept losing track of his punch lines. As his five-minute set ground forward, his mouth became increasingly dry and his voice quavered to the point of actual vibrato. The gaggle of friends he brought along applauded their support, but the entire room seemed to sigh in relief when he climbed down. It would take a good twenty minutes and several drinks before his face stopped glowing and he lost that just-survived-a-plane-crash expression. The second comic was hilarious, but not on purpose. He was a chubby college kid, affable, unoriginal, and mostly drunk. The crowd laughed at his expense, not at his jokes.

Simon introduced Oliver, peppering his resume with a few friendly cheap shots, then managed to evoke some hearty applause as Oliver ushered Wendy to a barstool in the middle of the stage. He took his time, positioning himself behind Wendy and pretending to study his set list—all in an attempt to make his new assistant feel even more awkward, which was the only way this was going to work, if indeed it worked at all.

In a stage whisper, Oliver said, "Just look at the people out there and repeat after me."

Wendy nodded, and Oliver imagined her looking wide-eyed and biting her bottom lip. After an uncomfortably long delay, he leaned in close enough to catch the mingled scent of some exotic lotion and nervous perspiration. Then he whispered a line from an old Steve Martin routine about learning to speak French.

Instead of repeating the line, Wendy said, "What?"

This elicited a few nervous laughs from the crowd. Oliver repeated the line, more softly than the first time.

"Look, you're going to have to speak up, Oliver. I can't hear a word you're saying."

This time the laughter was less timid. Oliver wished he could see Wendy's expression, then wished he'd thought to videotape this little experiment, then finally delivered the line so Wendy could hear it. Speaking through the monotone voice of Wendy Tatlinger, Oliver set up Martin's joke one stilted line at a time.

"*Oeuf* means egg ..."

Wendy's delivery was deadpan, stilted, a soft drone.

"*Chapeau* means hat ... It's like those French have a different word for *everything*!"

The response from the audience fell well short of uproarious. But they did laugh a little. So Oliver forged on, providing a guided tour of comedy's greatest hits, sampling on random bits from Bill Cosby, Woody Allen, George Carlin, Robert Klein, and Jerry Seinfeld. The point—Oliver finally realized midway through the exercise—was not to elicit big laughs, but to provide a novice case study comparing and contrasting the reaction of a comedian's material when divorced from his particular intangibles. Things like delivery, personality, point of view, timing, facial expression, body language, and strategic pauses. The experiment proved interesting enough, at least for the first few minutes. But Oliver became bored with the whole endeavor almost as quickly as the nice people listening to it. As he was preparing to end with a few of his favorite Steven Wright one-liners, Wendy stood up and turned on him.

"What is this supposed to be anyway?"

Smatterings of laughter rippled through the crowd. But most seemed to sense this was not part of the show.

"Stand-up comedy," Oliver said.

"But it's not funny."

"It wasn't really supposed to be."

"So the point was to get up and do comedy . . . at a comedy club . . . and for the crowd *not* to laugh?"

"Yes," Oliver said. "I mean, no, not really." When he'd dreamed up this little experiment, it seemed risky and avant-garde and progressive. Now it just seemed desperate, and kind of stupid. "I forget what the point was, actually."

The crowd found this admission much funnier than Oliver's recycled jokes. That's when he finally realized the point of this rather desperate comedic excursion—he didn't really believe his material was good enough for Downers.

"Well then," Wendy said, more to the crowd than to Oliver. "I quit."

This elicited a few inebriated whoops and catcalls from the crowd, even an obligatory *You go girl!*

"We were pretty much done here anyway," Oliver said, then stood and made an overly chivalrous gesture toward the steps on stage right. But Wendy planted her feet and crossed her arms. She looked anything but nauseated now. She looked like she was enjoying the attention.

"No way," she said. "I want my money first."

"Fine," Oliver said. "But can we do this over by the bar?"

"I don't think so." Wendy looked to the crowd—*her* crowd now—who began cheering for her. "I want witnesses. In case you try to stiff me."

Oliver shrugged, retrieved his checkbook from his hip pocket, and began filling in the blanks.

"I said cash."

"Sorry, I don't have any cash."

"Well, just go get your cut from the bartender and pay me out of that."

"I can't," Oliver said.

"Why on earth not?"

"There is no cut."

"You mean you guys do this for free?"

Oliver shrugged at Wendy, then at the crowd.

"Why am I not surprised?" she said. Oliver had to guess at how to spell her last name as he filled in the blanks. "Anyhow, I thought comedians had rules against stealing jokes and stuff." She delivered this like a punch line, but it fell flat. Wendy inspected her paycheck before jamming it into her jeans pocket and heading for the exit.

Oliver sensed the crowd turning on her. But then a tipsy guy wearing a dented fez stood, blocked her path, and said, "Will you marry me?"

Wendy paused, seeming to consider his offer, then said, "Maybe next time, sweetie." But when she tried to get around him, he grabbed her forearm and shouted his question again. An instant later Wendy had swept the man's legs out from under him and stood over him in a menacing karate pose. The only movement in the room was the pendulum swing of her braids.

When she turned to leave again, Wendy added a noticeable sashay to her gait, which caused a groundswell of applause to gather in her wake. Before pushing through the door, Wendy turned to her new admirers and offered a formal bow. Some smart aleck stood up, so several more followed suit, all men of course.

Still, it was the first time Oliver had ever seen a standing ovation on open-mic night.

. . .

"This seat taken?"

Oliver looked up, pleased to see Simon instead of an angry club owner or Wendy coming back to karate chop him for writing a bad check. Without waiting for an invitation, Simon stretched out opposite Oliver in the booth.

"You sulking over the girl?" he said. "Or the lame set?"

"My set wasn't that bad."

"It wasn't that good, either. At least not up to your standards."

"Thanks. I think."

"You're a funny guy, Oliver. But you can be your own worst enemy. When you get up there and tell jokes, it's good stuff. Sometimes it kills."

"I think I have a confession to make." Oliver spun his coffee mug until the handle was on the opposite side, then lifted it and sipped. "I hate my act."

"Hah, that's the funniest thing you've said all night."

"Maybe so. But it's definitely the most honest thing I've said all night."

"You do realize that there's a dozen other comics in town that'd give their left funny bone for your material? Half of them are sitting out there tonight, waiting their turn."

"They can have it."

"Present company included?" Simon said.

"You actually want some of my material?"

"Not all of it. But you have a few bits I'd steal if, you know, I didn't have such high moral standards. I'm not really crazy about that prayer bit you usually open with."

"Why not?" Oliver said.

"I don't know. Fake prayer just seems kinda sacrilegious or something."

"It's not fake, Simon."

"Oh, well . . . still not interested."

"Anyway," Oliver said. "I'm just tired of sitting around and dreaming up some funny observation about some mundane event, then running it through the mill."

"We're comics. That's what we do."

"All I am is a safe version of the nice-guy comics—Seinfeld or Romano or take your pick."

"Just a lot less famous," Simon said. "And not quite as funny."

"Gee, thanks."

"Look, your problem is that you've got the voice of Roscoe talking in your head. You can't let him get to you like that, man. And speaking of Roscoe, did you get the email?"

"I did."

"So?" Simon said. "I figured you'd be bouncing off the walls."

"I don't know. I may not even audition."

"You mind if I ask why? I mean, that's all you've ever talked about since the first time I met you. *Downers this, Roscoe that.*"

Oliver tried to think of a response that avoided the truth but still wasn't a lie. It was already a bad night. He wasn't up to admitting he'd been uninvited to his dream gig. "I probably wouldn't have a legitimate shot anyway. Heard it was all big names, A-list guys."

"Yeah? I heard it was all old farts and has-beens. Just like Roscoe. He doesn't even pay people, unless you count burgers."

"They're pretty good burgers," Oliver said.

"Look, I know you guys have a history, but all that legendary crap is overblown, a figment of your hyperactive imagination. Roscoe's a footnote, man. Seriously, Oliver, you're too good to worry about the approval of that old man."

"Thanks," Oliver said, choosing to ignore Simon's comments about his old friend. Besides, if he started defending Roscoe, he might not be able to stop. And he'd already lost one argument tonight. "Anyway, what's wrong with trying something fresh?"

"Not a thing. So long as it's actually fresh. And funny."

"You're telling me you didn't laugh once tonight?"

"Yeah, I did. We all did. But just like the chubby kid, we were laughing at you, not the material."

Simon pushed himself up from the table and said, "Time to get back up there and practice my craft. I, for one, have a big audition at Downers to prepare for."

"I thought that was beneath you, a bunch of old farts, has-beens, and footnotes."

"A gig is a gig, man," Simon said, but his voice sounded distant, distracted. He was craning his neck for a better look at the bottom of Oliver's set list. "Besides, some of those old farts are still pretty funny."

"Wait," Oliver said. "You didn't come over here to cheer me up at all, did you? You just wanted Wendy's phone number."

Simon replied with a guilty shrug.

"What happened to your flight attendant girlfriend?"

"She's attending to a flight at the moment."

"I don't think so, Simon." Oliver folded the set list and slipped it into his hip pocket. "I refuse to contribute to the delinquency of a serial womanizer."

"Too late," Simon said, reciting seven digits as he made his way back to the stage.

Chapter Twelve

SOMETIMES THE TRUTH sneaks up on you when you least expect it. Like when you're sipping coffee in a booth and one of your so-called colleagues plops down across from you and suggests that you may be wasting your talent, even *if* that so-called colleague is more interested in scoring some strange girl's phone number than in helping your career.

Oliver didn't mean to say it. As far as he knew, he'd never even considered it before. But as soon as the sentence came flying out of his mouth, he knew it was probably the most sincere thing he'd said in months. And now that he'd said it, he couldn't take it back. Or stop thinking about it.

He really did hate his act.

Not that he was ashamed of it. Objectively speaking, he'd come up with some genuinely funny stuff. After years of serious study, Oliver had certainly figured out how to manufacture laughs. But it was the "figuring out" part that didn't sit right. As if he'd reduced stand-up comedy to a Rubik's Cube, a crossword puzzle, or an episode of *Murder, She Wrote*. Like humor was something to be solved or decoded.

Oliver finished his midnight rounds and sat in the lobby, waiting for inspiration to strike. He scribbled the words "new material" onto an otherwise blank page and stared at it. Then he waited.

But inspiration was playing hard to get.

Maybe he needed more sleep. Or a better job. Maybe the hotel was too quiet. Or he was distracted by the new girl with her serious expressions and intermittent adding-machine pyrotechnics.

In a fit of frustration, Oliver stabbed his notebook with his pen. It felt so good, he did it again ... and again and again until the page was riddled with dark blue pockmarks. It wasn't funny, but it felt good.

Finally, he slouched on the sofa, closed his eyes, and waited for inspiration to overtake him. Or sleep. He didn't really care which.

What seemed to overtake him instead were the last cheesy tendrils of a familiar melody, courtesy of unseen speakers in the lobby ceiling. It took a few moments for Oliver's brain to unscramble the watered-down Muzak version of the classic tune.

"Reminiscing."

His mother adored that song, but that didn't make it funny. Unless she tried to sing it. Everything Delores Miles sang was funny, whether she meant for it to be or not. Especially when she would stalk around the living room singing the Iron Butterfly classic, "In-A-Gadda-Da-Vida." According to legend, this song title was actually a drunken mispronunciation of "In the Garden of Eden." The irony was too thick to miss.

Oliver started writing faster again. The first inklings of a decent joke began assembling in the basement of his brain for an inaugural AA meeting—making awkward small talk, building rapport, forming connections.

He knew better than to force it. So he coaxed it out one question at a time.

When was the first time Adam and Eve reminisced? Did they even realize it? Could you be nostalgic if you never had a childhood?

It wasn't brilliant, but it did have potential. He scribbled snippets of ideas as they occurred to him about their "good ole days" in the Garden of Eden ... in the days before chafing fig leaves, sibling rivalry, or phantom rib pain. But then a phone began ringing and completely derailed his train of thought. He eventually got up and followed the sound all the way to the security closet. It kept ringing, but Oliver eventually had to stand on the edge of his desk and move a pile of dusty phone books to find it. It was an old-fashioned phone—blocky plastic housing with a line of opaque buttons across the bottom. When he couldn't think of a reason not to, he answered it, assuming it was a wrong number.

"Hello?"

"Cool, it still works."

"Barry?" Oliver looked longingly at his notebook. He even considered faking a bad connection or some hotel emergency. "I didn't even know there was a phone in here."

"I set it up when I first got to Nashville. Actually ran a couple of different businesses out of that little broom closet. Anyway, how's my number-one client doing? Seen any ghosts lately?"

"What are you doing still up?"

"Working for you, baby. Speaking of which, do you have any idea how few comedy clubs there are in and around Nashville?"

"Two."

"Right, okay. And of those two, can you guess how many are willing to actually pay you, Oliver Miles, to come and do your act?"

"Exactly none," Oliver said, oddly pleased with his I-told-you-so tone. "I tried to warn you, Barry."

"Just so you know, I've left several voice mails with both club owners. But they haven't called me back yet. And if I haven't heard from them by tomorrow, I plan to start staking out both clubs and pleading your case in person."

"Please don't do that."

"No need to thank me yet. But I do need to swing by your place tomorrow and pick up some press kits."

"Press whats?"

"You know, head shots, CDs, a list of references, press clippings, the usual stuff." Barry had obviously been googling things like *stand-up comedian + manager*. "Just bring what you have to the hotel and I'll pick it up in the security closet."

"There are no CDs or press clippings."

Barry didn't respond. In fact, the only sound filtering through the receiver was canned sitcom laughter. Oliver's first impulse was to hang up. Instead, he said, "Barry? You okay?"

"Oh yeah, sorry. I was just thinking."

"Alright," Oliver said. "I'll let you get back to it then."

"Don't you want to know what I was thinking about?"

"Actually, I was kind of in the middle of—"

"I think I need some ethnic friends."

"Excuse me?" Oliver squared his notebook on the desktop and uncapped his pen, just in case.

"My friends are all too white."

"You have something against white people?"

"Mathematically speaking, yeah."

"I'm not sure I really want to hear this."

"It's true. I'm sure you've noticed I don't have a lot of quote-unquote friends—of *any* color. It's like, you know, me and people just don't get along. We irritate each other. But then it dawned on me that I'm surrounded by *white* people and figured maybe it's not people in general that bug me. It's Caucasians."

"So you're saying you think you'd get along better with other ethnic groups?"

"Statistically, I don't see how I could miss."

"Well," Oliver said, scrambling to find a way off this subject, which felt like the conversational equivalent of touching Barry's knot. "What do you plan to do about it?"

"Trash all my Weezer CDs for starters. And no more Gap or Abercrombie either, I suppose."

"Look, Barry, I really need to get back to work."

"That reminds me, I heard about your little greatest hits gig the other night."

It took Oliver a few seconds to catch up. "You did?"

"Apparently it didn't go over so well. But I also heard the girl was really hot. What was her name? Wanda?"

"Wendy."

"She taken?"

"Not your type," Oliver said. "At least not this week."

"What's that supposed to mean?"

"She doesn't meet your new ethnic profile."

"Oh yeah, right." While Barry seemed to mull this over, Oliver wrote "white people" in his notebook. "So what about Mattie then? Dark hair, dark skin, big almond eyes? I'll bet she's something or another."

"Yes, Mattie is definitely something," Oliver said, grinning at nothing in particular. "And I'll be sure to ask her as soon as we hang up."

"Thanks, man. I was kinda hoping I wouldn't have to come right out and ask."

"That was a joke, Barry."

Barry fell silent again. Oliver thought he heard channels being changed in the background. Finally, he said, "So, you want me to come down to the hotel to brainstorm or, you know, talk strategy or something?"

"It's after midnight, Barry."

"That's okay, I'm not doing anything."

"So why aren't you covering my shift for me?"

Barry's laughter faded as the line went dead.

"If you say so," Barry said, sounding genuinely hurt.

Oliver replaced the receiver and stared at his notebook, waiting for the comedy fairy to magically reappear. But Adam and Eve didn't seem so funny anymore. In fact, it seemed forced, contrived, and a bit ridiculous. He turned to a fresh page, wielded his pen, and was about to start stabbing again. But that felt even more forced, contrived, and ridiculous, like he was trying too hard. Just like the rest of his act.

At some point he realized he was drumming his ink pen between his teeth, just like Mattie. He considered barging in on her and striking up a conversation. That's when he realized he hadn't heard the clatter of her adding machines in a while. He walked across the lobby and let himself into the front desk area. Mattie was nowhere in sight. She probably went to the restroom while Oliver was on the phone.

So he sat at Mattie's desk and opened his notebook.

He started moving his pen across the page in hopes that it would move something in his imagination. That's when he realized he was transcribing his inane conversation with Barry about not having enough white friends. He read it again and realized it was funny. Or that it could be. So he kept writing. He made notes about Barry's movable knot, his new penchant for non-white girls, and how he wanted to be Oliver's manager to *avoid* doing work. This led naturally to thoughts about Mr. Sherman, a man obsessed with appearances who absentmindedly picked his nose, which segued to even more thoughts about haunted hotels, night auditors in silky pj's, unsolved robberies, getting pummeled by a drug-addled transvestite, not to mention Oliver's raging ineptitude as a security guard or the pretty girl with the dueling adding machines.

It dawned on him that he'd been looking in all the wrong places, or at least all the same places all the other comics were looking—airports, Burger Kings, television commercials, cereal boxes, and college campuses. He'd been mining the same ore, searching for common denominators, things that people could easily recognize and relate to.

Maybe it was time to take his mother's advice to another, more personal level. The material culled from his own life had resonance; it rang true. He was contemplating this minor epiphany when something else began to ring true. It was a telephone.

"Front desk," Oliver said.

The voice on the other end was breathless, bordering on panic. "I need to speak with hotel security."

"That's me," Oliver said.

"I'm calling to report a prowler on the fourth floor."

A prowler? "So there's someone roaming your hallway?"

"No, it was a bit more, um, *intimate* than that."

"Could you be a little more specific?"

"Look, I'm not crazy. I don't even believe in ghosts. But someone, or at least some*thing*, was in my room."

"I'll be right up," Oliver said.

He waited a few minutes for Mattie to return from the restroom, but decided to leave a note on her desk instead. It didn't take long to determine that, indeed, the guest was a little crazy, that she definitely did believe in ghosts. Her tale was a stilted retelling of one of the more popular Harrington ghost stories, the one where the Old Man visits unsuspecting virgins in the middle of the night and seduces them. In short, all the guest in 403 really wanted was attention.

When Oliver returned, Mattie was at her desk abusing her adding machines.

"Hey," he said, "you didn't happen to be wandering around the fourth floor scaring the guests, did you?"

"Well, I certainly didn't mean to scare anybody."

Oliver waited for her to crack a smile.

Chapter Thirteen

OLIVER SAT UP IN BED. The only evidence that he'd actually been sleeping was the last few strands of a dissolving dream. It was the recurring one where he'd finally been invited to do stand-up on *Letterman* or *Kimmel*, but found himself wandering aimlessly through a maze of studio corridors unable to find his way to the stage. Of course he never actually made it to the stage. On those rare occasions where his personal dream weaver did escort him to the stage, the curtain would open to reveal Oliver in his underwear or pajamas. Or worse, in his security uniform.

He thought about falling back into bed but knew it wouldn't do any good. Something about sleeping with the sun out made him hopelessly groggy while making it impossible for him to fall back asleep. So he grabbed his notebook and padded off toward the tiny bathroom at the end of the hall. After reconciling with his bladder, Oliver put the seat down (in honor of his mother), washed his hands, then began scribbling ideas in his notebook about stealing his education. He read from his notebook as he walked, mumbling potential one-liners about actually feeling *guilty* for skipping stolen classes.

That's when he stepped into the kitchen and saw Joey sitting at the table, choking to death on a peanut butter sandwich.

. . .

If Joey had a last name, Oliver had never heard it. Not once in the dozens of times the rotund little handyman had introduced himself had he mentioned his last name. Oliver had never asked because he didn't want to know. He was afraid the man would say "Miles." This was Oliver's singular thought as he piloted his mind from a creative trance to a more robotic progression of moving in behind Joey, gripping his midsection with interlocking fists, and thrusting hard.

He'd perfected this technique in health class, albeit on a much thinner, less pliable crash test dummy. The teacher had praised Oliver as being a "natural," going so far as to announce (far too loudly for Oliver's liking), "If my gullet ever needs a good plunging, I sure hope you're noshing nearby." He was the kind of teacher who named the dummies after famous inventors and carried fake plastic vomit in his pocket to help crystallize teaching moments. "Seriously, son, I have no idea who you are, but you would have made Herr Heimlich proud."

What Oliver had meant to do was keep quiet and disappear. But then he'd heard himself say, "Actually, Heimlich was from Delaware."

The teacher found this hilarious. Oliver never returned to that class.

Joey remained eerily quiet as he strained and writhed in Oliver's grasp. But no matter how hard he dug his thumb knuckles into the soft flesh between Joey's ribs, the man continued to *not* breathe. Oliver paused, regripped, and was just about to yank with all his might when Joey arced his fat little leg backward and swept Oliver's legs out from under him.

Feelings of anger and betrayal clouded Oliver's head as the two men plummeted forward toward the kitchen floor. But he didn't let go.

They landed with a breathless thud, which resulted in a strained belching sound, followed by a wet plop.

Both men stood awkwardly. Oliver was rubbing his aching hands when Joey extended one of his own and said, "Hi there, I'm Joey. And thanks for saving my life."

"Thanks for not dying," Oliver said, vaguely eyeing the gooey remains of Joey's sandwich. "Were you going to, wash your hands?"

"Hadn't planned on it. But if it'll make you beel fetter." As Joey lathered and rinsed, he called over his shoulder, "Heard you practicing your jokes. Just like your momma used to."

"I wish you'd laughed then." Oliver sat, his heart pounding in his chest as it dawned on him just how close Joey was to really choking. The back of one hand was really starting to throb. "Really loud, in fact. Might have prevented the heart attack I think I'm about to have."

"I only laugh on the inside."

And it was true. Oliver had seen Joey laugh at his mother's jokes dozens of times. He would shake hysterically, wheezing and bobbing and hissing but producing very little sound. Joey's vaporous laughter would expand inside him like steam under pressure, turning him into a human piston.

Oliver rubbed his chest, which caused real concern to bloom in Joey's expression. He waddled across the kitchen and sat down opposite Oliver. "I'm real sorry if I scared you."

"You know CPR?"

"I know how to spell it."

Joey jiggled and tittered and bobbed at the sound of his own joke.

"No offense," Oliver said. "But what are you doing here?"

"What do you think I'm doing? I'm the terminator."

Joey wet his grinning lips and leaned forward, expectant, obviously setting up another joke. Oliver wasn't in the mood.

"Oh, I get it. *Ex*-terminator, right?"

"No way, no sir. You ain't fired me yet!"

Joey laughed at his own punch line, but Oliver just grinned along, not wanting to encourage him. So he pointed to the calendar, magnetically clipped to the side of the refrigerator, and said, "You just sprayed last week. We shouldn't be due for a while now, right?"

"I suppose you're right. Got anything that feeds nixing?"

"You could take a look at the fridge. It's still making funny noises."

"I already looked at it. But there weren't much in there. That's how come I ended up coughing up peanut butter instead of ham and cheese."

"Well, anyway," Oliver said. "I really need to get back to work."

"Making up jokes?"

"Something like that."

"You need some help? You know, I used to help your mom too."

"I work better alone."

"You got any cookies then?"

"I think you ate the last one, the last time you were here."

"Okay then," Joey said. "I think I'll go root around the garage for a while." On his way out he paused, snapped his fingers, and said, "I almost forgot. You got a message from a hairy guy."

"A hairy guy?"

"He said he was a promotioner."

Oliver had to fend off dueling pangs of excitement and panic as it dawned on him that Harry McNabb had returned his call about the Downers audition, but that Joey was the one who'd actually taken the message.

"Harry McNabb called?"

"That's him," Joey said, clapping his hands.

"What did he say?"

"He said for you to keep quiet," Joey said. "And something about a mixer."

Oliver took a deep breath, hoping to expel his mounting frustration and breathe in some much-needed patience. "I need you to remember—*specifically*—what he said. This is important, Joey."

"I'm *trying* to meremember."

"Come on. Think, Joey."

"I am," he said. "It hurts."

"Did you at least write it down?"

"You know I don't know how to write nothing but my name on checks."

Joey was sniffling now, seemingly on the verge of a breakdown.

"I'm sorry, Joey. But this is really important. And I need you to calm down and help me figure out this message."

"Why don't you just listen to it?"

"Listen to what?"

"The message," Joey said, pointing with his thick forefinger. "It's on the answering machine."

Oliver scrambled to the kitchen counter and stabbed the button. First there was the familiar-yet-incongruent voice of Rodney, an insurance salesman practicing a new spiel, urging Oliver to call back at his earliest convenience to discuss new coverage opportunities. Then there was the message he was waiting for.

Hey, Oliver. Harry McNabb here. I'm the promoter for the Downers benefit. Got your message and there was no mix-up. The reason you're not on the audition list is because you don't need to audition. You're already in the lineup. Give me a call when you can and we'll talk about details.

Oliver saved the message, then called Harry's number immediately.

The squeaky-voiced man answered again and said that Harry was out of the office all day. Then he said, "Is this Oliver?"

"Yep, it's me. Again."

"Good," he said. "Look, sorry about the other day. I didn't really think to look at the other list, you know, because everybody else on the other list is, like, really famous and stuff. And like, you're not."

"Thanks," Oliver said. "Do you think you could check the other list now?"

"Don't need to. If your name is Oliver Miles you're already in the lineup, no audition required."

Oliver grinned at Joey and gave him a thumbs-up. Joey grinned back, then began a search for more cookies in the pantry.

"Anything else you need from me?" Oliver said.

"Just fifteen minutes of your best stuff. And it probably goes without saying, no jokes about cancer or any other terminal diseases."

"Fine by me," Oliver said. "You mind if I ask why?"

"Well, it is a cancer benefit. You know, for Roscoe."

Oliver said, "The email said it's a birthday party."

"It's both," the man said.

"Are you telling me Roscoe has cancer?"

"Apparently so."

When Oliver hung up, Joey offered him a vanilla wafer, quite possibly an antique, and said, "My name is Joey."

• • •

The urge to pick up the phone and call Roscoe started small, like a nagging sense of obligation. But how was he supposed to broach *that* subject? And what would he say once he did? The sensation began to morph from duty to sadness, then through various stages of worry, anger, and premature grief before settling into a debilitating case of hurt feelings. Oliver's heart instructed his brain to move his hand toward the phone. But it just sat there, limp and unmoving. The longer he sat there idling, the easier his inertia became to rationalize. Roscoe was a private man. He was probably just searching for the right moment to give Oliver the news. Or he could be waiting for lab results or a second opinion. Or more likely, he just didn't trust Oliver with such grown-up news.

Chapter Fourteen

AFTER THREE CONSECUTIVE open-mic nights of experimenting with material culled from his real life—mostly stories about his childhood, third-shift security work, stealing his education, and his superfluous hypochondriac business manager named Barry—Oliver woke one afternoon with what could only be considered an epiphany ... *he would tell the truth in his act.*

Oliver opened to a fresh page in his notebook and wrote:

> I, Oliver Miles, being of sound mind and body, do solemnly swear to tell the truth ... the whole truth ... and nothing but the truth ... so help me God.

He eyeballed this resolution, freshly inked into his notebook, with equal amounts of anticipation and dread. If he actually followed this new decree, he would effectively reduce his life's work to about three minutes of usable material. And the Downers gig was less than two months away.

For the next hour he studied his words. He edited, whittled, expanded, retracted, mentally wrangled, and eventually came up with this:

> I, ~~Oliver Miles~~, being of ~~sound~~ mind and body, do ~~solemnly swear~~ promise to tell the truth ... (not quite) the whole truth ... and nothing but the truth in my act ... so help me God (PLEASE!!!).

This new version was more accurate, but lacked the zing of his original. So Oliver drew a big X through it all and tried a different tack:

God grant me the serenity
to accept the things I cannot make funny;
courage to use the things I can (in my act);
and wisdom to know the difference.

After several moments of serious contemplation, he scratched that out too.

So far, he'd spent three hours working on his mission statement and zero hours on the actual mission. Finally, he remembered a rare but hilarious CD he'd picked up in a used record shop. It was by a guy named Rick Reynolds. And it was more of a one-man show than pure stand-up, called *Only the Truth Is Funny.*

So Oliver wrote that title down too. It was good but not terribly original, and—ironically enough—not entirely true.

Finally, he opted for something much simpler:

When in doubt, tell the truth. Amen.

So that's what Oliver would try to do.

Feature / ‘fē-cher / also known as the middle act. The feature generally will have more stage time than the emcee, but not as much as the headliner.

Chapter Fifteen

OLIVER WIPED THE SAUCEPAN with a paper towel, then rinsed the residue in the sink. After four purple drops of dishwashing liquid, he used a stiff-bristled brush to scrub the pan clean. As he rinsed the suds, he used his thumb to massage the pan's inner wall in search of any marinara remnants or melted mozzarella he might have missed. He inspected it once more with his eyes and placed it on a rack to dry. When you only used one dish, it made sense to keep it clean.

As he mopped up small puddles around the faucet, he caught a glimpse of his mother's handiwork outside the kitchen window. He smiled in spite of himself. And in spite of the torrential rains turning his backyard into marshland.

The cups had been her idea. It had been a particularly good day. He remembered his mother as being sober, rested; she'd even faked an appetite.

Oliver dried his hands on his jeans and carried a kitchen chair out the side door and into the backyard. He positioned it under the fattest limb of the Bradford pear tree, just like his mother had done a decade-and-a-half ago. It was raining even harder than he'd thought. Plus, the twist ties had rusted, both of which made getting the cup out of the tree way harder than he'd imagined. Back inside, it took him a good five minutes to change out of his soggy clothes, and another fifteen to find his version of his mother's mug at the bottom of a cardboard box marked *Dorm Junk*. He set the mugs on the table, side by side, and dialed his memory back about a decade and a half.

When he felt his eyes getting hot, he pushed back from the table and went to the garage.

He was surprised, and more than a little perturbed, to see a bundled sleeping bag, a battery operated lantern, and a few retractable tent poles littering the only clean spot on the garage floor. He made a mental note to yell at Joey about the mess as he dug through a pile of boxes that contained his mother's prized vintage clothing. Eventually he found a small plastic tub marked *Dot's Crafty Craft Box* and lifted the lid. He grinned at the familiar sight of permanent markers, yarn, construction paper, scissors, rulers, glue, and of course . . . three clear plastic mugs. His mother always bought extras—likely a conditioned response/internal urge to want to fix the inevitable mistakes she knew she'd make along the way.

On his way out of the garage, Oliver did a double take—he would have sworn that his mother's mannequins were wearing different clothes the last time he saw them.

Oliver poured a to-go cup of coffee, dropped the mismatched mugs into the craft box, and eventually found an umbrella that worked. The drive to Shady Grove took three times longer than it should have. The radio dial was filled with flood warnings.

Betsy was preparing to leave for the day when he breezed into the lobby. "How is it out there?"

"Wet," he said. "How's Mom?"

"Still on the ground floor."

This was Shady Grove shorthand for *still sane enough to take care of herself.* The higher the floor, the further removed from reality the patients were. The folks on the second level were no crazier than the first, but were far less ambulatory. Levels three and four housed the bedridden, the comatose, and the deranged. The fifth floor, at least according to legend, was one short step removed from actual prison, complete with locked doors and barred windows.

"So," he said. "You really think they're going to move her up?"

"Oh, I have no idea," Betsy said, her cheeks filling up with hot pink. "I was just making a joke. A rather insensitive one, I guess."

"It's okay," he said. "I don't suppose Dr. Strahan is here?"

She shook her head.

"Another meeting?"

"This time he's out of town. I actually booked the flight myself."

"Why do you think he's avoiding me?" Oliver said.

"I wouldn't take it personally," she said. "He seems to be avoiding everybody all the time. As a matter of fact, I wanted to tell you— "

The door to the patient rooms opened and the beefy security guard stepped through with two steaming mugs of tea. "Thanks, Tyler," Betsy said. Oliver offered a manly nod to the security guard who pretended like he didn't see it. Betsy blew on her tea and asked Oliver, "So what's in the box?"

"Memories."

"Good ones, I hope?"

"I think they're mostly mixed."

When it came to his mother, memories were never that simple. Although he had no intention of trying to explain all that to Betsy. She'd been acting weird lately, like maybe she wanted to ask him out or something. A month ago, this prospect would have thrilled him.

He found his mother watching TV when he entered the room and set the box on the edge of the bed. It seemed every channel featured colorful 3-D radar screens and anxious, bleary-eyed weather people.

It was official. Nashville was flooding.

"Hey, Mom. How are things?"

She glanced up at him suspiciously, then pulled her covers up a little higher, a little tighter. Oliver sat in the recliner and tried to think of something to say. He asked how she was feeling, if she was taking her medication, how her patients were doing. But her answers were either short or nonexistent. She seemed to be more in the mood to listen than talk. So Oliver told her things instead.

He told her about the upcoming Downers gig, how he'd decided to only tell the truth in his act, how he thought it might actually work, and that he'd even hired a manager. She didn't seem impressed. His voice cracked when he told her about Roscoe and his apparent cancer. But if she comprehended what he was saying, she gave no outward indication. She just kept staring at the television. He told her that the house was fine, that Joey was still coming by and fixing things, and he even manufactured a small chuckle when he informed her that he still hadn't unpacked his suitcase from his one failed semester of college.

"I still use the exact same dishes every day," he said. She responded by changing the channel.

At the next commercial break, Oliver said, "I've met this girl."

Nothing.

"Her name is Mattie. And I think you'd really like her."

His mother turned then, eyes narrowed slightly. She said, "Think you could fix me a drink?"

"Afraid not," he said. "But I did bring you something."

Oliver lifted the lid from the craft box, removed the trio of left-over mugs, and placed them in his mother's lap. There was more than a flicker of recognition as she picked them up, one in each hand, and studied them. For the first time in months she looked truly nostalgic about something. Her eyes darted from one detail to the next as she held a mug in each hand. Her lips kept flirting with smiles, but would then deflate into looks of confusion and distress. Apparently, her memories were as complicated and confusing as Oliver's.

Eventually she set the mugs down and fixed her wet eyes on the television screen. Undaunted, Oliver began unpacking various supplies and piling them in her lap.

"I thought we could decorate them. You know, like old times." Oliver placed a few colorful markers in her lap. "They're mood cups, remember?"

Apparently, she didn't. She clicked the TV off and turned onto her side. Eventually, her pretend snoring turned into actual snoring and Oliver put the supplies back in the box. But instead of leaving, he decided to follow her advice and try to find the funny in their situation. He opened his notebook and waited for inspiration to strike.

Decorating the mugs was another of her creative ways of apologizing. But Delores Miles never really learned how to apologize. Instead, she atoned, obfuscated, hinted at things, changed the subject, and made peace offerings. And since she never actually said she was sorry for anything, Oliver never really learned the finer points of forgiveness.

After a particularly nasty fight that started with the ten-year-old version of Oliver dumping an expensive bottle of some stinky brown liquor down the kitchen sink, included Oliver locking himself in the bathroom to keep his mother's fists out of his face, and ended with her slumped and sobbing outside the locked door, she was ready to make amends.

First, they split an extra-large, extra-gooey pizza. Then it was an afternoon of splurging on ice cream and video games and another new skateboard. Dinner consisted of sugary cereals and cinnamon toast, at least for Oliver. Delores mostly sipped her dinner.

After one such trip, she returned with an armload of supplies, announcing, "I have a little project."

Oliver pawed through the piles of permanent markers, blank pages, and large plastic cups that looked like frosted beer mugs. "What is all this?"

She bit the cap off a marker, then began writing on one of the mugs. She inspected her work, then pushed the pile of supplies toward Oliver.

He recognized the roles they were supposed to play. She was TV mom, sassy and smart and demanding. He was the lovable, neurotic son, torn between craving his mother's attention and pretending to be annoyed by it. So he did as instructed.

"Have you ever seen a mood ring, Oliver?"

"No," he said. "They only had those in the olden days, back when *you* were a kid."

"Well, Mr. Smarty Pants, we're making mood cups."

"So?" Oliver held his up to the light, squinting at it. "These are supposed to turn colors?"

When she didn't answer, he followed her gaze to a thumb-sized bruise on his wrist. Oliver pretended to have an itch and moved his arms under the table. Some days her heightened sense of regret made even his most innocent comments sound like indictments.

Oliver watched his mother work, her tongue tucked into the corner of her mouth, sweat beading on her forehead as she focused intently on coloring in the loopy letters of her name. He could have watched her for days. Although it was beyond the ability of his young mind to process, Oliver knew there was more to her fierce concentration than coloring inside the lines. This was his mother's version of penance. She was atoning, and she had to get it right.

Eventually she held her mug up for inspection and announced, "There, that's not bad."

On the side opposite the handle she drew a hash mark in the middle and wrote the word, *Half.* Near the bottom, she wrote *Empty.* And the word *Full* hugged the rim of the cup, as if she couldn't write it high enough.

Satisfied, she excused herself to the attic. He heard her humming a tune and rummaging through boxes. She returned with a rusty hammer, some fishing line, and a mouthful of nails. Oliver carried one of their kitchen chairs out into the backyard and watched his mother study the branches of their Bradford pear tree. It didn't take long to figure out what she was trying to do. She was going to hang their cups from a tree limb, and she wanted them to be high enough to see from the kitchen window. He volunteered to do the hammering, but she insisted he steady the chair for her while she worked. When she climbed down, her forehead was beaded with sweat and her skin pink and splotchy. She looked good, healthy for once.

She rested her hands on her hips and studied her work.

"There," she said. "Now, even on the rainy days, our cups will be half-full. And I don't know about you, but I think we could use some better days."

"What about mine?"

She looked from the decorated mug in Oliver's hand to the ladder and back again. "We'll keep yours inside. For emergencies."

"It's a good idea, Mom."

"And ..." She stopped to clear the tears out of her throat. Then she placed both hands on his shoulders and continued. "Whenever I get particularly hard to live with, maybe you can come out here and, you know, fill my cup up for me."

Oliver stared at his mother as she stared up into the branches, desperately wishing he could give her what she really wanted. But real forgiveness was beyond his adolescent ability to articulate. So he did the best he could with what he had. "I love you, Mom."

"I know that," she said. "But you still deserve better."

"Stop it, Mom. You're the best and I mean it. And when I grow up I'm going to find a girl just like you and live happily ever after."

He never saw the slap coming, but he would feel it for days.

"Don't you ever say that again, Oliver Miles. Don't even think it."

Hours later he found her in her recliner. The shopping network was on, the sound down. The lights were off, and she was sipping more stinky brown liquid from his recently decorated cup. In the glow of the television Oliver noticed it was empty. Then his mother retrieved a bottle from her lap and slowly filled her cup to just above the *Half-Full* mark.

"There," she said. "That's better."

But it wasn't, he thought, as he watched his mother dozing to the sound of thrumming raindrops. And probably never would be.

When Oliver felt himself begin to nod off, he closed his notebook and watched his mother sleep a while longer. He'd found very little funny in the memory of their mood cups. And *nothing* he could use in his act.

He flipped the television back on, muted it, and watched the footage pouring in of neighbors helping neighbors find higher ground. He wondered what would happen if his mother's house flooded. Did she have insurance? If not, how would he pay to replace the carpet? He decided to call Joey as soon as he got home. Then he remembered that he'd never called Joey before, that he had no idea where the man lived or what his phone number was. He just showed up a few times a week, ate all the cookies he could find, avoided fixing things, and messed up the garage.

Oliver had planned to find an open-mic night before clocking in at the hotel. But it looked like the city was shut down. So he leaned over and kissed his mother. He whispered, "I love you, Mom."

His heart nearly stopped when she opened her mouth. Then she replied by snoring in his face.

She *still* had great timing, even in her sleep.

On the way out he took his cup with him and made a halfhearted promise to keep it half-full. As he drove through the relentless downpour, Oliver put his window down and held his mug out in the rain. By the time he arrived home, the left side of his body was soaked. But at least he'd made good on his promise, if only for a day.

Chapter Sixteen

Oliver and Mattie were sipping coffee and swapping flood stories when he let it slip.

With a few catastrophic exceptions, the waters receded almost as quickly as they'd come, leaving most Nashvillians soggy but safe. Most, but not all. While Oliver napped through most of the deluge, Mattie had organized a task force of neighbors to help ferry valuables from ground-floor apartments to those on the second and third stories. Apparently some priceless antique vase was shattered in the process and now the neighbor directly above her was threatening to sue the neighbor directly below her.

"Seems to be a lot of that going around," Oliver said.

"Meaning?"

"Oh," Oliver said. "I'm not really supposed to say."

Sherman had summoned him to his office again for yet another detailed grilling about the robbery of Room 218. As they reviewed Oliver's written report in excruciating detail, Sherman mentioned a lawsuit, then realized what he'd said and sworn Oliver to secrecy.

"You didn't hear this from me," Oliver said, then told Mattie that the Johnsons from 218 had contacted General Sherman and threatened a criminal complaint.

"No way, that's ridiculous," Mattie said. A tiny bubble of maple syrup had formed in the corner of her mouth. Oliver had made pancakes. "They'll never go through with it. They were totally lying. Maybe not about the money, but about something."

"I wish Sherman had your confidence. Maybe then he'd get off my case. And frankly ... your case too."

Mattie swallowed her last bite of pancake, then clicked into the hotel's registration software. "You really want him off our case? Give me those first names again."

"I think it was Daniel. Or maybe it was Donald? I can't remember the wife's name."

"Didn't you write it down?"

"It's all in the report."

"And where is that?"

"In Sherman's office."

Mattie attacked the keyboard as if it were one of her adding machines. "You didn't keep a copy?"

"Nope. And Sherman keeps all the more sensitive stuff like that locked away in a special desk drawer."

After another flurry of keystrokes, Mattie said, "What about Dennis?"

"Who?"

"Dennis Johnson, former point guard for the Celtics, actually." She shrugged, then formed her next words into a kind of verbal parenthesis, "My dad was a big fan of the Celtics. But it also happens to be the name of the alleged victim from Room 218."

"I still don't get how you can be so sure they were lying."

"Looks like they checked in under a corporate account." Mattie checked her watch and frowned. "I need their home number."

"I remember writing it down in the file. But like I said ..."

"Guess we'll just have to break in and get that file."

Oliver laughed at her deadpan delivery. But Mattie didn't. She just dabbed the syrup from the corner of her mouth, licked her finger, and stood as if preparing for battle.

• • •

Once outside the executive office suite, Mattie gathered her hair into a ponytail. She then removed her hotel-issued vest and rolled her sleeves up to her elbows. After she fished a small velvety pouch from her purse, she looked at Oliver and said, "Ready?"

"I suppose." Oliver had to wonder if he looked as sick as he felt.

"Come on, Oliver. I promise this won't hurt a bit. Just tell me where he keeps the security files."

Oliver's mouth was so dry he had a hard time forming the words. "Credenza. Bottom drawer, right-hand side."

"You sure you don't have a key to his office?"

Oliver shook his head and tried to think of a way out of what they were about to do.

"Okay, get me into the executive suite then. And you stand guard."

Oliver unlocked the door and watched Mattie disappear inside. She flipped the switch that lit up the hallway, then shut the door behind her.

He stood in the foyer, his back to the wall, and tried to convince himself that there was no real crime in what they were doing. It's not like they were trying to profit from all this cloaking-and-daggering. Quite the opposite, in fact. If anything, they were trying to salvage the hotel's reputation. The more he thought about it, this was the closest he'd ever come to doing actual *security* work since Sherman hired him. Plus, with a little luck, he might be able to massage the entire ordeal into a few minutes of decent comedy.

Oliver was just starting to breathe normal again when a ghost appeared at the top of the foyer stairs. Oliver felt his knees buckling and his throat clenching into a scream when the apparition finally spoke.

"Whew, good thing I found you." The man had to be in his seventies, at least. His skin was so thin, so translucent that Oliver would have sworn he could see the blood coursing through the man's veins. And there was a lot of skin showing. The old man was wearing nothing but a pair of threadbare boxer shorts. "I'm afraid I've locked myself out of my room."

Oliver looked at the man, then at the door to the executive offices, then back at the man. He had no idea what to say, much less what to do.

But then Mattie emerged from the hallway looking exactly like she did when she'd gone in there, empty-handed. She was about to speak when Oliver motioned toward the man at the top of the stairs. He bent his knobby knees inward and covered his nipples with his hands. When he seemed to realize how ridiculous that looked, he shrugged and dropped his hands to his side.

"Don't just stand there, Oliver. Let this nice man back into his room."

. . .

The nice man's name was Cleve. He offered no explanation as to how he ended up stranded in the lobby in his underpants. And Oliver didn't ask. He was more worried about what kind of witness the old-timer would make should he and Mattie end up on trial for burglarizing their boss's office. Outside Room 623, Cleve stood there, pacing in place, muttering to himself.

"Did you just say something about Mr. Sherman?" Oliver asked as he inserted his plastic master key into the thin slit, waited for the mechanical click and the little green light, then opened the door.

Cleve glanced up, then back down at his veiny feet. "Please don't tell him you saw me."

"I won't if you won't," Oliver said. "It'll be our little secret."

Cleve asked Oliver to wait another minute, ducked into his room, then returned offering a twenty-dollar tip. Oliver refused it and just shook the man's hand instead, his palsied fingers unnaturally cold. Then Oliver ignored the elevator and hurried down six flights of steps to Mattie's office.

"So," he said, "you couldn't find it?"

"Of course I found it," Mattie said, giving her cell phone a small spin on the desktop. "It's all in here."

"Isn't it a little late to be calling these people at their home?"

"If you remember, *these people* like to party. Besides, they probably won't even answer. If they do, we'll have the element of surprise on our side. Calling after midnight will just let them know we mean business."

Mattie had already stretched another hotel phone over to the corner of her desk so Oliver could listen in. She checked the number again and began dialing. Between the thrill of the moment and the luxurious sound of Mattie's breathing in his left ear, Oliver's brain had almost completely disengaged. But that all changed after four long rings, when a vaguely familiar male voice answered.

Mattie's voice was stern, scary even. "Is this Mr. Dennis Johnson of Williamsburg, Virginia?"

"Who?"

"Am I, or am I not, speaking with the same Mr. *Johnson* who filed a criminal burglary complaint against the Harrington Hotel on April 9 of this year? And whose lawyers have subsequently filed, um, briefs without the express written consent of major league ... you know, like, legal authorities and such?"

Oliver felt his eyes bulging. And he fully expected Mattie to abort after stumbling over her words. But she actually looked more confident, not less.

"Oh, yeah, that's me." The man struggled through a wrenching yawn; Oliver and Mattie waited. "Do you have any idea what time it is?"

"Believe me, Mr. Johnson ..." She pronounced his name like an accusation. "I'd much rather be staring at *Letterman* over the tops of my bunny slippers than sitting in my office at this hour. But I wonder if *you* have any idea how many times we've tried to reach you during more respectable hours?"

Johnson swore under his breath. But the name he took in vain sounded like his wife's.

Mattie forged ahead. "And before we begin, I feel it's incumbent upon me to inform you that I have our chief investigator, Officer McCartney, on the line with us." Oliver cleared his throat for the sake of veracity; Mattie shot him a thumbs-up. "You should know that this call may be recorded for quality—I mean, like, for legal purposes. Do you understand, Mr. Johnson?"

"No ma'am, I really don't. Did you say you're some kind of lawyer?"

"Some kind, yes," Mattie said. "Now, would you like me to repeat anything for you, Mr. Johnson? I can go really slow if you think that will help."

"Whatever," he said.

Oliver mouthed the word *Wow* at Mattie, but she ignored him. She was in a zone.

"Tell me, Mr. Johnson. Are you under the influence of anything right now?"

"Does sleepiness count?"

"I'll be brief then. If you intend to move forward with what we, here at Harrison, Lennon, & Starr, frankly consider a frivolous criminal complaint against our client, then you are obligated under statute 3, section 2B of the Tennessee State Penal Code to allow us a rather wide purview in the pursuit of our due diligence against— "

"Calm down lady. You're making my head hurt. Just tell me what you want. And try to say it in English."

"We're asking you to cease and desist in this fraudulent litigation."

"What?"

"It means stop, sir. It means we want you to drop all legal action against the hotel."

He laughed, but not like he meant it. "Now why would I do that?"

"Do you watch *CSI*, Mr. Johnson?"

"I've seen it."

"Then I'm guessing you've seen what they can do these days with fingernail clippings. Not to mention skin fragments, pubic hairs, and all the other grimy little microbes people leave in hotel rooms."

"So what? We never denied being in the room."

"Who's the nail biter in your family? Is that you or Mrs. Johnson?"

"This is ridiculous. Did you find my money or not?"

"Among other things."

"What other things?"

"Are you familiar with Inositol, Mr. Johnson?"

There was a pause, long and suspicious. Oliver heard loud breathing in his ear, realized it was his own breath, and stopped. Finally, Johnson said, "No."

"It's a cutting agent." Mattie inserted a long pause of her own. "Commonly used to make crystal meth." Mattie let this sink in, then added, "If you cooperate, we might consider giving you the benefit of the doubt and assume you and the missus were on your way to a science fair."

"I don't know what you're talking about, lady."

"I think you do, Mr. Johnson."

"If you're so confident, why are you calling me? Why not just take it to court?"

"Trust me, the longer we talk, the more anxious I am to blister your sorry behind in front of a jury. But unfortunately for me, my client would prefer to avoid the publicity."

"I'll need to talk to my wife."

"I'm sure you will, sir. But if you'd like to avoid criminal charges, I'd suggest you talk to her tonight."

"She won't be happy."

"That makes at least two of us."

Johnson sighed, a long tortured sound. He mumbled a creative string of naughty words, then said, "Give me a number where I can call you back."

"Just call your lawyer, sir. Have them drop the charges."

. . .

Mattie hung up and released a gust of pent-up breath. Oliver stared at her, still in awe. "You think it will work?" he said.

"I have no idea." Mattie's cheeks turned pink and her eyes lost their ability to focus on any one thing. She seemed to have spent all her confidence on Mr. Johnson.

"The law offices of Harrison, Lennon, and Starr?" Oliver asked.

"You caught that, huh?"

"I did. And did I hear you say 'express written consent of major league ... what did you say again?' "

"What can I say? My dad was a big baseball fan too."

"Just remind me to never get on your bad side," Oliver said. "And how did you know about that Inosi-stuff?"

"I don't know," Mattie said. "They had all the obvious signs when I checked them out that morning—the acne, the random scabs and gaunt faces, and that constant wide-eyed look. Just seemed kind of obvious."

"So does your family, like, run a meth lab out of the basement or something?"

Oliver was laughing when he said it. But again, Mattie didn't laugh back.

"Something like that, yeah."

. . .

Hours later, Oliver nearly killed a valet on his way out of the garage.

He was fiddling with the car radio as he came down the ramp and didn't see the pink-faced car jocky standing there and waving at him with both hands. Oliver braked hard and the sound of shrieking tires haunted every concrete crevice of the entire parking garage.

Oliver rolled his window down and the panting valet said, "General Sherman needs to see you."

"Did he say why?"

"Nope, but he sounded pretty serious," the valet said as he opened the driver's-side door. "Better let me park this thing for you."

Sherman was studying something on his desk and didn't look up when Oliver entered. With his head still down, he said, "Was there some kind of problem last night?"

"A problem? I don't think so."

"Then maybe you could explain why when I arrived this morning I found the lights on *inside* the executive office suite. Unless I'm missing something, I was the last one out last night and the first one in this morning."

"Huh." Oliver resisted the impulse to bang the heel of his hand against his now throbbing head.

"Did you happen to enter the executive hallway on your rounds last night?"

"No, sir." Oliver checked his conscience as the words tumbled out of his mouth. And it was true. He never actually stepped foot in there. Mattie did. But Sherman hadn't asked about Mattie yet.

"And did you not notice the light pouring out around the doorway on your rounds last night?"

"No, sir. I can honestly say I didn't notice that."

"Isn't that part of your job, Oliver? To notice such things?"

"Yes, sir, it is. And I'm afraid I don't really have a good explanation—"

"Tell me this. Did you see anyone roaming the halls last night?

"Just an old man in his underwear."

"You think this is funny, Mr. Miles?"

"No, sir. Not at all."

Sherman cocked his head, then wrinkled his brow at Oliver, as if trying to figure out if he was joking or not. "Okay, I'll be a little more specific then. Did you see anyone from our executive team here after hours?"

"Oh no, absolutely not."

"Because we both know they resent having to 'check in' with the lowly security guard when they need to pop back into their office to grab their umbrella or lunchbox or whatever. This may not be the crime of the century, Oliver. But we do have rules about these kinds of things."

"Absolutely, sir."

"Very well then. I just wanted to make sure you had nothing to report before I hit Send on this rather scathing email about after-hours policies."

Oliver had every intention of feeling guilty about all this, but then the phone on Sherman's desk lit up. He whispered, "Excuse me," then answered. Oliver watched his boss's expression morph from an overly pleasant hotel manager face to one lined with concern and confusion, and maybe even a hint of relief. Sherman's side of the conversation was limited to punctuating bursts of *I see* and *yes, uh-huh* and *very well.* His only complete thoughts came at the end, a string of sentence fragments that amounted to variations on the theme of *Thank you.*

"Interesting," he said after disconnecting. Then he just sat and stared at the fancy mechanical pencil in his hand.

When he couldn't stand the silence any longer, Oliver said, "Everything okay, sir?"

"Oh yes, sorry. That was good news, actually. Odd, but good." Sherman opened his mouth to speak, then closed it again. There appeared to be some kind of internal debate raging behind his eyes. Finally, he nodded to himself and said, "Do you remember the name Dennis Johnson?"

"Isn't that the guy from 218?"

"Two-eighteen?" Sherman said. "Oh, yes, the scene of the alleged robbery. Nice memory."

"He called you?"

"Actually, that was his lawyer. And it seems they're dropping the charges against the hotel."

"Congratulations, Mr. Sherman. That's fantastic."

"Yes," he said. "I suppose it is."

"Something wrong, sir?"

"Not wrong, just curious. It seems the Johnsons' change of heart came after talking to one of the members of our legal team."

Oliver didn't see any obvious lapses in logic so he waited. And tried not to smile.

"The thing is," Sherman continued, "the Harrington lawyers were never apprised of the situation."

"They weren't?" Oliver said, mostly just to have something to say.

"Up to this point, all the communication has been limited to their attorney and me. My hope was to mediate this in-house before involving the Harrington legal team. As you can imagine, we don't need this kind of negative publicity. Sometimes, the less our superiors know the better."

Oliver could not have agreed more. "But now you don't have to worry any more, right?"

"I suppose not. But I still cannot fathom how or why the Harrington lawyers could have contacted Mr. Johnson. As far as I can tell, the only people who knew about this were my wife and myself." Then Sherman met Oliver's eyes and added, "And you."

Oliver almost blurted out, "And Mattie!" He could—and probably should—try and give her credit. But to do so would be to admit he watched her break into Sherman's office. Oliver decided that silence was the least of all available evils.

Plus, Sherman was still studying him, no doubt wondering if his lowly security guard had the necessary moxie to tangle with adversarial lawyers on the behalf of his employer. But then he laughed, something Oliver had never actually heard Sherman do before. It was not an altogether pleasant sound.

"Thanks for coming in, Mr. Miles. And have an outstanding day. I know I certainly will."

Chapter Seventeen

If Oliver was going to tell the truth in his act, he knew just where to start. He poured a strong cup of coffee, clicked his pen into action, and turned to a fresh page in his notebook. Across the top of the page he wrote *Officer Dan*.

As he scrolled back through nearly two decades of memory, Oliver reminded himself that writing jokes and telling jokes were two vastly different things. His mission this afternoon was to collect raw material, to *find* the funny. It wouldn't actually start to *be* funny until it simmered for a while. First he would need to tweak it, rehearse it, edit it, then edit it some more (hopefully without wringing all the funny out of it in the process). The only way to know if it was actually going to work would be to try it out in front of an actual audience.

First, he would need a way to transition into this particular story. But he could figure the segues out when it came time to put a set list together. He read what he had so far:

> … not that I'm one of those guys that blames my parents for everything. That's not my style—I'm way more passive-aggressive than that. I prefer to tell you my story in the most objective, even-handed manner possible, then sit back and let you guys blame my parents for me.
>
> This all began when I was six …

Oliver stopped and scratched out the word *six*. It was technically true, but it didn't sound as funny as *seven*. This was just one of many artistic liberties he would have to juggle along the way.

I was in second grade when I had my first brush with the law.
When the cops found me I was trying to light a cigarette by rubbing two sticks together. It was a little after midnight, and I was strolling through my neighborhood wearing a stolen dress.
Apparently, some concerned citizen called 9-1-1 when I unlawfully discharged a firearm into the Wilsons' swimming pool ... later, I would testify that I saw a shark.

Oliver struck through the line about the shark, then formed a large question mark at the end of the line. A domesticated shark didn't seem scary enough to actually be funny. Plus, it wasn't true.

The first cop says, "Okay, kid. Let's put the gun down. Nice and easy." He was the Good Cop.
So when I pulled the .40 caliber, 16-shot Glock 22 from the belt cinched around my flower print sun dress, the cop pulled his out too. He had a much better holster.
He asked me again to put the gun down, and I tell him I can't.

"Why not?" he wanted to know.

"Cuz when I put things down I always lose them. Just ask my mom."

He said he'd be sure to do that.

"If I lose it I'll be in big trouble. And I only need to be in a little bit of trouble."

That's when the Bad Cop came flying out of the shadows and tackled me in the dirt.
Good Cop tells Bad Cop to lighten up. Then they yell at each other for a minute or two, invoking the name of God and Jesus. And that's when it dawned on me why they were so mad ... I had probably interrupted a religious debate when I shot off the stolen gun.

Oliver paused and read what he had so far. It wasn't hilarious, but it wasn't bad. And it was accurate, at least in spirit. He underlined a few words he would want to emphasize, then made a note about not overdoing the stereotypical good cop/bad cop angle, where to put pauses, and the overall rhythm of the bit.

The first cop wanted to know how old I was.

"Seven," I said. "And a half."

The second cop asked why I was wearing a dress ... and how come his uniform was all wet?

"That's Old Milwaukee," I said, trying to be helpful. "You spilled it when you tackled me."

Oliver made a parenthetical note to tag this last bit if the crowd did their part and laughed. Just in case, he wrote, *Yeah, the Good Cop thought it was funny too.*

He unloaded my gun and showed it to his partner, then asked me, "Where'd you get this?"

"From the pants of Sergeant Dan Something-ski."

"Kowalski?"

"Yeah, that's him."

"You took this gun from a police officer?"

"No, sir. I took it from his pants."

"And how were you able to come into possession of Sgt. Kowalski's pants?"

"Easy. They were in a pile outside my mother's door. I got his badge too, see?"

Oliver made another note to mime showing off the shiny badge pinned to his dress. Maybe even add a curtsy, if he thought he could pull it off.

They were impressed, I could tell.

"Officer Dan told me to beat it then, said they were doing grown-up stuff. But I know that's just a nice way of saying he was about to adulterize my mother."

The Bad Cop wanted to know more about the pants. "Where are they now? Still outside the door?"

"Oh, no. I had to hide them. You know, in case he woke up and was mad that I took his gun. It's not even a very good gun. It only shot once."

The cops shared another lingering glance.

"And what about those cigarettes? Those his too?"

"Uh-huh. And that was his beer. He'll be mad you spilled it."

Bad Cop was grinning when he asked, "And what about the dress? Is that Officer Kowalski's too?"

Both officers thought this was hilarious. Which was good. Even at seven-and-a-half, I understood that things always go better when people are laughing.

I figured that was a good time to confess. "No, I got the dress off

Patty Brinkshire's clothesline next door. I was gonna put it back after I did my plan."

"Just what is your plan, by the way?" Good Cop wanted to know.

See, I was pretending to be asleep in my bed when my mom and Officer Dan came in. They sounded too happy and smelled like beer. And I don't think Officer Dan knew I existed until he saw me wandering the hallway playing with his cell phone. He'd left it on the kitchen table with his watch and his keys and his wedding ring.

Anyhow, he snatched the phone out of my hand and silenced it. Then he told me I should learn to mind my own business and keep my hands to myself. Otherwise I would end up just like my daddy.

"Wow," I said. "You know my daddy?"

"Sure, kid. I know them all."

"Really? You really know where he's at?"

"I'm sure he's in prison. Same as you if you don't straighten up and stay out of people's business."

"You're sure?"

"Sure I'm sure, kid. Now beat it. Your mother and me have some official police business we need to take care of. Why don't you go play in the yard for a half hour or so? Give us some privacy."

So I did.

On the way back to my house I asked my new cop friends if I was in a lot of trouble.

They said, "Not as much as Officer Dan."

So I asked if he got to go to prison too.

"I don't get it, kid. You make it sound like you want *to go to prison."*

"Of course I do."

"What in the world for?"

It seemed obvious to me, but I told them anyway. "To meet my dad."

Oliver spent the afternoon tweaking and editing and shuffling sentences around. He condensed the story by half, then by half again. He even recorded it on a tiny tape machine, then tried to imagine where the laughs would come when he played it back. He doubted the routine would kill, but he hoped it would resonate. Either way, it had to be better than his experimental gig with Wendy.

When he tried the routine at an open mic later that night, he never anticipated getting choked up on the final punch line. When the words wouldn't come he reached for his *half-full* tumbler of water, hoping that his casual sipping would appear nonchalant, a well-placed pause that allowed the audience to anticipate the payoff a split second before he delivered it. In reality though, he was trying to swallow the lump in his throat. He did finally manage to get the punch line out, but it was distorted, anemic, ineffectual. Not the high note he'd hoped to end on.

Thankfully he had the wherewithal to improvise a final line about the image playing out in his head.

> I did get to see Officer Dan one final time though ... when they escorted him back to the police car—they made him ride in the back.
>
> He was wearing handcuffs ... but no pants.

Chapter Eighteen

OLIVER STARED AT THE TELEPHONE until it rang again, then placed the soap-stained pan in the sink and wiped his hands on his jeans. Somewhere between the third and fourth ring he lifted the olive drab receiver and listened.

"Oliver?"

He slid the die revealing one dot directly in front of him.

"You know," the caller continued, "you're supposed to say something when you answer the phone. Like 'hello' or 'greetings' or 'Yo, whaddup dawg?' "

"Hi, Rodney."

Rodney called a minimum of once per week in a fruitless attempt at selling insurance. When Oliver actually answered the phone, their conversations rarely lasted more than a few minutes. Rodney was a terrible salesman, timid and apologetic and overly sincere. Oliver blamed this abject lack of confidence on Rodney's parents for having saddled their daughter with such a regrettably masculine name. (With a middle name like Rene, Oliver could relate.) Rodney, the youngest of seven girls, was apparently her parents' last shot at perpetuating the traditional family name that had survived for nearly a dozen generations.

"Good news, Oliver. We've expanded our family of products to include homeowner's insurance."

"Are you reading from a script, Rodney?"

"Not reading, I memorized it. Am I that obvious?"

"Sorry."

"So tell me, are you happy with your current homeowner's policy, Oliver?"

"Well I'm definitely not unhappy with it."

"Wonderful. Would you like me to run a comparison for you? Generate a quote?"

"It's up to you," he said. "I'm not really sure what you'd compare it to though."

"Oh, um." Oliver heard the sound of frantic tapping on a keyboard followed by a mechanical-sounding voice. "So, you're saying you don't currently have a homeowner's policy?"

"What I'm saying," he said, "is that I really don't know."

"Are you being obtuse?"

"Actually, I'm trying to be honest. It's not really my house."

"Your rejection would be a little easier to swallow if you put some thought into it. Take your time. Be creative. I'll wait."

The story of who actually owned the house Oliver lived in really was a long one. In fact, it shared the same punch line as the classic joke about the family who moved out of their home as soon as the kid went away to college.

They had moved so often that he was neither surprised nor offended to learn that his mother had migrated yet again without a forwarding address. He'd confronted her about her new living conditions, demanding to know how she could afford the rent on an actual house with an actual driveway and garage and working appliances or why they kept getting calls from bill collectors looking for a deadbeat locksmith company. There was no rent, she'd said; the house was paid for. When he'd asked for proof, all she could offer was more indignant staring.

Her failing memory had become a source of embarrassment for her and a source of friction for the two of them. She wouldn't be officially diagnosed for another month or two. Her vocabulary was dwindling, her eyes turning spastic, and somehow she was still losing weight. So her forgetfulness on top of all that just made her angry, confused, and afraid. By the time Oliver quit school and moved home, he'd already learned the hard way to tread lightly.

"Okay," Rodney said. "That's enough time. What's it going to be?"

"I'm sorry, Rodney."

"You always say that," she said. "But at least you sound sincere this time."

When the phone rang again minutes later Oliver had every intention of ignoring it. But *not* answering reeked of deceit, an off-white lie with darkening shades of gray.

He lifted the receiver and said, "Hello?" All he heard in reply was the bustling chatter of office workers. "Is that you, Rodney?"

He was about to hang up when he heard, "Nope, not Rodney." The voice was familiar, female, but he couldn't place it. "Just a pesky reporter."

"Is this Lindsey? From *The Rhythm*?"

"Guess you got my message then. So, you mind answering a few questions?"

"Absolutely."

"Absolutely you mind? Or absolutely you'll talk to me?"

"The second one."

"Really?" she said, sounding genuinely relieved. "And you're willing to go on the record?"

"I don't see why not."

"Cool. My last appointment stood me up and I just happen to be riding by your neighborhood. Mind if I drop in?"

"Oh, um ..." Oliver considered his house again, trying to view it with a reporter's eye. He'd never been all that concerned with image before. But there was nothing about this place that suggested "hip young artist," nothing that hinted at "bohemian chic" or even a starving wannabe comedian. What it looked like was what it was—an overly domestic, half-furnished house with all the good parts missing—and by good parts, he meant the intangible things that made a house into a home. "You think we could meet someplace else?"

"You know Flannery's?"

"Sure, I'll be there in thirty minutes."

• • •

Actually, Oliver knew Flannery's all too well. A month before his high school graduation, he'd insisted his mother put on her only dress and accompany him to their favorite neighborhood eatery. These ceremonial meals at Flannery's were typically reserved for big family announcements. Whenever his mother found a new job or new boyfriend or new apartment, Oliver learned the details over leafy greens, charred protein in puddles of A.1., and baked potatoes gaping with steam, butter, bacon, and chives. (When she *lost* jobs or boyfriends or apartments, they "celebrated" with Ben & Jerry's. Sadly, the porthole into Oliver's childhood memories was smeared with more Chunky Monkey than steak sauce.) This particular trip to Flannery's, however, had been Oliver's idea, his occasion, his treat. He'd finally figured out what he was going to be when he grew up. And he couldn't wait to see his mother's reaction.

He worked up his nerve during appetizers and lost it again when the waiter arrived with salads. His courage ebbed and flowed as he watched his mother expertly rearrange her food on the plate without actually eating much of it. When it came to *not* eating, Delores Miles combined the tactical precision of a master chess player and the grace of a con artist, a tutorial in misdirection and deceit.

At least she wasn't drinking. Not yet anyway.

Finally, with the first forkful of tiramisu poised inches from his mouth, Delores said, "Okay, Oliver. Out with it."

"Out with what?"

"Whatever's eating at you." Oliver could feel his face clenching into mock disbelief. "You scarfed your meal, keep wetting your lips for no good reason, and practically worried the stitching out of that fancy napkin."

He put his fork down, started to speak, then opted for a courage-inducing sip of coffee. "Well, I suppose I do have some news. And a big thank you."

Now it was her turn to look nervous. Any display of apology or appreciation made Delores Miles skittish. By her own sad admission, she preferred her intimacy after dark and under the influence.

"Is this about college?" she said.

"Sort of. I mean, I know you were worried about how we were going to pay for it."

"Hah! What worried me was how *you* were going to pay for it."

"Problem solved, then. I've finally decided what I'm going to do for a living."

"Pharmacist?" This was his mother's idea of a dream job—well-lit, smoke-free, steady paycheck, boring beyond belief, and a full arsenal of free narcotics should the need arise. To her mind, it was the exact opposite of her life's vocation as a waitress in a comedy club.

"Nope, something I think I'd actually enjoy. And I have you to thank for it."

"Honey, there's no future in security work. Besides, all I did was call in a favor to Glen. He was desperate enough that he would have hired you without any help from me."

"No, Mom. I'm not talking about the security job. What I'm talking about is ..." Oliver paused, trying to remember how he'd rehearsed it. It wasn't just finding the right words; he had to get them in the right order, with just the right inflection. Just like stand-up, delivery was everything. "You said once that I was born funny. Do you remember that?"

"Sure, yeah. How could I forget that?"

"I've thought about that a lot. And, well, I'm going to become a comedian."

The words felt funny coming out of his mouth. They must have sounded funny too, because his mother suddenly gripped the table with both hands and laughed like it was the most hysterical thing she'd ever heard.

But there was something else to her laughing conniptions, something cruel. Or was it crazy? When she finally gathered enough breath to form a sentence, she looked at her son and said, "I said you were born funny, not born *to be* funny."

"What's the difference?"

"You were born breech, Oliver." Her impish grin splintered into full-out laughter as she mimed tipping back a flask and said, "Bottoms up!"

Then she laughed again. It was a good sound, even if it was at his expense. He only wished he'd savored it more, because it was the last time he ever heard it.

• • •

After a quick four-point hygiene inspection of tooth brushing, whisker massaging (but no shaving), cologne spritzing, and deodorant slathering, Oliver changed into fresh jeans and a thin, hooded sweatshirt. He checked his reflection, then changed his shirt again.

He couldn't help feeling a bit like Sherman, longing for his own "feature" in a local rag. He spent the ten minutes it took to get to Flannery's strategizing. The last time he'd done an interview—the *only* time, really—Oliver had gotten so nervous and tongue-tied that he ended up coming off as uptight, panicky, and severely unfunny.

Lindsey was not hard to find. She was sitting in the foyer, biting her lip and feeding fresh batteries into a small tape recorder. She stood when she saw him, but it seemed to take forever. Despite Oliver's five-foot eleven-inch frame, he still had to look up to meet Lindsey's eyes. Her gaze was direct yet inviting. Oliver had to wonder how much of it was natural and how much was practiced. Then he decided to just focus on the inviting part.

"Thanks for meeting me on such short notice," she said. Despite her imposing presence, her handshake was surprisingly delicate.

"My pleasure," Oliver said with far too much enthusiasm.

They followed a grandmotherly waitress to a cozy leatherette booth where she then recited the daily specials in a strained monotone. Oliver was still scanning the menu when Lindsey ordered an Italian salad with house dressing on the side. When Oliver realized the ladies were looking at him, he blurted, "Just make it two."

"Hope you don't mind talking while we eat," Lindsey said. She placed her freshly batteried tape recorder on the table between them and foraged through her enormous leather purse for a notebook and pencil. "I have a hard deadline on another story I'm following."

"No problem," he said.

Lindsey pressed a button and the tiny machine whirred to life. The red Record light made Oliver's palms moisten, his mouth go dry, and his bladder tremble. They eventually fumbled their way through some patchy small talk—Oliver was born and raised in Nashville, Lindsey a transplant from Chicago; he was still working his way through school, she graduated with honors from Vanderbilt. It didn't take long to establish that they didn't move in the same circles, had vastly different tastes in music and movies and books (she used words like *art* and *literature* and *film*), and shared no friends or acquaintances. The only thing they had in common were the matching Italian salads that had mercifully arrived.

Lindsey finished a last unintelligible note on her pad, then had to clear a spot for the giant bowl of greens. Finally, she said, "So tell me about your work."

"What do you want to know exactly?"

"Whatever comes to mind, just your general impressions. Details are always good for adding credibility to the story. But mainly what I'm interested in is the fear factor."

Oliver wiped a greasy splotch of dressing off his chin and said, "You mean like stage fright?"

"Is that what it feels like?"

Oliver swallowed hard, chased the salad with a sip of water, then dabbed at his chin again. "Not so much anymore. I mean, I still get nervous sometimes. But I think that can be a good thing. It helps keep me on edge."

"Interesting," Lindsey said, but she was clearly distracted. She frowned at a spot on the table, then began working her tongue behind closed lips to dislodge a piece of something stuck between her teeth. It didn't appear to be working. Her voice still had the faraway quality when she said, "So you feel like you're on edge the *entire* time you're on the clock?"

"Well, I'm usually only up there like ten minutes or so." Lindsey raised her eyebrows, nodded absently, chewed, and scribbled another note. "But you don't want to lose your edge. Once you lose concentration, things can go south in a hurry."

"You said 'up there.' So I'm guessing most of the activity still takes place upstairs? On, what is it, the sixth floor?"

Oliver faked a cough, refolded his napkin, and tried to decipher whatever kind of journalistic shorthand Lindsey was using. She was hip, educated, and hard to follow, which when taken together, made her intimidating.

"I'll bet it can be so spooky sometimes," she continued. "I know it would scare the molasses out of me, but I would so love for you to take me up there some night."

"Molasses?" Oliver said, grinning to himself. Obviously she'd heard about his experimental gig with Wendy. Or maybe she'd been there and seen it firsthand. Either way, it had apparently left some kind of impression on this smart, forward-thinking reporter lady. He could almost feel the bubble of anxiety pop inside him. His food suddenly tasted better. The red light on the recorder seemed benign now, friendly even. If she wanted to assist him on stage, he'd be more than happy to oblige. Who knows? It might be funnier with a willing participant.

"I'm sure I can arrange that," Oilver said. "And it may not be as scary as you think."

"Really?" Lindsey dropped her pencil and gaped at Oliver. "You can get me into Room 623?"

"I don't think I know that club." Although he did have to ignore a twinge of something familiar ballooning up inside him. "I'd say our best bet is to start with an open mic or two."

"Open mic?"

"You want to go onstage with me, right?"

"No, I want you to escort me to Old Man Harrington's bedroom."

"Oh."

It was all he could think to say.

Lindsey tilted her head and said, "Something wrong, Oliver?"

"You're not doing a follow-up story on local comedians, are you?"

She shook her head, clearly confused by his question. "Didn't you get my messages? I told the girl at the hotel I was doing a story on the Harrington."

"Oh," he said again, trying not to let his disappointment show.

"You still work there, right?"

"As far as I know, yeah." He wanted to choose his next words carefully. "Can you tell me the, um, *angle* of your story?"

"Sure thing. I'm doing a feature on some of the area's best ghost stories. Kind of a haunted tour of Nashville."

"Why me? I mean, I'm just the security guard."

"I would think that would be obvious."

"Humor me. I'm still a little sleepy."

"You do work the overnight shift, right?"

"I hate to break it to you. I've seen plenty of freaky things, but no ghosts."

"That's okay, I'm sure you've seen something. Or at least heard a few juicy rumors."

"Um, maybe you should talk to my boss, Mr. Sherman."

"He won't return my calls."

"I'm not surprised," Oliver said.

"Look," she said, "I can tell you're disappointed—I am too, probably more so. And maybe we can work something out on the comedy front. But you have to know, we just ran a story like that."

"Not very well." Oliver heard himself mumbling. He was pouty and disappointed and suddenly wanted to sleep.

"What are you talking about? It was a cover story, eleven pages long. We interviewed every area comic we could find. We even tracked down a few in LA and New York."

Oliver heard himself listing all the things wrong and offensive about the *Rhythm's* coverage. He'd meant to defend the honor of his fellow amateur comics. But all he had were secondhand complaints, hearsay, and rumor. And even as the words tumbled out of his mouth he could hear how petty they sounded, how defensive and whiny and ridiculous. When his voice finally tapered off he realized he'd been talking into his salad bowl, scraping glistening pieces of lettuce into a little mound.

"So," she said, "you're not going to talk to me about the hotel, are you?"

Oliver shook his head. "I can't."

"I don't get it. Why won't anybody from that place talk to me?"

"Job security."

"It's not like I'm asking for you guys to air all your dirty laundry or tell embarrassing secrets about your guests. I just need a few people to corroborate the rumors and a few off-the-record quotes."

"Maybe there's nothing to tell," he said.

"Will you at least give me your honest opinion on one thing?"

"Off the record?"

She made that tortured sighing sound again. "Yes, Oliver. This is just between us girls."

"How credible is Barry Sherman?"

Oliver tried not to laugh but couldn't help himself. "I have no earthly idea. But when you find out, I hope you'll tell me."

Lindsey looked like she wanted to hit him. "Why is that, Oliver?"

"He thinks he's my manager."

"Okay, what about Gretchen Pendley, a former night auditor?"

"Have you already talked to her?"

Lindsey nodded.

"And did *you* think she sounded credible?"

"She sounded psychotic, like she was nursing a hardcore grudge."

Oliver shrugged his corroboration.

"That's what I was afraid of," Lindsey said. "Okay, last one. What about Matilda Holmgren?"

Oliver found himself staring into his bowl again. "What about her?"

"Am I wasting my time or is she worth talking to?"

"I really don't know her very well."

"Well what do you think about her?"

That was a good question, but Oliver didn't get to ponder it long because the waitress arrived and deposited the check, tucked neatly inside a fake-leather wallet. Oliver and Lindsey took turns assuring her that they didn't need any coffee or dessert. He was still thinking about her last question when Lindsey reached all the way across to *Oliver's* side of the table and snatched the check. She glanced at it and slipped her American Express inside.

"You don't have to do that." Oliver reached for his wallet and said, "At least let me get the tip."

She waved him off and said, "For what it's worth, I'm really sorry you didn't like the article, Oliver."

"Which article?"

"The cover story on the local comedy scene."

"Oh, it's fine. I was just blowing off steam. I'm sure you didn't have anything to do with it."

"Actually, I wrote it."

Chapter Nineteen

IT TOOK A MOMENT for Oliver to recognize the man loitering by the employee entrance as he sped up the ramp in search of a parking space. He had to assume the man didn't recognize him either. Otherwise the general manager of the Harrington Hotel would have risked more than a single sheepish glance in either direction before inching his right index finger up his nostril for a quick, surreptitious dig.

After parking and locking his car, Oliver hurried down the dank stairwell of the hotel's parking garage. Sherman was waiting for him by the door, each of his manicured hands now a sanitary distance from his nostrils. He'd swapped his customary monochromatic suit in favor of stylish jeans, a black turtleneck, and a fitted Red Sox cap. Somehow he seemed shorter in street clothes, but no less imposing.

Oliver smiled a greeting that Sherman either missed or ignored.

"Follow me," he said, ushering Oliver through the doorway. "I need to show you something."

Oliver did as instructed, pausing to clock in and wondering as they walked what sort of bad news awaited him. Had there been another robbery? Had Sherman somehow discovered that Oliver was playing make-believe in the ballroom when the last one went down? But once inside the security closet, Sherman commandeered the only available chair and began clicking through a complicated maze of screens on what appeared to be a brand-new computer. In the liquid crystal glow of the monitor, his pinched expression had melted into one of boyish animation. As improbable — nay, impossible — as it seemed, Sherman was positively giddy.

"The technician should be done about now," he said as one black-and-white image flickered into the next. "What you see here, Oliver, is a real-time shot of the hallway on the fifth floor."

A bearded guy sucking a lollipop stepped into view, then reached up to adjust the camera angle.

"That's Chuck," Sherman said. "He'll be here most of the night installing cameras and tweaking software."

"I don't understand. We're spying on guests now?"

"Not spying—surveilling. And it's not *on* the guests. It's *for* them."

"Is that even legal?"

"Perfectly." The grainy image of Chuck consulted a handheld device. As he used his lollipop hand to tweak settings, the image appeared less grainy. "We've had cameras in the lobby for years, as well as in the workout room, the parking garage, the laundry room, and the employee break room."

"I thought those were all dummy cameras." Everyone did. It was a running joke among the hotel staff.

"Oh no, the cameras are real. They just weren't recording anything. Not until tonight, anyway."

"So ..." Oliver said, telegraphing his punch line with an inviting grin, "... does this mean I don't have to make my rounds anymore?"

As usual, Oliver's attempt at humor boomeranged over Sherman's head unnoticed.

"Don't be ridiculous. You will obviously need to monitor the screen whenever possible, on the lookout for any suspicious behavior. Chuck will even show you how it all works—protocol, passwords, all of it. It's implausible to think you can simultaneously patrol the grounds and babysit your computer. That's why we plan to record everything, in case there's another, you know, incident."

"Are we going to install cameras in guest rooms too?"

This time Oliver's grin was overly ripe, conspiratorial, yet completely unseen. Sherman was still staring at the screen as if he were afraid he was going to miss something, as if he expected a masked burglar to step off the elevator and beat Chuck senseless with his own lollipop.

The tiny room had gone uncomfortably silent. Oliver wasn't sure what to say, so he just watched the jerky images on the monitor as Sherman continued to scroll through more screens, experimenting with the controls and managing to access various video feeds. It dawned on Oliver that it wasn't the silence he found so unnerving; it was the intimacy. He'd never spent so much time in such close proximity to his boss. But now he was trapped in a tiny room, close enough to hear the slight rattle of Sherman's breathing, to see the graying sprouts of stubble littering his cheeks. The casual clothes didn't help either, nor did the overdose of expensive cologne obviously applied to mask the accumulated staleness of the day.

Then the door opened behind him and he had to flatten himself against a filing cabinet to save his kidney from being impaled by the doorknob.

Sherman swiveled in his seat and said, "Oliver, meet Chuck. Chuck, Oliver."

Chuck saluted with what remained of his lollipop—a tacky pink nub clinging to the end of a soggy stick.

Oliver waved and said, "Nice to meet you."

Chuck stared at Oliver before finally squinting at him and saying, "Don't I know you from someplace?"

"I don't think so."

"No, man. I know I know you from somewhere. You a friend of Barry's?"

"Well ... aren't we all?"

Oliver didn't really consider Barry his friend, or even his manager, for that matter. The truth was, he didn't really consider Barry much at all. But that was not the kind of information he wanted to volunteer with Barry's uncle sitting two feet away.

Sherman stood and arched his back until it popped. "Where are we, Chuck? You about finished?"

"Hallways are done," he mumbled and slid past Sherman to commandeer the seat behind the computer. "Just need to check the feeds from the lobby, restaurant, loading dock, front desk, and outside entrances."

"Well then," Sherman said. He looked longingly at the image on the monitor, proud and expectant, but certain that all the real fun would start as soon as he left. "I guess I'll leave it to the two of you."

In one long motion Chuck waved over his shoulder, deposited the gnarled lollipop stick behind his ear, then opened another and popped it into his beard-fringed mouth. Sherman motioned for Oliver to follow him into the hallway. Once outside he lowered his voice to a whisper.

"One last thing, Mr. Miles. This needs to be our little secret. Not a word to anyone. Understood?"

"Okay, sir. But really, who would I tell?"

"Well, for starters, your co-workers."

"Oh, so you mean nobody else knows about this?"

"Just you and me and Chuck. And I'm counting on you to keep it that way, Oliver."

"Yes, sir."

Sherman tilted his head and pumped a little more air into his whisper. "And I do mean *anyone*, got it?"

Oliver nodded.

His boss clearly had someone particular in mind, but Oliver couldn't process any of that just yet. Something had clamped down around his fingers, inched forward into a firm grip, then began to pump. It was a handshake, the executive kind—weighty, significant, the kind of handshake reserved for generals, governors, conspirators, old friends. But all Oliver could think about was the hand itself—that one spelunking finger in particular—now gripping his, and all those nostril germs migrating antlike from Sherman's hand to his own.

He nodded again and tried to pry his hand loose. But Sherman held on. His relentless eye contact implied a pact, a newly minted brotherhood, and the alarming intimacy of a new deal. Although Oliver was left to wonder what he was going to get out of this deal, and what he might have to give up.

• • •

Oliver washed his hands four times and applied sanitizer twice. On his way back to the security closet he paused near the front desk to listen to the rattle of Mattie's adding machines. It was hypnotizing, more musical than he would have imagined, like a chattering lullaby. Or maybe he just needed a nap.

Back in the security closet, Oliver stood in the doorway and watched as Chuck toggled between two screens—one that revealed live feeds from various floors and another filled with some hieroglyphic programmer language. Eventually he landed on a screen that revealed a black-and-white image of Mattie sitting at her desk. On screen, she rattled a pencil between her teeth and studied a long ribbon of adding machine tape.

"Whoa," Chuck said. The fake leather chair squeaked as he sat up a little straighter. "What's *her* story?"

"Her name is Mattie, Matilda actually."

"On second thought, this project may take longer than anticipated."

Chuck tapped a few quick commands and the camera began to zoom in on Mattie. Oliver stared, simultaneously mesmerized by the image looming larger on the screen and wanting it to stop. Not that he minded getting a closer look at Mattie; what bothered him was Chuck getting a closer look. When her face filled the entire screen, the security tech began smacking his lips around his lollipop. Or maybe he'd been doing it all along and Oliver was just noticing it more. Either way, he had to fight the urge to slap it out of his mouth.

"Mah-teel-dahhh ..." Chuck said, no doubt intending it to sound sexy. "Turn to papa ... turn to papa ..."

Who actually says stuff like that? Apparently bearded, lollipop-loving security technicians who smelled like yeast and secondhand smoke, because he *kept* saying it. Without taking his eyes off the screen, Chuck tapped a few keys and the computer simulated the sound of a camera shutter.

"Did you just take her picture?"

"Just testing the equipment, big guy."

"Well I'm not sure snapping photos of employees is such a great idea, especially without their consent."

"Hey, feel free to jog up to floor number five and strike a pose for me."

"I think I'll just hang out here." Oliver meant this to sound menacing. But the journey from his brain to his vocal cords had a neutering effect on his words.

"You sure? Might give me a few minutes to go introduce myself to Mah-teel-dahhh."

"I'm sure the hotel has some sort of policy against employees fraternizing."

"Sounds like that's your problem, not mine. I don't work here."

"What do you call this then?" Oliver exaggerated a sweeping gesture meant to encompass the vast geography between the computers and the most remote camera on the top floor. But Chuck was still staring at the screen, playing with different angles, snapping more photos.

"A black-ops mission," he said. "I'm a ghost, Oliver. A phantom. General Sherman paid me in cash. So according to the IRS, I don't exist." Chuck zoomed in on Mattie's right hand, then her left. "Hmm, interesting."

"What's that?"

"See there? No ring."

"What difference does that make?"

"To guys like us, it could make all the difference in the world."

Oliver didn't know what offended him more—Chuck's soft-core voyeurism? Or the fact that he'd just assumed some sort of fraternal union between the two of them?

"Aren't you about done here?"

"Not quite," Chuck said. "I'm supposed to show you how everything works."

Chuck was a surprisingly thorough instructor. In a few short minutes he'd armed Oliver with enough passwords, procedures, and confidence to navigate the entire system. But when Oliver began taking notes, Chuck told him not to bother.

"Why not?"

"Nobody ever really goes back and watches these things."

"You obviously don't know Sherman."

Chuck gave an *I'll-believe-it-when-I-see-it* shrug. When he'd finished his tutorial, he gathered all his notes and instructions and tucked them into a fresh manila folder. Then he stapled his homemade business card to the outside, handed it to Oliver, and said, “You think you got it?”

“I guess so,” Oliver said, his newfound confidence already waning. “But can I, you know, call you if I get stuck?”

“Yeah, sure. You can call.” There was something mischievous in Chuck’s delivery. He paused on his way out to jiggle the doorknob, then added, “And don’t forget to lock the door when you leave.”

“Oh, right, the equipment. I guess this is pretty expensive stuff.”

“Nah, it’s mostly secondhand crap I pieced together. But didn’t I hear your boss tell you to keep this all hush-hush?”

“I guess you did.”

“Besides, you don’t want anybody to catch you staring at Mah-teel-dahhh.”

Chuck thought this was hilarious. Oliver didn’t; true maybe, but not funny.

Chapter Twenty

THE ONLY THING MORE PECULIAR than obligatory coffee breaks during third-shift hotel work was the idea of a mandatory lunch hour. Most nights felt like one long coffee break anyway. But that's what the employee handbook called for, and Mr. Sherman was a stickler for enforcing policy. So Oliver and Mattie had to cover each other's posts at least three times nightly. In practice, it was no big deal since they'd begun eating "lunch" together weeks ago. They usually took turns making sandwiches for each other. A few times he tried to be a little more creative, preparing novice interpretations of complicated salads or fancy pasta dishes. But Mattie seemed to possess the culinary sensibilities of a seven-year-old. She liked plain sandwiches, bland salads, and waffles. Her only surprise was the random ways she took her coffee.

Oliver thought he heard music as he neared Mattie's desk; however, it sounded less musical than music-ish. He paused outside the door to the front desk area and listened to Mattie strum a few chords.

She didn't sound very good. Or rather, she didn't sound good for very long. Mattie would meander through a chord progression, pause, crank one of the squeaky tuning keys, then play some more. She seemed to only be able to play well in spurts.

Oliver's mind drifted to all the terrified wannabe comedians he'd ever had to endure. It wasn't the trembling hands or warbly voices or painfully unfunny jokes that stressed him out. It was how much they cared. It was all that sincerity with no discernable talent to back it up. Mattie obviously had that same passion; he'd seen it in her eyes, heard it in her voice when she talked about writing songs, could hear it now in the fumbled notes.

As she fingerpicked another progression that eventually derailed, Oliver imagined himself having to offer lame encouragement about her playing, or maybe even dodge endless requests to come listen to her perform at coffee shops. That's when she stopped playing and said, "You know I can hear you out there?"

Oliver keyed the security code and let himself in. And despite every urge to the contrary, he said, "Sounds good."

"Poor, poor Oliver," she said.

"What's that supposed to mean?"

"Either you're tone deaf or have really peculiar musical tastes."

"Well, most of it sounded good. You just need to, you know, avoid the bad notes."

"That's actually much wiser than you know," she said. "But unfortunately, on this piece of junk, they're unavoidable. Do you know what intonation is?"

Oliver shook his head.

"Basically, the neck is all out of whack, making it impossible to keep it in tune for the length of the fret board. So if it sounds good down here ..." Mattie played a series of cascading arpeggios that sounded jazzy and sweet. "... then it sounds horrid up here." The further her fingers climbed the frets the more dissonant and harsh it sounded.

"Well it looks nice."

"I hate this thing." Mattie reached inside her guitar case, removed a torn-out magazine ad, and set it on the scarred Formica worktable next to her open guitar case.

Oliver studied the page and said, "What's this?"

"A Martin D-Series. Trish has one and I've been thinking about stealing it." Oliver checked her expression, prepared to laugh at her little joke. But Mattie's genetic wiring seemed to be missing the switch that allowed her jokes to register on her face. "Anyway, that's what I'm going to buy myself as a graduation present. *If* I ever graduate, that is."

"I know the feeling," he said. "So where do you go to school?"

"Officially, Belmont. But I guess I'm kind of taking the semester off."

"Kind of?"

"My GPA was nose-diving hard, so I dropped all my classes and decided to regroup for a few months before getting back into it. So right now I'm auditing a couple of music business classes, just in case. What about you?"

"The same," he said, thinking up ways to change the subject.

"The same, as in Belmont?"

"Oh, no, I meant I'm auditing classes too. Just like you," he added, but Mattie wasn't really listening as she alternated between plucking strings and trying to tune them. Finally, Oliver said, "If you know the intonation is off, why do you keep frustrating yourself like that?"

"I seem to have this doggedly persistent streak." As if proving her point, Mattie moved her hands deftly between frets and the tuning keys, determined to tune her untunable instrument. Oliver decided he liked watching Mattie's hands. "Plus, I can't really write songs without it nearby. It's like a big, wooden security blanket."

"But I thought you just said you hated it."

Mattie shrugged, "What's the difference, really?"

"Between love and hate?" Oliver was incredulous but tried to temper his question with simple curiosity.

"It's the same passion, really. Just has a different spin on it. I kind of think of them as interchangeable."

Mattie said this as if it were the most obvious thing in the world. And for a few fleeting moments, it was. But it had nothing to do with Oliver's comedy or Mattie's music, and everything to do with his mother's misguided passions and sloppy atonements. In one quick instant Oliver felt the phantom pain of every slap or bruise she'd ever inflicted, then felt them wash away again.

"Anyway," Mattie said. "Where have you been hiding out lately?"

"Oh, you know, just hanging out in the security closet," he said. "Sherman has me working on a special project."

"Something to do with ghost hunting, I presume?"

"That reminds me. You remember giving me that message from a reporter lady named Lindsey?"

"Yeah, the night I found you doing stand-up in the ballroom."

"Right. So why didn't you tell me she wanted to interview me about a ghost story she was working on?"

"I would think that's obvious," Mattie said.

"Humor me."

"Because, Oliver. We're not supposed to talk about ghosts." Mattie gripped one of the thinner strings and yanked on it, hard. She strummed what Oliver remembered as a D chord, tweaked a tuning peg, then played a quick succession of chords before announcing: "Close enough for rock and roll."

"Are you going to play me a song now?"

"Not a chance. I'm taking a much-needed break." Mattie stood and gingerly laid the instrument in its velvety case. She closed the lid and snapped four brassy clasps into place. "Anyhow, I didn't really want to leave my office until you got here to babysit this for me."

Oliver followed Mattie to the door and watched her hit the Down button on the elevator. The elevator dinged open immediately and she stepped inside the empty car. "I don't suppose you're making coffee down there?" he said.

"The fiscal health of the hotel depends on it."

"Tough audit?"

"They're pretty much all the same. Just numbers." The thick metal doors lurched inward. Mattie elbowed them open again. "The tough part is just staying awake."

Oliver watched the elevator doors swallow her up and take her away. He kept watching until the L went dark and the B lit up, then imagined her stepping into the darkened restaurant, navigating the maze of tables, and feeling along the kitchen wall for the light switch.

Gretchen only made that trip alone once. She swore she was followed through the restaurant, heard voices in the echoey kitchen, then was visited by Old Man Harrington on the elevator ride back up. Oliver could hear the screams before the doors opened. For the next three weeks, she refused to be left alone in the hotel and even accompanied him on his rounds. Only after Oliver brought her a canister of mace (she was convinced that this had to be purchased from some special law enforcement shop) did she allow him out of her sight at work. Still, except for bathroom breaks, she remained barricaded behind her desk until the night she was fired for good.

Oliver concluded—*again*—that third-shift work is for crazy people.

He spent a few minutes checking out the front desk area. But after a quick tug on the cash drawer and a meaningless spin on the dial of the hotel safe, there wasn't much else to do. So he made his way to Mattie's chair and sat down.

A cursor blinked from the column of a half-filled-in Excel spreadsheet. Oliver stared at the numbers, but they didn't really register. Mainly because all available brain cells had been put on emergency olfactory duty.

They say that the sense of smell is most closely related to memory. And there was something about Mattie that made Oliver want to remember things. He'd only been within hugging distance a few times. And as far as he could tell she didn't wear perfume or overly aromatic lotions. There was never a hint of cigarette smoke or garlic or sweat, just that delightful Mattie scent, earthy and organic and sweet. He was trying to imagine what her skin smelled like when he began picking up random things and sniffing them—Mattie's pencil, one of her adding machines, her miniature bottle of hand sanitizer. He was wondering what infatuation smelled like when it finally dawned on him what he was doing.

He dropped the tiny plastic bottle and shooed it away. After a quick glance at the not-so-hidden camera, he made a mental note to rewind the security tape and see if it captured the mentally unstable night watchman sniffing the night auditor's stapler. If so, he would need to figure out how to erase it. Once his initial humiliation wore off, he could attempt to turn his deranged sniffing expedition into a comedy bit.

He stood up, too quickly, and walked around the room. He put his hand on the guitar case, as if he needed proof that it was still there. Then the phone rang in the security closet.

Oliver gripped the handle of the guitar case and jogged the hard diagonal through the lobby, up two creaky steps, and into his own tiny office. He snatched the phone up and said a breathless hello.

"Working hard?" It was Barry, of course.

"Just covering Mattie's post for her."

"Lucky you," he said. "Look, I don't have much time to chitchat. I just took a bunch of sleeping pills and I'm sure I'll turn loopy any second."

"Please tell me this isn't a cry for help."

"What? No, don't be ridiculous. I'm too vain to kill myself. I just have this incessant ringing in my ears. It's driving me nuts and nothing seems to help. So I figured I'd knock myself out."

"Why are your ears ringing, Barry?" Oliver glanced at the computer monitor, but the flickering split screen instantly made his eyes itch.

"I think it has something to do with that knot on my arm. You ought to feel this thing now; it's getting bigger every day."

"I think your speech is starting to slur."

"Right, yeah. Okay, write this address down."

Oliver set the guitar down and looked for something to write on. "What's this all about?"

"An audition." Barry sounded like his batteries were dying. "Be there at two p.m. Sharp."

"Okay, I found a pen."

Whatever Barry said sounded French.

"Are you sure you're okay?" Oliver said.

But the line went dead. Oliver stared at the phone a moment longer, then tucked the note in his front pocket and lifted the guitar case off the ground. On his way out, he indulged a few second thoughts about calling 9-1-1 for Barry. He even turned to stare at the phone again. And that's when he noticed a shadowy image on his computer monitor that looked eerily like Mattie Holmgren. Oliver leaned in, squinting. It was indeed Mattie.

But she wasn't in the kitchen getting coffee. She was on the fifth floor with something in her hand.

Just as she reached for the doorknob of Room 504 the image jumped to a shot of the laundry room.

Oliver sat down and scrolled through various menus trying to figure out how to switch the angle back to the fifth floor. He should have ignored Chuck's advice and taken notes anyway. Eventually he retrieved the homemade business card and dialed the number. But he reached the operator instead. *The number you have dialed has been disconnected or is no longer in service . . .*

By the time the camera angle panned back to the fifth floor, there was no sign of Mattie. Or anyone else for that matter. The hallway was deserted.

Oliver was waiting at Mattie's desk when she finally returned fifteen minutes later with a large platter of coffees, teas, and buttered toast.

She placed it next to the guitar case with a flourish and said, "Brunch is served, my lord."

"That's okay," he said. "I'm not really thirsty anymore."

"Who drinks coffee when they're thirsty?"

"I don't know," he said. "I'm not sure."

"Everything okay, Oliver?"

"Yeah, I'm fine. I just really need to get back."

"Suit yourself," Mattie said, pausing to take a large bite of toast. Her lips glistened when she smiled and said, "More for me."

Oliver didn't jog back to the security closet; he trudged. Then he spent three fruitless hours trying to figure out how to rewind the security tape of the fifth floor. And no matter how many times he dialed Chuck's number, the operator repeated her mantra. By the time he clocked out he'd convinced himself he'd imagined the whole thing.

Chapter Twenty-One

THE PREVAILING THOUGHT in Oliver's brain when he turned onto his street was: *I* knew *I should have gone to class this morning.*

Because the last thing he wanted to see as he pulled into his driveway (or more accurately, the driveway of the house where he did most of his sleeping, noshing, showering, and flushing) was Barry Sherman sitting on his front stoop. All he really wanted to see were his two fluffy pillows and one thick quilt. He considered backing out and driving away. Instead, Oliver locked the car door, then stopped by the mailbox to perform an elaborate pretend search for mail that he knew wasn't there (since he'd already gathered yesterday's mail on his way to work). He tried not to resent Barry's shiny black BMW parked across the street.

When Oliver finally looked up again, Barry was still there, lounging on the steps, squinting at his iPhone. Oliver ambled up the cracked sidewalk, marveling at the resemblance—Barry's dopey grin was the mirror image of his uncle's frown.

"I don't mean to be rude, Barry. But what are you doing here?"

"Managing."

"On my front porch?"

"Well, since you don't answer my calls I'm not sure how else to do it."

"What are you talking about? I answered your call last night."

"Did I call you last night?"

"At the hotel," Oliver said. "Right after you allegedly popped a bunch of sleeping pills. You were going to give me an address before you sort of faded out."

"I think you were dreaming."

"I don't think so," Oliver said, not really sure what he believed. He moved his duffel bag from one hand to the other, then back again. "So what sort of managerial duties are you here to perform?"

"Actually, this is more of a rapport-building visit. You know, strengthening the manager-client relationship."

"I was hoping you booked me on *Letterman*."

"I'm working on it."

"You know, I'd settle for a headlining spot at Downers."

"I'd say you probably have a better shot at *Letterman*, actually."

This was obviously not news to Oliver, but he was more than a little surprised to hear it coming from Barry. "If you don't mind my asking, how could you possibly know that?"

"I stopped in and talked to that Roscoe guy again."

"I really wish you wouldn't do that."

"Why not? According to Google, he's a legend, like some kind of comedy Yoda. And I don't know what you're worried about. He seems to really like you."

"It's not me I'm worried about."

"Hey, what's not to like about me?"

Oliver considered the question as he watched Barry finger the lump on his forearm, but decided that sometimes the truth hurts too much. And unnecessarily. "It's not you. Roscoe kinda hates everybody."

"Well if you guys are so tight, why won't he let you play his club?"

"It's a very long and very complicated story."

"I have time."

"I thought you were working today. I would have sworn I saw the word *Barry* followed by the word *Sherman* on the schedule."

"I'm taking a personal day."

"Any chance you could cover for me tonight? Or tomorrow night? Or, you know, ever?"

"There's always a chance, Oliver."

"So how many personal days do you get anyway?"

"It's kind of a birthright thing. Anyway, aren't you going to invite me in?"

The first excuse that popped into Oliver's mind was to claim the house was a mess. But for all he knew, Barry had already peered through the windows. "Haven't we built enough rapport for one day?"

"Come on. How about a quick beer?"

Oliver bristled at the idea of alcohol inside his mother's house. She was never much of a beer drinker. But most of the men she brought home were.

"It's 8:30 in the morning."

"I'll take orange juice then." Before Oliver could turn him down again, Barry gripped his elbow and began escorting Oliver up the steps. "This won't take long, I promise. And we really do have some business to discuss. I got you an audition."

"Yeah, you mentioned that last night."

Barry looked at Oliver as if *he* were the one recovering from a sleeping pill hangover.

"Whatever." Barry said as he clicked through a series of screens on his fancy phone. "Here, write this down ... two p.m. today, at Jesters. You should be there by—?"

"No thanks, Barry."

"What do you mean, *no thanks*? I worked hard to get you on the list."

"It's an open audition, which means anyone can, and usually does, show up. And it's for that new reality show, a knockoff of *Last Comic Standing*."

"Yeah, so? That's a huge show with national exposure."

Oliver was too sleepy to explain abject lack of "reality" in reality TV. The producers invite any and every wannabe comic to show up and stand in line for hours. Their goal is twofold: one, to create hype by having the cameras pan to the hundreds of alleged comedians lined up around the building for their shot at the fabled fifteen minutes of fame; and two, more importantly, to shoot scads of embarrassingly bad footage of embarrassingly bad stand-ups. This footage is then spliced between that of the real comics who actually have a legitimate shot at getting on the show. The part they don't tell the viewer is that these seasoned comedians don't have to stand in line with everybody else. Their auditions have set appointments.

"Trust me," Oliver said as he fished his keys out of his pocket and opened the door. "Unless they gave you a specific appointment time, it's a total waste of time."

"If you say so." Barry brushed past him and stepped inside. It was more than a little surreal to have a "guest" in his house. Oliver followed close behind, overly aware now of any potentially embarrassing sights or smells. But there were no piles of dirty laundry, no moldy pizza boxes, no musty smells or overflowing garbage cans or unsightly stains on the carpet—not a single domestic faux pas or unflattering detail worth memorizing and blabbing to the gossip-mongering staff of the Harrington Hotel. If anything, Oliver was most embarrassed by how thoroughly uninteresting it all seemed. If Barry had any opinions about Oliver's living conditions, he kept them to himself. Instead, he said, "Well, let's get down to business."

"Don't I have to generate some income for this to qualify as an actual business?"

Barry unfolded a check and handed it over. It was payable to Oliver Miles. Oliver had to look at the amount twice.

"And that's just the retainer. You get twice that amount once your services have been rendered. That is, if you don't feel like it's a waste of your valuable time."

Hope ballooned inside him but developed a slow leak at once. Oliver had long held the belief that if something sounds too good to be true, just wait for the other shoe to drop.

Oliver pocketed the check and pulled a chair out from the table on his way to the refrigerator. This was less an invitation for Barry to sit than an invitation for him to *not* go nosing around in Oliver's business. Barry took the hint and Oliver drained a carton of Tropicana into the only two glasses in the cupboard. The refrigerator rumbled, then belched, then seemed to expire altogether.

"That thing okay?" Barry said.

"Give it a sec." As if on cue, the compressor resurrected itself. "So what's this gig all about? Where is it? And when? And who is it for?"

"It's a corporate thing, next Wednesday night. Some kind of fund-raiser for a big insurance company."

"Can you at least tell me how long my set is supposed to be?"

"All I know at this point is that you're one of several comics on the bill. And that it's a paying gig. As soon as I get more information I'll send you an email."

"Good, okay," Oliver said. "And thanks."

Barry lifted his glass, as if proposing a toast to his own success as a manager. Then he said, "Man, you must really love that hotel."

"Why do you say that?"

"Your place is just like it."

"Gee, thanks."

"Look, I wasn't going to say anything. But this place is weird. And kind of *old* too. It's just . . . I don't know, functional. There's no personality, no soul. Just like the Harrington."

Oliver considered reminding Barry that he was free to go whenever he liked. But then Barry said, "Speaking of the hotel . . . what do you think of her?"

"Think of who?"

"Mattie, who else?"

"Your segues are as bad as mine," Oliver said. "So is that why you're really here? To ask about Mattie?"

"This is the rapport-building part," Barry said.

"I think she's nice enough. Seems to be a hard worker."

"Don't give me that, Oliver. I know you like her. I can tell by the look on your face."

"Sure, I mean, yeah. What's not to like? But I don't *like her* like her."

"Well I think she's totally hot," Barry said.

"You've mentioned that before."

"Come on, admit it Oliver. Don't you think she's hot?"

"I haven't really thought about it."

"That's too bad, 'cause she really digs you."

Oliver pretended to take this in stride. "How could you possibly know that?"

"It's kinda hard to miss. Every time I tried to steer the conversation onto me, she just kept steering it back to you. So finally I say, 'You really dig Oliver, don't you?' But then it dawned on me that she could have been playing hard to get. You know, using you to get to me. To be fair, she didn't start going on about you until I asked her out."

It occurred to Oliver that Mattie might be using him to get *away* from Barry. But he kept that to himself. What he really wanted to know was how she answered the question, or even if she answered it. But before he could find a way to ask, Barry was cradling his chin in his hand and wincing.

"Oh man," he said. "Did you hear that?"

"Hear what?"

Barry didn't answer at first but darkened his already blank expression while moving his jaw from side to side with great deliberation. "I think my hinge is busted."

"Your hinge?"

"Yeah, listen." He reversed the direction of his cocked chin. "My jaw pops whenever I move it like this."

"Have you considered not moving it like that anymore?"

Barry ignored the question and continued trying to break his own jaw.

"Okay," Oliver said. "I think I did hear a little something." This was not entirely true; he just wanted to ease Barry back onto the right conversational track, specifically what *else* Mattie might have said about him. "But why do you feel the need to keep moving your jaw like that?"

"To see why it keeps cracking. Why else?"

"It's probably in protest. Because I really don't think it's supposed to move that way."

"Oh, man. You think I have a bone disease? I'll bet it's cancer."

"Put me down for brain damage," Oliver said, still trying to figure out how to steer the discussion back onto Mattie. Or at least get rid of Barry and get some sleep.

"There! Did you hear that? It was more of a click that time."

"Could we change the subject?" Barry's face was turning red and there really was a dimple on his left jaw that was starting to quiver. "I can see your pulse beating in your hinge and it's creeping me out."

"But did you hear it?"

"No, Barry. Not really."

"Well, listen. You need to hear it."

"Why? What difference does it make? If you say it hurts, I believe you."

"Who said anything about pain? I never said it hurt, only that it's making this weird creaking noise."

"Maybe it's haunted then. Maybe you have a haunted hinge."

"You think this is funny?"

"Yeah, sort of."

"Fine. That's just fine. My bones are disintegrating in my face and you're making jokes. If that's how you're going to be, you can just be your own manager."

"All because of your clicking jaw?" Barry slid the bottom half of his face so far to one side that it made Oliver's own jaw hurt. Then it did pop.

"Okay. Alright. I did hear that."

"Too late now. My feelings are already hurt."

"That was kind of gross, actually. Like you cracked a big knuckle in your face."

Barry lined his teeth up again, then opened and closed his mouth several times in quick succession. When he cocked it to the side again, there was a short creak, followed by a small click, then another loud pop. Oliver was about to make some wisecrack about his new manager turning his face into a percussion instrument when panic lit up in Barry's eyes.

"I hink ih tuck."

"What?" But then the audio caught up to the visual and made the necessary translation.

"I HINK IH TUCK!"

"Should I call 9-1-1?"

Barry shook his head so hard, he spritzed the table with tears. "Hake ee to da EEE ARR."

"What?"

"HAKE EE TO DA EEE ARRRR!"

"To the ER?"

In his mind, Oliver said, *I'm not driving you to the hospital, especially not for some idiotic, self-inflicted facial injury. What I am going to do is show you to the door and go catch up on some much-needed, well-deserved sleep.* What actually came out of his mouth was: "Can I pee first?"

Barry just shook his head.

"Okay," Oliver said. "Give me your keys."

Barry mimed a question, painfully.

"I've never driven a BMW before."

Once they were buckled in and Oliver started the car, Barry cradled his jaw in his hand and began to cry in earnest.

• • •

Oliver spent the morning dozing in a plastic chair in the ER's waiting room. He'd brought his notebook along in case inspiration struck. But there was nothing funny about the county ER. Unless sad was funny.

When Barry finally emerged hours later, he looked disheveled, defeated, and more than a little embarrassed.

"What's the prognosis?" Oliver asked. "Are you going to live?"

Barry walked toward the exit, as if he couldn't get out of there fast enough. He ended up banging his shoulder on one of the sliding doors, then teetering into Oliver on the rebound, and nearly falling on his face on the sidewalk.

"What did they do to you in there?"

"Muscle relaxers," Barry said, moving his lips like a bad ventriloquist. "I guess all that flexing caused my face to cramp up." Barry righted himself, took a deep breath, then gripped the crook of Oliver's elbow before starting off toward the car again. They toddled toward Barry's car like an old married couple. "Gonna need to crash on your couch for a while. Till the drugs wear off."

He wasn't asking permission, but rather stating his intentions as a foregone conclusion. Oliver suspected it was a by-product of growing up rich. That's when it dawned on him that what bugged Oliver so much about Barry wasn't his money or his laziness or even his glaring chauvinistic tendencies. It was his hyperactive sense of entitlement. Barry was a spoiled brat and Oliver didn't like him very much. But he did feel sorry for him.

As they rode in relative silence, Oliver sensed movement in the seat beside him. Barry had lifted Oliver's notebook and was thumbing through the pages.

"What are you doing? Put that back."

But Barry held up a silencing hand, then used it to massage his jaw again.

Oliver heard the scratch of pen on paper. Then Barry was holding the notebook up where Oliver could see it.

There was an address in big letters, followed by the date, time, and contact number.

"What's that?" Oliver said.

Barry added: *Insurance gig.*

Oliver nodded and Barry snapped to a clean page and wrote some more.

BTW . . . She said yes.

"Who did?"

Mattie did, dummy. Barry scribbled faster, then held up the notebook where Oliver could see the words without having to take his eyes off the road. *I said, You really dig Oliver? And she said yes.*

"Huh," Oliver said, trying not to blush.

She thinks you're funny.

"She said that?"

Barry nodded, cradled his face again for a long moment, then scratched out another message.

Sorry I messed up your sleep.

"It's okay," Oliver said. But Barry was already writing again.

Thanks, Oliver. You're a REAL PAL!

He'd underlined the last two words. Oliver didn't respond, focusing instead on the traffic in front of him, conveniently slowing for a traffic light. Only after they were at a complete standstill did Oliver turn to look at Barry. He was slouched and sleeping with a thin line of drool forming on his chin.

It took real effort to wake Barry and get him settled on the couch. Oliver kept trying to ask for more details about Barry's conversations with Mattie, but only seemed capable of slurring nonsense.

"What are you saying?" Oliver asked. "You want me to call your brother?"

Barry nodded, pointed at his jaw, then his watch.

"I didn't even know you had a brother."

Barry struggled through various syllables that sounded like "Jen—Rull—Shoe—Man."

After the fourth attempt, Oliver said, "General Sherman?"

Barry nodded again.

"You mean your uncle, right?"

Barry nodded a final time, then nodded off completely.

Oliver called the hotel and left his boss a brief message about Barry, then padded off to his bedroom for an afternoon nap. But he couldn't sleep. His mind ping-ponged between what Mattie had *actually* said about him and imagining tactful ways to kick Barry out of his house. He fluffed and refluffed his pillows and eventually vowed to figure out both as soon as he woke up.

Hours later, when he finally padded out to the living room to check on Barry, he was already gone.

Chapter Twenty-Two

MATTIE WAS ON BREAK, hopefully making a fresh pot of strong coffee, when Oliver heard someone knocking on the lobby door.

Ever since the infamous robbery of Room 218 (and his ill-fated encounter with a local transvestite), Oliver had begun enforcing the Harrington's policy of locking the outside doors at midnight.

As he approached the door he assumed his authoritative security guard posture—slower pace, inflated chest, shoulders squared in that way that made his arms swing like a cowboy about to draw. The guy on the other side of the glass smiled as if he was used to getting his way. Oliver held up his credit-card-sized master key, made a swiping motion, and arched his eyebrows into a silent question. The grinning guy on the other side of the glass shrugged helplessly and knocked again.

They stared at each other until Oliver finally opened the door a crack and said, "Can I help you?"

"I believe you just did."

"Are you a guest?"

"I *am* visiting," he said. "But I don't plan to stay all night, if that's what you mean."

"Mind if I ask what you're doing here?"

"Here to see Eleanor."

"Is *she* a guest?"

"Oh, right, sorry." His face slithered into a polite smirk, as if he knew a joke and was simply waiting for Oliver to catch up. "I forget that she goes by Mattie in the civilian world."

"You make her sound like a soldier."

"Not quite. She's the bass player in my band."

"Oh, I guess that makes you the brother then?"

"Actually, it makes me the other guy in the band. The fiancé, to be exact."

Mattie's engaged? Oliver wasn't exactly sure if he'd said this or merely thought it. Judging by the smarmy look on the guy's face, he still wasn't sure.

"I'm Max," he said, without offering his hand.

"Okay then, if you'll follow me." Oliver still found it difficult to imagine Mattie strapping on an oversized electric guitar and holding down any kind of groove. But he found it impossible to imagine her marrying this preppy guy with the great hair and perfect teeth. He led Max up the short flight of stairs, keyed the security code, and ushered him into the empty offices. "Guess she's still on break."

Max sat in Mattie's chair and immediately began flipping through an open file on her desk. When Oliver reached across the desk and closed the folder, Max smirked again and leaned the chair back until it groaned. He laced his fingers behind his head and closed his eyes, silently dismissing Oliver and his folders and his hotel.

They sat in silence for several long minutes until Mattie arrived. Oliver had to hide a rather proud smirk of his own when Mattie noticed Max and rolled her eyes.

"Looks like you have a visitor," Oliver said, unnecessarily, but it just seemed like something needed to be said. "I'll be in the lobby if you need me."

Oliver left them alone, at least physically. He made his way to the lobby, to what he called the eavesdropping sofa. It was the least comfortable piece of furniture in the hotel but was strategically placed so that sounds from the front desk area traveled up and over the wall, then filtered down to where Oliver was now seated. He then opened his notebook, clicked his pen into action, and pretended not to care about the conversation starting up on the other side of the partition.

"So," Max said. "What's up with your boyfriend out there?"

"I keep telling you, I don't have a boyfriend."

"So what does that make me?"

"A pain in the butt."

Oliver managed to intercept the laughter bubbling up in his chest and convert it into a light cough. When Max spoke again, his voice was noticeably softer.

"Alright, I get it. I probably deserve that. I just don't like the way he was looking at me. Like he was looking *through* me to see you."

Oliver felt his face flush.

"Oliver's the hotel security guard." Mattie powered up an adding machine, then another. "It's his job to be suspicious."

"Hey, I see what I see. And believe it or not, I can be pretty insightful when I set my mind to it."

"What exactly are you doing here, Max? Besides spreading your insight around?"

"I came to apologize. I even brought flowers, but I guess I left them in the car."

"What are you sorry for this time?" Papers shuffled, a chair squealed, then fingers banged on adding machines.

"It's kind of a blanket apology. I realize I've been kind of a jerk lately. You know, inattentive, lazy, distracted."

If she responded, Oliver didn't hear it. He imagined Mattie studying something on the screen and rattling a pencil between her teeth.

"So do you accept?"

"Accept what?"

"My apology."

"I don't know that I've actually heard one yet."

"Okay, I'm sorry, Mattie. Now do you accept?"

"Will you leave me alone if I do?"

"You know I can't do that. Besides, what would happen to the band?"

"The same thing that will eventually happen to this band, only sooner."

Oliver tried again to conjure Mattie onstage. The image was grainy, a low-definition rerun of a scene from the early days of *American Bandstand*.

"Don't say that, babe. The Family will be our ticket out."

The Family? Oliver jotted it in his notebook and tried to imagine why Mattie hated it so much.

"I've already booked my ticket out," she said.

"Right, I forgot. Your girlhood dream of making it big in the Big Apple."

"The plan is to make music, not make anything big."

"Why can't you do that here? Isn't Nashville supposed to be like the songwriting capital of the world?"

Oliver sat still and listened hard. He had to admit, it was a good question.

"Too many distractions, for one thing," she said.

"Are you talking about me?"

"Well I do have work to do. And you are still distracting me."

"Speaking of work. Are you sure this is such a great job for you? You know, with your, um, proclivities?"

If Mattie answered, Oliver didn't hear it.

"Right," Max said. "That's cool. I'll just nap while you finish up. I've got a couple of good song ideas I thought we could work out later."

"This is a hotel, Max. Not a rehearsal hall."

"Did I ever tell you you're sexy when you're mad?"

It took a few seconds for Oliver to recognize his competing urges—one to barge in and punch Max, and another to run to the security closet and zoom in on this ostensibly sexy look. Instead he sat still and listened.

"I think you may be confusing me with someone else."

"Okay, I can take a hint. I'll get going. But first I want a kiss."

"From who?"

"Come on, Mattie. You have the best kisses."

This reminded Oliver of a radio commercial for one of those alleged reality TV shows about bachelors choosing from a smorgasbord of eligible ladies. It also made Oliver wonder what it might be like to kiss the new night auditor.

"The best?" she said. "How very superlative of you."

"Yeah, so? What's wrong with that?"

"Nothing, nothing at all. It makes sense now. What some consider infidelity was really just some kind of comparative smooching contest. But hey, at least I came out on top."

"Come on. Not this again, Mattie."

"What did I win, Max? Golly gee, I hope it's Tupperware."

Oliver tried the laugh-suppressant coughing maneuver again but failed miserably.

"How many times do I have to apologize for my, you know, lapses in judgment?"

"I think the Bible mentions seventy times seven."

"Hah, that's how many times you're supposed to turn the other cheek. Besides, she threw herself at me."

"I know. They all do, Max. You're irresistible."

"Then why do you continue to resist?"

"It builds character."

Oliver didn't realize it until then that he'd been transcribing bits of their conversation. Nor did he realize his envy. Mattie was way funnier than Oliver felt. And she didn't even seem to be trying.

"Come on, babe."

There was movement on the other side of the wall—the creak of a chair, the shuffle of feet, a muted slapping sound. Oliver froze, cursing his lack of security guard instincts.

"I'm serious, Max. Knock it off, or . . ."

"Or what? You gonna call your boyfriend to come run me off?"

"Yeah, Max. That's exactly what I'm going to do."

Oliver's grin faltered when he realized that she was talking about him. That he was the only security guard on the property. And that if she did call upon him, that he would actually have to do something about Max, who was much bigger than Oliver. At least it would be two against one.

"What do you see in that guy, anyway?"

"Grow up, Max. The world is not one big singles' bar."

"You know, you used to make that same face at the sound of my name, back in the day, back when I mattered."

"You still matter, Max. Just not to me. Or at least not in that way."

• • •

Oliver pretended to be engrossed in the mostly blank page of his notebook when a more sheepish version of Max appeared and said, "I'm guessing you need to let me out."

Mattie was waiting at the top of the steps when Oliver locked the door behind the retreating silhouette of Max, the fiancé. "Sorry about all that," she said.

"No worries."

The conversation skidded to a clumsy stop before it actually began. Which was okay with Oliver. He just wished Mattie appeared as awkward as he felt. Finally she said, "So, whose turn is it to get the coffee?"

"Let's say it's mine," Oliver said.

Mattie followed him to the elevator. He pushed the Down button, and she said quietly, "I'd really rather not talk about it."

"About what?"

"Him."

The elevator doors dinged opened and Oliver climbed aboard. In the mostly dark kitchen, Oliver multitasked his way through the preparations. He dumped grounds into the filter with one hand and loaded a tray with the other. He realized he couldn't wait to get back upstairs and *not* talk about Max.

When he returned, Mattie checked a series of numbers on her computer monitor as Oliver poured two mugs and stirred in the mystery amount of condiments. He felt an absurd amount of pride in the fact that he knew exactly how she liked her coffee—different every time. He was willing to bet Max was not so attentive. He probably fixed her coffee the way *he* liked it. Mattie swiveled her chair, lifted the mug, and slurped loudly.

"Perfect," she said. After another noisy sip she added, "He's not really my fiancé, you know."

"Good," Oliver said.

"Why is that good?"

Oliver raised his cup but didn't drink. Instead he breathed in a head full of steam. Finally he said, "Because I don't think I liked him very much."

"Most people don't. Max is spoiled, obnoxious, too cute for his own good, and will probably make a ton of money someday soon."

"Well, now I like him even less. But I thought you said you didn't want to talk about it."

"I don't," Mattie said. "But it seems rude not to. And just so you know, the whole engagement thing was a publicity stunt for the band. My brother's goofy idea."

"But Max takes it seriously?"

"Only when it's convenient for him."

"So are you guys even, you know, in a relationship?"

"It's in remission."

They talked until the coffee ran out, then talked some more after that. They discussed her music and his comedy, and the longer they talked the more he envied her passion for her art—apparently Oliver only *thought* he loved writing and telling jokes. Eventually they talked about what it was like growing up in Nashville, marveling that they had lived less than a mile from each other for a brief while but had apparently never crossed paths and didn't know any of the same people. She smiled a lot and even laughed at a few of his jokes. At one point she'd stared at him hard and said, "You really are funny, Oliver. But only when you're being real."

Before he could think of a response, she said the absolute last thing in the world Oliver would have expected to hear.

"Do you have plans for Saturday?"

"I honestly don't know," he said.

To Oliver's untrained ear, it sounded like Mattie Holmgren had just asked him out on a date. But that couldn't be right. Surely she had something else in mind. She probably wanted him to help her move, or maybe watch her cat for her. "As far as I know, my calendar is clear."

"Well, think about it and let me know," she said. "I need a date."

Oliver nodded, hoping he didn't look as dumfounded as he felt.

"But I should probably warn you," Mattie continued. "It's for a wedding."

"I don't know," he said. "I think I hate weddings."

"You're not sure?"

"Well it's been awhile since I've been to one. But it sure seems like the kind of thing I might hate."

"Oh, it'll be dreadful. No doubt. But I'll make it up to you by buying you dinner or washing your car or doing your taxes for you."

"I don't know..."

"Come on, it's the least you can do after eavesdropping on my conversation with Max."

He opened his mouth to deny it, but Mattie warned him off with arched eyebrows and a one-sided grin. "Will he be there too?"

"He was invited, but who really knows?"

"Do I need to bring anything?"

"Nope." Mattie began fishing in her big floppy purse, then produced a Hello Kitty ink pen and a tattered envelope. As she scribbled what looked like a crude map, she said, "Of course you will need to prepare a toast for the bride and groom, then do a short set of stand-up at the reception. Twenty minutes ought to be enough."

Oliver tried to wipe the horrified look off his face before she looked up. She was still grinning at him when she handed over the envelope.

"See?" she said. "You don't laugh at my jokes either."

He stared at the envelope, then folded it in half and tucked it neatly in his hip pocket.

At some point Mattie said, "So what's on your mind now, Oliver?"

"Why does something always have to be on my mind?"

"I can't answer that. But a minute ago we were talking like normal. Now you have that slightly crazed, faraway look in your eye... and you keep pinching your bottom lip... and you're bouncing your knee like a tiny jackhammer."

"Well, I was curious about something. A couple of things, actually."

"Just spit it out."

"From where I'm standing, I see a full tray of copy paper, at least two legal pads, and a pile of sticky notes; not to mention a half-dozen pens and pencils."

"And?"

"Just curious why you'd dig around your purse for scrap paper and a pen with all those other options in front of you."

"Because, Oliver." She said this like he was the silliest person on earth. And with the sound of his name floating around the inside of his skull, he just might have been. "That would be stealing."

"Oh, okay. That makes sense."

"You said a couple of things."

Oliver had every intention of confronting her about what he thought he saw on the security camera the other night. He'd rehearsed the question in his head until he thought he could utter it with the exact right proportions of authority and grace. *Would you mind telling me what you were doing outside Room 504 last Tuesday night?* But as he stood and stared into her unblinking eyes, he couldn't seem to get the words back into the right order.

Finally, he said, "Sorry, I guess I miscounted."

Chapter Twenty-Three

DELORES MILES WAS SLEEPING when Oliver entered her room. It seemed she was sleeping in more and more lately. Oliver sat in her recliner and watched her breathe, wondering exactly when she started to look her age. When his own eyelids grew heavy and sagged, he forced himself up and out of the chair. He kissed his mother on the forehead and made his way back to the lobby.

Betsy looked up and said, "What? No breakfast this morning?"

"She's still sleeping."

"I heard she was up late last night. Revival week."

"Oh no," Oliver said.

"Apparently she climbed onto the dinner table and started rebuking all the vile fornicators and gluttons in her midst."

"Did she use the cooler?"

Betsy nodded, then relayed the details. Apparently his mother had enlisted a guy named Simon, a former Green Beret, who had already filled the oversized Igloo with generic fruit punch. The orderlies arrived as his mother and Simon hoisted the big jug over Mrs. Hazeltine, who was nibbling a piece of jelly toast unsuspectingly in her wheelchair.

"They really doused her," Betsy said, "like a couple linebackers splashing their coach at the Super Bowl."

Oliver allowed his chin to plummet dramatically to his chest, partly out of genuine shame for his mother, but also so Betsy wouldn't see him smile.

"I think it worked too," Betsy said.

"How so?"

"They say Mrs. Hazeltine stood up for the first time in years, raised her hands to heaven, and yelled, 'Jesus wept!'"

Oliver didn't have to feel guilty for smiling. Betsy thought this was much funnier than he did.

"So, is she in trouble?"

"Not as much as the orderlies," Betsy said. "They were watching *SportsCenter* instead of the cafeteria."

"In light of all that, I kind of hate to ask. But is Dr. Strahan here?"

"I think he's in a meeting." Betsy made talon-like quote signs when she said the word *meeting*.

"He seems to be in a lot of meetings lately."

Ever since the untimely death of Ms. Tompkins, Oliver had tried to call the good doctor no less than ten times. But every time he called, Strahan was either in a meeting or he let the call go to voice mail.

Betsy looked conflicted, as if there was something on her mind. But all she said was, "I'd be happy to give him a message when I see him, if you think that would help."

"Just tell him to call—"

Before Oliver could sarcastically state his full name and phone number, the thick door behind Betsy opened revealing the hulking security guard followed by none other than Dr. Strahan himself. He propped the door open with one foot while reaching toward Betsy with a thick, legal-sized envelope.

"Could you see that this gets in today's mail?" he said, then noticed Oliver standing there. "Oliver, hey good to see you. And I apologize. I did get your messages, but things have been kind of crazy around here lately."

"A lot of meetings?" Oliver said.

"I'm on my way to one right now, in fact." To prove his point, he glanced at his watch.

"I need to talk to you about my mother."

"I agree. And unfortunately, I don't have a lot of time right now. But you would do well to remind her that she's not going to get better if she won't take her meds."

"Are you saying she's going to get better if she does?"

Strahan retreated back through the doorway until only his head and shoulders were visible. "We can only hope."

"She's convinced you guys are poisoning her," Oliver said to the now closed door.

He looked to Betsy for help. She opened her mouth to speak, but then swiveled her gaze toward the recently closed door behind her. The burly Shady Grove security guard was perched in his customary spot by the door. Betsy closed her mouth again. It seemed the best she could offer was a sympathetic shrug.

Oliver stepped out of Shady Grove and squinted into the morning sun. He was surprised to see Roscoe there, leaning against his enormous Lincoln, squinting cross-eyed at the glowing tip of his cigarette.

"Here to see Mom?"

Roscoe looked up, startled. His attempted smile gave way to a series of small twitches. After a final, and seemingly painful, drag, Roscoe exhaled a long column of smoke and flicked the spent butt out into the parking lot. "Morning, Oliver. How is she?"

"You do realize you just littered?"

"Sorry," Roscoe said. "Bad habit."

"I'd say that's at least two bad habits."

Roscoe bent and picked up the smoldering butt, stubbed it on the bottom of his shoe, and tossed it through the open window of his car. "There," he said. "Feel better?"

"I would feel better if you just quit smoking."

"And I would feel much worse."

"Are you coming inside?" Oliver said.

Roscoe stared at the building and seemed to tremble at the thought of actually stepping inside. Instead he said, "Let's go get some breakfast."

"They serve breakfast here. And Mom is probably up about now—"

But Roscoe was already ambling down the sidewalk. Oliver caught up and they walked in relative silence. Two blocks later they entered the parking lot of a donut shop Oliver had never noticed before. He made his way between a pair of shiny black cars. The first was a bulky Mercedes, very new and probably very expensive. But the more interesting car was parked alongside it at an odd angle. Oliver didn't know cars, but he did recognize the sleek silvery wildcat leaping from the hood as a jaguar. The car was definitely old, but in immaculate condition from its taut convertible top to the flawless wine interior.

"Man, this thing is older than me," Oliver said. "And in way better shape."

"Probably closer to my age," Roscoe said. "And worth more than my house."

"That's not really saying much," Oliver said, watching his own playful grin in the reflection of the Jag's window.

"What's that supposed to mean?"

"Same argument as your car. You could afford much better."

Roscoe raised his hand to open the door but withdrew it again to pound a series of labored coughs up and out of his chest. Oliver wondered if he'd be able to muster the courage to ask Roscoe about his cancer. Why hadn't he told Oliver about it before? Knowing Roscoe, he probably didn't want to be a burden.

A cowbell dinged over the door when he finally held it open for Oliver. They approached the counter and ordered a pair of thick apple fritters and two coffees from a bored teenager who appeared to be trying to cure her ravaging acne with acupuncture—her pale face had more piercings than Oliver had ex-girlfriends. Roscoe paid for their breakfast and Oliver dropped a couple dollars in the tip jar. But the teenager never looked up.

They sat in a creaky booth near the door, elbows propped on the scarred table, and ate. Roscoe still seemed pensive, as if trying not to think about Shady Grove. Oliver wanted to ask how he was feeling, if there was a lot of pain, if he could do anything to help, but he knew it would just make Roscoe grumpy. The man did not abide unwanted attention well.

"How's the donut?" Oliver said.

"It's no Roscoe Platter. But it'll do."

"I know it kills you to hear this. But you're famous for spotting talent, not frying burgers."

"I'm not famous for anything, Oliver."

"Of course you are. You're a legend, and you know it."

"But that's not the same as famous."

"How so?"

"I'm just a guy who owns a restaurant with a stage and a microphone." Roscoe took a long, hard swallow of coffee. "Cenodoxus was a legend."

"Who?"

"My point exactly. Now eat your donut."

Oliver never tired of Roscoe's paternal scoldings. Although he would never admit it, he kind of craved them. He followed Roscoe's gaze toward a noise behind the counter where the thinnest, darkest man Oliver had ever seen ambled around the pierced adolescent, with a broom in one hand, a dustpan in the other, and a thoroughly confused look on his craggy face. He seemed to be searching for crumbs that weren't there. Finally he shrugged and started moving the broom around. Oliver was about to whisper a reminder to Roscoe that it was rude to stare. The guy with the broom sensed it too. He blinked once, then again. His expression brightened, then exploded into a big smile.

The broom clattered to the floor and the man gathered Roscoe's extended hand in both of his, pumping madly and saying over and over: "I can't believe it. Roscoe? Is that really you?"

Instead of letting go of Roscoe's hand, the guy cupped the back of his head and pulled him close, planting a loud kiss on his forehead.

"Ain't that sweet?" the man said. "Roscoe's blushing."

Then Oliver caught himself flinching at the large brown fist arcing in slow motion toward his face. But the man was offering him a fist bump, not a punch in the schnoz.

"I'm Eddy Murphey," the guy said, trying not to laugh at Oliver. "Eddy with a Y; Murphey with an E ... the *original* Eddy Murphey. You tell him, Roscoe."

But Roscoe didn't need to tell him anything. Oliver recognized Eddy from Downers, from a decade ago. His face had weathered, his hairline retreated, but there was no mistaking the boisterous force of his personality. He used to refer to himself as a one-man cult. But the thing Oliver remembered most was how thoroughly hysterical the man was. His material was erratic, often ranging between zany and cerebral, but always funny.

Oliver was about to show his belated admiration when Eddy leaned in close and said, "Wait—is that the little paper football man? Oliver, right?"

"Good to see you again, Eddy," Oliver said. "You still doing comedy?"

"Every day. But these young punks nowadays don't get it. All that hip-hop done made 'em too dull to appreciate the finer points of my comedic sensibilities." Eddy jerked his thumb at Oliver and said to Roscoe, "He your new funny man?"

"He is funny," Roscoe said, like he actually meant it. Oliver knew better than to indulge the pride swelling inside him. If Roscoe really thought he was funny, Oliver would have headlined at Downers by now. "We're still working on the man part however."

"He'll get there." Eddy squared himself in front of Oliver. "You just listen to what Roscoe says and you'll be fine."

Oliver nodded. Eddy stared thoughtfully at his broom, then picked it up and started sweeping a few donut crumbs into a neat pile.

Roscoe cleared his throat and said, "Bleak House here?"

Oliver remembered the name from an autographed black-and-white headshot. It was tacked up near the stage of Downers and revealed a wide face on an impossibly thick neck, a thin Casanova mustache, and one gold tooth. His signature read: *Bleak as a tomb-stone, big as a house*. If there was a real name attached, Oliver couldn't remember it.

Eddy with a Y shook his big head.

"Off counting his money?" Roscoe said.

"Preparing to tell it goodbye," Eddy said. "He in court again."

"Another divorce?"

"Practice makes perfect."

"Will he get to keep the cars?"

"I hope so. He already gave up the house. As soon as he got out of rehab, he moved into his office out back."

"Rehab?" Roscoe said, real worry etched into his expression.

Eddy mimed tipping a beer mug to his lips, smiling. But it was a sad smile.

"Tell him if he needs anything to call me," Roscoe said.

Eddy nodded and moved his broom around.

Roscoe said, "Stop in and see me sometime."

"I'd like that, Roscoe. You know I would. But I'm afraid all those demons hanging around might recognize me, invite me back in, you know?"

"You need anything, Eddy?"

"No, sir. I'm as good as it gets."

"Well you let me know if that changes."

"You'll be the first."

Roscoe offered his hand, but midshake Eddy pulled his old friend to his feet and wrapped him in an awkward man hug, trading backslaps. He turned to say something to Oliver but squeezed his shoulder instead. Then he collected his broom and disappeared back into the kitchen.

"You ready?" Roscoe said.

"You didn't finish your coffee."

Roscoe blinked at his mostly full cup, then drained it in a single loud slurp. Then he slid out of the booth and dinged the bell again on his way out the door. Oliver finished his breakfast slower than necessary and watched Roscoe through the dirty glass as he leaned on the hood of the Jag and lit up another cigarette.

When Oliver finally made his way out into the sunlight he said, "Should we get it over with?"

"What's that?" Roscoe said.

"The lecture. Or parable, or whatever you call this. I feel like Scrooge being shown my own miserable future as a comedian."

"Oh, I thought we were here so I could buy my friend a donut." When Oliver didn't reply, Roscoe added, "He was the funniest one of the bunch, you know."

"Who?"

"Eddy. He had real talent. But he was never going to make any money at it."

"Money's not everything, Roscoe."

"Agreed, but it is something."

"So are you going to tell me the point of all this? Or do I have to guess?"

"You're a smart kid. I don't think I have to spell anything out for you. I will tell you that, at some point, guys like Eddy and Bleak and a bunch of others ended up broke and homeless. They were still funny, mind you, but had no plan B when the comedy thing didn't work out."

"Bleak House appears to be doing alright. He owns his own donut shop, right?"

"He actually took my advice."

"You mean he took your money?"

"And then he paid it all back. With interest."

"Okay, so you helped a few former comedians get back on their feet. But in case you missed it, I already have a job."

"And how long do you plan to be a security guard?"

Finally, Oliver said, "As long as it takes. It beats sweeping donut shops. Bleak House ended up divorced, drunk, and sleeping on a couch in his office. Seems like he could have accomplished all that without your help. Maybe if you hadn't talked him out of a comedy career he'd be even more successful."

"That's the point, Oliver. I never told him to quit comedy. I encouraged him to think about his future. Most guys need a contingency plan."

"And I'm one of those guys?"

"Yeah, Oliver, you are. We all are."

"Hey, I'm already thinking of my future. I even hired a manager."

That's when Roscoe's features creased in disgust. Evidently, Barry really had made an impression.

Oliver didn't realize they were walking again until Roscoe stopped at the corner to allow a delivery van to pass.

"You're a funny kid," Roscoe said. "Always have been. But you allowed your expectations to outgrow your actual talent. That's exactly what happened to Bleak House and Eddy and a hundred other guys."

"Okay, if I'm so funny, why can't I play your club?"

"I've told you a dozen times."

"Tell me once more. I can be a little slow."

Roscoe pointed toward the brick structure looming in front of them. "I promised your mother."

Oliver resisted the urge to stomp his foot, stick his tongue out, and tell Roscoe that, for his information, he'd be playing his stupid club in a few weeks anyway. With or without his consent. But the emailed invitation had been explicitly clear that Roscoe's benefit gig was to be kept secret.

Instead they just stood there in silence, staring up at the building. Roscoe alternated from an almost prayerful stillness to nonstop fidgeting. He fondled his lighter, smoothed whiskers, picked invisible flecks off his pant leg before settling back into another long stretch of forced tranquility. Every time he looked up at the building he seemed surprised to see it still standing there. Finally, he cleared his throat, then again. "I don't know how you do it, kid. I honestly don't."

"Come on, Roscoe. Let's just stop in and say hey. She doesn't bite, I promise."

"She used to."

Roscoe chuckled at the confused expression on Oliver's face, then offered his left hand for inspection. When it was obvious Oliver didn't see anything, Roscoe pointed at a curved line of purplish scars that ran along the webbed meat between his index finger and thumb.

"She did that to you?"

Roscoe nodded, soundless and rueful and grinning like mad.

"Well come on then," Oliver said, reaching for the ignition. "Seems like she owes you an apology."

"I'm sorry; I wish I could. And I do try sometimes. But I can't." He rubbed the stubble on his chin and said again. "I just can't."

"Thanks for breakfast, Roscoe."

"You're welcome. And sorry if it sounded like a lecture."

"It's fine, Roscoe. A little preachy on your part, but fine."

"You know I just want to help."

"I've been asking for your help for years."

"No, you've been asking to play my club. Big difference."

Roscoe gave Oliver's shoulder a squeeze, then turned and walked away from his hulking Town Car.

"Where are you going?"

"St. Anthony's," Roscoe said, pointing toward an ornate bell tower in the distance. "Been awhile since my last confession."

"You're going to walk?"

"It's only eight blocks or so."

"But you're ... you know ... sick."

Roscoe set his jaw, narrowed his eyes, and eventually looked away.

"Why didn't you tell me?" Oliver said.

"What's to tell? I have a disease." He pointed toward the bell tower again and said, "I'll do what I can and leave the rest up to Him."

"You sure I can't drive you?"

"I have lung cancer, son, not dementia. Besides, the fresh air makes my cigarettes taste better."

Chapter Twenty-Four

OLIVER COULDN'T FIND HIS NOTEBOOK anywhere. He'd turned his house upside down, searched his car three times, and had called the hotel twice. But the front-desk manager assured him that it *still* wasn't in the lost-and-found box. His search had turned ridiculous, as he was now double-checking places like the refrigerator and bathtub. Oliver was searching the pantry when the phone rang. After exchanging a few pleasantries he said, "Have you seen my spiral notebook, Simon?"

"Yep."

"Lately?"

"Nope. So anyway, I hear you're on the docket tonight?"

"The insurance convention?"

"That's the one," Simon said. "And you're very welcome."

"Um, thanks?"

"Whimbush had to back out. Then I ran into your so-called manager at Jesters one night and I put in the good word for you about this gig."

This only confirmed what Oliver suspected. Barry hadn't ferreted this gig out on his own. Someone had canceled and the promoter was forced to go to the bench, to find a second-stringer and put him in the lineup.

"Thanks for thinking of me."

"Think you could express your gratitude in the form of a ride?"

"Your place is not exactly on the way."

"It is now. I'm staying at my uncle's for a while."

Fifteen minutes later, Simon piled into Oliver's Integra and snapped his seatbelt into place.

Oliver said, "So what happened to your car?"

"Donna kept it."

"Donna the stewardess girlfriend?"

"Donna the ex."

"What happened?"

"She found out about your little assistant friend."

"Wendy?" Simon nodded with a big stupid grin. "So why can't she give you a ride?"

"She found out about Donna."

As soon as Oliver saw the room he considered bailing out. The stage was no mere afterthought, nothing like the six-inch platforms wedged into corners between tables at his local comedy haunts. This was a massive structure, three feet off the ground, painted black and replete with monitors and a rack of blinding gel lights. And there wasn't a blue collar in sight. No beer mugs or rude waitresses or comedy groupies. It was a roomful of suits and ties and champagne flutes.

Simon elbowed him in the ribs. "Pretty cool, eh?"

"If you say so."

"Oh, that's right. I forgot about your stage fright."

Oliver had long since conquered his fear of speaking in public. But he did still harbor a handful of more specific fears, one of which was lofty, wide-open stages in well-lit rooms. But he didn't have time to obsess over it because the mustached master of ceremonies was approaching."Childress, right?"

Simon nodded and accepted a stack of paperwork.

"And you must be Miles?"

"That's me."

"Thanks for helping us out on such short notice. Trust me. You're going to have a ball."

"What's this?" Oliver said, scanning the handful of pages.

"Just a few formalities. The first is a waiver in case one of those lighting trusses falls and caves your head in. Then there's a tax form in there somewhere, and a check. And that last bit there is the list of topics."

"Topics?" Oliver said.

The emcee laughed, obviously pleased that the promoter had sent him such a funny, funny man. He gave Oliver a hearty pat on the back and was off to shake other hands.

"Yeah," Simon said. "I was really surprised you agreed to do this. Don't you hate improv?"

That's when the list finally registered in Oliver's sleepy brain. Instead of taking the gigantic stage and blowing through his best ten-minute set, he was about to share the spotlight with several of Nashville's finest stand-ups and invent brand new material on the fly. The only thing he hated more than giant stages in well-lit rooms was forced improvisation. He'd seen Roscoe force comics to abandon their well-honed material many times, insisting they do a set of nothing but "crowd work." Witnessing this had filled Oliver with awe and dread, but mostly dread.

He was still scanning the room for emergency exits when the comics were called to the stage. Simon gripped his arm and dragged him against his will.

"You'll be fine," Simon said. "Like my uncle used to tell me when he was learning to fly planes, 'If it doesn't kill you, it will make you stronger.'"

"Didn't your uncle die in a plane crash?"

"See? That was funny. And you just made it up on the spot."

"Seriously, Simon. Isn't that how your uncle died?"

"Sure, but that doesn't make it any less funny."

Five stools stood in a line across the platform, one for each of the assembled comics. Each had his own microphone as well. Oliver angled for a stool on the edge but ended up in the middle of the stage. The emcee stroked his curly mustache as he thanked everyone for coming and promised a festive night of hilarity. He explained the format for the night's proceedings. The comics would each do a short set of stand-up material. After which they'd engage in a free-form set of improv, based on topics supplied by the organizers. Oliver couldn't help thinking it was going to be a sloppy version of *Whose Line Is It Anyway?*

But he did breathe a small sigh of relief. He could do five minutes in his sleep. And since most every comedian he'd ever met was an attention hog, he could simply fade into the background when the comics started riffing on each other's material. This would no doubt turn into an exercise of one-upmanship. He'd seen this before at Jesters and knew it could get brutal.

Oliver sat through three good sets before his name was called. After a rather bumpy start where he muffed a punch line, things went better than he expected. He calmed down and settled into his material. He didn't kill, nor was he killed. On balance, he got as many laughs as the other comics. When the last comedian finished his short set, the emcee made his way back up to the stage, sporting an inebriated glow. Oliver had seen this before too, where a closet stand-up drinks some courage and tries to go toe to toe with real comedians. He found himself simultaneously hoping the guy would stay out of the fray, but mostly wanting to witness the comedic roadkill.

Once the first topic was thrown out, the assembled talent wasted no time bucking for attention. Oliver had guessed right. He settled onto his stool and tried to become invisible, which actually worked for nearly thirty minutes. But eventually the emcee turned to Oliver and said, "So what about you, Mr. Miles? We haven't heard from you yet."

Oliver waved good-naturedly, as if to say, "Go on without me." But the emcee flipped to his next topic and said simply, "Everything I ever learned about picking up chicks . . ."

The crowd laughed. The other comics looked at imaginary spots on the ceiling as they searched their internal vaults for some trusted material to recycle. Everyone else in the room stared at Oliver, waiting. That's when he noticed the giant TV camera in the back of the room, its illuminated "record" light mocking him. The only thing he hated more than improv was performing on camera.

Oliver stood, raised the microphone, opened his mouth, and then closed it again. This made the crowd titter. Then he opened his mouth a second time, but his tongue had turned to parchment paper. Instead of actually speaking, he lowered the mic again. A few people laughed, which made a few more people laugh. Oliver could imagine his expression—shell-shocked and forlorn—but couldn't seem to send the right combination of signals from his brain to his face. A smattering of applause broke out near the back. Clearly, they thought this was an act, that he was feigning indecision or inexperience or some crisis of confidence about his ability to pick up girls. The truth, however, was that he was feigning nothing at all. He was genuinely terrified. Mentally, he kept hitting rewind, pause, then play, searching for any scrap of real-life experience he could quickly parlay into some semblance of a joke.

But the more he fidgeted, the harder they laughed.

By the time he shrugged and sat down again, he was enjoying the biggest laughs of the evening—by far. When he hung his head, thoroughly humiliated by his thorough lack of creativity, the laughter swelled.

At some point he looked up, only to see a tableful of folks down front, on their feet and applauding. As Oliver's head dipped again he risked a quick glance at his fellow comedians. Two rolled their eyes in disgust, one shook his head in silent admiration, and Simon gave him two thumbs up.

• • •

Later, while sharing a pot of coffee with Mattie, recounting the more embarrassing parts of the gig, Mattie laughed harder than the roomful of inebriated insurance agents had.

Sherman wasn't laughing at all when he intercepted Oliver in the parking garage. His face looked grim, his eyes imploring, moving like two small searchlights. But there seemed to be a smile tempting the corners of his mouth.

"Good morning, Oliver." But it didn't sound good.

Before Oliver could reciprocate, Sherman removed a folded sheet of paper from his jacket pocket and handed it to Oliver. It was a photocopy of the hotel's phone bill.

"Correct me if I'm wrong, Mr. Miles. But I do believe that is a Virginia area code?" Sherman pointed to a specific entry on the printout of the phone bill. "As you may recall, our last night auditor was relieved of her duties for—among other things—abusing the hotel's telephone policy."

Oliver nodded. Gretchen's fiancé was a traveling computer salesman. And she used to indulge her paranoid streak by calling him wherever he was staying to make sure he was in his room—alone—and not out carousing.

"So, Mr. Miles. You're obviously hiding something. I just can't decide if it's to protect yourself or someone else."

"I'm not sure what you mean, sir."

He nodded as if he understood. "Funny, that's exactly what Mattie said. Don't you find that funny, Oliver?"

"No, sir, not really. And if you'll pardon me for asking, why did you hire her if you don't trust her?"

"I didn't hire her," Sherman said. "Monty did."

"Your brother?"

"Seems that he's an old college friend of Mattie's father. So I agreed to bring her on board as a favor. But I don't have to—" Sherman paused. He seemed to be considering his words carefully. "She has a past, Oliver."

"We all have pasts, sir."

"True, but they don't all include class-2 misdemeanors for breaking and entering."

Sherman seemed to enjoy Oliver's shocked expression. But it passed quickly and he seemed to regret having said it.

"That is obviously confidential information," Sherman added. "And I assume you'll keep it that way?"

Mattie's criminal past was still sinking in when Sherman said, "You know, it's a shame that no one wants to take credit for making the call. *Occasionally*, the ends really do indeed justify the means. So let me just say, in the most nonspecific way I know how ... thank you for your loyal service to the hotel."

Sherman waited until he had Oliver's full attention, then winked.

As he walked back to his car, Oliver couldn't help imagining his boss getting up early and rehearsing his winks.

Chapter Twenty-Five

OLIVER HAD FINISHED HIS ROUNDS and Mattie had finished her audit. The lobby was mostly quiet as they hung around her desk talking about nothing in particular. Oliver was trying hard not to think about her alleged criminal past when Mattie picked up the phone and began to dial. "Guess I'd better check my messages. See if anyone's interested in leasing my apartment yet."

She dialed and listened, her pen poised over her Hello Kitty stationery. Apparently no one called because she didn't write anything down. When she hung up, Oliver said, "I should probably do that too."

"What? Lease my apartment?"

"Check my messages."

"Give me the number," she said. "I'll dial it for you"

He recited his phone number along with the access code, secretly enjoying the intimacy but trying not to show it. When she offered the receiver, he waved her off. "Go ahead, you can listen for me."

"Sounds like two messages," Mattie said. "One from a place called Shady Grove, someone named Betsy, and she wants you to call her back. And the other one sounds like a wrong number."

She scribbled the words "Shady Grove" followed by the name "Ida" and slid it across her desk to Oliver. He was staring at Betsy's name in Mattie's handwriting, feeling oddly guilty for the small crush he used to have on the friendly receptionist.

"What's this Shady Grove place?" Mattie asked.

"Kind of an old folks' home," Oliver said. "My mother lives there, although she's not really that old."

"Tell me about her."

"I was planning to change the subject."

Mattie crossed her arms and stared. She used the non-blinking one.

"Okay." Oliver sighed, collected his thoughts, and plunged in. "My mother was arrested several years ago for assaulting a couple of cops. At some point a police shrink claimed she had suicidal tendencies, so they sentenced her to a minimum-security nut house. She was in there for a couple of years until the new governor started making budget cuts and talking about overcrowding. I was afraid they were going to move her across the state, but then I got a call one day from a doctor named Strahan who runs Shady Grove, asking if he could move my mother into their new facility. It took about ten minutes of walking the grounds for me to agree."

"Guess that explains your moonlighting. Those places are typically pretty pricey."

"Oh, I'm not paying for it. Frankly, I was so happy to get her out of the dingy jailhouse conditions, I never really thought to ask about the details."

"Okay, so now I know where she lives, but nothing about your actual mother."

"There's not much to tell, really. She never finished high school, but she's convinced she's a nurse. She claims she had an affair with a famous novelist from New England. And the last time she actually recognized me was more than five years ago."

"*That* explains it," Mattie said.

"Explains what?"

"Why you like to hear your name so much." Oliver opened his mouth to respond—to deny or excuse or maybe even defend himself—but ended up closing it again when Mattie grinned at him and said, "So, *Oliver* ... is your mother sick?"

"It's mostly self-inflicted. I used to think she just checked out, that she chose to drink herself into oblivion."

"And now?"

"It seems more complicated than that. A lot of bad choices about bad men, some feeble self-esteem, a rickety batch of genetics."

"How much do you blame yourself?"

"Depends on the day."

"What about today?"

"Today, I'm hungry. I try not to do guilt on an empty stomach."

"How about breakfast instead?" Mattie asked. "My treat?"

"Why do I sense there's a catch?"

"What's that lady's name again? Edna?"

"Ida."

"Have you ever talked to her?"

"Not on purpose. But apparently there was a locksmith named Clifton who used to rescue Ida when she locked herself out of her car, her house, her tool shed, probably her high school locker. I've tried to explain to her that whoever she's trying to reach has moved or changed their number or gone out of business. But she always ends up saying, 'Just tell Clifton I called.' "

"So let's call her back."

"What? Who?"

"The lock lady."

"You're kidding, right?"

But he knew she wasn't. It took some goading, but Oliver eventually recited the number. As Mattie dialed he said, "By the way, you didn't see my notebook lying around the hotel, did you?"

"Yep, you left it on a table in the lobby the night Max came by."

"Really? Do you know what hap—?"

Mattie shushed him. She handed the phone to Oliver and started dialing.

"What am I supposed to say?"

"Tell her we're going to come look at her locks for her."

"You know how to fix locks?"

"I know how to google it. Come on, Oliver, how hard can it really be?"

The phone rang in his ear.

"What if we get there and it doesn't work? All we end up doing is getting this lady's hopes up."

"If we can't actually fix it, we'll call a real locksmith. Or maybe just buy her a new set of locks and have them keyed like her old ones. It's not like her key ring will know the difference."

"Just like that?" The phone rang again. "Just buy her new locks?"

"Try to think of it as an investment in character."

When Ida finally answered, she sounded more suspicious than grateful, and kept insisting to speak to Clifton. Eventually Mattie commandeered the phone, claiming to be Oliver's supervisor, and promised Ida that they would be there within the hour to solve her doorknob problems.

They stopped by Home Depot on the way, where Mattie picked out three identical boxes of the most expensive lockset in the store before proceeding to the self-checkout line. As she scanned items and swiped her card, she said, "So how's the comedy career coming?"

"Good," he said, trying to sound casually professional. But it sounded childish and proud in Oliver's ears. "I even have a manager now."

The machine kept beeping and asking Mattie to swipe her card again. "Yeah?" Mattie sounded distracted, bordering on frustration. "Who is it?"

"A guy named Barry."

"Not Barry *Sherman*, I hope."

"Well ..."

"Good luck with that," she said. "That man is a snake."

Oliver was fighting the urge to defend Barry when Mattie jammed her credit card back into her wallet in frustration. "Don't suppose you could float me a loan?"

He bellied up to the machine, feeling much more heroic than he deserved, and swiped his Visa card.

Mattie alternated between perusing the lockset instructions and giving Oliver directions to Ida's house. The lady proved to be even more suspicious in person, wanting to know where their work van was, why they weren't wearing coveralls or carrying clipboards. But Mattie had a soothing excuse for everything. She began twisting locks and inserting keys as soon as she stepped inside. Oliver was struck by the smell—a sickening combination of chicken soup and cough drops—as Ida guided him to the parlor. While Mattie worked, Ida treated Oliver to blow-by-blow descriptions of the diagnoses and treatments of goiters, gout, two failed hysterectomies, glaucoma, hemorrhoid surgery, several bouts of pneumonia, root canals, and various infections caused by dirty instruments and inexperienced doctors. Between anecdotes, Ida offered Oliver a candy dish filled with moldy mints and diseased cashews. She was asking his opinion on plastic surgery (she was thinking of having her eyes done) when Mattie mercifully announced that she was finished.

It took Ida three tries to extract herself from her recliner. Mattie's pride was apparent as she showed off her handiwork.

"You mean I can use the same key for all three doors?" Ida said.

"Yep," Mattie said as she began piling all the old hardware into the Home Depot bags.

"Wait," Ida said. "What are you going to do with those old locks? I mean ... I realize they're forty years old. But they've been with me a long time."

"I understand," Mattie said, then placed the bag on Ida's sofa. "Guess we'd better be going then."

"But what am I supposed to do with all of these?" Ida's hand shook as she opened her palm to reveal four shiny new keys.

"If it were me," Mattie said, "I'd keep one in my purse, hide one on the porch, give one to a neighbor, and give one to your favorite relative."

Ida went so still that Oliver wondered if she'd fallen asleep on her feet. When she looked up her eyes were moist. "Would you keep one for me?"

"I'd be happy to," Mattie said. She wrapped Ida into a warm, lingering hug as Oliver inspected a hangnail.

When they turned to leave, Ida said, "Wait, what do I owe you?"

"Oh, there's no charge," Mattie said. Then she leaned in close and said, "Actually, can I tell you a little secret?"

Ida nodded.

Mattie cupped her hand, motioned toward Oliver, and whispered, "This is his first day on the job."

Ida looked scandalized. "You mean he's never done this before?"

"A total rookie," Mattie said. "So it just wouldn't be right to ask you to pay for his education."

• • •

Back in the car, Mattie said, "Guess we'll have to eat breakfast at the hotel later."

"I'm not sure I can wait twelve hours for breakfast." That's when Oliver looked at the dashboard clock and realized they'd been at Ida's house for over two hours. Moldy mints and decaying nuts never seemed so appetizing before.

Mattie motioned toward her purse and shrugged. "You take rain checks?"

"I guess I have no choice."

"You know," Mattie said, "you should put some of those Ida stories in your act. She was pretty hilarious."

In truth, Oliver had been logging away potential material all evening. But most of his attention had been focused on the adorable philanthropist who decided to forgo dinner and impersonate a locksmith, not the old lady with her funky party favors and faulty locks.

It wouldn't dawn on Oliver until days later, as he watched the simulcast version of Mattie roaming various hallways of the Harrington, that maybe there was a reason she was so proficient with locks. It also made him wonder what Mattie had planned for Ida's spare key.

Chapter Twenty-Six

BETSY WAS ALREADY ON HER FEET when Oliver breezed into the plush lobby of Shady Grove. Her typical smile was being held hostage by a worried frown and a series of deep crevices that started between her eyebrows and disappeared under her bangs. She glanced at the spot where the beefy security guard usually sat, then motioned Oliver forward with a series of quick shoveling hand gestures.

"Did you get my messages?"

"I guess not," Oliver said.

"Huh, I checked the number twice. And I would have sworn that was your mother's voice on the machine. Anyway, your mother has been moved."

"As in, moved out of Shady Grove?"

"Not out, up." She pointed her index finger skyward and pumped it a few times.

"Unofficially?"

"I'm worried about her."

Now Oliver was too. "Worried how?"

"Well, she has been kinda depressed lately. Mostly because she can't remember things. She complains about the way she's being treated, says she feels like she's dying."

"When was someone going to tell me about this?"

"I'm sorry, Oliver. I figured Dr. Strahan would have called you already."

The security guard roamed back into the lobby, and Oliver would have sworn the guy gave him a dirty look. It occurred to Oliver that the tight security at Shady Grove should make him feel better about his mother's welfare, not worse. Betsy cleared her throat. The worry lines were gone and the corners of her mouth had magically risen to reveal two rows of perfectly crooked teeth.

"So ..." Betsy reverted to her chirpy tour guide voice again. "Just take the elevator to the third floor, go left, and she's three doors down on the right."

When Oliver arrived in his mother's new room she wasn't there. It was a miniature copy of her old room—same wallpaper, same linens and curtains and bathroom fixtures. But the bed was bulkier, more industrial. And most of her personal stuff was missing. It was obviously too small to accommodate her recliner and love seat and favorite coffee table. All that remained were her imitation oriental rug, rolled up and leaning in a corner, and her bookshelf. The floor was littered with nearly a dozen boxes marked *Miles 322.* Only one had been opened.

Oliver knelt and used his car key to break the seal on the remaining cartons. He took his time moving the contents of the boxes onto the shelf. Someone—probably Betsy—had gone to the trouble of blowing the dust off the pages of her books.

When he found the tape recorder, he listened to a few seconds of his eleven-year-old self doing comedy—a few seconds was all he could take—before lining it up on the top shelf alongside his favorite photos of himself and his mother. He grinned when he realized her chest of drawers was also missing, wondering where his mother would hide the photos when he left.

The last two boxes contained her prized (and very expensive) collection of John Irving novels. Oliver suspected that these were the only books she actually pulled down and read with any regularity. He used to track her bookmark as it moved through *The World According to Garp* and into *Widow for One Year* or *Imaginary Girlfriend.* Today though, he wanted his eyes to travel the same literary terrain as his mother's. He took his time then, paging through slowly, allowing his fingers to graze as much of each page as possible. He looked for smudges or stains on the pages and tried to imagine her making them.

Oliver was fanning the pages of *A Prayer for Owen Meany* when the handwritten letter fell out and fluttered to the floor.

He'd seen this before, or something very much like it. She'd included the month and day, but not the year. So Oliver had no way to know how old it was. The tone felt familiar, scripted in deliberate upright strokes. The ink was black, no-nonsense. And the stationery was the same she'd been using since Oliver could remember. She never ran out because Delores Miles didn't write letters. She wrote suicide notes.

He was sixteen the first time he found one of her notes. She'd been running late for work when she saw him sitting at the table reading a single sheet of paper. When he hadn't responded to her goodbyes, she walked over and stood across the table from him. She didn't ask what he was reading; apparently she could see it in his face. She eased the paper from his hand and scanned it.

"Oh … this old thing?" She had tried to make her voice sound frothy and droll, but missed badly. "This isn't mine, I swear. I was, um, writing this for a friend."

"Not funny, Mom."

"Seriously, honey, you can make good money ghostwriting suicide notes."

"Still not funny."

He would eventually find eleven more notes, all dated within the previous year. Apparently, she blamed her suicidal tendencies on her failure as a mother, as a lover, and her inability to make a "decent living." One recurring theme was her undying love for her son. Oliver wasn't so sure.

"Look, I have to run, sweetie. Can't really afford to be late for work again. Just promise me you won't worry."

Oliver hadn't promised anything.

"Think about it," she said. "Have I *ever* left you without saying goodbye?"

"Not when you were sober."

"Touché. Still, logically speaking, I can't kill myself with you watching because you'd try and stop me, right?"

"Yes, probably."

"So my only alternative would be to write my farewell, then do the deed while you were at school or something. But that simply is not going to happen."

"And why is that?"

She tapped the unfinished note and said, "Writer's block."

He hadn't meant to laugh. But Roscoe was right. She was either the funniest sad person he'd ever met, or the saddest funny person.

Oliver scanned the note a final time and tucked it into his hip pocket. He searched for more, but found none. The closest he came was another handwritten page titled "Sermon Notes" where his mother had scribbled random ideas about parents not exasperating their children and the value of training kids up in spiritual disciplines. Near the bottom, in all capital letters, she'd written: *Possible title? The Healing Power of Forgiveness.* Apparently Delores Miles was still coloring in the lines of her penitence, her tongue still tucked into the corner of her mouth, sweat still beading on her forehead as she continued to work out her salvation with fear and trembling. Oliver's gaze angled toward the heavens as the conflicting emotions roiled inside him and finally bubbled up into a one-word prayer that seemed to cover both his mother's illness and all his own raging inadequacies. "Help," he whispered.

After alphabetizing his mother's books, Oliver divided his time between breaking down cardboard boxes and resisting the urge to study the fresh suicide note tucked into his hip pocket.

When he heard his mother's voice wafting through the open door, he walked to the hallway and watched as she berated a pair of young nurses. She gripped her Fisher-Price doctor kit in one hand and used the other to pound the desk of the nurse's station, demanding to know what they had done with her patient and threatening to quit. When they finally tried to explain that Ms. Tompkins had passed away, Delores Miles just pounded harder and yelled louder.

What Oliver should have done was calmly escort his mother back to her new room. But all he really wanted was to see her, to make sure she was still okay. So what he did instead was put his head down, ignore the elevator, and hurry down the echoey stairwell.

Betsy was speaking into her headset, giving someone directions to Shady Grove. The security guard was in his customary spot, leaning his chair back on two legs. Oliver didn't look at him but felt his gaze nonetheless, certain it was focused on his hip pocket.

Chapter Twenty-Seven

OLIVER FINALLY STOPPED READING his mother's suicide note. But that didn't keep him from obsessing about it. He was already tucked into bed and staring at the ceiling before he realized he'd skipped breakfast. He'd also neglected to brush his teeth or change out of his uniform. He turned onto his side and stared at the alarm clock, considered setting it, then decided there was no real point. His showcase at Jesters was twelve hours away.

He couldn't be sure, but he thought it was the sound of his stomach growling that finally woke him up—eleven hours later.

His first thought was that the clock was broken. But then the sensations hit him in waves—drool on the pillowcase, tongue pasted to the roof of his mouth, limbs that felt like chopped lumber, howling pangs of hunger, and a bladder screaming for relief.

Skipping a shower before work was not an option. Neither was missing his spot at Jesters. So Oliver decided his best option was to borrow a room at the hotel for a quick shower and shave before clocking in. He only owned two security uniforms—one now severely wrinkled, the other one dirty. He decided to unwrinkle the less stale one if, that is, he could figure out how to work an iron.

The next ten minutes were an exercise in multitasking. Oliver brushed his teeth as he loaded three pieces of bread into the toaster oven, laid out his gig clothes alongside his uniform, and crammed his shaving kit into a duffel bag. He wasted another three minutes wetting his hands and attempting to reverse the effects of rampant bed head. As Oliver Miles fluffed and patted and hand-combed errant shocks into submission, he mentally rehearsed the handful of new jokes he wanted to try out tonight. When it dawned on him that his strong-willed hair was funnier than his jokes, he gave up on both. His stomach growled as he approached the refrigerator—a bowl of cornflakes had never sounded so good. But when he opened the door, the warm stench hit him like a punch in the mouth. The fridge had finally died. He slammed the door and made his way to the toaster, grabbing a knife, the tub of fake butter, and a bottle of water from the pantry along the way. That's when he realized he forgot to plug the toaster in. He eyeballed the unused iron hungrily, but eventually wrapped three untoasted pieces of bread in a napkin. He patted his pockets for his keys and wallet. And just before heading out to his car, Oliver Miles paused to kick his refrigerator.

Thankfully, he had plenty of gas and just enough time to get to the club.

He only nodded off twice on the way—once while driving and again while waiting for a traffic light to cycle back to green. The last thing he should feel after eleven hours of uninterrupted slumber is sleepy. But years of graveyard shifting had taught him that too much sleep was almost as bad as not enough ... almost.

Oliver made it to the club with nearly five minutes to spare. Out of habit, he reached into the passenger seat to retrieve his notebook. But of course it wasn't there. As far as he could tell, Mattie was the last one to have seen it, perched on the end table in the lobby. Oliver knew his notebook was a crutch. But it was *his* crutch, and he still wanted to have it around.

Inside the club, he leaned against the bar, hoping to order a large basket of chicken tenders and fries before the emcee called his name. But the bartender either didn't see him or was ignoring him on purpose. That's when Oliver caught sight of his face in the bar mirror. The right side of his hair had crept back up into a prickly wave. He was mashing it back into place when Simon appeared in the mirror behind him. Their reflection looked like two heads floating above a fleet of fancy liquor bottles.

"Still experimenting, I see."

Oliver followed Simon's gaze down to the shiny badge clipped to the wrinkled security guard uniform he'd slept in. He blinked at himself in the mirror, then checked again to make sure he wasn't dreaming.

"I may have been wrong about you," Simon was saying. "The more I think about that greatest hits gig you did with Wendy, the funnier it seems. And that whole stuttering thing you did at the insurance convention gig—what with all those pathetic looks and whimpers—that was gold, man."

"I did not whimper."

"No? Ask Doug."

Doug Whimbush, a youngish white comic who wanted more than anything in the world to be a black comic from the seventies, had materialized on Oliver's left. Somehow he got the bartender's attention and ordered a beer. He glanced at Oliver, then Simon, and said, "Oh yeah, baby. That was some serious whimperin'."

"How do you know?" Oliver said. "You weren't even there."

Whimbush shrugged. "I got sources."

"Trust me," Oliver said, running his hands down the front of his not-so-fresh uniform. "This is not shtick. In fact, I'm thinking about bailing on the whole thing."

Simon grabbed Oliver by the arm and wheeled him around. "You can't go, man. This is a showcase. Invitation only."

Showcases were the comedic equivalent of a networking mixer or job fair for up-and-coming executives. Basically, it was a glorified audition, but one with the potential to multiply your exposure exponentially. The audience was allegedly littered with booking agents, talent scouts, and promoters. A decent showcase set could keep a comedian working for months. If the set killed, it could keep him in gigs for a year or two.

The emcee made announcements and introductions, thanked everyone for coming out, and began working his way through some tired material.

"I'm not going on like this," Oliver said.

"Trust me," Simon said, rubbing Oliver's shiny badge between his thumb and forefinger, "*that* is funny."

He looked at Whimbush for confirmation, who then nodded begrudgingly. "Sho' nuff, that's pretty funny, man."

The bartender finally looked at Oliver. "What'll you have?"

"I changed my mind," Oliver said.

The barkeep shrugged and turned to leave. But Simon yelled out an order for a couple of cheeseburgers and fries, then tried to remind Oliver that he'd wanted to leave the improv gig too — and hadn't that worked out okay?

But Oliver wasn't listening. In fact, he was picking his way through a maze of tables toward the illuminated exit when the emcee called his name. He kept his head down and his feet moving. But the guy working the spotlight found him and trained his dusty beam on Oliver. At least a handful of people in the room recognized him, because a smattering of applause erupted somewhere in the dark.

Oliver made his way to the stage and told the crowd about the cute girl at work that may or may not be breaking into rooms and stealing stuff. And despite his spiky hair, crinkled uniform, and howling hunger pangs, his set absolutely killed.

Chapter Twenty-Eight

He thought he'd be nervous by now. But after thinking about it for a few days, Oliver had convinced himself that Mattie's use of the word "date" had been innocuous. She'd simply used flirty language precisely to emphasize the fact that she was *not* flirting with him. Besides, how much pressure could there be in a big church with loads of strangers? If nothing else, it should be a goldmine of potential material. He imagined an overly benevolent priest, chatty bridesmaids, jokey groomsmen, a rival pair of weepy mothers, a horde of bratty kids, tipsy uncles, and nostalgic wives on the arms of bored husbands.

The first needling twinge of apprehension struck when he saw the steeple rising up in the distance. But Mattie's directions led him past the church and through a quaint neighborhood that eventually opened up into a collection of small, sprawling estates.

Oliver eventually matched the number on the mailbox to the number on Mattie's Hello Kitty envelope. The driveway was long and circular and swarming with valet parkers. It felt odd surrendering the keys of his dilapidated Integra to the valet that had just leapt from an idling Hummer—odder still that he recognized him from the hotel. In fact, Oliver was fairly certain he'd run over this guy's foot before on his way out of the garage.

If the valet recognized Oliver, he didn't act like it. Instead he pointed to an open gate on the east side of the house. As Oliver approached the sound of happy voices, he felt an overwhelming urge to adjust something—his shirttail, his hair, his wallet. But he was already as put-together as he was going to get at this point. And adjusting his wallet wasn't going to make it any fatter.

Mattie spotted him at once, almost as if she'd been looking for him. Oliver was only a little disappointed when she didn't jog to his side and take his arm. Instead she waved him over and introduced him to a group of four couples that Oliver could only describe as geeky chic. He assumed that at least a few of them played in her band, but no one mentioned music. And so far there was no sight of Max, the smarmy non-fiancé. Oliver answered a few obligatory icebreaking questions—he was fine, thank you; he worked with Mattie; he was "between" colleges at the moment; and that, no, he was not the new drummer. Mostly, he just listened to their banter and inside jokes until the wedding planner yelled at everyone to take their places.

Mattie directed him toward neat rows of white foldout chairs facing a gazebo the size of Oliver's garage. It too was white, strung with some kind of evergreen garland and dotted with what appeared to be real magnolias. Mattie deposited him on the outer end of the last row and told him to have fun. He couldn't tell if she winked or if the sun was in her eyes. Then she took her place among a group of what he assumed were bridesmaids.

Despite the ridiculously opulent surroundings, the festivities were surprisingly informal. The preacher was youthful, but not all that young. The string quartet was stellar. And the vows were plain, unaffected, and obviously written by the bride and groom. During the solemn exchange, tissues sprouted, then bloomed—mostly on the bride's side of the aisle.

When the preacher started speaking again, Oliver's mind began to drift back in time to the first wedding he could remember attending.

. . .

He couldn't have been more than six or seven. And he couldn't remember ever seeing his mother so happy, or beautiful. She had never *not* been pretty, even after she lost all the weight and her eyes fell out of sync. Even now, she wasn't pretty for her age. She was pretty in spite of it.

But the morning of the wedding she'd been stunning, radiant, like a TV starlet from one of her soap operas. And she'd dressed him up in a secondhand sport coat and clip-on tie too. The most vivid image from this batch of memories was the way her face seemed on the verge of laughing and crying at the same time.

She kept calling him her little man and promising that things were going to be different from then on. And not just different, but better. But Oliver couldn't imagine anything much better than a happy mom and Krispy Kremes and chocolate milk.

When they finally piled into the strange black car, she answered all his questions about the wedding they were going to. When he finally got around to asking who they were going to watch get married, she'd bitten her bottom lip and told him that they were finally going to get his wish. Which seemed more than a little peculiar that she would use such a formal occasion to inform Oliver that he was *finally* going to get the trampoline he'd been begging for and that she was going to finally get her farmhouse with the wraparound porch and baby goats. But he wasn't going to argue. It made sense why she seemed so giddy. Weddings, it seemed, were like Christmas.

Just before they climbed out of the biggest, blackest car ever, Delores Miles took her only son's face in her hands and said, "You are going to be surprised, Oliver. And we are going to be so happy."

Only the first part came true.

As Oliver sat, swinging his feet in the first pew of the tiny chapel, he finally learned what a wedding was. Even better, his mommy was the bride. But the groom never showed up.

Neither did the trampoline, the big porch, or the goats.

Later that night, Oliver used all his newfound knowledge to make things better again. He sat down cross-legged on his bed with construction paper and a few freshly sharpened pencils. After several false starts and piles of balled-up paper, he finally finished his note.

His mother was sitting in the dark, still in her pretty cream-colored dress, staring at nothing on television, and nursing a bottle of something that smelled like bathroom cleaner.

He offered her the note. She unfolded it and read his proposal. He volunteered to be her groom and get a good job as a mailman and buy her the farmhouse and goats. He promised to always clean up his toys and dress nice and be a really good and nice groom. His favorite paragraph was the one that took the longest to write, the one where he told her what a beautiful bride she was.

But when she finished the note, she didn't smile or laugh or cry. She just folded it up and let it fall from her hand to the sofa, then from the sofa to the floor.

She said simply, "Go to bed, Oliver."

He'd seen his mother drink her "medicine" before. He'd experienced the blanked-out expressions, dreamy speech, the long stretches of apathy. But he'd never seen her be so mean. Unfortunately, he would see a lot more of it in the future, all of it.

He'd poured out his milky little heart, hoping to nourish his mother. But all he really managed to do was stain the carpet.

Oliver finally snapped out of his own memory when the preacher told Reese he could now kiss the bride.

• • •

The first marital smooch was chaste, sweet even, the way their foreheads touched and all the pent-up wedding day tension seemed to blissfully drain away. But then a pair of groomsmen destroyed the moment by whooping and whistling, which prompted Reese to attempt an impromptu make-out session. Two boys in the row in front of Oliver made retching sounds. Mattie seemed to be caught in a perpetual eye-roll. Oliver followed her gaze upward, half expecting to see a sky-written message up there.

The cellist cued the rest of the quartet, who then pounded out a strident recessional. Before the newly minted married couple had disappeared through the portable archway, staff members materialized in droves—caterers, waiters with hors d'oeuvres and wine bottles, and serious young men assembling some tables, disassembling others, and moving chairs to encircle an enormous makeshift dance floor. Oliver surrendered his folding chair and went in search of some inconspicuous place to blend in as the wedding party posed for pictures. Mattie found him leaning against the trunk of a willow tree. She handed him a flute of champagne, then sipped her own as they watched people congregate around the newly assembled dance floor.

Oliver said, "We don't really have to dance, do we?"

"Just once. It's basically a photo op for the wedding party. But it'll be a slow number. We just zombie waltz for three-and-a-half minutes, then our duties here will be done."

The wedding planner seemed to be pulling imaginary strings and levers from the edge of the dance floor. During the traditional bride-and-groom dance, she coordinated more and more couples in what appeared to Oliver as the on-deck circle—the bride with the groom's father, the groom with the bride's mother, then increasingly complex pairings of the bride's stepparents and best men and maids of honor and grandmothers. Eventually the entire wedding party was invited to join in and Oliver found himself embracing the Harrington Hotel's new night auditor. He held one hand aloft and perched the other self-consciously on the small of her back. Mattie rested her head on his chest and hummed along with whatever sappy song the DJ was spinning.

A minute into the song, Mattie angled her face up toward his, and for one delightfully alarming moment he thought she was going to kiss him. He tried *not* to think about the taste of champagne on her lips. The longer she looked at him the harder he tried to think about anything else. But nothing worked.

Finally, she said, "You okay up there?"

"Sure, yeah. Why do you ask?"

"Your heart's playing a drum solo." She tapped his ribcage with her finger. "And your hand's all clammy."

"Sorry. I'm a little out of practice. I think the last time I danced was with my mother, about a hundred years ago."

"Maybe you should do it more. If you could relax a little, you'd be quite good at it."

"Thanks. I'll just be happy if I don't break any of your toes."

Actually, that had been his mission when the song started. Now it was to keep breathing in the smell of her hair and pray the song never ended. But the song did eventually fade and the DJ began yammering instructions for the bridesmaids to stay put and do the Chicken Dance.

Mattie finally pulled away, shrugged, and rolled her eyes yet again. Oliver backed to the edge of the dance floor, savoring the warm spot on his chest, watching the girl who'd made it. She looked bored, just going through the motions until the grinning bride grabbed her hands and exaggerated the wacky dance moves. The more she lost herself in the madcap choreography, the harder it was for Oliver to take his eyes off of her. He was conniving various ways to ask her to slow dance again when he felt someone bump his elbow.

"You're Oliver, right?" It was Reese, the groom, Mattie's brother.

"That's me." Oliver offered his hand, but Reese did a poor job pretending not to see it. "Anyhow, congratulations. The ceremony was beautiful."

"You do realize that, technically speaking, you weren't invited?"

"I don't know," Oliver said gamely, still holding out hope that Mattie's brother was just messing around. "I have a pretty vivid memory of Mattie asking."

"Well it's not exactly her wedding, is it?"

"Are you asking me to leave?"

"Just making friendly conversation," he said. "So tell me, what are your plans with Mattie?"

"As far as I know we don't have any. But she did say something about dinner later."

"She mentioned your sense of humor," Reese said. "I have to say though, that so far I'm not impressed."

"Look, I didn't come here to start trouble. Mattie asked me to come and I came. I promise I'm not trying to ruin your big day or break up your band or whatever it is you think I'm doing here."

"So did she feed you that load of crap about staying in the band to save her kid brother?"

"Not exactly," Oliver said.

"Despite what my sister tells you, my alleged addiction was basically a two-year stint of relatively normal fraternity life. Excessive partying, failing a few too many classes, and maybe a drug test or two. But it was a weird time for all of us, and we all found our own unhealthy ways of dealing with it. *All* of us."

"Okay," Oliver said, unsure how he'd been so easily sucked into such a one-sided argument. Evidently, Mattie wasn't the only Holmgren who said everything that came to mind. He'd already decided his best line of defense was to just stop talking when the elder version of Reese appeared, grinning too wide, speaking louder than necessary, and pumping Oliver's hand much too hard.

"I'm Walter, Mattie's father."

"The difference," Reese said with way more drama than the situation called for, "is that I *admitted* I had a problem. Unlike everyone else in this family." Then he ambled off without even acknowledging the man still gripping Oliver's hand. He appeared to be talking to a guy that looked suspiciously like Max.

"I'm Oliver Miles. It's a pleasure to meet you, sir."

"Mattie's told me quite a lot about you."

"She has?"

Walter Holmgren stared at his drink as if seeing it for the first time. "Actually, no. But I'm sure she meant to."

That's when Mattie finally broke away and hurried over to Oliver's side. Her face was flushed from dancing, her forehead damp as she rose up on tiptoes to kiss her father's cheek. "Love you, Pop," she said.

Walter smiled into his drink. Mattie gripped Oliver's arm and escorted him toward the gate by the side of the house.

"Does this mean you're coming to my rescue?"

"Actually, I'm coming to kick you out."

"Funny, your brother just tried that."

"Well, I'll be much nicer about it. And you'll just have to believe me when I say it's for your own good."

Mattie shot her brother and Max a dirty look as she ushered Oliver past piles of amplifiers and guitar cases. Once outside the gate she nodded toward the nearest valet and told Oliver, "Give me your ticket."

"Why the rush?" he said. "Looks to me like a band's about to set up."

"Which is exactly why I'm rushing you out of here." She took the claim ticket out of Oliver's hand and placed it into the valet's.

"Hey, don't I know you guys from the Harrington?" he said.

All at once Oliver nodded and Mattie said no, that he must be confusing them with someone else, and to please hurry. When the valet ran off to fetch Oliver's car, Mattie turned and said, "By the way, thank you."

"For what exactly?"

"For being here to help me endure these people."

"Who? Your family? Or *the* Family?"

"See why I hate that name?"

"No," Oliver said. "I really don't."

"Don't get me wrong. We love each other. But did you get the sense from anyone you met here today that we'd ever actually *choose* to spend time together if we weren't related?"

"Now that you mention it," he said. He wondered if she had any idea how sad that sounded, if she had any clue how lucky she was to actually have an intact family. But he decided to play along, to be a good sport, to keep his envy to himself. "If I didn't know better, I'd say you're going to stand here in the driveway until I leave."

"That's exactly what I'm going to do."

"Mind if I ask why?"

"You already know. Yes, that's my brother's band setting up in the backyard. No, I had no idea they were going to do this. But I'm not surprised either. And if it weren't his wedding day I'd jump in your car with you and treat you to that dinner I promised. As it stands now, I hope you'll take another rain check."

The valet pulled Oliver's wheezy Integra alongside them. He fished his wallet out of his pocket, more than a little dismayed to see only one bill tucked inside—a twenty. He stared at it, willing it to break into a pile of singles. It didn't move, and neither did the toes of the valet's Nikes. Oliver surrendered the obscene tip with his eyes clenched. The valet practically shouted his thanks, then stood at attention, holding the door as if Oliver were the prince of Nashville.

Finally, Oliver turned to Mattie and said, "Why don't we just go after you guys play?"

"I'm sorry," she said. "You really need to go."

"But why?"

"Because ..." She gripped his arm with one hand and placed her other hand on the top of his head, just like a cop on TV. Then she playfully yet forcefully shoved him inside his car. "You can't see me this way, Oliver."

"You know, I could just drive around for twenty minutes and come back while you're already playing."

"But you won't."

"Why not?"

"Because you're going to promise me you won't."

"I am?"

That's when Mattie punched him in the shoulder. Her expression was playful, but the pain was rich and intense.

"Ouch!"

"Promise me," she said, her lopsided grin now in full bloom, her fist still clenched. "Or I'll have to do it again."

"Okay, I promise, Mattie."

He watched her shrink in the rearview mirror, arms folded and unmoving until they were out of each other's sight. Oliver turned the radio down so he could replay Mattie's last three syllables in his head. Then he spent the rest of the trip trying to devise more ways to get Mattie to hit him again.

Oliver got lost on the way home. Or maybe his subconscious had commandeered the wheel. Either way, he found himself taking the Second Avenue exit away from the city, through a few of Nashville's seedier neighborhoods, and eventually idling outside a nondescript three-story brick building. Although he'd never actually been here, he'd made the trek dozens of times in his mind's eye.

Oliver killed the ignition and sat, staring and doubting and wondering what he thought he was doing here. Maybe it was meeting Mattie's father, or just an inconvenient rash of curiosity.

Roscoe had warned him numerous times that it was probably a bad idea to track his father down. Now he was about to find out.

Chapter Twenty-Nine

ONE OF THE MORE MEMORABLE SETS in Oliver's comedy career was also one of his shortest. It was the kind of night biographers might refer to as transcendent, cathartic, or even seminal. Although he doubted biographers would ever refer to it at all.

His mistake—if it could really be called a mistake—was not allowing the material to age properly. Improvising a line here or there was one thing; creating an entire routine in a single afternoon, then attempting to perform it that same night, was another. Stand-up comedy is dynamic. It's give and take, a transaction, as much about the effect as it is about the cause. The best editors are time, attention, and honest feedback—the more brutal and objective the better. That night however, it wasn't the crowd's reaction that led to Oliver's undoing. It was his own.

The weirdest thing happened today. I met my father for lunch …

Literally.

You see, we'd never been formally introduced before … or informally either, for that matter.

So far it was working. He was taking his time, allowing the material to breathe, thinking a few lines ahead, impregnating his pauses and carrying them to term. The real key would be to trust the crowd with his subtleties.

It was awkward at first, you know. We tried some small talk. My dad did that nervous-laugh thing and said, "So … it's been a while, huh?"

I did some quick math, hoping he'd be impressed …

Let's see, I was born twenty-six years ago, give or take a few months ... add nine more for gestation ... carry the two ... and it comes to a neat quarter-century.

The audience did their part. They tracked along with his story, allowing him some leeway to set things up, laughing through obvious pauses.

Oliver still had confidence in the material. What he hadn't banked on were his memories. As he milked each one for maximum comedic effect, he was forced to relive it. And the images were still too raw. For this bit to really kill, he would first need to build some emotional calluses. But it was too late now. He was onstage, mouth open, mind racing, heart rending, exposed. He tried to drown the bulge in his throat with a sip of water. But seeing the *half-full* mark on his homemade mug only made it worse.

A few good punch lines hovered on the horizon. So he tried to focus on those.

Finally meeting his father had been more than awkward. It was pathetic and sad, more bitter than sweet. There was nothing deep or insightful about the exchange. No healing, no catharsis. Roscoe had warned him that meeting his dad was probably a bad idea, that he'd be disappointed and end up with more questions than answers. And as usual, Roscoe was more right than not.

Oliver's father was a sad little man named Gerard, way more interested in talking about himself than learning about the son he'd never met. Apparently he'd lost all of his money, most of his mind, and three fingers to frostbite. He wasn't quite homeless, but it was close. He seemed exceedingly proud of his apartment and his job bagging groceries. Oliver tried hard to ignore the eerily familiar mannerisms, the deep-set canal of skin that sloped between his nostrils and full lips, and dozens of other subtle manifestations of their shared DNA.

He hadn't gone looking for an Oprah moment or some overly emotional reunion. But he'd been determined to scrape past the superficial epidermis of names, ranks, and serial numbers. What he'd wanted was simple: a few childhood anecdotes to memorialize and to finally check "Meet Father" off his mental to-do list. But Gerard seemed to have a one-track mind. When Oliver finally worked up the nerve to broach the subject of his mother—how they met, what she was like, her losing battle with alcoholism, and her resulting illness—Gerard had steered the conversation to the only topic that seemed to interest him, what amounted to a master class of variation and theme.

"So, like I was saying," my dad said, although he hadn't really said much the entire time. "Been going through a rough patch lately. And if you could, you know, spare a few bucks till my next check . . . ?"

If it's true that only the truth is funny, then it's equally true that the truth hurts.

As Oliver's crying turned to outright weeping onstage, the crowd ate it up. The harder he cried, the louder they laughed. Much later, he would remember to be thankful for the crowd's collective hilarity. In the moment, however, he wanted to climb down from the stage and individually strangle the ones laughing the hardest. Instead he dropped the microphone and left the stage.

Mattie had the night off. So Oliver spent most of his shift in the Harrington's Business Center, googling himself. Barry had apparently been busy. There were three YouTube videos from three different angles, only one with decent sound. A groundswell of happy gossip was already building on Facebook, referring to Oliver as the Crying Comedian. There were Tweets and re-Tweets, hyperlinks, blogs, and one actual article review of a recent show on the front page of the *City Rhythm* website—byline Lindsey Whittaker. But she did refer to him as the "world's saddest funnyman," which horrified him. That was uncomfortably close to the way Roscoe described his mother. And not only was he still terrified of turning into his mother, he could now say the same thing about his father.

Oliver then googled his father for the thousandth time. And came up empty yet again.

It seemed he was stuck with his mother's version of his biological father—a brief-yet-promising comedy career as a stand-up, followed by a longer stint in narcotics where he served as maker, seller, user, addict, and eventual informant. And of course Oliver now knew his father moonlighted as a bagboy and indiscriminate panhandler.

At least the man could multitask. This struck Oliver as profoundly funny. But he didn't really feel like laughing.

Chapter Thirty

Oliver had never "met the family" before, not officially, not like this. Sure, his dating resume included passing introductions to this parent or that, and he'd had to endure a handful of pointed questions from suspicious fathers or doting mothers—and even one veiled threat from an overly muscular uncle or two. Pesky siblings had been deployed to spy or eavesdrop or disrupt any potential make-out sessions before they could heat up. But there had been no family picnics or sit-down dinners, no fatherly rounds of golf or trips to amusement parks. Looking back over his romantic past, the most enduring familial relationships he'd managed to forge had been with his girlfriends' family dogs. Which was fine, because Oliver usually liked other people's dogs. There was no subtext with dogs, no pretense or angles or hidden agendas.

So Oliver was almost disappointed when he rang the doorbell and wasn't greeted by a husky bark. In fact, there was no sound at all. No buoyant shouts of "I got it," no curtains dropping, not a single muted footfall approaching. He did think he smelled something burning.

When Mattie had suggested dinner, she'd mentioned an informal evening of pineapple pizza and root beer. Somehow it had morphed into dinner at her parents' house, which was fine, but a little nerve-wracking.

He was trying to decide between ringing the bell again, knocking, or just going home when he heard the muffled hoof beats of someone bounding down stairs. Mattie opened the door seconds later and Oliver's first thought was, *She didn't tell me she had a sister.* Then she smiled her lopsided Mattie smile and Oliver felt like he was seeing her through Barry's eyes. She had reverted back to the little-girl haircut from their first, unremarkable introduction—a puffy bouffant with a shoulder-length flip. But now she looked like a grown-up girl from a half-century ago. He allowed a small laugh to escape as he surveyed her outfit.

"Are you making fun of me, Oliver Miles?"

"Absolutely not," he said, still unable to stop grinning.

"I think you are." Mattie began pushing the door closed, but not like she meant it.

"I'm not, I promise." Oliver put his foot on the slow-closing door and said, "In fact, I'll prove it."

Mattie leaned on the still-cracked door and waited.

"Your paisley print shift dress is authentic. Probably rayon and probably not very comfortable. The style is a mid-sixties hybrid, kind of a crossover between the tailored Jackie O influence and the mod look. I'm guessing you picked it up at B&V's, or some online boutique, and probably paid a small fortune for it."

Mattie eased the door open another few inches and said, "Impressive."

"The go-go boots are imitation, probably from some retro shop near Vandy."

"Okay, now you're just showing off."

"Sorry, my mother always dreamed of opening a vintage clothing store." It dawned on Oliver that bringing up his mother and her dreams would naturally invite unwanted questions about his family. So he quickly added, "And those bright orange leggings are a nice touch. Although I have no clue where you got those."

"Second-hand store," she said with a hint of apology. "But there is a point to all this. We have a gig tonight."

"Does that mean I finally get to hear The Family?"

"Absolutely not."

"Okay, fine. You can't come see me do stand-up then."

Mattie made a thinking face. She even rested her finger on her chin, then said, "If that's what it takes." She extended her hand and Oliver shook it. "We'll call it a pact."

"That didn't quite work out like I'd hoped."

"Too late now. You already shook on it." Then Mattie sighed dramatically and said, "Hope you're ready for this."

The smells were delightful—garlic, freshly baked bread, the scent of something charred, which Oliver hoped was coming from the fireplace and not the kitchen.

Mattie made a grand sweeping gesture toward the tall man with the sharp nose and silver hair hunched near a stone hearth. "You remember my father from the wedding?"

Sparks glowed and tumbled upward as he gave the fire one last poke and stood. He wore a tweed jacket, starched button down, and fuzzy bedroom slippers. After pausing to blot each corner of his mouth with a silk handkerchief, he tucked it away and extended his hand.

"Evening, Mr. Holmgren."

"Please," he said, "call me Walter."

Voices wafted in from another room. Oliver couldn't make out the words. But judging from their cadence—and their heat—it sounded like an argument. Mattie and her father shared a knowing frown that Oliver pretended not to notice. Instead he surveyed the room, noting the enormity of the dining room table. It was large enough to seat ten, but only six places were set. Tall candles burned on either end and several dishes sat steaming between what looked like fine china. Oliver could already imagine himself breaking something expensive.

Mattie's mother entered the dining room carrying a large casserole dish. Mattie made a quick introduction as Mrs. Holmgren placed the dish in a vacant spot on the table. Then she took a quick inventory, biting her bottom lip and dotting the air with an index finger as she counted off place settings and gravy boats and wine goblets. Satisfied, she smiled and said, "It's a pleasure to meet you, Oliver."

Walter said, "Everything looks lovely, Vonnie."

She didn't respond, probably because she was already engrossed in realigning the cutlery.

Walter squeezed Mattie's shoulder and said, "Why don't you let Reese and Trish know it's time to eat?"

"Do I really have to?" Mattie said.

"I heard that." Oliver recognized the animated whine of Reese's voice from the wedding.

The first inklings of a joke about honeymooning with the in-laws tickled Oliver's subconscious, but he ignored it.

"He wasn't even invited." Mattie directed this at Oliver, as if trying to justify.

"Of course he was, dear," Yvonne said, now seated and waiting. She appeared to be inspecting the glasses for spots.

"As you know," Mattie said with an air of conspiracy. "This was supposed to be a casual dinner at my place. Pizza and whatever sweet stuff I could find in the fridge. But then I made the mistake of joking about being too broke to make good on those rain checks I owe you. So they insisted we get together here. But I promise to make it as quick and painless as possible."

Oliver was about to respond, but Walter Holmgren beat him to it. "I do hope we'll still have time for a quick Scrabble match?"

"I should have warned you, the only thing Daddy likes better than playing Scrabble is beating people at Scrabble."

"Not true, dear," he said, clearly offended. He focused his overly earnest defense directly at Oliver. Mattie then turned so only Oliver could see her and mouthed the next words along with her father. "I just find the game stimulating. And a darn fine judge of character. You can tell a lot about a man by the words he chooses."

Oliver stuck close to Mattie as they migrated toward the table. But Yvonne had already planned the seating arrangements. Walter Holmgren assumed the head of the table with Oliver at his right, his wife on the left. Mattie was directed to the seat next to her mother. This seemed to Oliver like a tactical move, making it impossible for him to see Mattie and her parents at the same time. The remaining place settings were to Oliver's right, ostensibly for Reese and his new bride. But their argument had awkwardly ceased in the next room.

The resulting silence finally broke when Yvonne aimed a series of deliberate throat clearings at her husband. Oliver sensed a more overt signal under the table.

"Right, yes," Walter said. "I suppose grace is in order."

All four heads bowed as Mattie's father stumbled and stuttered his way into a prayer. Once he finally found his groove, the sentences grew longer and more complex until he sounded like he was warming up for a Scrabble competition. He continued to lecture God until his wife kicked him again under the table. When the family said Amen in unison, Oliver was surprised to hear Reese settling into the seat next to him.

Walter said, "Good of you to join us, son." There was no trace of irony in his tone. He looked and sounded sincere.

Reese said, "Not every day a guy gets to eat with a celebrity." There was more than a trace of irony now. "Could you pass the potatoes, Yoko?"

A thousand and one snarky comments scrolled through Oliver's brain. But mostly he had to wonder again why regular people routinely thought it wise to trade insults with comedians. Dealing with hecklers was part of the job description. Thankfully, Mr. Holmgren responded first.

"Reese, don't you owe Oliver an apology? From your rather rude introduction at the wedding?"

"Oh yeah, right." Reese sounded like he was working from a script. He glanced in Oliver's direction and said, "I owe you one, buddy."

Walter looked grim, Yvonne disappointed. Oliver smiled politely and passed the potatoes. Mattie ignored her brother and scooped leafy greens into her salad bowl. This ignited a flurry of passing, spooning, ladling, salting, and peppering.

Finally, Yvonne said, "So how is Trish feeling?"

"She's fine," Reese said.

"I am *not* fine," Trish called from the living room. "I'm nauseous."

Mattie's mother called, "Can I get you anything, dear?"

Her offer was drowned by the sound of Trish clicking the TV on in the other room.

"Does she have to do that?" Yvonne said, pleading.

"I think she does," Reese said, his mouth full of chewed bread. "Takes her mind off vomiting."

This time everyone glanced at Reese before aggressively ignoring him.

"So ..." Mattie's mother began. She appraised various serving dishes and nodded a silent approval to herself. Oliver was pleased for her too but couldn't quite shake a twinge of pity. Her relief seemed out of proportion, fleeting, as if she'd cast herself as the underdog in an unwinable battle. The rest of the Holmgrens seemed not to notice or even care. Or maybe they were just used to it? When everyone wielded their cutlery and began buttering and scooping and cutting, Oliver followed suit. "Does everyone have what they need?"

"It's all very lovely, Ms. Holmgren," Oliver said. "And delicious."

"Why thank you." She used one hand as a shield and the other as a pointer, then pretend whispered to Mattie, "I do believe this one's a keeper."

"He's not a pet, Mom."

"No, but he is a marked improvement over you know who."

"We all know who, Mom," Reese said. "Speaking of which, Max might be stopping by later."

"Whatever for?" Yvonne said.

Mattie added, "Yes, Reese. Whatever for?"

"I asked him to drop off our latest demo."

"Won't you see him in a few hours at your concert?"

"It's not a concert, Mom," Reese said. "It's called a gig. And it's at a really crappy bar."

"Language . . ." Walter said.

"Sorry, a really defecatious bar. Is that better?"

"That's not a word, son."

"Hey, like the book says, everyone poops."

"But not at the table," Mattie said.

Scandalized, Yvonne said, "Could we *please* change the subject?"

"Anyhow," Reese said. "I figured I should probably listen to the demo before the gig, to refresh my memory."

Mattie stopped her fork on the way to her mouth. "You're talking about 'Cuts Both Ways,' right?"

Reese nodded, but didn't look up.

"We're not even playing that tonight."

"You never know," Reese said. "We might."

"Well, I'm not playing it," Mattie said.

"Me neither."

All heads turned in unison at the sound of Trish's voice. She wobbled into the room, cast a queasy glance at the empty seat next to her husband, then sat next to Mattie.

Proving that chivalry wasn't quite dead yet, both Walter and Oliver rose from the table to help her into her seat. Trish's father-in-law busied himself ferrying platters and bowls toward Trish. In his haste, Oliver bumped Reese's elbow, ran his own sleeve through a puddle of gravy, then bumped Reese again on his way back down. When he saw Mattie's gaze, Oliver was more than a little pleased to see her laughing at him.

"Thanks, Pop," Trish said. The endearing nickname made Oliver turn wistful at once. He felt homesick, but it was by proxy, nostalgic about someone else's past. The better word, he supposed, was jealousy.

Trish ate voraciously, her knife and fork working in tandem, preparing the next bite before she swallowed the last. Without looking up she said, "Would everyone please stop looking at me?"

"No one's looking at you, dear." Yvonne's voice bordered on panicky. "Why would anyone be looking at you?"

"Oh, I don't know. Maybe because I'm fat and waddly and shoveling food like a refugee."

She didn't seem fat to Oliver, but he kept that to himself.

"Nonsense," Yvonne said, grabbing the bowl nearest her and spooning a mound of green beans on Mattie's plate. Several bounced off the back of Mattie's hand and spilled onto the table.

"What are you doing?" Mattie said.

Yvonne ignored the question and reached for the potatoes. "You don't eat nearly enough, Mattie. You're nothing but skin and bones."

"Just so you know," Trish said, looking directly at Oliver, "I didn't always eat this way. This pregnancy thing has thrown my hormones all out of whack."

"Patricia!" Yvonne said.

"He already knows, Mom," Mattie said. She sounded either bored or embarrassed or some of both.

Reese glared at his sister. "What gives you the right to blab all our personal business to your new boyfriend?"

"He's not my boyfriend."

Oliver felt various sets of eyeballs drifting toward him then flitting away. He wanted to confirm Mattie's statement, to rally to her defense. But in the heat of the moment he couldn't figure out if that meant nodding his head or shaking it.

"Besides," Mattie said. "I'm pretty sure Oliver took biology in high school. And he knows how to count to nine."

"Still, if I want people to know about our … our … situation, I'll take an ad out in the paper. Right, Trish?"

Trish regarded her new husband pitifully, "You're such an …" She eyed each of her in-laws in turn, and finally settled on "jerk."

"What did I do?" he said.

"First you made me pregnant. Then you made me marry you. Now you're making my morning sickness a twenty-four-hour phenomenon."

Several tense moments passed. Then Mattie said, "In case you weren't able to follow all that, Oliver, my mother is offended that Trish mentioned her pregnancy to a relative stranger. Reese is offended that I told you, although he's been bragging about it from the stage since the little pink line showed up on the pregnancy test. And Trish is offended that my brother is apparently more upset about you knowing that he knocked her up than he ever was about knocking her up in the first place."

Reese opened his mouth to speak and Oliver braced himself for an eruption. But he simply pointed his fork at his father and said, "So what's his deal?"

All eyes shifted to the head table where Walter Holmgren seemed to be indulging some deep or distant thought. Finally, Mattie said, "He's waging an epic Scrabble battle in a faraway land."

Everyone chuckled at Walter Holmgren's expense, and most of the previous tension magically evaporated. When the silence began to crescendo, Mattie said, "And here's where we change the subject and pretend our family flare-ups didn't happen. Trish, would you like to do the honors?"

"Sure," Trish swallowed and wiped her mouth with a napkin. "You find a roommate yet?"

Mattie shook her head.

"Too bad," Trish said. "The sooner you break the lease, the sooner you can hightail it out of here." She cupped her hand conspiratorially at Oliver and said, "I'm planning to stow away when she moves to New York. But don't tell anyone; it's a secret."

Mattie kept her gaze down, chewed her food with more deliberation than necessary, and pushed beans around on her plate.

Finally, Walter blinked himself back into the present and said, "So, tell us about yourself, Oliver. What do you have planned for this life of yours?"

Up to then, Oliver had been free to enjoy the meal and domestic fireworks display as a mere spectator. But now he had the floor, whether he wanted it or not. "Well short term, I was hoping to get seconds on those mashed potatoes."

There was some polite laughter as Yvonne scooted the large bowl in Oliver's direction. He wasn't really that hungry but had no choice now but to scoop out a fresh dollop.

"Save room for dessert," she said.

"How about long term then?" Walter said.

Reese swallowed and said, "What he's asking now is, 'Surely you don't plan to be a security guard forever, do you?' "

"Hey," Trish chimed in. "Maybe he hails from a long line of proud security guards."

There was more laughter, less polite this time. In an attempt to head off the next potential flare-up, Oliver added, "The first thing I need to do is finish my education."

"Good man," Walter said, raising his glass in a mimed toast. Reese grumbled something under his breath. Mattie rolled her eyes at no one in particular.

Oliver made the mistake of following up on his own comment. "I promised my mother I would."

Mattie's mother stopped chewing and patted her heart.

Walter said, "So what's your major?"

"At this point I'm still undeclared."

"Well surely you have something in mind."

Reese said, "What he's asking is, 'What do you want to be when you grow up?' "

"Actually, I'm thinking about following in your children's footsteps and working in the performing arts."

Something passed between the Holmgrens then, something ancient and weather-beaten. This was clearly another wrong answer. Walter found it suddenly imperative to start clearing dishes. Oliver watched him leave with an armload and wondered if the man was offended or disappointed.

"I hope you don't think you're joining the band," Reese said. "Is that what this is about, Mattie? Recruiting band members without my consent?"

"He can take my place," Trish said. "You play drums, Oliver?"

Oliver shook his head. "Nope, sorry. Mattie already asked."

"Why am I not surprised?" Reese said.

"Why don't you tell us about your family?" It was Yvonne, beaming again.

"There's not much to say, really." Oliver looked at Mattie for help, but she looked as curious as her mother. Walter came back, along with his benevolent smile and bemused expression, a Scrabble board tucked under one arm.

"I'm pretty much an only child," Oliver said.

"Pretty much?" Reese said, clearly mugging for what he considered *his* crowd. "You're not sure?"

"Well I'm the only one I know of." This elicited a round of courtesy laughs. Oliver's unease was becoming glaringly apparent. And the harder he fought against it, the worse it got—too many awkward pauses, too much heat in his cheeks, and he couldn't quite figure out what to do with his hands.

Yvonne said, "Let's hear about this mother of yours," obviously trying to help.

When Oliver seemed at a loss for words, Mattie said, "She's in health care."

"So your mother's a nurse then?" Walter said.

"Gee, that's not very sexist." This came from somewhere in the vicinity of Mattie and Trish.

"I was just going with the odds," Walter said. "Statistically speaking, there are ten times as many nurses as there are physicians. And

I certainly meant no offense, Oliver. So what does your mother do exactly?"

"She doesn't really practice medicine anymore," he said. "In fact, she retired recently."

"How about your father?" Walter asked. "What does he do?"

Oliver almost said, *He works in food service.* Then he considered, *He's a money manager—but apparently not a very good one.* Finally, he said, "I don't really know him all that well."

Someone said, "Oh." Maybe a few someones.

Then there was more clearing of dishes and Walter unpacking the Scrabble box. It was the most animated Oliver had seen him all night. Mattie noticed Oliver noticing the exorbitant number of letter tiles.

"Pop adores Scrabble," Trish said.

"So I have, like, no chance?" Oliver said.

"None," Mattie said.

"Nonsense," Walter said. "He has just as much chance as anyone at the table."

Once all the tiles were facedown on the table, Oliver collected seven of them and began lining them up on the little wooden easel. The object of Scrabble when he played with his mother was not to score the most points, but to see who could make the other one laugh the hardest. A winner was declared when the other person had to excuse his or her self to the restroom, which always gave Oliver a distinct advantage.

Walter scooped up a large handful of tiles, at least a dozen or more. He took his time arranging them onto a pair of little wooden racks. Occasionally he would frown at one tile, place it back in the pile, exchange it for another.

Reese said, "Dad has his own rules."

Mattie tried to explain but finally said, "Just grab fourteen tiles and brace yourself for a beating."

"And be prepared," Trish said. "Pop likes to use words that are both abstruse and recondite."

"Yes," Mattie said. "He plays the game with great erudition."

"Go ahead and mock me," Walter said. "But your vocabulary is obviously improving as a result."

"Is your mother going to play?" Oliver asked.

"She abstains for the sake of the marriage."

"The woman is a saint," Walter said with no small trace of reverence. He even stared off toward the clattery sounds in the kitchen.

The game itself moved quickly. Mattie, Reese, and Trish plunked down whatever obvious word came to mind, words like "pea" and "snoop" and "also." All the Holmgrens played with urgency; the ones not named Walter added large doses of irony. Oliver couldn't tell if their small words and seemingly little effort were in homage to the master or to indulge his inflated sense of competition. Or maybe they were just trying to make it harder for him by giving him so little to work with. Regardless, when his turn arrived he was always ready with another word Oliver had never heard of. This time it was *veracious*.

"Put me down for twenty-seven points, please."

"Wait a second," Reese said. "Did our illustrious father figure just make a spelling error? I do believe *voracious* is spelled with an *o*, not an *e*."

He reached to remove the offending tiles, but Walter batted his hand away. "A veracious man is one who habitually tells the truth. He can't help himself. Whereas a voracious man is unnaturally eager, usually about food."

"Is he making fun of me?" Trish said.

"Although," Walter mused, "I suppose it is possible that one could be voracious about one's veracity."

"How's it going in here?" Yvonne entered with an enormous tray of coffees and thick slabs of key lime pie and began passing them out.

"What she really means is," Mattie explained, "just how bad is it?"

Walter used the time between turns to lecture Oliver. He explained the meaning of the words he used, words like *louche*, *abstemious*, *yeomanly*, *peripatetic*, and *monogamous*. He parlayed each definition into a miniature dissertation on character and integrity, especially as it pertained to the sanctity of marriage. Oliver wasn't sure if this was directed at him or at Reese or to Walter himself.

His next word was *fealty*. "It means loyalty, fiercely loyal."

Reese whistled and said, "Losing your touch there, Dad?"

"Only two syllables?" Mattie said.

Trish added, "And about eight measly points."

They were having fun at Walter's expense. And he seemed to be taking it in stride. Then Yvonne chimed in with, "Yeah, are you feeling okay, dear?"

The room broke up at what was obviously an inside joke, one rife with history and family irony. The laughter was infectious and Oliver found himself laughing along with them, although he didn't actually get it. He allowed his gaze to rest on each family member before studying his fourteen tiles. He began shifting tiles, in a near frenzy, as he tried to form the words scrolling through his brain—*ambivalent, bittersweet, melancholic, nostalgic, wistful*—but the tiles wouldn't cooperate.

When it was Oliver's turn, the best he could come up with was *whatnot*.

The game ended when Trish announced she needed a shower before the gig.

"That wasn't so bad," Oliver said.

"That's because Daddy was more interested in lecturing you than beating the rest of us. That's why he only tripled our scores instead of really trouncing us."

"You kids run along," Walter said. "I'll spot Oliver everyone else's points, which ought to even things out. Then he can represent your team while the rest of you kids get ready for your jig."

"It's a gig, Dad," Reese whined.

"I think Oliver's had enough," Mattie said.

"Probably so," Oliver agreed. "But that really was fun."

Everyone looked at him curiously, as if the word "fun" would never have occurred to them.

After an enthusiastic round of thank-you's, great-to-meet-you's, and promises to do this again real soon, Mattie walked Oliver to his car in silence. She hugged herself against the chilly night air and finally said, "I'm resisting the urge to apologize."

"For what?"

"For, you know ... *that*." She swept her arm back toward the house.

"Are you kidding? I had a great time."

"Don't make fun, Oliver. I already know my family is weird."

"I promise," he said. "There were some tense moments. But mostly it was strange and wonderful."

She looked suspicious, scrutinizing his face for any trace of irony or hidden punch lines.

"Anyway," Oliver said. "Thanks for inviting me."

An awkward silence descended, thick and bloated with possibility. Then Mattie leveled her most penetrating stare and said, "Look, I realize that if this were a movie, this would be the part of the scene where you're trying to figure out whether to kiss me or not."

"Well, I was wondering ..."

"Please don't, Oliver."

"Don't wonder, or don't kiss you?"

"It will only complicate things. I promise."

"Which things?"

"Just about everything."

Oliver was surprised to feel relief flooding his veins. There was no getting around the fact that he wanted to kiss Mattie. But he didn't want the pressure that came with it, what it might mean, how it might change things. Besides, he liked having something to look forward to. And then he thought of her moving to New York. He was trying to figure out a nondesperate way to shoehorn that into the conversation when Trish came hobbling out, zombielike, eyes closed, arms extended in front of her. Her long gown and full bouffant created a Bride of Frankenstein effect.

Mattie said, "What are you doing, Trish?"

"You guys done kissing yet? I can't bear to look."

"Yeah, Trish. We're done. You can open your eyes now."

"Sorry, I just can't stand to see happy right now. I don't think it's good for the baby. Anyway, it was really nice to meet you, Oliver. I'd tell you to run for your life, but it's obvious that Mattie's too far gone for that."

Oliver looked at Mattie for confirmation, but she was staring at her sister-in-law with virtually no expression whatsoever. He thought of Barry and wondered how everyone else could tell how Mattie felt about him but him.

Trish leaned in close and said, "But if you do make a run for it, take me with you. I can drive the getaway car, cook the meals, just whatever."

"I'll try to remember that," Oliver said.

That's when Max pulled to the curb in a gleaming Saab. His windows were down and he was spinning a compact disc on the end of one finger.

"Hello Security Guard," Max said.

Oliver served up his most sarcastic wave and said, "Guess I'll be going. Thanks again, Mattie. For everything."

Oliver climbed reluctantly into his car and was about to shut the door when he heard his name again.

"Technically," Mattie said, "I do still owe you dinner. You know, since I didn't really pay for this one."

"Is this another rain check?"

"You can collect them," she said. "Like trading cards."

As he neared the end of the block Oliver was surprised to realize he was thinking of Mattie's father, specifically the man's fierce loyalty to his family. By the time he reached the four-way stop, he was mired in a bog of secondhand envy—Walter was just the kind of man his mother always needed, but never found. But of course, she looked in all the wrong places. The Holmgrens seemed to take their intact family for granted. And why wouldn't they? They didn't know any better.

Oliver turned at the corner, and as he looked back toward the house his envy turned to outright jealousy. Mattie was on her way to a gig with Max while Oliver would be stranded at the hotel for hours, alone with his unreliable imagination.

Chapter Thirty-One

Oliver could smell the man before he saw him.

So just moments after clocking in, he was only a little surprised to see Sherman sitting in the security closet searching the computer for surveillance videos. Apparently he was having no better luck than Oliver. Each consecutive camera feed looked exactly like the one before it—endless shots of empty hallways. Sherman wasn't complaining out loud, but his frustration was apparent in the way he'd gone from tapping the keyboard to pounding it. At one point Oliver thought he actually heard the mouse squeak. His boss was dressed in jeans and a turtleneck and had the sweet and sour smell of perspiration and an overdose of expensive cologne. Obviously Sherman didn't yet realize he was being watched, as he was using his free hand to forage in his nostril. Oliver took two large and quiet steps backward, then executed a considerably more noisy approach, which included throat clearing and gum popping. By the time he rounded the corner a second time, Sherman's foraging hand had disappeared under the desk.

Oliver noted the time on the computer screen; thankfully he wasn't tardy yet. "Everything okay in here?"

Without looking up, Sherman said, "At least for the time being."

"That doesn't sound promising."

"We received a rather ominous call from Memphis this afternoon."

"Memphis" was a code word for the "future owners of the Harrington Hotel." It never ceased to amaze Oliver how Sherman could be so in awe of his brothers. Although their ailing father, the infamous Claude Sherman, was still the CEO, brothers Morty and Montel Sherman had been running the daily operations for more than a decade. The family portfolio consisted of four luxury hotels, a dozen or so economy hotels, a small chain of dry cleaners, and a few assorted golf courses, liquor stores, and car washes. Wherever possible they installed family members to manage their interests. Oliver had met the elder Sherman brothers twice. And despite their tenaciously amiable dispositions, they somehow managed to strike a special brand of fear in their kid brother. It had only gotten worse since Claude's most recent stroke. Rumor had it he was slipping in and out of a coma, and may not make it to the end of the fiscal year.

"Something security related?"

"I'm afraid so. Somehow they got wind of our latest ... um, incident."

"Are you saying the Johnsons un-dropped the charges against the hotel?"

Sherman seemed to study Oliver's expression for a full minute. Once he was satisfied that whatever he was looking for wasn't there, Sherman said simply, "So I take it you were not aware that we were robbed again last night?"

Oliver accidentally swallowed his gum. His primary thought as he watched his boss watching him was: *At least Mattie wasn't working last night.*

Sherman continued. "But instead of reporting it to the front desk—or even the police—the alleged victim called Montel on his cell phone."

"Your brother, right?"

Oliver realized it was a stupid question before he even finished it. Sherman's bunched-up facial features merely confirmed it.

"It seems Monty had comped a room for an old college roommate who was in town on business. When he realized he'd been robbed, he called Monty instead of the police, obviously trying to help us avoid the negative publicity."

"But that's good though, right?"

"In theory, I suppose. At least it is for the hotel. But since we cannot control information we don't have, this news is not especially good for me. Or for you either."

"What was taken?"

"I believe it was a Rolex and a few hundred dollars."

"So what does this mean? You know, exactly?"

"I have been informed, in no uncertain terms, that one more such *incident* will force Memphis to bring in outside help."

Oliver was touched. He'd never considered Sherman as any kind of father figure, but the man looked genuinely worried, even more than normal. The fact that Sherman appeared so outwardly concerned about Oliver's vocational welfare made Oliver's heart beat a little sideways. He said, "Wow, I really appreciate your concern, sir."

"*Concern*, Mr. Miles?" Sherman's voice was bloated with real conviction, and Oliver had to squelch a sudden urge to hug the man. "Outsourcing hotel security is merely the first step in outsourcing everything else around here—*including* management."

"Oh," Oliver said. "I see."

"I should hope you do. For both of our sakes."

Sherman's conviction and concern made sense now. It was all about self-preservation. With their father slipping deeper into a coma every day, the brothers inched ever closer to owning the small Sherman empire outright. Apparently, General Sherman was feeling like an outsider looking in, and not liking what he saw.

"Do we have any theories?" Oliver said.

"I do." Sherman swiveled back around and scrolled down the menu until he found the tab labeled "Front Desk." One click later Oliver stared at the image of Mattie pounding out numbers on both her adding machines. Sherman clicked his fingernail on the computer monitor.

"Mattie? But she wasn't even here last night."

"Tell me, Oliver. When did this recent rash of robberies begin?"

"About the same time as Mattie?"

"Look, I'm not accusing her of anything untoward. Honestly, I have no idea what's going on here. But I'm convinced the clues we need have already been captured on videotape." Sherman tapped the computer monitor for emphasis, but it was already cycling through feeds from various floors. When it panned the sixth floor, Oliver saw a familiar form ambling down the hallway.

"That's him." Oliver spoke before he thought.

"Who?" Sherman said as the man in the hallway stopped in front of a door and began patting his pockets.

"The underwear man," Oliver said as the man found his key. "Barely recognized him with his clothes on. He said his name was Cleve. From Room 623, I think."

Sherman seemed to bristle at this, but then stood and arched his back until it popped. "I'm sure you realize we have a policy against that kind of talk, Oliver."

"What kind of talk?"

"You know as well as I do that 623 has been shut down for decades."

"I do?"

"Six twenty-three was Old Man Harrington's private suite."

"But I'm sure that's the room I let him into."

"And I'm sure you're mistaken."

"Oh, I guess I, um, got the number wrong."

"I'm sure you did," Sherman said as he moved toward the door. "Now please just focus on the task at hand. Or else we'll both be finding new jobs."

. . .

An hour later, Oliver was still watching the split screen. On the left, Mattie sat staring at a spreadsheet and tapping her teeth with a pencil. The right side revealed alternating angles of empty hallways, an empty restaurant, and an empty lobby.

He tried calling Chuck again, to no avail.

Eventually Oliver found a tape that wasn't just an empty hallway. It started like all the others—a motionless shot of carpet and walls and door handles. But then a shadow emerged on the bottom of the screen and eventually morphed into the baskside of a chubby guy in a flannel shirt and flip-flops disappearing into a room. Oliver watched it twice, then moved on. Ten minutes later he found a second tape that wasn't just an empty hallway. It was the same guy in the same flannel shirt disappearing into the same room. Oliver found the exact same footage eleven more times, all with different labels and different dates. He didn't know what it meant and he was tired of thinking about it.

He changed the camera feed to the front desk and spent the next hour watching Mattie work. Oliver liked watching Mattie work.

At some point she left the office and got on the elevator. Tracking her movements via simulcast became like a video game. He changed the angle to the lobby, assuming she'd head toward the ladies' room, but she moved to the elevator instead. When the door closed, Oliver clicked to the basement feed, assuming Matttie was making an impromptu coffee run. But she never appeared in the basement.

So he set the monitor to split screen and began searching for Mattie, viewing two angles at once.

He eventually spotted her roaming the halls of the third floor. She would occasionally pause, tilt her head as if listening to some faint siren song, then start walking again.

Oliver double-checked the date and time to make sure he was viewing Mattie in real time. Then he clicked various keys until the scene unfolding on the third floor filled the entire screen.

The black-and-white version of Mattie paused again. She sat down—her back pressed against the expanse of wall between Rooms 311 and 313—pulled something from her purse, and placed it on her lap. Next, she retrieved a pencil from behind her ear and drummed it lightly against her pursed lips.

He stared until the pencil stopped. A smile tugged at one corner of her mouth, then migrated. She opened the spiral notebook in her lap and began to write.

Oliver sat and watched and wondered. He wondered what she was up to, what possessed her to roam the halls at night. He wondered if he might be imagining the whole thing, if maybe the hotel really was haunted. Mostly, he wondered what she was writing—and why she was writing it in his lost notebook.

Chapter Thirty-Two

OLIVER WAS SITTING in his mother's room at Shady Grove, fruitlessly soliciting advice about Mattie—her criminal past, whether or not she might have stolen his notebook, and what he should do about it—when the telephone rang. As far as he could remember, he didn't think he'd ever heard his mother's phone ring before. Judging by her blank expression, he didn't think she had either. When he couldn't think of a reason not to, Oliver answered it.

"Joey?" he said, when the odd noises coming through the receiver started to make sense. "Where are you?"

"In the kitchen. You need to— "

"Listen, Joey, I'm glad you called." Oliver learned along ago to take charge of conversations with Joey before they rambled into oblivion. "I need your advice on something."

"Can't you ask your mom?"

"That's what I've been doing for the last two hours. But she's engrossed in a *Little House on the Prairie* marathon."

"Oh, um, alright. Go ahead , but try to hurry."

"Okay, here goes. There's this girl at work, see? And, well, I'm not sure I should trust her."

"How come?" Joey said. His voice sounded strained, mixed with small grunts and even a few distant squeals.

"She kind of has this habit of sneaking around the hotel at night. And she seems to be really good at picking locks and stuff. And well, I think she may have stolen my notebook."

"Uh huh."

"And I caught her writing in it, sort of. On a security camera."

"Uh huh."

"Are you listening, Joey?"

"Uh huh."

"So do you have any thoughts, you know, about the girl?"

"Did you *ask* her if she stole your notebook yet?"

"No, not yet."

"I would just ask her."

"You're right, Joey. I should probably just confront her about it."

"Only if you really care about her," Joey said. "At least that's what my Sad used to day."

There was a fumbling sound on the other end of the phone, followed by more of Joey's grunting and another high-pitched voice. "What's that noise, Joey?"

"You need to get here soon. I don't think I can hold her much longer."

"Hold who?"

"I caught a burglar. That's why I called you at your mom's."

Oliver thought he heard a distant, yet familiar voice shouting, "Hello, Oliver." He heard himself laughing when he asked, "Is her name Mattie?"

"I don't know."

"Is she pretty?"

"Gosh, *yes!*"

"Okay, I'll be right there, Joey. Make sure you don't hurt her, but don't let her go either."

Oliver kissed his mother on the cheek and promised to come back soon. He wondered if she'd even heard him through her TV coma. When he was almost out the door, she mumbled something that sounded like, "So long, Wayne."

Mattie's car was in the driveway when Oliver got there, but he still was not prepared for the scene unfolding in his living room. She'd been rolled into a sleeping bag, and Joey was sitting on the edge of it to keep her from getting up. But she wasn't struggling to get free. In fact, Joey was holding a copy of *Are You My Mother?* so Mattie could read it to him.

"Hi, Oliver," Joey said. "My name is Joey. I still got your robber."

"Hi, Oliver," Mattie had said. "My name is Mattie. And I really have to pee."

Oliver pulled a forlorn Joey to his feet as Mattie scurried out of the living room. Joey said, "You think she can binish the fook when she comes back?"

"That will be up to her. Now do you mind telling me what happened?"

"Sure. I was working on the fridge—man, it was really stinky—and anyway, I heard something in the garage. When I went out to instigate, I catched her digging through your mama's boxes. That's when I captivated her and brought her in the house."

Mattie returned then, grinning sheepishly.

Oliver said, "So what do you have to say for yourself, young lady?"

She shrugged and said, "Busted."

"You broke into my house?"

"I was making a delivery," she said. "Plus, I didn't think you were ever going to show me your mom's collection of vintage clothes. Which, by the way, is stellar."

"So you were the one changing the clothes on the mannequins?"

Mattie's eyes widened and she shook her head. "Nope, not me. This is my first trip, scout's honor."

Oliver turned to Joey, who was now staring at the floor and blushing from the crown of his head. He mumbled, "You got a message on the phone machine. It's from the bank."

They adjourned to the kitchen, and while Mattie made coffee, Oliver listened to his voice mail. It was indeed the bank, his mother's bank in fact. And apparently, the account was overdrawn.

"Hmm," Oliver said.

"That doesn't sound good," Mattie said.

"I'll bet that's why my check bounced," Joey said.

"Which check?" Oliver said.

"The last one you wrote me for fixing things."

"I'm sorry, Joey. But why didn't you tell me?"

"I didn't want to hurt your feelings."

"So were you, you know, able to pay your rent and buy food and stuff?"

"I don't have rent. And I usually just eat your food."

"Why don't you have rent, Joey?"

"My house is paid for."

That's when Oliver noticed the big, lopsided grin on Mattie's face. "What's so funny?"

"Keep going," she said. "You're getting really warm."

"How do you know so much?" he asked her.

"I've been Joey's prisoner for over an hour," she said. "And Joey likes to talk."

"Okay," Oliver said. "I'll bite. Tell me about your house, Joey."

"You already know."

"No, Joey. I really don't."

"Sure you do. You're standing in it."

"This is your house?"

"Since I was eight." For proof, Joey held up four fingers on each hand. "I inheritanced it when my mom died."

Oliver said, "And all that stuff in the garage?"

Joey shrugged.

Mattie said, "I do believe that's his stuff."

"Are you saying you sleep in my garage?"

"Nope," Joey said with his own version of Mattie's lopsided grin. "I sleep in *my* garage."

"Not anymore," Mattie said. Both Joey and Oliver swiveled their heads at Mattie. "I think Oliver has a new roommate."

Joey looked as troubled as Oliver felt about that prospect. Apparently he liked sleeping in the garage.

Mattie poured three coffees and set them on the kitchen table. She sat and motioned for the boys to do the same. Once everyone was comfortable, she picked up Joey's book and started it again from page one. Her voice was animated and sincere, with nary a hint of condescension.

As she read, Oliver alternated his gaze between Mattie's mouth, Joey's enraptured expression, and his own wringing hands.

"I did have a mother," Mattie read. "I know I did. I have to find her. I will! I WILL!" Joey made a snuffling sound. His eyes had grown large and wet. Oliver camouflaged his own tears by pretending to have a pesky dust mite in his eye.

When he finally recovered from the story, Oliver asked Joey, "So how did my mother come to live here, anyway?"

"We met in the hut nouse," Joey said. "She was on the way in and I was on the way out."

"So, she paid rent?"

"Sort of," Joey said. "She paid for all the repairs."

Mattie gasped, then again like a ratchet. After a final wheezy gasp, she sneezed her delightful cartoon sneeze. Joey fished around in his pocket and handed Mattie a tissue. Then he matter-of-factly said, "Of course it was your mother's idea for us to get married."

Oliver stared, open-mouthed, as his mother's husband inspected whatever residue Mattie sneezed into his hanky.

"I think Oliver has a stepfather," Mattie said.

"You knew about this?"

"We didn't talk *that* long."

. . .

Oliver had the entire afternoon to think about it. And no matter how he spun it, he had to admit that Joey was right. If he really cared for Mattie, he would need to confront her. Plus, the more he thought about it the more indignant he became—why would she so flippantly put his job at risk? And he didn't have to wait long for his opportunity. Twenty-four hours after spying on Mattie as she read his notebook, he watched her embark on another unauthorized stroll through the hallway, this time on the fifth floor.

He tried not to think on the ride up. But not thinking only made his brain work harder. It's impossible to have thoughts and not think them, or at least not consider them a little before shoving them aside. It helped to imagine a closet door, like in cartoons, where he could cram each unwanted thought before it found its footing. But the mind is a vacuum; it won't remain blank long. So every time he stowed a new thought into his imaginary closet, another more insidious one took its place. They were accumulating so fast now that he had to imagine leaning his entire bulk against the bulging door to keep them hidden away and out of his head.

He decided it might help to think about something else entirely, something unrelated to confronting Mattie or hotel robberies or losing this job or having to find another one. Which is why, by the time Oliver rounded the corner near the ice machine, the whole of his brain was occupied with trying to figure out the last time he'd had a bologna sandwich.

Mattie was midway down the hall, standing still, and staring at something in her open palm. She must have heard Oliver's footsteps scuffing along the carpet because she looked up, startled, both hands closing into fists as she braced herself for whomever or whatever was wandering the halls at two a.m.

She blinked once, recognition blooming in her face. She seemed to unclench everything at once (everything but the hand she'd been staring at), her smile warm and genuine. And Oliver almost fell for it too. She obviously wasn't smiling *at* Oliver Miles. Rather, she was smiling because it was *only* Oliver and not Sherman or a real cop with handcuffs.

She said, "Hey, you."

When he opened his mouth to speak, his closet full of unwanted thoughts came spilling out in a flurry of run-on questions ...

Where were you? Why didn't you answer my radio call? Don't you know how it looks when you go traipsing around the halls in the middle of the night? Do you even care? Has it even dawned on you that you could get us both fired? Then his imaginary cross-examination turned accusatory: *Admit it, Mattie ... you're just using me. You obviously stole my notebook. Do you think I'm so naïve that I don't see what's going on here? That you're going to fund this ridiculous move to New York by robbing guests because you know I'm too smitten to try and stop you?*

... he couldn't be sure which ones he'd actually asked aloud.

"Are you okay, Oliver?"

"Don't patronize me." Oliver hated the shrieky sound of his voice. So he took a long, cleansing breath and tried again. "Just tell me what you're doing up here. I mean, we're supposed to have a system. Didn't you agree to let me know when you're leaving the front desk so I can cover for you?"

"Sorry, Oliver. I just didn't think— "

"And what's that you're hiding in your hand?"

Mattie opened her hand and stared at the crumpled five-dollar bill. "I believe this is called a tip, Oliver. I've never really gotten one before so I'm not exactly sure what I'm supposed to do with it."

Oliver heard the scrape and rattle of a chain behind the door of room 541. It opened a moment later and a forty-something woman in a thick, fluffy bathrobe leaned out into the hallway. "Is everything alright out here?"

"Yes, Ms. Jacobs. Everything is fine."

"I thought I heard shouting."

"I'm afraid you did. But I think everything has settled down now." Oliver could hear the smile in Mattie's voice, but when she turned to face him, it had been hijacked by a cold, hard stare. "Isn't that right, Mr. Miles?"

"Um, yes. Sorry to disturb you, Ms. Johnson."

"It's Jacobs," Mattie said. Oliver watched her expression transform again as Mattie turned to address their guest. "Is there anything else I can get you?"

"No, I don't think so. And thanks again for bringing me the toothbrush at this hour." Ms. Jacobs shared a look with Mattie, then addressed Oliver again with a nervous chuckle. "I'm still embarrassed I forgot mine, but I'd rather be embarrassed than sleep with dirty teeth."

"Nothing to be embarrassed about," Mattie said. "And if you need anything else at all—anything—you know my number."

Mattie turned her fist into a large zero. Ms. Jacobs looked confused for a second, then smiled at Mattie's joke.

Mattie didn't speak to him on the elevator ride down. She wouldn't even look at him. But that didn't stop Oliver from trying to make sense of things, to make amends, to make that sick feeling in his stomach go away.

"A toothbrush, eh?"

She didn't answer. A Muzak version of "Hard to Say I'm Sorry" tinkled out of unseen speakers. When Oliver couldn't stand the ironic serenade any longer, he tried again.

"I'm sorry, Mattie, I just thought ..."

The music faded, then a cheery female voice encouraged elevator riders to stop by the hotel restaurant for one of Nashville's premiere dining experiences from a world-renowned chef. The door opened and Oliver watched Mattie go. When he stepped out, she turned and looked at him, hard.

"For your information," Mattie said, her voice quiet. "Ms. Jacobs isn't forgetful. She's afraid."

Oliver didn't know what to say, or where to look. So he said nothing and stared at the tops of Mattie's red and yellow saddle oxfords.

"That's the third time she's called tonight. I've had to bring her a toothbrush, a comb, fresh towels, more soap, hairnets, just whatever she can think of."

"I'm sorry, Mattie." Her silence made his heart cramp. "Are you going to be mad at me forever?"

"I'm not mad, Oliver."

For once, hearing her say his name sent the wrong kind of thrill through him. "What are you then?"

Oliver was preparing for *disappointed* or *conflicted* or *disenchanted* or even *you really hurt my feelings*. What she said was much worse; the way she said it was heartbreaking.

"Apparently, I can't be trusted."

And as luck would have it, he found his notebook a few hours later.

It was in the garage, perched atop his mother's pile of cardboard boxes. There was a Hello Kitty sticky note affixed to the front that said simply: *Oliver*.

She'd obviously left it there when she snuck into his garage and spent an hour as Joey's prisoner. But Oliver had been too distracted by all of Joey's new information to notice it.

He leafed through the pages, both stunned and exhilarated to see her handwriting mingled in with his. She used colorful pens—neon pinks and glittery purples—where Oliver wrote exclusively in black. Her loopy cursive lilted and cascaded, impishly darting between his blocky paragraphs, sometimes even daring to resurrect his scratch-outs. She'd even found the page he'd mutilated with stab marks and connected the dots into a cartoonish version of Oliver onstage with a fat, old-fashioned microphone.

It didn't take a great deal of imagination to figure out when she'd left it.

• • •

Mattie sustained her silent treatment until their shift ended. She didn't even acknowledge his goodbye.

Oliver skipped school again, deciding instead to confront his mother about her clandestine marriage. But she was sleeping in her recliner when he arrived. He considered waking her up, but what would he say? Did she really need his permission to get married? Or his blessing? Would she even *remember* getting married? He'd assumed Joey was confused, or just making it all up. But all that wishful thinking had dissipated when Joey bounded off to the garage to find his marriage certificate.

The longer he watched his mother sleep, the harder it became for Oliver to cling to his hurt feelings. But when he began to sense an emotional U-turn, he quickly kissed his mother and left. There was no sense harboring resentment over his mother's decision to marry the handyman. But he refused to be happy about it.

He spent the rest of the morning at home reading through his notebook and dialing Mattie's apartment. She didn't answer and he didn't leave a message because he didn't really know what to say.

Eventually he closed his notebook, placed it atop his unpacked suitcase, and tried to sleep.

Chapter Thirty-Three

ONSTAGE, OLIVER WAS LOOSE, focused, and had full control of his mouth, his memory, and that mysterious part of the brain that makes ordinary things funny. He followed his opening prayer—which grew more sincere every time he uttered it—with a heartfelt promise of full disclosure, the whole truth, and nothing but the truth, whether they wanted to hear it or not. "I promise," he said, "I won't lie to you once tonight."

Simply saying this out loud, actually promising to confide in a roomful of strangers, was as liberating as it was terrifying.

He paused then to consider his crowd. And for the first time in his short comedy career, Oliver did consider them *his*—at least the ones facing the stage and paying attention. He tried to ignore the oblivious people talking amongst themselves or watching muted sports highlights or poking their BlackBerries.

Ever since he started adding truth to his repertoire, he'd noticed several things. There were "regulars" now—not quite groupies, but a dozen or so actual fans who brought their friends to see this new comic who swears most of the stuff in his act is true, who sometimes pretends to get stage fright or forget his lines or even shows up wearing a ridiculous security guard uniform. And as much as he hated to admit it, he had Barry to thank for some of his recent notoriety. Not only had the quality of Oliver's gigs improved since "hiring" a manager, but Oliver was actually making a little money. Not only that, his confidence was back. The upcoming Downers gig still terrified him a little—it was less than a month away—but at least now the fear was manageable.

Even his fellow comics looked at him a little differently now, not quite in awe of his newfound talent or eaten up with petty jealousies, but like they'd begun to genuinely respect him.

The best part, however, was the actual laughter. It no longer seemed like a conditioned response, one where the guy on stage relies on subtle physical cues or the pitch of his voice to help the crowd figure out where they're supposed to laugh. Finally, after years of doing stand-up, it had become less about playing assigned roles and more about the actual material, what he said and how he said it.

The amazing thing about telling the truth onstage was that it worked. It really did set him free. Oliver did five solid minutes about third-shift security work at an allegedly haunted hotel, detailing the nutty things that happen while most normal people are sleeping, which included getting beaten up by a guy in a dress. From there he launched into a brief character sketch of his uptight, paranoid, publicity-obsessed, nose-picking general manager, then segued into a series of hollow rationalizations about the security guard who steals his college education. He flirted with the idea of improvising a joke or two about his roommate-cum-stepfather capturing Mattie and making her read *Are You My Mother?* Not that it wasn't funny; it was just too raw to work onstage yet.

Oliver realized midway through his set that his gaze kept drifting to the only couple in the room that seemed oblivious to the guy telling jokes in the front of the room. The silver-haired man huddled around a young blonde as if he were afraid someone would steal her. They sat in gloomy profile, on the same side of a darkened booth, quietly animated with lots of whispering and stolen kisses. Oliver thought about calling them out, trying to embarrass them from the stage. But crowd work was never his strong suit. So he did his best to ignore them and tried not to resent their lack of interest in his craft.

"Tonight I want to tell you guys a story . . ."

Oliver noticed an auburn-haired thirty-something elbow the girl next to her, then point at the stage. Her gesture said *See? This is the part I told you about. This guy tells great stories and they sound like they might actually be true.*

". . . a true story," he said. "It's the classic tale of girl meets boy . . . boy catches girl stealing."

Then he told them about Mattie, skirting as close to the "whole truth" as he could without actually naming names. He started with the night that she found him playing make-believe in an empty ballroom. From there he connected the dots from that initial meeting through two robberies, from Sherman's covert installation of security cameras to Mattie's heroic phone prank where she convinced a meth addict to drop criminal charges against her employer.

"You see, the problem with my girlfriend is that she has this odd habit ... just a little quirk, really ... something the legal system likes to call breaking and entering ...

"But that's just one of her problems. The main problem with my girlfriend is that she hasn't realized it yet ... you know, that she's my girlfriend ...

"Despite all that, she is the most adorable kleptomaniac you have ever laid eyes on."

He segued into finding Mattie in his house, rolled up like a burrito and held hostage by an enormous captor who reintroduced himself every sixty seconds. This new material worked, but it didn't kill. Probably because the real-life version was way funnier than any jokes he could cull from it.

The end of his set was approaching and he wanted to finish strong. He glanced at the digital clock by the soundboard, then allowed his gaze to drift to the oblivious couple in the back. Something about the man's profile looked eerily familiar. For a second Oliver thought it might be Professor Laramy, or maybe another of his mother's former lovers.

As he stared though, the crowd—*his* crowd—had gone silent, expectant, waiting. So Oliver dismissed the non-laughing couple and forced himself back on script.

As he approached what should have been his culminating punch line about the lovable burglar who'd obviously stolen his notebook, then broken into his house to return it, Oliver realized his voice had stopped working.

Why am I so upset? he thought. Was it Mattie's silent treatment? His mother's matrimonial betrayal? His new roommate-slash-stepfather? His stupid notebook?

But then his brain began to catch up with his heart. As the real reason began to dawn on Oliver, the crowd continued to laugh at the comedian on the verge of tears. Everyone but the couple in the back of the room.

The non-laughing man stood to allow his date out of the booth. As she disappeared toward the restroom, he sat on the edge of the booth and began thumbing his cell phone. The faint glow was enough to make out the man's features. Oliver thought he was imagining things until the man removed a silky handkerchief and dabbed each corner of his mouth.

Oliver made himself look away, to try and salvage his waning momentum. But it was no use. He would finish this set by rote.

He tried again, starting with the basics. He opened his mouth, had his brain dispatch the order to his lungs to begin moving some air upward and outward. He synchronized his lips, his tongue, and the muscles in the back of his throat. The words had found their form, but couldn't seem to make it past the giant knot in his throat.

The room grew quieter, leaning forward in anticipation. A few people tittered, assuming Oliver's forced silence was just another wacky part of the show. It dawned on him then that if he could see his face from where the crowd sat, he would see a quivering bottom lip, flared nostrils, eyes wide and panicky—a thick-voiced man fending off heaves and sniffles and prickly wetness gathering in his right eye.

The audience assumed he was acting. And of course they were eating it up. A few people even shook their heads, obviously marveling at his uncanny thespian abilities.

What he should have done was fake a cough, maybe even pound his chest for good measure, before turning and gulping ice water—then, after some self-deprecating aside, finish the punch line he'd worked so hard to perfect. What he did instead was strain harder, finally producing a tortured, squeaking sound.

Oliver gave his voice one final push, but it just cracked.

That's when the non-laughing man looked up, met Oliver's gaze, then blinked away the tinge of recognition that flashed across his features before turning his attention back to his date.

Oliver clipped the microphone atop the stand, grabbed his half-empty mug and drained it, then left the stage. But instead of waving thanks at the generous applause and commiserating with his comedian buddies in the back of the room, Oliver walked straight for the exit. Which, for some reason, the crowd cheered even louder.

His crowd.

Before pushing through the door, he took one last glance at Mattie's father as he fondled and flirted and traded small kisses with the young lady that was clearly not Mattie's mother.

Chapter Thirty-Four

If there was an upside to Mattie's silent treatment, it was this: how could he possibly be expected to look her in the eye and inform her he'd caught her father cheating on her mother if she wouldn't even speak to him? He didn't want to tell Mattie. But he didn't want *not* to tell her more. However, the more she ignored him, the easier it was to justify. Was it his place to deliver that kind of tragic news? Was it even any of his business? It's not like they were a real couple. She would barely look at him anymore.

But she wasn't rude about it either. In fact, their every exchange was rife with overly polite answers and bittersweet smiles. And this was not his mother's passive-aggressive brand of sly manipulation. Mattie seemed more sad than scheming, genuinely miserable. So Oliver did the only thing he could think of—apologize. He found legitimate excuses to drop by the front desk and ask her questions. While there, he would apologize for interrupting her, for speaking too loud or not loud enough, for not offering to cover the front desk for her sooner, for offering too soon; then he apologized for being so apologetic all the time. (He unconsciously hoped that the accumulation of lots of small apologies would eventually reach the critical mass of one big meaningful one, one that mattered.)

Her response never wavered. "That's okay," she would say.

But it wasn't okay, nothing was. Not as long as she was still mad or hurt or whatever she was feeling that made her not want to talk to Oliver anymore. And he didn't want the excruciatingly pleasant, matter-of-fact Mattie. He wanted the fiery, opinionated, straight-talking, sneak-off-in-the-middle-of-the-night Mattie. He wanted his friend back.

If she needed to use the restroom, she would go straight there and back. No more elongated walks or disappearing for thirty minutes at a time. If he suggested she make a run to the kitchen for coffee or a sandwich, she politely declined. Then he would bring her trays of soups and sandwiches, coffees and teas, and even one elaborate fruit salad that took him twenty minutes to make. But when he came back later to retrieve her dirty dishes, he would find the tray untouched.

Thankfully, she didn't *look* like everything was okay either. His biggest fear was that she would keep saying she was okay until she started to believe it. At that point, Oliver would have no chance.

Her unbridled indifference lasted for more than a week. And it might have gone on forever if Oliver hadn't heard Mattie sneeze.

At first he thought he was dreaming. He was sitting in church, quietly paging through his spiral notebook. The more he read, the more he felt like a creep. It was obvious now that Mattie hadn't stolen his notebook; she'd simply found it. And although it may have been a blatant violation of his privacy for her to read it, he liked to imagine something a bit less sinister. His last entry was the night Max stopped by the hotel. Oliver had been eavesdropping, transcribing all of Mattie's witty replies to her non-fiancé's desperate appeals. When Max interrupted him and asked to be let out, Oliver must have left his notebook sitting on the couch in the lobby. That was the last time he remembered seeing it.

He imagined Mattie finding it later, her off-kilter smile as she fanned the pages, her wide-eyed curiosity when she glimpsed her own name. Of course she read it. Anyone would.

When the offering plate came by, Oliver emptied his wallet. It wasn't quite a tithe, but it was all he had. He knew God couldn't be bought off. But he did hope he was watching.

Oliver tried to read his own handwriting through Mattie's eyes. He'd transcribed bits of conversations, what she'd been wearing on certain days, little reminders to himself, things like how Mattie liked her coffee (different every time), her birthday (December 24), her favorite song (the original John Hiatt version of "Have a Little Faith in Me"), and her favorite color (the shade of green that bleeds into yellow on a ripening banana). With the benefit of hindsight, he could see her logic. She obviously assumed that Oliver wanted her to find his notebook, that it was his way of flirting with her. Because, based on her own entries, it sure seemed she was flirting back.

The preacher began his sermon and Oliver tried to pay attention. But it was no use. There was something deliciously intimate about the pages that contained his private thoughts on one side and hers on the other. She had underlined certain passages or drew smiley faces in the margins. His joke ideas sat in alongside her song lyrics—all of it half-formed, malnourished, embryonic, vulnerable.

Oliver was surprised to see how much more he'd written than jokes. There were stories about his mother, how much he missed her and wanted her back. He'd confessed his pathetic need to hear his own name every day. He wrote about his frustrations with his comedy career, whined about wanting to quit, even crafted an elaborate chart that recorded all the classes he was stealing. He didn't even remember writing most of it. But it looked like Mattie had read it all.

The last third of the notebook was filled with what appeared to be her random journal entries and snippets of lyrics. Some were dated, most not. The margins were laden with elaborate doodles of faces, geometric shapes, footnotes, and flowers. Mattie seemed to have a thing for leafy vines that wound their way along the perimeter of the page.

He read her first entry again. It said simply:

I still can't believe he's speaking to me after meeting my family.

In the margin next to one of his more pathetic admissions about how much he missed his mother and how envious he was of Mattie's family, she'd written:

If he only knew ... Mom's working on her fourth nervous breakdown, paranoid that the cancer will come back. Between the baby and the eventual breakup of the band, Reese will probably end up back on meth. Daddy is a goofball, but he's also our rock. There was a time when Reese suspected he was having an affair. I refused to believe it. Because that would not only break my heart ... but break our family's back.

This must be the "rough time for all of us" that Reese mentioned at the wedding.

Oliver couldn't quite tell if this odd sensation was his own, or if he'd subliminally borrowed it from Mattie. But flipping the pages felt a bit like walking down the darkened hallways that connected Mattie's heart to her brain. Each entry faced him like a locked door, one he could choose to pass by, or break in and explore. Oliver didn't hesitate much; he studied, savored, wallowed, and cast himself as the object of every "he" or "him."

He deserves better. He needs a girl who can bake cookies, a girl who separates her darks and whites, a girl who at least has a shot at growing up and into an actual woman.

I am neither moth nor rust
I break in, but never steal,
Only borrow.
And return, always returning ...
To the scene of the coming Kingdom.

Sometimes I feel like he's watching me when I go on my little excursions. Or maybe the hotel really is haunted, because someone's watching. I can just tell. And ultimately, that's probably a good thing. It might actually make me behave.

He's falling.

I suppose I could catch him. But I think I'll just wait and see if he gets back up again.

I finally met his mother. She's funny and sad and delightful. Not surprising.

My knitting really sucks.

And the entry he kept coming back to ...

I had a dream last night where Oliver paused over a bed of oxeye daisies, each more exquisite than the next. He took his time, considering them all in turn before selecting the perfect one. Mouth closed, eyes open, he drew a long, savoring breath. As if trying to commit the aroma to memory. Then he did it again, eyes closed this time. Finally, he began plucking petals one at a time, alternating joyous she loves me's *with increasingly dismal* she loves me not's. *His face defined bittersweet, personified it. With only a few petals left, his expression tightened into a single flat line. His eyes glinted, glassy and wet with dread.*

I never saw how the dream ended. The camera in my mind's eye panned away from the action and slowly zoomed in on Oliver's slow-motion lips. The soundtrack whispered two final syllables before fading to a wakeful black.

She loves . . .

I sat up in bed and reached for my journal. But my hand found this one instead. We'll call it Providence.

In the dream, I was the daisy. I suppose I should be happy that at least he picked me. But those last two words worry me.

And all that plucking hurt like hell.

That's what he was reading when she sneezed again. There was no mistaking it this time—that sibilant squeal, the adorable backfire.

Oliver ignored the perturbed faces as he excused himself out of the aisle midsermon. He found Mattie sitting in the grass beneath an open window, her back against the clapboard building, an open journal in her lap, and sipping something steamy from a stainless steel travel mug. Oliver didn't say anything as he approached. As much as he wanted to go and sit beside her, he stopped just below another open window and sat, cross-legged, his back against the same clapboard wall. Still fifteen feet away, it was the closest he'd felt to Mattie in nearly a week. They sat and listened, each with their own window. When the preacher stopped and the singing began, Mattie said, "I really hate it when that happens."

"When what happens?"

"Weren't you listening to the sermon?"

"To be honest, I was a little distracted." Oliver tapped the notebook resting in his lap and risked a glance at Mattie. "It was the sneeze."

"Allergies," she said.

"Me too," Oliver said.

"Thought you said you didn't have allergies."

"Late onset," he said. "And very specific."

"Is that so?"

"Yep, I'm severely allergic to you ignoring me all the time, acting like everything is okay when nothing is."

She nodded, masking the tiniest hint of a grin with a long sip. Finally, and without looking up, she waved a folded sheet of paper at him and said, "I got your note."

"Oh." Oliver felt the color in his cheeks. He'd written dozens of notes, then missed quite a bit of sleep trying to figure out which one to slip into her purse. "And?"

In the end, he settled on the one that got right to the heart of the matter, albeit like a third grader. He'd ripped a sheet of lined paper out of a spiral notebook, not bothering to remove the fringy pieces, and used a #2 pencil to write:

I like you. Do you still like me? Check one:

Yes ____

Maybe later ____

Not yet, but I forgive you anyway ____

"Well," Mattie said. After checking all three lines and scribbling a short note along the bottom, she motioned Oliver over and handed him the note. "According to the preacher, I guess I don't have any choice, do I?"

Confused, Oliver found his copy of the church bulletin tucked between the pages of his notebook. He scanned the order of service until he found *Today's Message: The Healing Power of Forgiveness.* He resisted the urge to give God a thumb's up.

Then he read her five-word note and said, "*What's* not my fault?"

"Your mother's incarceration, her drinking or troubles with men, none of it. You were just a little kid, Oliver."

"Did I really say it was my fault?" Of course he'd always blamed himself for his mother's problems, but he didn't remember writing any of it down.

Mattie eyed his notebook and said, "Not in so many words."

When she was gone, Oliver stood in the parking lot and finally gave voice to another one-word prayer welling up inside him. He gazed heavenward and said simply, "Thanks."

Part Three

Headliner / 'hed-,lī-ner / the final and "star" performer, the climax of the show.

Chapter Thirty-Five

OLIVER TRIED TO GIVE MATTIE SPACE. Just because she opened up to him a little outside the church window didn't mean things were back to normal. So in an effort to not push too hard (or to not seem too desperate ... or to not say anything too dreadfully stupid), he spent most of that Sunday night/Monday morning shift avoiding her altogether.

Yet as he drove down the ramp of the parking garage, Oliver replayed his conversation with Mattie in his mind. He couldn't help feeling like he'd blown it, that he'd let eight golden hours of opportunity pass him by. The note-swapping moment outside the church had been magical, sweet, and vulnerable, and the perfect time to ask Mattie out on an official date. But he'd let it slip by and now the magic was gone. It wasn't a fear of rejection—he felt reasonably certain Mattie would say yes if he asked. It was the added pressure of having caught Mattie's father in the throes of some ludicrous affair. And now every time he opened his mouth, he feared it would all come spilling out. He would have to tell her eventually. But he just couldn't fathom bearing the news that would break her heart and her family's spine.

His brakes squealed as he paused at the mouth of the garage to let his eyes adjust to the sunlight. The Harrington faced a narrow, one-way street. So Oliver only needed to glance the other way for oncoming traffic.

That's when he saw Mattie on the sidewalk outside the hotel's main entrance. Oliver sat there, idling, indulging daydreamy thoughts, until a horn blared behind him. He eased his Integra onto the street, hugging the curb and watching Mattie in his rearview mirror. When he couldn't stand it any longer, he put his car in park and hopped out.

He'd only made it a few steps in Mattie's direction when he heard another car horn, much closer this time. Oliver was barely aware of the big yellow streak passing on his right. It didn't dawn on him that he'd left his car door open until he heard the awful crunching sound.

He turned in time to see his driver's-side door snap off and skitter across the pavement and into an empty parking space.

The big yellow streak was a taxicab. It didn't even slow down.

For one brief moment, the world went silent. The street still bustled, only now it was in slow motion. Oliver Miles was aware of the stares from guys with briefcases and tourists and rubber-necking drivers as time resumed its normal speed. He didn't move toward his car, but inspected the violent wreckage from where he stood, still unsure what to make of what just happened.

When he turned, Mattie was still standing on the sidewalk, covering her gaping mouth with one hand. As he closed the distance between them, she said, "I hope it's important."

"What?"

"Whatever it is that made you stop in the middle of the street like that."

"Oh, it's just … I wanted to tell you something."

Oliver had seen that look before, just not on Mattie. It was a cloudy mixture of hope and resignation. Oliver tried to focus on Mattie's unblinking eyes as he searched the dusty catacombs of his memory for the last time he'd seen that expression. He kept expecting to see it on his mother's face, but he couldn't make it fit. He was about to give up when it hit him—it was the collective expression of every girl he'd ever dated. When it came to former girlfriends, Oliver was not just tentative, he was afraid, a perennial bench warmer. It was easier to follow, to avoid the risk of emotional injury. Relationally speaking, Oliver was a bit of a sissy.

So he not only recognized the expression; he finally knew what it meant. He was supposed to *do* something.

"Forget the rain check," he said. "All of them."

Mattie blinked, released a subliminal sigh, and said, "Excuse me?"

"Well, not forever. Just, you know, forget it temporarily."

"Are you okay, Oliver?"

"I have no idea. Maybe, I don't know, I'm not sure. Will you go out with me?"

In a movie, this is where the soundtrack would change and the camera would shift to some oddly sympathetic angle. Instead, a city bus belched out exhaust and elicited one of Mattie's delightful sneezes.

"Bless you?" He didn't mean for it to sound like a question.

"So this is it, then? You're finally asking me on a real date?"

"Yes, Mattie Holmgren. That's exactly what I'm doing. I'm even prepared to beg, if necessary."

"You do realize that this will probably ruin everything?" She stared off in the direction of his ruined car still idling at the curb.

Oliver watched, waiting for Mattie's expression to soften, suppressing urge after urge to blurt out hollow promises that, no, they wouldn't ruin anything. At some point he said, "So, it's a yes, then?"

Another small eternity passed.

"Yes, Oliver. I do believe this is a yes."

"You don't sound so sure."

"It's not that." As Mattie seemed to search the street behind him for the right words, Oliver offered tiny prayers that she wasn't going to change her mind. "It's just that, honestly, my head and my heart really are in conflict here."

"Can I ask you one small favor then?"

"Sure, you can ask."

"Just this one time, you think you could leave your head at home?"

"Sorry, Oliver. I'm afraid my heart needs a chaperone."

. . .

He opened his trunk, but there was no way his battered car door was going to fit. So he left it by the curb and drove up the ramp, feeling the cool rush of air coming from where the door used to be. It was shocking just how loud the outside world was. Back on the street, Mattie helped him lug the mangled steel appendage to the garage elevator. They eventually leaned against the back bumper of his car and Oliver removed a few scant valuables from the glove compartment—four CDs, a phone charger, and a fistful of paperwork.

As they turned to head back down to the curb, Oliver hit the Lock button on his key fob.

Mattie didn't start laughing at him until she realized he wasn't trying to be funny. It was a good sound, even better as it echoed off the drab concrete walls of the garage.

"I guess you need a ride home too?" she said.

"Too?"

"My car's in the shop," she said. "Alternator. Reese is on his way to get me."

"Well, I was going to call my friend Roscoe, see if I can borrow his car until I figure out what to do about mine."

"Nonsense," Mattie said. "We'll just drop you off at his place."

Oliver wasn't all that eager to see Reese again. But he didn't plan to protest much. When they stepped out of the gloom and into the blinding sunlight, he caught Mattie frowning at a dented Subaru wagon parallel-parked across the street from the hotel. Chuck-the-security-camera-guy sat, drumming his thick fingers on the steering wheel. He had one lollipop in his mouth and a spare tucked behind his ear.

"You know that guy?" Oliver said.

"That's Chuck," she said. "Barry's pal. He stops by at least once a week to ask me out."

"How come I never see him?"

"Probably because he doesn't want you to."

To quell a sudden flush of envy, Oliver mentally scrambled for some droll comment about Mattie's not-so-secret admirer. But she was already pointing toward a dark sedan idling where Oliver's Integra had been just minutes before. She let herself into the passenger seat and motioned for Oliver to ride in back.

But it wasn't Reese behind the wheel. It was Walter Holmgren, Mattie's cheating father.

Their eyes met in the rearview mirror. Walter's narrowed, then widened, then blinked in recognition. Just like they'd done across the nightclub.

Mattie tried to make small talk, but her father kept his eyes on the road and his mouth shut. He seemed tense, brittle, about to crack into a million tiny pieces. Oliver sat back and bit his lip, afraid of what might come out if he opened his mouth.

Finally, Mattie said, "You okay, Pop?"

Walter shook his head, but just barely, more like a tic. Oliver braced himself for an awkward confession. But Walter checked the rearview again and said, "It's Reese."

"What about him?" Mattie said.

"Your mother caught him using again."

Oliver stared at her profile, thinking back to her confidence when she accused the couple from 218 of being meth addicts. But Mattie didn't react. She just stared.

Oliver wanted to say something, but there was nothing to say. He knew the cycle all too well—disappointment and rage giving way to fear and resignation. Oliver had found liquor bottles hidden in hampers, tucked inside rain boots, duct-taped to the inside of toilet tanks. He'd uncovered entire meals buried in the garbage can. He'd found his mother passed out in the bathtub, behind the wheel of her parked car, and sprawled in the front yard. It always felt like a kick in the chest.

He wanted to give Mattie a hug but was still trapped in the backseat. And it probably wouldn't help anyway. Nothing would.

Somewhere along the way he realized he was praying for Mattie's family. It was familiar, yet scary, terrain.

Chapter Thirty-Six

THERE WAS A PART OF OLIVER that didn't want to actually go through with dinner. In part, because he didn't want to say anything stupid. It didn't help that he'd had to borrow Roscoe's big, smelly Lincoln. But mostly because he wouldn't have it to look forward to anymore. And what if it didn't go well? What if she liked work Oliver better than regular Oliver?

But all such doubts vanished when she answered the door of her apartment. She was only slightly retro, opting for jeans, a colorful peasant blouse, and a few tiny braids that swayed when she moved. Somehow she managed to look casual, muted, *and* stunning.

If Mattie's heart needed a chaperone, Oliver's was going to require a bodyguard or a military escort or maybe its own Secret Service detail.

He considered taking her to Downers. His logic was that the familiar surroundings might ease the pressure of their official "first date." But the last thing he needed was Roscoe hovering around the table asking doleful questions about his mother; or worse, any of the handful of Downers waitresses Oliver had known since birth. He imagined them inventing excuses to stop by their table like flirty, meddlesome aunts, making wisecracks about his love life or asking obvious and conspiratorial questions, like *Who is* this *lucky lady? Ooh, I can't believe my eyes ... Oliver Miles on a date? Where have you been hiding this little beauty?* Inevitably, one of them would say, *If only your mother could see you now.* And Oliver really didn't want to cry on their first date.

So he'd opted instead for the mom-and-pop elegance of Flannery's. The food was always delicious and the prices steep enough to earn credit for splurging without seeming garish. The various dining nooks were intimate and homey, replete with white tablecloths and aging wait staff in black ties. Mostly, Flannery's was safe, and familiar *enough*.

It didn't dawn on Oliver until they were seated and perusing oversized menus that every "special" occasion he'd ever toasted in this room had one thing in common — they were all doomed.

Oliver sipped ice water and reminded himself he didn't believe in superstition. Mattie kept scanning the room as if she'd lost something.

"Looking for someone?" Oliver wished his voice sounded as light and airy as it had in his head. For some childish reason, the idea of Mattie focusing on anything other than him made his feelings hurt.

"As a matter of fact," she said, "give me a number between two and six."

"Three," he said.

Mattie bit her bottom lip and glanced around the room again, a bit more surreptitious this time. Before he could ask why she needed a number, or exactly who she was looking for, Mattie lowered her menu and said, "What looks good to you?"

The obvious answer was *Mattie*. Mattie Holmgren looked good to him. But thankfully he had the wherewithal to bottle that thought up before it came spilling out and casting some awkward flirtatious pall on the evening. So he settled for a more benign truth. "It all looks good from here."

"Well, well ... isn't your mug half-full this evening?"

Oliver looked up sharply, but Mattie was busy studying the list of side items. He thought he saw her trying to hide a self-satisfied smile. "I'm thinking Italian," she said. "But I don't want to be the only one afflicted with garlic breath all night."

"I brought gum," he said. "Besides, garlic might help if we bump into a pack of vampires. Or Old Man Harrington."

"I thought we weren't allowed to talk about him."

"That only applies to work," he said. "Which reminds me, how do you like working at a haunted hotel so far? Has it made you believe in ghosts yet?"

Mattie spun her water glass a half turn, then back. "Sure, why not?"

"You sound serious."

"Well, when you really think about it, everybody's haunted by something—dysfunction or worry or some other kind of addiction."

Oliver knew he should ask about Reese, but he wasn't ready for the conversation to get that heavy yet. Instead he considered his own dysfunctional obsessions—his mother, his stand-up career, and the sound of his own name, not to mention the bass-playing, glasses-wearing, breaking-and-entering, ambidextrous night auditor sitting across from him—when their waitress arrived with a steaming basket of bread.

Her name was Cecelia. She was clearly the youngest server at Flannery's, and she seemed enamored with the sound of her own voice. Her smile was big and bright and infectious, practically glistening with all the charm and grace and the unbridled optimism of a wannabe country star. She had an elaborate eighties soap opera hairdo, manicured nails, and one dead tooth in front. As she ran down the memorized list of specials it became clear her southern roots ran much deeper than Nashville. Oliver was guessing Mississippi.

"Y'all know what you want? Or you need another minute to think about it?"

Oliver arched his eyebrows into a question. Mattie said, "You go ahead; I've narrowed it down to two."

Oliver ordered chicken parmesan and a Caesar salad. Mattie said, "Make it two," then turned to Cecelia. "Tell me your favorite color."

"Red," she said, pronouncing it *ray-ed*. "The deeper the better."

Then they were alone, candlelit, cozy, with nowhere to look and no one to talk to but each other. And Oliver thought he could just stay there forever. This wasn't like work where Mattie had to spend time with him. She could have been doing anything she wanted right then, but she'd chosen to go to dinner with Oliver. He'd already resolved to keep the conversation casual, low key, to avoid any mention of robberies or sneaking into rooms or stolen notebooks or his parents or her parents ... and *especially* not her adulteress father. That would have to wait. He lifted the basket of bread and offered it to Mattie. She took one and said, "My parents made me promise to say hello."

"Oh, well, hello to them as well. How are they doing?"

"They're kind of nuts about you."

"Really?"

"Absolutely. They think you're nice and respectful and attentive."

"In other words, they're glad I'm not Max."

"That too," she said. "At first, I think my dad worried that you're not ambitious enough. But then he was getting a little weird on the phone this afternoon. He must have asked me fifty questions about you."

"That is weird."

"For some strange reason, he seems to care more about what you think of him than the other way around. I mean, he's always been pathologically vain. But he usually does a better job of hiding it."

As Oliver tried to banish the image of Mattie's father huddled around the girl half his age, Mattie said, "Do you realize you start squirming whenever we talk about parents? Anyway, I suppose you're wondering what's up with Reese."

"I was wondering that, actually."

"But you didn't want to upset me or put a downer on the evening?"

"That too," he said.

Apparently, Mattie's brother was still in denial. He claimed the drugs his mother found belonged to "a friend" and swore that he wasn't using. But no one in the family was buying it. Reese had never been a good liar. They all seemed to assume it was the stress of becoming a father. Either way, it didn't sound like happy times at the Holmgren house.

"Anyway," Mattie said, "enough of that. How's your new roommate?"

"Same as ever. I keep moving him into the house and he keeps moving himself back out to the garage. What about you? Any luck finding a new roommate?"

"Funny you should ask."

Cecelia arrived then with armfuls of entrees and a mouthful of banal restaurant-speak—*Careful, those plates are hot. Care for some fresh-grated parmesan? More bread? More water? Y'all need anything else? No? I'll be back in a jiffy to check on you then.*

"You were saying?" Oliver said.

"Oh, right. I did interview a potential new roommate today. Turns out she's a friend of yours."

"A friend of mine?" Oliver said, wisely stopping before admitting, *But I don't have any friends.*

"Her name is Betsy Something-or-another, from Shady Grove."

He wanted to ask if all this roommate talk meant she'd changed her mind about moving to New York, but he was afraid she would say no. So he opted for safer terrain. "How do you know Betsy?"

"Oh, well we just seemed to keep bumping into each other. Anyhow, her job situation is changing and she might need to downsize."

"She's quitting?"

"No, she was fired. And I think the whole thing is kind of fishy if you ask me."

"What do you mean, fishy?"

"I don't know, just a feeling I got after talking to her. I used to visit my great aunt in one of those places. They look and feel like a hospital, but no one ever seems to get better there."

"Shady Grove is more of a—what do they call it—a retirement community or an old-folks home?"

"But your mom's not that old. And apparently not even that sick. At least not like everyone else there."

Oliver had mentioned his mother's illness, but only in passing. But he didn't recall ever discussing her age. "Just how long did you guys talk?"

"An hour, maybe two. Anyway, I think maybe you should talk to Betsy about it." Mattie looked up then, frowning as her eyes tracked a couple's progress as they packed up all their baby gear and headed toward the exit. When her eyes met Oliver's again her grin was big and playful. "Anyway, Betsy seems to think you're avoiding her."

"I guess maybe I am a little," Oliver said. "I kinda think she might want to ask me out."

"Is that so?" Mattie seemed to be biting back a smile. "I wonder what her fiancé would have to say about that?"

"Betsy's engaged?"

"Apparently he's some kind of body builder. I think he works security at Shady Grove."

"So she wasn't flirting with me?"

"I have no idea," Mattie said. "I wasn't there."

"Wow, I feel kind of dumb now. Do you think maybe you could flirt with me a little now? To make me feel better?"

"Sorry, Oliver. I don't believe in flirting."

"You think there's no such thing?"

"Oh, it exists. But it usually comes off as disingenuous, somewhere between a shifty marketing ploy and outright lying."

Oliver's first instinct was to respond in some cutesy, overly flirty way. But he could tell by the way she kept stabbing her chicken with her fork that she may not fully appreciate his not-so-subtle sense of irony.

"Are you telling me you've never flirted with a boy?"

"Of course I have."

"And you didn't like it?"

"At the time, sure. It felt great. But so do therapeutic shopping, gorging on donuts, and recreational dope smoking. At some point I grew up and realized those are a waste of valuable time too."

"Funny, I've never really thought of flirting as a gateway drug before."

Mattie shrugged. "That's not exactly the metaphor I was going for, but I suppose it fits. All I'm saying is that it's insincere. I could try and impress you and you can try and impress me. But at some point, we have to live up to our own hype."

"So you've sworn off flirting altogether?"

"Absolutely not," Mattie said. "I just think we get it out of order. I'd rather find my soul mate first, *then* indulge in copious amounts of flirting and doting and other childishly romantic behavior. Sorry, don't mean to get all preachy. I just think—when something's on your mind, you should say it."

"Interesting," Oliver said, trying hard not to sound flirty. "So based on your logic, I guess it's okay to just blurt it out and ask how you really feel about me?"

"You can ask."

"Okay then, how do you feel about me?"

"Pretty good, actually. But that's all subject to change, especially if you start pestering me about how I feel all the time. Frankly, I'd feel better about you if you change the subject again."

As if on cue, Cecelia returned, wielding a sweaty pitcher of ice water. "I didn't mean to eavesdrop or nothing. But did I hear y'all mention the name Betsy? I just love that name, so soft and delicate. The ironical thing is, I had a turtle named Betsy once." She refilled Mattie's glass and said, "Anyhow, is that your name, honey? Betsy?"

"Mattie, actually."

"Mattie? That's such an interesting name." She pronounced it *Inner-sten.* "Is that short for something?"

"Matilda."

"Ooh, even better. See, I just love how names go together. In fact, my daddy used to always say you could predict the success of a couple by listening to their names."

Oliver flashed a grin at Mattie, then asked their philosopher waitress, "So what about Mattie and Max?"

Cecelia beamed. "Now that's about a perfect match. Really and truly. Fact is, they go together like apple pie and ice cream. Can I innerst you kids in some?"

When they declined, Cecelia produced their check and began clearing dishes. Oliver glanced at the bill and handed over his Visa.

He was dying to know what Mattie thought of their server's redneck psychology, but she was preoccupied with scanning the room again. When her gaze circled all the way back to Oliver, he said, "So what would you like to do after dinner?"

"Funny you should ask ..."

"Care to elaborate?"

"Not really," she said, staring tight-lipped at Cecelia as she tried to charm a bigger tip out of an elderly couple at a nearby table. "It's a surprise."

"Why do I get the feeling you're not overly fond of our waitress?"

"She's been flirting with us all night," Mattie said. "I just don't like imposters."

Cecelia arrived moments later to return Oliver's credit card and deposit a pair of foil-wrapped mints. "Just curious," she said. "Is Max like a nickname or something?"

"An ex-fiancé," Oliver said.

Cecelia began verbally backpedaling at once, denouncing Max as a goofy name and trying to make the names "Oliver and Mattie" sound like a love song. Finally she said, "Anyhow, no offense or nothin'."

"None taken," Mattie said, "but we could use a favor or two."

"Okay," Cecelia said.

"First, help us settle a little bet and tell us where you're from?"

Oliver said, "I'm guessing Jackson, Mississippi."

"Nope," Cecelia said.

"And I'm going with Brooklyn," Mattie said. "But it was really hard to tell with all that syrupy sweetness."

Oliver checked Mattie's reaction, then watched Cecelia's smile relax. "Jersey," she said. "I start Vanderbilt in the fall."

"Not majoring in theater, I hope?"

"Medicine," Cecelia said, her voice an octave lower and decidedly more Yankee. "I am auditioning for a local production of *Fried Green Tomatoes* next week though. Anyhow, you had another favor?"

"Don't everybody look at once," Mattie said. "But you see the couple in the corner? By the window?"

Oliver was turning to look, but Mattie kicked him under the table, then smiled sweetly, daring him to break eye contact with her as Cecelia found the couple in question.

"Man with a beard, lady in a red beret?" Cecelia said. "And the toddler with alfredo sauce in his hair?"

Mattie nodded and slipped her own credit card into Cecelia's hand. "It's on us ... *anonymously*."

"Okay, I guess," Cecelia said, her eyes alternating between Mattie and her credit card, her voice filled with unasked questions.

"And for your *full* ... and *anonymous* ... cooperation, add thirty percent for your trouble."

Cecelia said, "Yes ma'am," her voice batter-dipped in fake southern charm again.

"Better," Mattie said. "More nuanced."

"What are we doing?" Oliver said when Cecelia left to ring up another meal.

"The first thing we're doing is keeping our voices down. The next thing is to play it cool. No suspicious activity or big smiles, just a normal couple enjoying some coffee and waiting for our check."

"Do you know those people?"

Mattie shook her head.

"So then why are you buying dinner for total strangers?"

"Lots of reasons. But mostly for the thrill of it."

"But why them? They certainly don't look destitute."

"Because, Oliver, you said three and Cecelia said red."

"So, do you do this often?"

"When I can afford it."

"No offense or anything, but it doesn't sound like you can really afford it right now."

"Actually, it's the other way around. I can't afford not to." Oliver was about to ask her to explain when Mattie said, "Cool, Cecelia's delivering the news."

Oliver snuck a glance at the serendipitous family. But Mattie reached across the table and squeezed his hand. "Just keep your eyes on me, Oliver."

For the first time all night, this was actually difficult to do. Oliver watched Mattie watching the couple and felt his world tip forward, then back. He wasn't quite dizzy, but it was close.

Mattie cut her eyes back to Oliver. "Have to play it cool now. They're looking around the room trying to figure it out."

"You are one strange and wonderful girl."

"Are you flirting with me, Oliver Miles?"

"I suppose I am. Is that okay with you?"

"Probably."

"Was that the big surprise then? Buying dinner for strangers?"

"What? Oh, no. This will be even more fun." Mattie glanced at the couple again, half smiled, then fixed her gaze on Oliver. "I think we should go see your mother."

He chuckled and said, "I'm afraid visiting hours are over."

"Oliver Miles, where's your sense of adventure?"

Chapter Thirty-Seven

EMOTIONALLY SPEAKING, Oliver completely missed the inauguration of his criminal career.

Mattie told him where to turn, where *not* to park, and had to remind him twice to lock the car. It took Oliver a full minute to realize exactly where they were—outside the rusted gate in the far corner of the expansive backyard of Shady Grove. Mattie wasted no time kneeling beside it and slipping two metal tools into the bulky padlock.

"Don't watch me," she said.

"That's much harder than it sounds."

He tried to look casual as he absorbed their surroundings. The sidewalk was buckled with weeds sprouting up through the cracks. A disco band played somewhere in the distance. A lonely traffic light cycled impotently through reds and ambers and greens at the nearest intersection. An occasional breeze filled the air with ripe Dumpster smells.

Oliver turned when he heard the metallic clink of a lock giving way; Mattie was already putting her tools away. He had to lean his full weight on the chain link gate to raise the forked gate hatch. Even after all that, it wouldn't budge.

He was saying something about too much undergrowth when Mattie produced a sizable knife and began slicing through thatched vines and weeds.

"Just keep pushing," she said. "We only need a crack."

The gritty rusted metal was making Oliver's palms burn. But

then it started to give way. Mattie yanked with one hand and sliced with the other as the gate inched farther and farther.

"I think that's enough," Oliver said. "We can crawl through there."

"Probably so, but we may need more wiggle room on the way out."

"Why? Won't we be about the same size when we leave?"

"Yep. But it won't feel that way if we're being chased."

Oliver checked to see if Mattie was serious, but she'd been nothing but serious since they left the restaurant. When they were on the other side, she pulled a shiny new padlock from her purse and locked the gate, making sure the key was secured around her wrist with a coiled wristband. Then she hid the old lock in the undergrowth with its key still inside.

"You're locking us back in?"

"We don't want to be responsible for someone else breaking out, do we?"

"So why are you changing the lock?"

"I have a key for this one," Mattie said, as if Oliver were the silliest boy in the world.

He didn't know whether to be impressed or terrified at Mattie's criminal aptitude. So he settled on awe and followed her along the darkened perimeter to a large metal door. As she studied the lock with a tiny flashlight, Oliver walked along the back of the building. Mattie whispered something about staying put and out of the light. She was on her knees now, flashlight between her teeth, and manipulating her tiny instruments. Moments later she opened the door and said, "Oops."

"What is it?"

"Boiler room."

Because he didn't have anything better to do with all the nervous energy roiling inside him, Oliver walked to the only other metal door on the backside of the building, twisted the handle, and pulled. The weather-stripping scraped as the door swung open.

"What's in there?" Mattie said as she relocked and closed the first door.

"Looks like the kitchen."

Oliver realized at once how absurd—and completely unearned—his pride was. That he'd simply turned the knob and gotten lucky. Absurd or not, however, he wallowed in his meager contribution.

They tiptoed through the kitchen to the rattle and hum of compressors, navigating a stainless steel maze of ovens and steamers and tabletops, then through the carpeted cafeteria. Mattie peeked out into the main hallway, then motioned for Oliver to follow to the stairwell at the end of the hall. After a brisk three-flight climb, Oliver was winded and prickled with sweat. Mattie looked unfazed as they made their way to his mother's room.

Delores was sitting up in bed reading her autographed copy of *The Cider House Rules.*

Her one-word response to the two after-hours visitors simultaneously thrilled and broke Oliver's heart. After looking directly into his eyes, his mother shifted her gaze and said, "Mattie!"

Delores Miles patted the bed in invitation. As Mattie closed the distance between them, Oliver watched his mother's face light up, igniting a heartrending memory that he couldn't quite place. She spread her arms wide, as if she were about to take flight, then wrapped Mattie into a taut, lingering embrace. They hugged for a long time, rocking gently, whispering things Oliver wanted to hear. He realized there was no default mode available to diffuse his conflicting emotions. So he just watched.

"Here," Mattie said as she rummaged through her purse. "I brought you another shawl."

Delores held it up and inspected it. "It's lovely, dear."

"Thanks," Mattie said, clearly struggling not to look too proud as she retreated to the lone guest chair, leaving nothing but space between Oliver and his mother.

By the time Oliver assumed the now dimpled spot on the bed next to his mother, her nostalgic expression had depreciated into polite confusion. Oliver followed her gaze into her lap where her hands aimlessly twisted the edge of her new shawl. That's when Oliver realized he was crying again. And just like on stage, he couldn't quite figure out why. Or how to stop.

Delores finally looked up at Oliver but spoke to Mattie. "So, he knows?"

Mattie nodded, then looked again at Oliver with her signature stare—penetrating, unblinking, tinged with some secret, shared message that Oliver was trying not to miss. But there was something else in her expression, something new—Mattie was nervous, as if she were risking something terribly important. Her wide, unwavering eyes seemed to be pleading with him to just play along and see what happened, to trust her on this one. Although he felt slightly ambushed, he was in no condition to defy her silent instruction.

As it turned out, there was no choice to make really. His mother cleared her throat and said, "So how did you know my boy?"

"Your son?" he said.

He didn't realize just how badly he wanted to hear her say his name until she didn't. Instead, she smoothed the wrinkled edge of her blanket across her lap with hands that looked impossibly old and fragile. Finally, she responded with a nod. And somehow it was enough, for now anyway. For the first time in six years, his mother acknowledged she had a son.

"Oliver, right?" he said.

He didn't mean to say it. It just slipped out. It was a risk he wasn't really ready to take, but it was too late for that.

"He was a good boy," she said. "The best. He deserved better."

"Better than what?"

"Me," she said simply. "He deserved better than me."

"That is not true, Mom." Oliver glanced at Mattie when he realized his mistake, but she was hovering in the doorway, standing vigil. "I'm sorry, I mean Delores."

"That's okay. I kind of like the sound of it. And please pardon my poor memory, but aren't you that friend of his from school?"

Oliver had to scramble to come up with the name. During his one semester at college, he roomed with a kid named Wayne from Missouri who insisted on spending that first Christmas break with Oliver and his mother. He was a theater geek, always ready with impressions from Broadway shows that Oliver didn't recognize and his mother found hilarious. At some point Wayne started referring to Delores as "Mom." Oliver never really liked Wayne, but he was more than happy now to borrow his identity to get some semblance of his mother back.

"What have you been up to since college?"

"Oh, um ..." Oliver wished Mattie would come back and help. He lacked the emotional wherewithal to reinvent a new persona all by himself. "I work in show business."

"You were really into musical theater, if I remember right?"

Now Oliver's jealousy shifted from Mattie and glommed onto a fictitious character that happened to share the first name and a few interests of a former roommate. "That's right. But I never quite made it to Broadway."

"Well don't give up. It's important to follow your dreams. My Oliv—" A tear sprang from his mother's left eye. She wiped at it clumsily with her fingers, then again on the other side. Oliver plucked a stiff tissue from the box and handed it to her. "I'm sorry. What I was trying to say is that my boy had a gift for comedy. He could have been a brilliant stand-up."

"Really?" It was utter disbelief that bottled up Oliver's throat, but pride that finally pushed the words out. "You really think so?"

"He was born funny," she said. She stared at her hands without really looking at them. She heaved her way through a long sigh and said, "Such a waste."

"What's that?"

"Losing my only son that way, to that ... that *drunk*."

They sat silent for a while. Then, when Delores Miles finally composed herself, she told him all about the accident. How her son had finally switched his major to pharmacy, mostly to appease his nagging mother. How he was making great grades and loving the college experience. How he was driving home after finals and was killed by a drunk driver. How the woman who murdered her son was a waitress with a drinking problem and a notorious reputation for sleeping around. Oliver was almost convinced.

"And what do you think they did to her for taking my son away from me?"

It was not a rhetorical question, but not one he was supposed to answer either.

"Nothing. Not a single thing. She put on this crazy lady act and they just let her go."

Mattie cleared her throat from the doorway. "Um, I hate to say this, but there's a nurse roaming the floor, apparently making rounds."

Oliver leaned forward, wondering just how long she'd been torturing herself with this filicidal myth. He took one of his mother's hands in both of his. He said, "You need to forgive her."

"Who?"

"The lady who killed Oliver."

"Never," she said, then again. "Never."

Mattie put her hand on Oliver's elbow. "We probably need to get going. Like, now."

Oliver stood, still holding his mother's hand. "Well, would you at least think about it?"

"What exactly do you think I do here all day? I consider things. I sit here and consider *every*thing. And nothing I consider ever changes."

"I'm sorry," Oliver said. And he was.

"Me too."

"Look," he said, "is there anything you need? Anything I can do for you? You do have a birthday coming up."

She studied him for a long beat, then whispered, "Get me out of here."

When Mattie tried to hug Delores, she remained stiff and stared blankly at the wall. Mattie hit a few buttons on the remote control until the TV screen filled with angry talking heads. Then she grabbed Oliver by the hand and pulled him to the doorway. They stood, waiting for the nurse to emerge from one room and enter another. Oliver glanced back; his mother still looked small and confused and pitiful. Then Mattie was tugging his arm toward the stairwell.

They retraced their steps, exchanged padlocks, and drove away much faster than necessary. Oliver didn't catch his breath until he was behind the wheel with the engine running. That's when he finally turned to Mattie and said simply, "Thank you for, you know ... *that*."

"She thinks we're sisters, you know."

"But that makes no sense. She never even had a sister."

"Apparently she always wanted one." Mattie was quiet, apparently letting that sink in. Then she said, "You do realize you need to take your own advice, don't you?"

"What do you mean?"

"That drunk, distraught mother who killed her son? You need to forgive her too."

Oliver pondered this, long and hard. Finally, he said, "I already have."

"Trust me, Oliver. Loving and forgiving are not the same thing."

They drove in silence until the Nashville skyline filled the windshield.

Oliver finally said, "I do, you know. Trust you."

"Just be careful with that. I do kind of have a history of disappointing people. Especially the ones I care most about."

Chapter Thirty-Eight

Oliver gripped the door handle but couldn't bring himself to pull it. "I'm not sure this is such a great idea."

"Would you stop worrying so much?" Mattie said. "You're going to give *me* an ulcer. Besides, if I recall correctly, you didn't think our other adventure this morning was such a great idea either. And how did that turn out?"

Oliver stared at her.

"Never mind," she said.

Mattie had volunteered to give Oliver a ride home after their shift. But instead of driving toward his house, she had paused at the mouth of the parking garage and said, "So what do you think? Is it time to crack Vandy?"

"What are you talking about?"

"I read your notebook, Oliver. You've 'audited' classes at every college or university in a thirty mile radius, *except* for Vanderbilt. I believe you called it your holy grail?"

Mattie removed a folded printout from her purse and tossed it into Oliver's lap. It was a comprehensive class schedule that she had gleaned from the internet. "I highlighted a few choice options. But it really needs to be your call."

In the end, they decided to ease into things. After parking illegally, they ate a quick breakfast in one of the many campus dining facilities. When Oliver grew weary of Mattie calling him a big chicken, he took a caffeinated swig of courage, pointed toward a nouveau-hippie girl at a nearby table, and said, "That's the one."

Mattie followed his gaze and said, "She is cute. But I thought we were here to complete your bucket list, not help you score chicks."

The hippie girl finished bussing her own table, shrugged into her messenger bag, and headed for the exit. "We'll follow her and sneak into whatever class she's going to."

"No, *you* will. I'm going to stand guard."

Oliver was almost disappointed when he saw the enormity of the auditorium-style classroom. He'd missed the name of the class, but the lecture was peppered with profuse amounts of polysyllabic scientific jargon. Oliver had nestled into his seat and was nodding off when he heard a loud knock at the door. The professor looked more befuddled than Oliver felt when Mattie strode purposefully toward the lectern.

"Please pardon the interruption, Professor," she said, very stern and professional. "My name is Matilda Holmgren from Admissions, investigative branch. We have it on good authority that your class may have been infiltrated by an interloper."

The professor responded by scratching his bald spot. Oliver slunk further into his seat.

"This should only take a minute," Mattie said. "Do you have your roll sheet handy?"

The professor looked around for a teaching assistant, who did eventually step forward with an orange binder. She flipped to a particular tab and waited.

Mattie said, "Do you show an Oliver Miles registered for this class?"

A thousand eyeballs tracked along with the assistant's fat finger as it traced the long line of names. "Nope, no Oliver Miles."

"Just as we suspected," Mattie said like a bad actor in a worse movie. Then she cocked her chin toward the darkened auditorium. "Okay, Mr. Miles, you can make this easy on yourself. Or we can do it the hard way."

Oliver considered ignoring her and trying to see how she wormed her way out of the public spectacle she was making. But she was looking right at him, which meant that, one by one, everyone else in the room was too. So Oliver stood, excused himself down a long line of students, and shuffled down the steps. When he slipped his hands into his pockets, Mattie said, "And please keep your hands where I can see them."

This created a wave of suspicious murmurs that ended as Oliver approached the double doors. That's when Mattie grabbed his arm and started running for the exit.

Once outside, Oliver faced Mattie and said, "Why on earth did you go to all that trouble to sneak me into class if you were just going to barge in and drag me out again?"

"For the thrill of it," she said. "Besides, you looked totally bored in there. I think you may have even nodded off a time or two."

"Does that mean you were watching me?"

"That was strictly research, Oliver Miles."

Now here she was, four hours later, asking him to trust her with another of her harebrained schemes. Oliver shook his head and said, "I'm afraid this idea might be worse."

"Don't make me call you a sissy." Mattie reached across Oliver's lap and opened the passenger door of her mother's borrowed minivan for him. He had to resist competing urges to sniff Mattie's hair, run his finger along the curve of her neck, and kiss the back of her head. "Look," she continued, "all you have to do is go flirt with the new receptionist a little. And keep one eye on the beefy security guard."

"Maybe *you* should go flirt with the security guard and keep an eye on the new receptionist?"

"I don't believe in flirting, remember?" she said. "Besides, you really think you're up for sneaking upstairs and breaking your mother out of this place all by yourself?"

"Never mind."

"It will be fine, Oliver. Just play it cool."

"But I already *am* playing it cool."

The grin started on the right side of Mattie's face this time. She planted the tip of her tongue into the smiling corner, as if trying to stem the laughter welling up behind it. But it was no use; she cracked up anyway. As she finally shooed him out the door, Mattie said, "Hate to tell you this, but that may be the funniest thing you've ever said."

Oliver wandered into the lobby in time to watch the changing of the guard, literally. The regular daytime security officer stood towering over his diminutive replacement, delivering an official briefing of the many security concerns the night watchman might encounter. They intentionally ignored Oliver for what seemed like five minutes, which was fine with him. Finally, the big guard acknowledged Oliver's presence with a curt, "Can I help you?"

"Just here to see my mom."

"Visiting hours just ended."

Oliver looked at his watch, then feigned surprise. "Huh, would you look at that?" Then he lifted the watch to his ear, proving again that his vapid improv skills were obviously not limited to the stage. It was a digital watch.

The skinny guard alternated his anxious gaze between Oliver and his bulky comrade, his hand absently fingering the can of mace on his belt. Oliver suppressed an overwhelming urge to whistle something tuneless and banal. Instead, he said, "Mind if I use the restroom then?"

"I'd rather you not." It was the guard with the muscles. "Cleaning crew just left."

"It's kind of an emergency."

"Just be quick about it. Like I said, visiting hours are over."

Oliver ambled toward the restroom, turned, and pressed his shoulder blades against the door. He was halfway inside when he saw headlights flash, then the front of Mattie's mother's Odyssey appear under the portico. Oliver was walking—entirely too quickly—toward the exit when the big guard (with the equally big voice) said, "I thought you needed the men's."

"I can hold it."

"I thought it couldn't wait? That it was some big emergency?"

"It comes and goes." Oliver walked quicker now. "Anyway, guess I'll see you guys laterhaveagreatdaygoodnight!"

He sprinted the last few steps, bounded out of the lobby, and leapt into the already open van door. When he finally caught his breath and snapped his seatbelt into place, Oliver noticed his mother perched in the captain's chair behind Mattie, belted in and smiling at nothing in particular. It dawned on him that, as far as he knew, she hadn't ridden in a car in years.

"That was fast," he said.

"I had a key." Mattie eased the van out from under the portico, then looped around the building.

"Where are you going?" Oliver said.

"Back around to the gate."

"Did you forget something?"

"Sort of, yeah." Mattie eased to the curb and put the van in park. Then she got out and motioned for Oliver to climb across to the driver's side. Through the open window she said, "You guys go ahead. I'll catch up later."

"Wait, no, we're not leaving you behind."

"Of course you are," she said, taking a quick inventory of her backpack purse. "I just need to check on a few things. Besides, Roscoe's expecting you with cake, and ice cream that's probably melting as we speak."

"Please tell me you're not going back inside?"

Mattie shrugged, as if helpless against her own illicit instincts. There was no fear or exaggerated pride in her flushed expression. She was simply doing what needed to be done. Oliver's imagination suddenly leapt forward a half decade to a placid scene—him sitting sidesaddle in an idling getaway car outside an old-fashioned bank, one hand on the wheel, the other extended into the backseat feeding a baby bottle to the cooing form in the bulky car seat, as a ski-masked Mattie comes running out of the bank with a backpack full of money, firing scattershot over her shoulder while cradling her pregnant belly with her free hand.

She said, "That doctor's name is Strahan, right?"

"I don't think this is such a great idea."

"Trust me, Oliver. It will all work out fine."

As he pulled away he wondered what it would be like to do stand-up in prison.

. . .

Oliver had no idea what to expect as he escorted his mother through the darkened foyer of Downers. She hadn't said much since leaving her Shady Grove cocoon, and he didn't try to push it. So far, her outward reactions had been limited to a single expression — marvel. She wore the blissful look of some interplanetary explorer experiencing the sensory rush of an exotic new world for the very first time. In the movies though, that wondrous expression never really lasted. Things always grew weird or dark or some of both.

Most unnerving though was that she kept calling him Wayne.

Roscoe was nowhere in sight, probably still hiding in his office trying to work up the nerve to come out and face an old friend. Oliver steered his mother toward an elongated table near the back of the restaurant. The word "reserved" was printed on a series of homemade table tents. By the time he had his mother seated, Oliver's expectations had flatlined and he was wondering if this was such a great idea. He sat beside her, unsure what to say or do next, silently reviling Mattie for talking him into this ridiculous scheme and Roscoe for not talking him out of it, then both of them for abandoning him to do the heavy lifting. Mostly he was surprised how sitting alone with his mother in public made him so uncomfortable.

Delores's attention seemed riveted on a flurry of activity near the stage. A large crowd had materialized and apparently caught the wait staff off guard. Oliver wondered if one of the stand-ups had invited everyone he knew to come see the show. Then he remembered that Downers didn't do comedy on Wednesday nights.

He faced his mother and said, "Are you okay to stay put here for a few minutes?"

She nodded, still fascinated with all the bustling activity. Oliver picked his way through the labyrinth of tables toward Roscoe's office. He didn't knock.

Roscoe sat behind his desk, thick-veined hands gripping the armrests of his chair, eyes closed.

"You're not dead, are you?"

Roscoe shook his large head.

"Sleeping?"

"Praying, actually."

"For what?"

"Courage, I think. Maybe a sign?"

"Is it working?"

"I guess it just did."

"How's that?" Oliver said, genuinely curious.

"You showed up."

"Funny, I don't think I've ever been an answer to prayer before."

Roscoe blinked at Oliver, then again. "I think you might be surprised."

"And I think you'd better get out there. Looks like a chartered bus just broke down on your doorstep."

Roscoe did not look rattled. He never did. However, when he pushed back from his desk, Oliver noticed that he did look old. And weary. And a little frightened.

They emerged from the short hallway together, paused to take in the peculiar scene unfolding in front of them, then regarded each other with equal measures of shock, confusion, and cautious delight.

Delores Miles stood at the end of the bar. And for one horrifying moment, when Oliver saw his mother's arms hovering behind her back, he thought she was being arrested. Instead, she was tying apron strings into a bow. Two of her former colleagues appeared by her side. They seemed to be swapping pleasantries, waitressing strategies, and even a few jokes. It felt like watching an old home movie as she settled into what she used to refer to as her preflight routine. She popped a stick of Big Red into her mouth, scribbled on the back of her hand to make sure her ink pen worked, then checked her hair and makeup in the mirror behind the bar. Before taking off again, she lathered on some lipstick, then thumbed the excess from the corners of her mouth. Oliver wished he could pause the tape, or at least sit and watch it in slow motion for a while.

"Wow," Oliver said. "Would you look at that?" But Roscoe was already huddled up with his assistant manager, no doubt trying to figure out what to do about their unexpected guests and uninvited waitress.

Delores narrowly averted colliding with a tray full of drinks as she quick-pivoted toward the activity down front. Instinct took over as she simultaneously pushed tables together, memorized drink orders, and politely bossed people around. She seemed incapable of talking to anyone without also touching them, from playful attention-getting jabs to lingering shoulder pats to scooching herself into already full booths to flirt with patrons. In an attempt to ward off a creeping sense of jealousy, Oliver averted his eyes. They landed on the front door, which only made him wonder what Mattie was up to.

With nothing better to do, Oliver sat at the table reserved for his mother's party and watched. Eventually Roscoe eased into the seat beside him.

"So what's the plan?" Oliver said.

"I guess we keep an eye on her. Lord knows, we can use the help tonight."

At the kitchen window, Delores clothespinned an order to a sagging metal wire. She shouted something unintelligible at the fry cook. When an aging Korean busboy ambled by, she pinched his butt, then feigned innocence when he grinned up at her. On her way back to her section, Delores Miles detoured by the mostly empty party table and plopped onto Roscoe's lap.

"Busy night, eh boss? Feels like I haven't seen you in ages."

"It has been a while," Roscoe said.

She rested a hand on Oliver's shoulder and squeezed. "Good to see you again too," she said. He had no idea if she was talking to her son or her son's former roommate or some other compensatory figment of her imagination. Frankly, he didn't really care. She had initiated contact. And her hand felt warm again.

"So what are you boys drinking?"

Roscoe bleated out the word "coffee." Oliver managed a "me too." Delores accused them of boring her to death, then promised to put on a fresh pot.

Watching his mother was like looking into the sun. After a while it began to hurt, to make his eyes water. But Roscoe never took his eyes off her. Oliver was considering a field trip into the parking lot for some fresh air and a pointless look around for Mattie when she finally pushed her way into the foyer. He waved her over and introduced his newest friend to his oldest one. After they assured each other that they'd heard so much about the other, Mattie sat and followed their collective gaze to the bustling form of Delores Miles.

"She looks happy," Mattie said.

The men nodded in unison.

"Who are all these seats reserved for, anyhow?"

Oliver looked at Roscoe who looked back, baffled. Even in her healthiest days, a party for Delores Miles wouldn't warrant a dozen seats. She didn't have friends; she had ex-boyfriends, co-workers, Roscoe, and Oliver.

Mattie and Oliver moved tables as Roscoe motioned for the hostess to start sending guests to all the newly available seats.

Then they sat and sipped their coffees and watched Delores Miles work. When she did stop by the table she called Roscoe and Mattie by name, but avoided calling Oliver anything. She did stare at him a lot though with a feline curiosity, as if trying to solve him. And at one point she said, "I haven't felt this energized since, you know, since Oliver was . . ."

Her voice trailed off when she realized what she'd said.

Oliver sensed Mattie's and Roscoe's blatant attempts at *not* staring. It had been a small eternity since Delores Miles had said her son's name. Finally he said, "I'm sure wherever he is right now, he's got his eye on you. Probably both."

"You think?"

"Yeah, I pretty much know."

Delores winked toward heaven and said, "I'll bet you're right."

Then she did the unthinkable.

First, she leaned forward and planted a soft, sweet kiss on Oliver's forehead. In a stage whisper, she told Mattie, "Whatever you do, honey, do *not* let this one get away."

Then she stood, cracked her back with a grimace, and announced to Roscoe she was going to take a smoke break. When Oliver tried to protest, both Mattie and Roscoe stared him down. As they watched her disappear into the kitchen, Oliver was struck again by how much she resembled her old self. And how that made him miss her even more.

Roscoe got up to go tend the business of his restaurant.

"Are you okay, *Oliver*?" Mattie said.

"I'm not sure. It's been a long, long time."

"Believe it or not, she says your name all the time. Just not when you're around."

Oliver nodded, then said, "So where have you been? And please don't tell me you snuck back into Shady Grove."

"You want me to lie?"

"Okay, then. *Why* did you go back?"

"Research."

"What kind of research?"

"The kind we're going to talk about later. You have more important things to occupy your mind tonight."

Mattie could have no idea how right she was. She excused herself to the restroom and Oliver watched her go, able to observe the two women he cared most about in this world at the same time. That's when he realized he'd reduced them both to props and punch lines. It was not a pleasant realization. And Oliver resolved once again to come clean. He was going to tell Mattie about her dad, confess to using her in his act without her consent, confront her about her breaking and entering, and maybe even tell her exactly how he felt about her. If, that is, he could actually figure it out.

Roscoe returned to the table first. "You up for doing a set tonight?"

"A what?"

"Comedy. You've been bugging me since forever to work this room. So how about it?"

"I don't think so," Oliver said, not sure if it was regret or relief that was making his insides tingle.

"You sure? I've been hearing some good things about your new material. And it might actually help her remember."

"Wouldn't that break your secret pact with my mother?"

Roscoe seemed to think about this, then said, "That was a promise to a friend. Tonight she's my employee again."

Oliver shook his head. "Even if I managed to get up there and open my mouth, I'm not sure I could actually squeeze the words out past the lump in my throat."

"You too, huh?"

They sat in silence, watching Delores Miles in action. As it dawned on Oliver that he'd just casually dismissed his lifelong dream, it also occurred to him why. Aside from the obvious distraction of his mother waiting tables, Mattie had never seen him do stand-up. Plus, all his good material either impugned or incriminated everyone in the room that he actually cared about. Mostly though, Roscoe's offer reeked of pity. And Oliver did have enough professional pride to actually still want to *earn* his spot at Downers.

"You think she's really back to normal?" Oliver said, mostly to change the subject in his own mind. "Or that she could be someday?"

"Who knows? But before you get any ideas, Oliver, you know I can't let her work here. Not after tonight."

"Can't? Or won't?"

Roscoe's face tightened. He kept his eyes on Oliver as he motioned toward the bar with his stubbly chin. "Have you smelled her breath?"

Oliver shook his head, suddenly mortified.

"She's been sampling all night, just like old times."

Mattie resumed her seat next to Oliver and said, "I don't believe I've ever seen two more maudlin faces in my life."

They didn't argue. Nor did they pretend to snap out of it. All three simply sat and watched Delores Miles, each nursing their own thoughts. Finally, Mattie said, "Hate to break up this little party. But we do need to think about getting her back."

It was true. Her complexion had gone waxy and pale. And as the night wore on she was moving much slower than before. Her playful banter had taken on a testy edge. And when she tried to blow her bangs out of her face, they remained pasted to her forehead in little ringlets.

"What about the party?" Oliver said. "And the birthday cake?"

"I'll take care of that," Roscoe said. He then intercepted a passing waitress and delivered a series of animated instructions. Moments later, Delores Miles was shepherded to the small stage as a candlelit cake seemed to float out of the kitchen and the entire room broke into song.

Back at the table, Delores seemed more interested in counting her tips than eating her cake. But she couldn't seem to stop thanking everyone for remembering her birthday. She stared at the ceiling and did a few calculations, then slid a wad of bills across the table and made Roscoe promise to give the busboys their fair share of her tips.

After three or four small bites she said, “I’m really tired, boss.”

When it was time to actually leave, she hugged Roscoe. But he wouldn’t let go. They held on, swaying gently, slow dancing to a song nobody heard but them. By the time Oliver and Mattie had her strapped back into the van, Delores Miles had resumed that spaced-out look of marvel. Three blocks from the restaurant she was snoring softly in her seat.

Chapter Thirty-Nine

HOTELS ARE NOT HAUNTED; people are. Someone much wiser than Oliver said that. He thought it was probably Mattie, but he was too sleepy to remember. If his calculations were correct, Oliver had been averaging fewer than three hours of sleep per night the last couple of months.

It finally dawned on him what bothered him about Harrington ghost stories. They were never the same. If the spirit of Old Man Harrington really was roaming the halls of his old hotel, why were the alleged encounters so vastly different? According to the more popular rumors and online accounts, Harrington ghost stories seemed to reveal more about the storytellers than their creepy encounters. Old Man Harrington had been portrayed as benevolent, benign, somewhat bored, and downright evil. He'd appeared to some as an old-world Italian with a thick accent and to others as a Tennessee redneck. Sometimes he was tall, thin, cigar-chomping, with a severe limp. Other times he was short, pudgy, pipe-smoking, and missing an arm. More times than not, Old Man Harrington wasn't even that old. Oliver had begun to suspect an altogether less intimidating version, a spindly armed old man in his boxers. But every time he stopped by Room 623 and put his ear to the door, it was as still and silent as a tomb. He wished now he'd accepted Cleve's fifty bucks. At least that way he'd know he wasn't completely crazy.

Oliver decided that ghosts only appeared to those with eyes to see and ears to hear. That supernatural encounters were the result of wishful thinking. And that if he ever did bump into the Harrington's pet apparition, he'd want to know: Why so bashful? So selective? So nocturnal? Could he really walk through walls? And if so, what did that feel like? And if it wasn't too much trouble, how about a demonstration?

These were the trivial thoughts occupying Oliver's mind as he made his rounds. On the elevator ride back to the lobby, his thoughts shifted to the haunted people in his life. Sherman continued to be vexed by his idea of reputation, Roscoe by regret and the disease gnawing away at his insides, Delores Miles by her deranged notions of romantic love and a past she couldn't quite remember, and Mattie by whatever prompted her to sneak into other people's rooms.

When the elevator doors opened into the lobby, Oliver was haunted by an eerily familiar voice. It was intimate, otherworldly, and punctuated with an authentic-sounding laugh track. Oliver followed the sound to the hotel's "Business Center."

Mattie didn't move as he approached from behind. The image on the screen was as surreal as the sound emanating from the tiny speakers, maybe more so. In the center of the monitor, Oliver watched a grainy, miniature version of himself performing stand-up comedy. Down the right side of the screen, a thumbnailed menu offered a dozen more selections of the "crying comedian" or "security guard comic" or the one he hated most of all—"Miles of Smiles." Oliver didn't have to squint at the hyperlinked username to know who posted the videos. Still, he made a mental note to strangle Barry when he saw him next.

Oliver groaned, conspicuously loud. He then lobbed a series of self-deprecating comments, all of which missed the mark, and eventually asked Mattie if she didn't have something better to do than watch those silly videos. He even reached over her shoulder and tried to commandeer the mouse. But Mattie simply tightened her grip, continued to stare forward, unmoving. The words—his words—continued to pour out of the speakers. But they were drowned out by the sound of Mattie *not* laughing.

When the video ended, she slipped out of the chair and walked away.

"Mattie?"

She didn't respond.

"What's wrong? Where are you going?"

He heard her punch the security code, then the door clicked shut behind her. A few seconds passed in silence before she began her assault on the adding machines. The Business Center chair was still warm when he sat and began scrolling through the videos. After searching in vain for a YouTube button that said "Delete All," he eventually lowered the volume and forced himself to watch the video Mattie had been watching when he found her. It was always painful to see himself performing stand-up, but it was agonizing to watch himself joke about his kleptomaniac girlfriend, her criminal record, and catching her father in a nightclub with another woman. There was nothing funny about any of it.

When the last video ended, Oliver let himself into Mattie's office. He didn't say anything; he just sat and waited and watched her work. It felt like an hour before she spoke.

"Am I the 'girlfriend' in your routine?"

There was no good answer to that question.

"I'm not stupid, Oliver." Mattie turned in her chair, but only halfway. She seemed to be studying an ancient gray stain on the carpet.

"I never said you were, never even thought it."

"You were acting weird. He was acting weird. So I followed him."

"You followed your dad?" Oliver wasn't really that surprised. He just wanted to stoke the momentum, to keep tossing coal into the conversational furnace. And try not to get burned.

"I even took pictures," her profile said. "Nothing illicit or anything. Just, you know, proof."

"I'm sorry, Mattie."

"Guess I should post them on the internet since that seems to be the hip new way to deal with hard things."

"I wanted to tell you, Mattie."

"But you did tell me, Oliver," she said. "Along with a roomful of people I don't know and whoever else happens to click onto your YouTube page."

"Look, I had no idea Barry was going to do that. I didn't even know he was filming me. And when I see him again, I'm— "

"Stop," she said, finally looking at him for a brief moment. But it was enough. "Just stop it."

"I know it was probably wrong to talk about that stuff onstage. But you said I was funniest when I was telling the truth."

"I see. So this is somehow my fault? Or Barry's, for posting it in the first place?"

Oliver opened his mouth to speak, but there was nothing there. He was empty, hollowed out, a blank.

He was trying to muster the strength to stand when Mattie said, "And what I *actually* said was that you're funnier when you're being real, and that I like you better when you tell the truth."

"Guess I kind of ruined that."

"I know you think I'm overreacting, Oliver. But I'm not. I'm simply *re*acting. And you don't like it."

"..."

"You want to keep saying you're sorry until I tell you everything is okay. But it's not okay. Nothing is okay. Not anymore."

"..."

"See, Oliver. I gave you the benefit of the doubt. Somehow I knew that you knew what he was up to. I just figured you were working up your nerve to tell me, maybe trying to preserve my feelings, that maybe you couldn't bear to see me hurt. I was even foolish enough to think you might confront him about it; that you might actually sit my father down and tell him what you thought of his adultering ways, what he was doing to his family. I always expected that kind of behavior out of him, but not from you. But it looks like I gave you too much credit."

"I am so sorry, Mattie. And you're right. I should have told you."

"You said you would always tell me the truth. You promised, actually. But all you ever really say is you're sorry."

"But I didn't lie. I've never lied to you."

"I'm talking about honesty, Oliver."

"So am I."

"No, you're talking about not lying. Big difference."

"I wanted to tell you, Mattie. But it's not the easiest thing in the world to tell someone you care about that you caught her father with another woman."

"Easy?" It was more than a simple two-syllable question. It was an indictment that echoed in his head, conjuring all the not-so-easy things she'd done for him. Not the least of which was giving him his mother back.

Returning her gaze was the single hardest thing he could ever remember doing. Then she did something he'd never seen her do before.

Mattie blinked. A single tear glistened on her cheek, then fell. Oliver had to look away. Then she stood and began gathering her things.

"You're leaving?"

"The audit's done."

She powered down the computer, gathered her purse, and headed for the door. Then she circled back around her desk as if she was searching for something.

"But it's three o'clock in the morning."

"I'm taking a sick day." Mattie was moving more quickly now, checking under tables and every available surface.

"But where are you going?"

Mattie stopped her search and faced Oliver.

"You really want to know?" She wasn't mad anymore; she seemed defeated. "I'm going to check on my mother, Oliver. Not that she needs me to; she's not stupid either. But sometimes it's just nice to have someone care enough to sit and hold your hand and whisper compassionate lies."

"Wait, Mattie." Oliver was up now, following Mattie toward the time clock. "Can't we just talk about this?"

"We just did."

"But there's, you know ... stuff I think I need to tell you."

She paused. And for one brief instant he thought she might stay. Then she said, "Save it for your act."

"Wait, Mattie?"

She stopped but didn't turn around.

"What were you looking for in there? Maybe I can help."

"I doubt it," she said. "Unless you're the one who stole my guitar."

Oliver watched her car until the taillights disappeared around the corner. He ducked into the security closet and watched surveillance feeds halfheartedly until he heard the phone ringing at the front desk. As he stood to leave, he noticed a gnarled lollipop stick pasted to the lip of his wastebasket.

The phone was still ringing when Oliver finally made it to the front desk. He knew better than to hope it was Mattie calling, but it was still difficult to find his voice when he answered.

"Front desk, can I help you?"

"Yeah, this is Cliff Houlihan in Room 621. Someone just tried to rob me."

. . .

By the time Oliver dragged himself up to Room 621, Houlihan was ready for him. He invited Oliver to read over his shoulder as he finished writing up a full "incident report" on hotel stationery. But the smell in the room—a gag-inducing musk of incense and burning rope—made it hard for Oliver to focus. Still, he got the gist of it. Houlihan's account was riddled with details and times and official-sounding language, referring only to "the perpetrator."

As Oliver scanned the report, a creepy, operatic sound came from the other side of the wall. Oliver looked at Houlihan, who remained unfazed, and said, "It was a guy, right?"

"Excuse me?"

"The perpetrator? Just making sure it wasn't a girl."

"If it was a girl, it was a butt-ugly one. Whoever it was used a key. The shower was running, so he probably assumed he had time. Turns out, he didn't. It's all in the report."

"Did he manage to take anything?"

"He tried."

"How come it's not in the report?" Oliver had scanned the handwritten document twice and all it mentioned was "contraband." But it was hard to concentrate with that quivering falsetto ebbing and flowing in the next room.

"I'm afraid that's classified."

"Can you give me a hint?"

"You know anything about medicinal marijuana?"

"Sure," Oliver said.

Houlihan stared directly into Oliver's eyes, then covered his mouth with a loose fist, arched his eyebrows knowingly, and faked a series of pathetic coughs. Then he said, "Do you have an email address?"

Oliver was about to recite it when the muted voice on the other side of the wall turned shrill. This time Houlihan scowled at the wall. "So," Oliver said, "you heard it too?"

"How could I miss it?" Houlihan said.

"What do you think it is?"

"It's an old man practicing ghost noises."

"How do you know that?"

"We have an agreement," Houlihan said. "I indulge his howling and he ignores the woody fumes that seep through the vents."

Oliver scribbled his email address on a blank sheet of hotel stationery and handed it to Houlihan.

"Lucky for you, I managed to snap a few photos while he was still on his back. Once I clear out of here, I'll send them to you."

"It would really help if I could have them now."

"Not me."

"So is your name really Houlihan?"

"That's classified too."

"Are you always so cryptic?"

"Have you ever heard of the witness protection program?"

"Yeah," Oliver said. "But I thought it was mostly a myth."

Fake Houlihan shook his head, tight-lipped and chiding.

"Okay then," Oliver said. "Is there anything else I need to know?"

"Yeah, if you happen to find this guy in the next week or so, his left eye should be good and purple."

"Why's that?" Oliver asked.

But Fake Houlihan just stared at his balled fist and massaged his knuckles.

• • •

Oliver paused outside Houlihan's room, then walked the few short steps to the closed door of #623. He stood and listened, but heard nothing. Then he put his ear against the door and listened harder. Still nothing.

He was about to leave when he thought he saw a flash of light in the door's peephole. Oliver knocked, cleared his throat, and used his most authoritative voice. "Security. Open up."

He knocked louder and added, "I just need to have a quick word with you."

Oliver removed the master key he kept clipped onto his security belt and slid the credit card-sized plastic into the slot. There was a mechanical whir, followed by a series of flashing red lights, but the door remained locked. He paused and reinserted the key three more times with the same result.

Maybe General Sherman was right? Maybe he'd gotten the number wrong? Or maybe he was destined to end up in Shady Grove alongside his mother?

Chapter Forty

OLIVER WENT TO WORK every night at eleven and conjured up new and creative ways to go apologize to Mattie that he would then abandon before he could work up the nerve to execute them. The security camera feeds flickered and idled by in the security closet unwatched. He couldn't really bear to see Mattie doing something naughty. Not that she ever strayed very far from her desk anymore. She seemed to have lost all interest in playing her guitar or knitting or even pounding on her adding machines.

So instead of watching her, he listened.

He spent countless hours sitting in the Business Center cubbyhole, playing computer Solitaire as he waited for Mattie sounds—adding machines, elongated sighs, unconscious humming, or one of her delightful sneezes—to waft over the wall. Her mother was calling a lot now too. Mattie never really said much of substance, mostly, "I know, Mom" and "I'm sorry, Mom." Or maybe that was all the substance that was required. Oliver had no idea. And it didn't matter, because no matter what she said or how she said it, it hit Oliver like an accusation. Maybe if he'd confronted Mattie about her dad instead of telling a roomful of strangers, he'd be consoling her as she consoled her mother. Lord knows, she needed it. Every time she hung up the phone, she released this pitiful sigh, as if trying not to cry, which of course made Oliver feel like crying.

When computer Solitaire got old, Oliver would google himself, still amazed to see how much of him was on the internet. With nary a keystroke from Oliver, he had a MySpace page, two Facebook pages (with over a thousand fans), two Twitter accounts (both imposters, and neither very witty), and dozens of YouTube videos. He'd seen most of them at least once. But they were hard to watch, not just because of the poor sound quality or because he hated the sound of his recorded voice. Mostly, he was embarrassed to see how far he'd taken the truth. He'd used everyone he ever knew and every experience he could remember and made them all fodder for his act, grist for the comedic mill. And now, thanks to modern technology, the entire world could watch the Crying Comedian ply his trade on the internet.

The more he thought about it, the more apt the mill analogy seemed. He'd taken those experiences—which he now realized were only half his—and ground them into dust, pulverized them to feed his own selfish whims. The fact that he'd used people didn't bother him. It was how mercilessly he'd done it.

It was no wonder he didn't have any friends.

Some unknown amount of time passed and the phone rang again. Mattie answered, and after an elongated pause she said, "It's just New York, Mom—not Ethiopia."

Oliver decided to go make his rounds.

• • •

He spent most of the morning working himself into a righteously indignant lather. His plan was to unload on Barry for having posted all those YouTube videos without his consent. But his confidence wavered when he heard his manager's groggy voice—after all, Barry wasn't the one who took the stage every night and exploited his friends' personal lives just to make a few strangers laugh. His confidence faltered altogether when Barry announced he'd landed Oliver a feature spot at Jesters.

"Very funny, Barry." He resisted the urge to hang up on him.

"Let's hope so. That's what they're paying you for."

"You actually sound serious," Oliver said.

"That's because I am actually serious."

"But I've never even emceed Jesters before."

"Right," Barry said.

"And it's a Friday night."

"Right again."

"And unless I'm remembering wrong, Tracy Morgan is headlining tonight."

"Also correct," Barry said. "So wake yourself up and let's meet for an early dinner. We need to talk about your set list and hammer out a few other details."

"What other details?" Oliver said, still waiting for the catch.

"Things like money. And other gigs. You know, I hate to say 'I told you so,' but it seems the Oliver Miles phenomenon is going viral."

Oliver sat up straighter, tried to clear his throat, and wiped at his eyes with the heel of his hand. Apparently he wasn't dreaming. And he really was going to be playing a real gig at Jesters in about six hours, not just another showcase or last-minute emcee spot.

"Okay," Oliver said. "I'm awake now. So let me just state for the record that if you woke me up just to jerk me around, I'm going to inflict some serious bodily harm upon you."

"It's no joke, Oliver. And don't get too carried away either. You're doing a feature, not headlining. And it pays, but not *that* well. It's more about exposure. And we just happened to be in the right place at the right time."

"So what did happen? A last-minute cancellation?"

"Not exactly," Barry said. "I was making rounds with your press kits—no thanks to you, by the way—this morning. When I stopped in to see Tony at Jesters, he didn't even hesitate. He said, 'Ain't that the crying comedian?' I tell him, 'Yeah' and he says, 'It's your lucky day, pal.' "

"What does that mean?" Oliver asked, trying to keep his enthusiasm under control.

"It means there was some kind of personality conflict between Tony and the scheduled feature. It means I was working the street like any good manager should, and we got lucky. And it means you need to grab a shower, a fresh security uniform, and meet me for dinner."

"No, no way, Barry. I'm not wearing the uniform."

"It's part of the deal."

"How so?"

"The last thing Tony said before I signed the contract was, 'He'll be in uniform, right?' I told him no, that you're not doing that shtick anymore. He says, 'If he wants to feature at my club tonight, he does.' When I grin and tell him it's not in the contract, he takes a Sharpie marker and writes it in, right in the middle of the page. 'It's in the contract now,' he says. Before I make it out the door, Tony says, 'And make sure he cries a little. I just love that crying bit.' "

Oliver let all this sink in, not sure what to believe. "I don't know, Barry."

"Yes, you do. Now get a shower and let's meet at seven. Show starts at nine, which means you'll go on about nine-thirty. I'm working on getting you a radio interview prior to the show. Local DJ is a friend of Chuck's. But that's still iffy."

"Speaking of Chuck, why won't he return my phone calls?"

"Why on earth are you calling Chuck?"

What Oliver thought was, *To confirm whether or not Mattie's actually been sneaking into occupied hotel rooms in the middle of the night.* Thankfully, all he said was, "There's a pretty major glitch in the security cameras he installed."

"What kind of glitch?"

"The archives don't work. There's no way to go back and see what's already been filmed."

"That sounds about right," Barry said. "Chuck's a bit of a scammer. And he has this habit of disappearing when he feels like people are on to him. But if I see him I'll tell him to call you. In the meantime, you have a gig to get ready for."

"I suppose this will be a good warm-up for the Downers benefit on Saturday."

"No, Oliver, I think it's the other way around. Downers is old news. Frankly, I think it's a waste of your time. In fact, I have a lead on a gig in Atlanta Saturday night—an actual paying gig if you'll—"

"Sorry, Barry, I'm doing the Downers thing." Just saying it out loud filled Oliver with both pride and trepidation. His dream gig was less than two days away.

"I don't get you, man. It's just a silly benefit for a grumpy old man who obviously doesn't think much of your act."

Oliver hung up the phone. He kept telling himself he was thrilled, ecstatic, wildly enthusiastic, that he was nearly as happy as he was nervous. Mostly though, he wanted to call someone to help him celebrate. But Mattie wasn't returning his calls. Simon would only pretend to be happy for him. Roscoe would probably lecture him about gigs that sound too good to be true. Oliver didn't have Rodney's number. And of course, his mother thought he was dead.

Before getting up to shower he called information and got the number for Jesters. Three rings later he heard someone say, "Jesters Comedy Club. This is Amanda."

"Um, yeah, Amanda, I'm thinking about coming down to the show tonight. Could you tell me who's on the bill?"

"Tracy Morgan from *30 Rock*. You should come out. It'll be a good show, I promise."

"Is there an opening act?"

"Let's see . . . yep, says here that the emcee is a local act called Jake & John. I've seen them before; funny stuff. And it looks like there's a feature tonight too, um, Oliver Miles. I've never heard him before, but Tony says he's hilarious. Some kind of weeping policeman or something like that."

"Okay," Oliver said. "Thanks."

"Hope you can make it out tonight."

"Oh, I'll definitely be there."

• • •

He'd actually been on the Jesters stage before, but only during comedy workshops and an occasional showcase. The dressing room was tinier than Oliver remembered, replete with old high school lockers, cigarette-burned sofas, and a cracked mirror. The emcees were already warming up the crowd—a very large crowd. And the headliner hadn't shown up yet. So Oliver had the dressing room to himself for the next fifteen minutes. Right after he changed into his uniform, someone knocked on the door. It was Simon.

"I just heard, man. Why didn't you call?"

"I don't know," Oliver said. "I just found out about it awhile ago myself."

"I brought everybody I could find—Whimbush, Freddy, Buster, all the usual suspects. We even canceled our open mic at the Sheraton, put up a big sign that told everyone to head to Jesters tonight. I called Wendy and she says she's bringing a bunch of sorority sisters. And don't worry; she promised not to get onstage and yell at you again."

"Wow, thanks Simon. I really don't know what to say."

"Then you'd better figure it out, pal. Looks like you're on in about ten minutes."

Oliver glanced at the face of Simon's watch and gulped hard.

"Nervous?"

Oliver shook his head, too nervous to speak.

"I am," Simon said. "And I'm not even going on tonight. But you're gonna kill. I just know it, man."

Oliver finally managed to say, "I'll settle for not *getting* killed out there."

"It's going to be tremendous. Just do your thing." Simon held out his fist for a bump, then decided to wrap Oliver into a loud, manly bear hug. "I'm proud of you, man. We all are."

"Thanks, Simon."

"And didn't I tell you the uniform thing was golden?"

He left Oliver alone with the sweat-stained pages of his notebook and trembling fingers. A few short minutes later, Oliver heard his name on the PA system, followed by enthusiastic applause that actually seemed to swell. He sat there a moment longer, waiting for his nerves to overtake him. But as Jake & John came bounding in through the stage door, he realized he'd grown remarkably calm. He filled his mug to the half-full mark and took the stage.

The applause grew louder as he approached the mic stand. The emcees had done their job well. It was a live crowd. Oliver took the microphone in both hands, paused thoughtfully, and said, "Let us pray."

And he did pray, hard. Twenty-five minutes of comedy feels like a lifetime—or two—especially when you're thinking about a girl instead of your material.

Then he told the crowd about his job at the hotel, about his nose-picking manager, about getting paid to watch a pretty girl work. He did five minutes of material about his mother, how she baptized old people against their will, how she retired from her pretend job as a nurse, how his nonexistent girlfriend had to metaphorically murder him so that his clinically insane mother would acknowledge her only son. He explained the uniform he was wearing and used it to segue into his story about Officer Dan, which he then segued into a bit about finally meeting his panhandling father. And somehow he managed all this without getting choked up.

And then it happened.

As soon as he started talking about Mattie his esophagus cramped up. His throat was a clenched fist and his mind a bowl of Jell-O. He stared at the crowd—*his* crowd, and completely froze. For what felt like a full minute, everything looked blurry. There was no sound, or rather, the room sounded like the inside of a seashell. He felt his jaw, hinging and unhinging, and thought of Barry. Then he spotted Barry in the crowd, elbowing a guy that looked remarkably like Chuck-in-sunglasses and pointing up at the stage. Oliver's roaming, bleary eyes found a few other familiar faces. None of them looked worried for their panicking, choked-up friend. They mostly marveled, laughed harder than necessary, and cheered him on.

Oliver tried to speak again, then simply clipped the microphone onto the stand and climbed down off the front of the stage. He obviously should have exited through the stage door, but it was too late now. He picked his way through the maze of tables, squinting through the tears in his eyes.

Oliver was a few feet from the front door when someone grabbed his shirtsleeve and tugged hard enough to stop him. He expected to see Tony when he turned around, maybe with his fist cocked. But it was a petite blonde girl with big brown eyes. She looked like she'd been crying too as she pulled him close and whispered in his ear, "Go tell her."

Chapter Forty-One

THE STRANGE GIRL'S WORDS were still echoing in his head, along with all the ambient sounds of laughing and talking and clapping. Those same sounds followed him out the door as it closed behind him. Oliver stood on the sidewalk searching for Roscoe's car; he could still hear their muted applause, although he couldn't really tell if he was hearing the lingering appreciation for his set or anticipation for the headliner.

He checked his watch and frowned.

Roscoe's hulking Lincoln Town Car was right where he'd left it. So he fired the ignition and aimed it at the nearest Dunkin' Donuts.

He ordered a pair of blueberry donuts and a large coffee. Then he added a second coffee in case he found Mattie. Before ducking into the men's room, the cashier said, "How do you take your coffee?"

Oliver opened his mouth to add his customary *two creams, one sugar*. Instead, he grinned and said, "Surprise me."

It was his first smile since leaving the club. The guy behind the counter did not return it.

Oliver returned to collect his donuts and coffee and paused to grab a handful of napkins on his way out the door. He tried to sip his coffee, but his taste buds and throat conspired against him. As Oliver finally managed to swallow the sugary sweet mixture in his mouth, his grip tightened on his cup, causing the lid to pop off and hot coffee to tumble over the side and down the front of his uniform. It tasted like cotton candy.

The guy behind the counter grinned back at Oliver. He moved

his toothpick from one side of his mouth to the other and said, "Surprised?"

Oliver sipped the second coffee, which was nearly perfect. He dumped the first one and drove toward Mattie's apartment. From the curb he could see that the lights were on and someone was moving around inside. He considered eating his second donut but decided to save it for Mattie, a confectionary peace offering. After draining his coffee, he climbed out of the car, the wet parts of his idiotic uniform clinging to his skin. It dawned on him then that he'd left his civilian clothes in the dressing room and wondered if he'd ever see them again.

He mustered enough courage to start walking and made his way to Mattie's door. He knocked much louder than necessary. The footsteps approaching on the other side turned his insides into an amusement park—everything loud, raucous, spinning, on the verge of nausea. The peephole darkened, then the doorknob turned, and he realized he should have scripted something to say.

"Oliver?"

"Oh, hey, Betsy." He spied a pile of moving boxes behind her, which sent his stomach down the first hill of the rollercoaster. "I guess I kind of owe you an apology. You know, for not returning your call."

"That's okay. Mattie told me about your little misunderstanding. And frankly, I was more than a little flattered. And I really do need to talk to you about some of the shenanigans going on at Shady Grove. But you seem a little preoccupied at the moment. Guess it'll just have to wait."

"Speaking of Mattie, is she here?"

"Haven't seen her," she said. "Haven't really seen much of her since I moved in here. Starting to think she doesn't like me anymore."

"I know the feeling."

"Oh, no," she said. "That's not your problem with Mattie."

"Please tell me what my problem is then."

"Your problem is that Mattie likes you too much. And for what it's worth, that's her problem too."

"I don't think so."

"Trust me, Oliver. I'm a trained health care professional. Or at least I was."

"I thought you were the receptionist."

"Close enough," she said. "Anyway, I'm also a girl who knows what it's like to fall too hard for a boy."

She held his gaze, but he couldn't quite hold hers. "So, you really think she's falling for me?"

Betsy shrugged. "She's definitely lost her footing."

Oliver thought about this. Then he thought about the moving boxes. Betsy must have followed his gaze and read his thoughts.

"Do you have any idea where she might be?"

"Nope, not really. But I'd check your mother's room."

"You think she's really going to move to New York?"

"I think she's still thinking about it."

"Got any advice?"

"You know that face you're making right now?"

"I guess," Oliver said.

"Just make sure that when you do find Mattie, that you make that same face."

• • •

Shady Grove took up an entire city block. Oliver drove around it several times, sipping coffee and searching for Mattie's getaway car. He considered trying to break in and sneak up to his mother's room, just to be sure. But if he didn't break his leg climbing over the gate, he'd probably get shot trying to break into the facility. He checked the clock on the dashboard and figured he had exactly enough time to check one last place before reporting for duty at the Harrington. He put the car in gear and drove away toward Mattie's parents' house.

Walter Holmgren answered the door. He was wearing striped pajamas and corduroy bedroom slippers. His face looked haggard and sleepy and he smelled of pipe tobacco. When he recognized Oliver he stepped out onto the porch, easing the door closed behind him.

"How are you tonight, Oliver?"

"Good, sir. And you?"

"Lousy, if you want to know the truth. And if you'll pardon me for saying so, you're not looking much better."

Oliver didn't answer.

"So how do we do this?" Walter said, sounding weary and a little frightened.

"I'm sorry? Do what, sir?"

"Are you going to take a swing at me? Yell at me in front of the neighbors? Or just shame me with a quiet lecture?"

"Not sure I understand."

"Well, I assume you're here to exact some form of retribution, to teach me some kind of arcane man-to-man lesson. Not that I don't deserve it; I'm just trying to mentally prepare for whatever's coming."

"Actually, I was just looking for Mattie."

Walter Holmgren seemed to relax a bit. "I'm afraid I haven't seen her in a while. Not since ... you know ..."

"I know."

"I am sorry that you had to see that. That I put you in such an awkward position."

"Is that all you're sorry for?"

"Of course not, Oliver. I'm sorry for, well, everything." He inspected his fingernails, as if they held some sort of answer. "Truth is, I've never been sorrier in my life."

"Sorry is good," Oliver said. "But unless you actually do something about it, it's just a word. And showing it is way better than saying it." Oliver thought of his mother, Roscoe's cancer, and the adorable girl with the little boy's name, the little girl's haircut, and the lopsided smile. "If you put it off though, you might lose your chance to make it right."

"Thank you, Oliver. That is wise counsel indeed. And I think I needed to hear it."

"No offense," Oliver said as he turned to leave. "But I wasn't talking to you."

Searching for Mattie seemed a little pointless, since they were scheduled to work together later that night. In fact, he wanted to keep looking for Mattie. But he had to go to work. And besides, she obviously didn't want to be found, not right now anyway. He aimed

Roscoe's boat of a car toward his mother's house and sped away. Once inside he had a decision to make—either wear his coffee-soaked uniform to work or pull a dirty one out of the hamper. He decided he preferred the smell of stale coffee to day-old sweat. So he stripped down to his skivvies, rinsed the coffee stains, and tossed his uniform in the dryer.

He'd never been late to work before, at least not more than a few minutes. So he wasn't sure what the protocol was. He called the Harrington, but neither of the front desk employees volunteered to hang around until he got there. One had to walk her dog and the other claimed to have a hot date. There was no second shift security guard, so Oliver had no other choice but to call Sherman at ten forty-five on a Friday night.

As he headed for the phone in the kitchen, he noticed Joey sitting at the table with a Monopoly game spread out before him. Oliver dialed information, hoping his boss was out walking his dog. Or on a hot date of his own. He was eventually connected to what he hoped was the correct Douglas Sherman (after accidentally referring to him as "General"), and began preparing excuses.

That's when Joey covered his eyes and whispered in a sing-songy voice, "Ollie's in his undies," then slid one hand down from his eyes to stifle a giggle.

By the time Sherman answered, Oliver was more than a little distracted.

"Oliver?"

"Oh, good evening, Mr. Sherman. How'd you know it was me?"

"Caller ID. Do you know what time it is?"

"Yes, sir. And I hate to call so late, but unfortunately I'm going to be a little tardy tonight."

"I see," he said, but not really like he understood. He sounded suspicious, more so than normal. "I'm not stupid, Mr. Miles."

"Of course you're not. Who thinks that?"

"Apparently, you do. And your little girlfriend."

"My girlfriend?" He knew exactly what Sherman meant; he just liked hearing everyone else say it.

Joey opened his fingers just wide enough to peep through. When he saw Oliver watching him he giggled again and clamped his fingers over his eyes. He rocked gently in his chair and repeated, "Underpants, underpants . . ."

"I just got off the phone with Ms. Holmgren. And it seems she's going to be a 'little late' for work tonight as well. I don't know what the two of you are up to, but I don't like it. And I don't plan to tolerate it much longer."

"I have no idea where Mattie is."

"I do," shouted Joey.

"Please," Sherman continued. "She just told me five minutes ago that you'd be bringing her to work."

"She did?"

"Just get yourself together and get to the hotel. We can sort it all out then."

"You're going to be at work tonight?"

"Do I have any choice? Until I can find suitable replacements, it looks like I'm the new night auditor and security guard."

"If you don't mind my saying so, sir, that sounds a lot like a threat."

"Yes, Mr. Miles. I thought the same thing when I said it."

When Oliver hung up, Joey stood and said, "Hi there, my name is Joey. And Oliver's not wearing any pants."

"I'm sorry, Joey. I'm kind of in a hurry."

Oliver turned to go get ready for work, but Joey put out a restraining arm. Oliver was amazed yet again at just how strong Joey was. "But you didn't get your message yet."

"What message?"

"From Mattie."

"Mattie called? What did she say?"

"That you need to come down to the police station and bail her out."

"She said that?" Under normal circumstances, the idea of Mattie wasting her one phone call on Joey would have struck Oliver as hilarious. But Joey seemed deathly serious. "She said bail her out?"

Joey nodded. "But that's not all she said. It was a long message and I didn't want to forget none of it."

"Okay, good. What else did she say? And take your time."

Joey handed Oliver a *Get Out of Jail Free* card. Only he'd marked out the word *free.*

"She said bail her out? Are you sure?"

"Yes, I already told you." Joey handed over a stack of colorful pretend money. "That's how much it's supposed to cost. I counted it twice."

Oliver counted it twice as well. Then, more to himself than to Joey, he said, "Where am I supposed to get that kind of cash at this hour?"

Joey handed Oliver a plastic apartment building. He'd taken a Sharpie and written M-A-T-Y on it.

"She has bail money in her apartment?"

"Uh huh, that's what she said."

"Did she say *where* in her apartment?"

Joey grinned big, held out his meaty fist, then dramatically turned it over and opened his fingers. On his palm sat the old shoe game piece. He said, "In her closet."

Oliver hugged the big man. "You did a good job, Joey."

Joey rested his head on Oliver's shoulder, then yelled, "Oliver's still in his undies!"

Chapter Forty-Two

THE POLICE STATION was just like the ones on TV—noisy, crowded, hectic. Behind the counter was an air of calm proficiency and order. Everywhere else felt hopeless, heartless, and desperate. It was like a bus station with a lot of cops.

Oliver had never felt more inadequate as he approached the desk and timidly announced he was there to bail his friend out. The female officer was unimpressed. She didn't even look up as she explained the procedure. Apparently, by signing the paperwork, Oliver was accepting responsibility for Mattie showing up for her eventual court date. If she skipped out, that made him financially liable for the rest of her bail. Oliver surrendered his ID, filled out a series of forms, and eventually handed over all but fifteen of Mattie's dollars. Thanks to Joey, the money hadn't been hard to locate. After Betsy let him in, Oliver had found a battered pair of work boots tucked near the back of Mattie's closet. Jammed into the toe he found a Ziploc freezer bag with a giant wad of cash, wrapped in Hello Kitty stationery and emblazoned with the letters *NYC.* He didn't bother counting it, but simply tucked it into his pants pocket, then abused the speed limit all the way to the police station.

Oliver pocketed the receipt and sat in a scarred wooden chair against the wall, ignored a flood of memories, and waited for Mattie to be released into his custody. A decade ago he'd sat in a similar chair in a similar room and fended off similar emotions as he waited for the police to escort his mother from a holding cell to the waiting area. At least back then he had Roscoe to mollify him, to lie and say everything was going to be okay. He didn't believe it then, and he wouldn't believe it now. But it would still be nice to hear.

Not much had really changed since the last time. Oliver found himself surrounded by worried mothers, angry fathers, paranoid friends, indifferent bail bondsmen, and a steady flow of police officers. Everywhere he looked, he saw despair, regret, and disappointment. Saddest of all was the African American lady sitting opposite Oliver. Her outfit appeared to be worth more than his car, especially the leather handbag she kept clutched to her chest. She seemed to alternate between trepidation, dismay, and near hyperventilation before recomposing herself into a kind of forced serenity—then the cycle would repeat. It was too sad to watch. So Oliver nestled into his chair, planted his chin on his fist, and closed his eyes. There was no way he was going to fall asleep. And if there was indeed anything funny to find in the room, he didn't feel like looking for it. So he clamped his eyes tighter and tried to mentally prepare for the Downers benefit gig. But it was no use; he kept thinking of Mattie, occasionally lifting one eyelid to see her when she came out.

That's when he noticed a priest several seats to his left. The white-haired holy man had his chin on his chest and was either sleeping or praying. Oliver shut his own eyes again and tried to tap the priest's open line to heaven. But to his own surprise, Oliver didn't trouble God with a long list of needy requests. He just thanked Him for stuff, Mattie mostly.

He didn't realize he was muttering to himself until he heard her say, "Are you okay, Oliver?"

When he looked up she was sitting in the chair next to him, her purse in her lap and her feet propped up onto her battered, bumper-stickered guitar case. She looked weary, a bit war-torn, scraggly, and more beautiful than he would have imagined.

"So," he said, "how are you?"

"Fine. Embarrassed. A little sleepy."

Oliver nodded, unsure what to say next. So he said the first thing that popped into his head. "You're in pigtails."

She took one in her hand and stared at it like she'd never seen it before. "I suppose I am."

"Fashion statement?" Oliver said.

"More of a silent protest. Aren't you going to ask me how I ended up in jail?"

"I don't think so," he said."

"Well, aren't you curious?"

"Quite a bit, actually."

A plainclothes cop ushered a screeching middle-aged man through the waiting area. The officer paused and chatted with the lady cop behind the desk. The officers laughed at something, ignoring the shrill barks of the prisoner who kept insisting he'd been framed. Mattie made no move to get up, so Oliver didn't either.

"The short version is this. I broke into Barry's condo, snooped around on his computer and through stacks of paper, and ended up hiding behind the couch when Chuck-the-security-camera-guy came in and started playing 'Stairway to Heaven'—on *my* guitar. I recognized the fifth fret buzzing on the B string."

"So you knew about the cameras too?"

Mattie grinned. "I liked to sit in your little closet and watch you make your rounds. " Oliver knew he was gaping but couldn't seem to stop. "I thought it was cute the way you talked to yourself. I always wanted to know what you were saying."

"What were you doing in Barry's condo?"

"Confirming a hunch. Like I told you, he's a snake. Anyway, I was prepared to hide there all night, but the dust behind the couch made me sneeze. So I stood up, told him to freeze, that I was dialing 9-1-1."

"No way."

"Yep, but he tackled me. By the time he snatched my cell phone, the 9-1-1 operator answered and Chuck told them he caught a burglar."

"Did he hurt you?"

"I'm fine. But he'll be icing his groin for a few days."

Oliver realized he was still staring, still slack-jawed, and still unable to stop.

"Well, he kept calling me *Mah-teel-dahhh*. Anyhow, the cops arrived ten minutes later and here we are."

"So," Oliver said, "were you able to confirm your hunch?"

"It's all in here," Mattie said, holding her cell phone aloft. "Believe it or not, Barry is really organized. He has files on everything. And it looks like he might actually be a decent manager for you. If, you know, he wasn't such a creep. But at least he gets it honestly."

"How so?"

"For starters, Barry is not Sherman's nephew."

"They're not related?"

"They're brothers." Mattie paused, letting this sink in as Oliver thought back to Barry's drug-induced trip home from the ER. "Half brothers, actually. General Sherman and his older brothers are from the first wife, which makes Barry the spawn of the trophy wife. When the elder Sherman got sick, the hot young wife took off, and Gladys — the original Mrs. Sherman — moved back in. She's been running things ever since. It seems our boss and your manager have a terminal case of sibling rivalry."

"Guess that explains why General Sherman is so uptight all the time? Having to babysit his young brother while trying to compete with his older brothers and eventually claim his part of the family fortune."

"That's my guess," Mattie said.

"But why all that business about nephews and uncles and such?"

"I don't know. Vanity? Collective psychosis? Your guess is as good as mine."

"And all of this was in Barry's files?"

"Not exactly," Mattie said, breaking her normally relentless eye contact to stare at the tops of her boots. "Most of it was in here."

"What's that?"

"Barry's journal."

"You stole his journal?"

"Not exactly," she said. "It was in my guitar case."

Oliver thought contrition looked good on Mattie. But then he thought *everything* looked good on Mattie. He decided to keep that to himself. "That kind of puts Sherman in a no-win situation."

"Yeah, every time Barry screwed something up or disappeared, their mother blamed Sherman for not being a better role model or something. And once Barry got it into his head that his half brother was trying to oust him from the family business, he launched his own campaign, basically trying to convince his ailing father and stepmother how incompetent General Sherman is."

"So you think he's responsible for the hotel robberies?"

"I'm sure of it," Mattie said. " Apparently he had Chuck do all the dirty work in exchange for free rent and groceries. But other than my guitar and a little creative deduction, I'm not sure I can really prove any of it."

"But your guitar was sitting right there. Didn't the cop see it?"

"Chuck claimed I brought it with me when I broke in. And under the circumstances, he did appear a bit more credible than me. I'm the one with a criminal record, after all."

"I know," he said. "Sherman told me. So why didn't you tell me all this Sherman business before?"

"I didn't know some of it till a few hours ago. Plus, you know, I'd kind of stopped speaking to you."

Mattie was about to say something else, but Oliver interrupted her. "Hey, did Chuck have a black eye when you saw him?"

"It was more yellow than black. Why?"

"Confirming a hunch of my own."

The African American lady was called to the counter where she engaged in an intense but quiet conversation with the officer behind the desk. After a series of sad nods, she hugged her purse and left. This time she didn't even try to compose herself.

"At least you have proof," Oliver said. "Now maybe we can go to Sherman for help."

"We could," Mattie said. "But now it looks like he doesn't trust you anymore either."

"How do you know that?"

"Because he sat me down and said, 'I don't trust him.'" Oliver managed to grin in spite of his bruised feelings. This was the same conversation he'd had with Sherman months ago. Only the pronouns had been changed.

"Did he threaten to fire you?"

"He tried. But then he seemed to remember how hard it was to replace the last girl, so he started backpedaling. But I plan to save him the trouble. After all, he doesn't trust me either. And, as you may have already noticed, I don't hang around where I'm not trusted."

"I did notice that."

"Anyway, I'm sorry if I got you fired. Or, you know, in some kind of legal trouble. Sherman is right; none of this started until I showed up."

"Sounds to me like it all started years ago," Oliver said. "And I really should have quit that job a long time ago. Anyway, I do have a lawyer we can use, if we actually need one."

Mattie's laugh was more bitter than sweet. "I can't afford a lawyer."

"Trust me, you can afford this one. He kind of feels like he owes me."

"We'll see."

"So what do we do now?" Oliver said.

"I was hoping you could give me a lift home."

"What about the hotel?"

Mattie just shook her head. On their way out, Mattie elbowed Oliver in the ribs and said, "Hey, isn't that your girlfriend?"

It took Oliver a second to realize he was staring at the handcuffed version of the transvestite that he'd scuffled with at the Harrington. His pink leotard was natty, stretched tight over his pallid skin. And he needed a shave—arms, legs, beard, even the knobby bulge that bobbed in his throat when he talked.

Oliver said, "Please tell me you see that that's a man?"

Mattie squinted, as if really studying the odd figure, but eventually shrugged, noncommittal. Her grin started on the left side of her face, but never fully bloomed. Still, it was the first time he'd seen Mattie smile in weeks. But it faded almost as quickly as it appeared.

"Okay," she said. "If it makes you feel better."

They rode with the windows down. He asked if Mattie was hungry, but she said she didn't feel like eating. He asked if she wanted to pick her car up from Barry's condo, but she said she didn't feel like driving either. When he finally asked what she *did* feel like doing, she said, "Sleeping. Or crying. Or maybe some of both."

"I know you're tired of hearing it, but I really am sorry, Mattie. About everything."

"I know that, Oliver."

He meant to say something, anything at all to cheer her up, to explain how things were probably not nearly as bleak as Mattie imagined. But then he remembered her police record and her troubled family and the fact that she just blew her New York money on bail.

"I just want you to know that, despite all the evidence to the contrary, I'm really not a thief, Oliver."

"I know that."

The outside air was warm and thick as it tossed Mattie's hair around the edges of her face. Oliver had to concentrate to keep his eyes on the road as she seemed to be staring off at nothing in particular. Then she started speaking again.

"The first time was when I was about ten or eleven. I snuck into Reese's room looking for my calculator, the one he borrowed and never gave back. I ended up finding dirty magazines, bags of pot, stuff he'd stolen from the mall. When I read in Reese's journal that he had a crush on Trish, I started working behind the scenes to get them together, hoping she might give his life a little direction."

Mattie spoke slowly, her voice less deliberate than normal, as if she were discovering the words a split second before saying them. It took real effort for Oliver to keep from interrupting.

"I was just playing around at first. But then the family started to fall apart. The same week I found Dad's love letters from his mistress I found out Mom had breast cancer. She started her chemo and Reese graduated to harder and harder drugs. So I nurtured my own private addiction along with them. I loved the secondhand intimacy of other people's stuff. But things didn't get out of hand until my neighbor asked me to feed her pets and check her mail while she was on vacation. I couldn't help nosing around, looking at photos, reading their mail and letters and business papers. It didn't really feel wrong or sneaky because I wasn't doing it to gain anything. From there, it just sort of escalated. And every time I did it, I swore it would be the last time. But it never was. I think I thought I was connecting with someone. I told myself I was risking for my art, 'cause my snooping almost always resulted in at least one good poem or song."

If Mattie realized that Oliver was taking the longest possible route from the police station to her apartment, she didn't comment. It sounded like she still had things she needed to say.

"And just so you know, I never actually broke into a hotel room.

Not that I wasn't tempted, or that I didn't want to. I just, you know, didn't want to get you in trouble."

"Why are you telling me all this now?"

"Because you need to hear it. You deserve to hear it. And because I might not have another chance."

The longer they rode in silence the more Oliver tortured himself with regrets and thoughts of Mattie moving away. When he couldn't bear it any longer, he said, "So, how'd you learn about picking locks and stuff?"

"The library, the internet, a lot of trial and error. Anyhow, I don't really expect you to get this, not totally. But when I break into places, it's more about fixing things than taking things. Sometimes I fold laundry, take out the garbage, finish unfinished projects, leave little gifts behind that I know will have some kind of meaning. I've even cleaned a toilet or two. Sometimes, I'll get a sense that someone is hurting or sad or needs encouragement and I'll send them an anonymous letter to cheer them up. One time, I even wrote a poem, put it to music, and sent that to a lady who was losing her husband to Alzheimer's. Anyway, it's amazing what you can learn about people when you watch them sleep."

"You sneak in and watch people while they sleep?"

He seemed to know what Mattie was going to say before she said it. "Just like you do with your mom."

And she was right. The most intimate time he'd spent with his mother in recent years had been while she was sleeping. When she was awake, they just frustrated each other.

"I know this will sound strange," Mattie continued, "but the best way to pray for someone is sitting alone in the dark, listening to them breathe. God feels a little closer then, or maybe less distracted. Or maybe it's me. Anyway, I realize this is all very creepy and weird and borderline criminal. But I just wanted you to know that I'm not a thief. And I'm really not crazy. And ..."

"Yes?"

"Please don't read too much into this, but ..."

"But what?"

"But you're really cute when you sleep."

"I … you watched me sleep?" Mattie nodded, somehow managing to look sheepish and adorable at the same time. "So, did you pray for me too? Or just sit and marvel at my slumbering cuteness?"

"Maybe a little of both."

"What did you pray for?"

"Lots of stuff," she said. "But mostly that you'd find some courage."

"Courage for what? Or do I even want to know?"

"To help people."

"Any people in particular?"

"Your mom, your manager, Roscoe. But mostly you and me."

"Maybe I still can?"

"I don't think so, Oliver."

"But why? I mean, I may have entertained a few doubts. I know you're not a thief."

"That's what you tell people when you have a microphone in your hand. And it seems to me that everything else in your act is 100 percent true."

"You've seen my act too? Like, in person?"

"Once, after we first met. I don't have to pick the locks on comedy clubs, Oliver."

"Hey, I thought we had a pact." His attempt to lighten the mood failed miserably. She didn't even smile.

"You're right, by the way, about the truth."

"What about it?"

"It's way funnier than your old material. But you just took it too far. You hurt people," she said. "Including me."

"I know it doesn't change anything, but I swear I only did that bit about your dad once. It just felt wrong."

"It was still one time too many."

He wanted to apologize again. But even he was sick of hearing his lame apologies. And he didn't think she would accept anyway, not now. Instead he said, "So are you going to see my act tonight?"

"I don't think so, Oliver. I appreciate you coming to my rescue and all that. And I'm glad I finally got some of this off my chest. But really, nothing has changed. You still don't trust me."

"That's nonsense. Of course—"

"Stop it, Oliver. I like you much better when you tell the truth."

They were sitting outside her apartment now. Oliver checked his watch and realized the Downers gig was a mere nineteen hours away. He braced himself for the ensuing panic. But it never came. He didn't want to think about it, but he also didn't know what to say or do next, so he sat and watched Mattie. She seemed to be deliberating, then reached into her purse, retrieved a folded sheaf of papers, and handed them to Oliver.

"What's all this?" Oliver paged through the papers, his mind barely registering words like *Shady Grove* and familiar names like *Strahan* and *Miles*.

"Every time I broke into that place it seemed like they were more interested in keeping people out than guarding the actual premises. Your mom kept telling me everyone there was taking the same medication. Then I found these in the bottom of her doctor kit." Mattie handed over a baggie filled with pale blue tablets, then a small opaque bottle with no label. "Then I found some more just like them while nosing around in Strahan's office."

Mattie bit her bottom lip as Oliver scanned the papers in his lap. He couldn't tell if she was proud or embarrassed or scared.

"But what does it actually mean?"

"It means you can finally get your mom out of there."

Oliver still didn't grasp the details, but the gist of it sure sounded good. He wanted to thank Mattie, to hug her, to take her hand and dance a little jig in the street. "It's not all good news, Oliver."

"What? Why?" He was flipping pages now as if he'd missed something obvious.

"Your mother is sick, Oliver. Sicker than you think."

• • •

Oliver watched Mattie until she disappeared. Then he opened the paperwork in his lap until he saw the words "Delores" and "Miles" and "cancer" in the same sentence. Then he put the papers down, put the car in drive, put his mind in park, and drove away.

Chapter Forty-Three

He didn't really want to go to the hotel. But he couldn't think of a good reason not to, at least not one that didn't reek of cowardice. Before looking for Sherman, Oliver made his way to the Business Center cubicle and checked his email. He deleted all the cures for baldness, erectile dysfunction, and credit woes, then scanned a few emails from Barry about upcoming gigs. He nearly deleted the message from Houlihan by accident. As promised, the dope-smoking, witness-protected, government spook from 621 sent pictures. Oliver opened the first one and was not at all surprised to see Chuck sitting on his butt in a familiar hallway, his chubby hand pressed to his recently punched eye and a lollipop stick dangling from his open mouth.

Oliver found Sherman in the security closet, still scouring video footage in search of hotel bandits. He glanced up over the top of his rimless bifocals at Oliver, then back at the screen.

"You're more than a *little* late, Mr. Miles."

"I'm sorry, sir. It was an emergency, one that had to do with hotel security, actually."

Sherman typed a few keys, frowned, then hit the Delete key a few dozen times.

Oliver said, "I'm afraid you're wasting your time, sir. Those tapes are bogus."

"And how do you know that?"

"Educated guess. I've watched them all a dozen times, and I'm convinced it's all the same footage over and over again, probably from the night Chuck allegedly installed the software."

"And you think you can prove this?"

"I'm not sure *I* can prove anything, but I'm fairly certain your brother can. Or is Barry your stepbrother? I can't keep it all straight." Oliver paused to make sure this sunk in. He was tempted to spill everything he'd learned about the dysfunctional Sherman clan. But there was no point telling Sherman what he already knew. And it wouldn't change anything. "So anyway, are you going to fire me now?"

"I haven't decided yet."

"Okay, I'll save you the trouble and just quit then."

"I see." Sherman said. "You're calling my bluff?"

"Not really. I should have done this a long time ago."

"Well, I'll be honest. I hadn't really planned for that contingency. And since I don't really have a backup plan, I'll just come out and say it—I'd really rather you stay."

"How about a deal then?" Oliver said.

"I'm listening."

"I think I can solve your robbery problem." Oliver paused for effect. "Which might go a long way in getting the Memphis Shermans off your back."

"And what do I have to do in return?"

"Make sure Mattie stays out of trouble. A glowing letter of recommendation wouldn't hurt either."

"I'll see what I can do."

"I was thinking more along the lines of a promise."

"And if I don't?"

"I could threaten to blow your cover about planting your own ghost in Room #623?"

Sherman opened his mouth, probably in denial, then thought better of it. "You realize, Mr. Miles, that the ghost mythology is all we really have at the Harrington. We claim to be a four-star property, but Memphis refuses to spend the necessary dollars to make us a bona fide three. When people talk about ghosts, we sell more rooms. It's as simple as that."

"Which is why you harp on your employees to not talk about it?"

"Exactly. The stricter I am about it, the more they talk."

"Makes sense to me."

"Anyway, Mr. Miles. I don't really see where you have any leverage here. Furthermore, I'm not convinced Mattie's not responsible for the recent rash of robberies."

"I am," Oliver said as he unclipped a shiny Rolex from his left wrist and handed it to Sherman.

"What's this?"

"The watch that was stolen from your brother's college roommate. I'll bet my last paycheck the inscription on the band will match his description."

"And where did you find this?"

"I didn't. Mattie did. And she found it in Barry's apartment, along with plenty of other damning evidence."

"The fact still remains, however, that I just don't like her very much."

"Okay, you leave me no choice then. If you can't promise to help keep Mattie out of trouble, then I can't promise I won't post videos on YouTube of you picking your nose."

• • •

It took Oliver more than two hours to find Lindsey's phone number. He left several messages for her at work, but could never find anyone there willing to give up her cell number. In the end, it was Joey that came up with her business card.

It was on the fridge, held aloft by a smiley-face magnet. There was no name with the number, just the word *Reporter.*

Oliver had hung it there after his lunch with her months ago. He'd gotten so used to seeing it hanging there that the sight of it didn't actually register any longer. Either that or he really needed more sleep. She answered on the first ring.

"Oliver Miles? Did you have a change of heart?"

"Sort of," he said. "But I think I did finally find your ghost."

"And you're going to tell me about it?"

"I am. Plus, I think I have another story—a bigger one—you might want to dig into as well."

"Perfect. I'll buy lunch and you can tell me all about it. Flannery's sound good?"

"Sorry, we'll have to do this over the phone. I have a pretty huge gig in a few hours and I still don't have any clue what I'm going to actually say."

"The Downers benefit thing?"

"You know about that?"

"I am the culture editor for the *City*. Anyhow, congratulations. That's big time. But you don't sound very excited."

"I'm sleepy," he said. "And a little terrified."

"Take a nap; you'll do fine. Now tell me what you've got."

Oliver told her everything he could think of about Barry and Chuck and their scheme to make General Sherman look bad with a series of petty robberies. It felt a little creepy to narc on his own manager like that. But he kept telling himself he was doing it for Barry's own good. Oliver realized there were plenty of blanks that needed to be filled in, and that Houlihan's pictures may not actually prove anything, but she was an investigative reporter. It was her job to dig deeper and fill in the missing parts.

"I have to admit, Oliver, a story about robberies is not nearly as interesting as one about ghosts."

"I tend to believe it's the same story. Anyway, his name is Cleve. And I'm pretty sure my boss installed him in Old Man Harrington's room to perpetuate the myth, just in case."

"And you have proof?"

"Nope, I thought I'd let you dig it up yourself. Cleve agreed to meet you at Flannery's at noon today … on one condition."

"What's that?"

"You have to buy. He's recently unemployed."

"Will he go on the record?"

"You'll have to ask him," Oliver said. "But he does like to talk."

"Okay, so what's the other story?"

"Have you ever heard of a retirement community called Shady Grove?"

"Nope."

"The primary doctor there is a guy named Strahan. Back in the eighties he got in some trouble in Kentucky, something about administering experimental drugs. Allegedly, he was on the payroll of some big pharmaceutical company. He got caught doing some 'independent testing'—the kind the FDA really frowns upon. He was never officially charged. But I think he might be up to the same tricks in Nashville."

"And what makes you think that?"

"My mother," he said, absently bending and unbending the corners of the paperwork Mattie had pilfered from Strahan's office. Dr. Strahan had apparently become Delores Miles's legal guardian when she moved from the state facility into Shady Grove. Oliver was still a minor, and his mother not yet married. According to Professor Laramy, Oliver could petition the state for guardianship, but it could take months to sort it all out. The quickest way to get his mother home for good would be to prove that she was indeed legally married to Joey, an idea Oliver still couldn't quite wrap his sleepy mind around. "She tried to tell me, but unfortunately I didn't believe her. She's been a little crazy for the last decade or so."

"I'm sorry about your mom. But so far, I'm not all that stoked about that story either. One is just a couple of petty thieves and some sibling rivalry. The other just sounds like wild speculation. Both of which have the potential to make me look stupid."

"I have a friend, a former employee, who can corroborate a few things. This is a first-rate facility with a long waiting list. But—and here's where it gets a little sketchy—another friend of mine actually broke into the place and dug up some interesting information."

"How interesting?"

"Nearly half the patients admitted in the last ten years have a particular kind of lymphoma. It's very aggressive and the survival rate is normally very low."

"Okay, that is a bit more interesting. And you can get me details on this information your friend acquired?"

"You'll have it tomorrow. Along with a suspicious bottle of pills and a photo of the guy who's been robbing the hotel. I'm not sure it's all admissible in court. But at least you'll know what to look for."

"And your friends will be willing to talk? On the record?"

"Again, you'll have to ask them."

"Fair enough," Lindsey said. "But I do have to ask though—if your mom is there, then she must be getting this treatment too. And just because it may be illegal doesn't mean it won't work. So, by telling me about it, aren't you kinda putting your mom at greater risk?"

"Maybe," he said. "I don't know."

"Then why are you doing this?"

"They should have told me my mother had cancer. I was just hoping the publicity might help get her out of there a little faster. And because I promised I'd get her out of there."

Lindsey said, "I'll do what I can, Oliver."

It didn't sound like much.

Chapter Forty-Four

So maybe Simon was right. Downers had lost most of its legendary cache over the years. Stand-up comedy had gone mainstream, corporate; even had its own cable channel. The mythology of Roscoe Downs remained cultlike, and probably for good reason. In the final analysis, his modest establishment in Nashville would be considered little more than quaint, an interesting exhibit whenever they got around to building an official comedy hall of fame.

All of which made Oliver's ultimate career goal seem rather ordinary. Or at least that's what he thought before he showed up for the gig, before his lifelong ambition started to feel more like a surreal dream.

His first problem was finding a place to park. It seemed half the lot was filled with panel vans emblazoned with big logos, each sporting giant retractable antennae pointing toward the heavens. Oliver parked two blocks away, slung his hanging bag over his shoulder, and was already starting to sweat when he tried to let himself in through the kitchen door in the back alley. But for the first time in twenty years, it was locked. When he made his way to the front door, he was greeted by an athletic blonde with a clipboard. After an embarrassing exchange that included Oliver showing his license to prove that he really was the lone nonfamous comic on her list, she gave him a lanyard with a laminated ID and ushered him inside.

There were camera crews everywhere. And lots of people dressed in black. Oliver found the promoter on stage, squinting into the lights and arguing with someone on his cell phone. He waited for the man to hang up before introducing himself.

"Oliver Miles, glad to finally meet you in person. I see you've got yourself checked in. Here's a copy of the lineup tonight. Looks like you're sandwiched between the Steves."

Oliver nodded, as if he actually knew who "The Steves" were. He assumed it was an improv troupe or a ventriloquist act. Then he scanned the list of comics on the itinerary and realized that he would be performing between Steve *Martin* and Steven *Wright*. He concentrated on not throwing up. The lack of publicity for Roscoe's benefit gig was making more and more sense now. With this kind of star power crammed into this size room, there was no need to advertise.

"You okay, Oliver? You look like you need a nap."

"No, sir, I'm good."

"You sure? I could try and scrounge up a cot."

Oliver did some quick math—he'd been awake for at least thirty-two hours, maybe more. "No, I'm good, thanks."

"I take it you know where the dressing room is?"

Oliver trudged away, wondering how so many bodies with so much talent were going to fit in the eight-by-eight dressing room. Then he opened the door and saw that someone had propped open the other dressing room door, the one that led to the parking lot. He stepped through that doorway, down a few concrete steps, and found himself in what appeared to be a circus tent with dozens of partitions along either side that formed a maze of makeshift dressing rooms. When Oliver found the large sign that said "Miles," he ducked inside his assigned cubicle and sat down. The tiny room was supplied with a folding table, a telephone, a mirror, and enough snacks and drinks to feed a preschool for a month.

Running away was not an option, because Oliver wasn't sure he could actually stand up. Tunneling out might work if the tent hadn't been pitched on a blacktop. The number and intensity of voices increased outside his tiny cubicle, which made Oliver wonder just who might be milling around out there, swapping war stories and catching up on old times. But his breathing had just returned to some semblance of normalcy. And he didn't think it wise to endanger his respiratory system for a little stargazing.

So he tried to distract himself by picking up the schedule and reading from the top. Despite the obvious generation gap—Oliver was the only comic under thirty on the docket—the list still read like a veritable who's who of comedy greatness. Along with the two Steves, it appeared Oliver would be sharing the bill with Robert Klein, Cheech Marin, Richard Belzer, Dennis Miller, Larry Miller, Carol Leifer, Jeff Foxworthy, George Wallace, and David Brenner. By modern standards, these were neither the hippest nor the coolest comics working today, but an intimidating list nonetheless.

It didn't dawn on Oliver that he was only one of a small handful of other local comics on the list until a young guy with a headset simultaneously knocked and stuck his head into the cubicle.

"Hour and twenty minutes to showtime. Need anything?"

Oliver croaked out some kind of response and the guy moved on.

He decided to test his legs. And to his great surprise and delight, they seemed to work fine. Then the effects of gravity manifested in his bladder. Oliver had to pee—really bad and really soon. But he wasn't quite ready to go mingle with a bunch of famous comedians either. He glanced around his cubicle, as if a urinal was going to suddenly appear on the carpeted wall. Then he noticed his hanging bag and grinned.

Two minutes later Oliver emerged in his security guard uniform and strode unnoticed to the men's room. He passed at least three television crews on site—the local NBC affiliate, the Biography Channel, Bravo. And there was plenty of gossip to be overheard along the way as well. Supposedly, there were correspondents from *Rolling Stone*, MTV, and even Comedy Central. He even overheard a credible-sounding rumor floating around that Seinfeld and Cosby had gotten together and videotaped a tribute to Roscoe Downs.

When Oliver finally bellied up to the urinal, he overheard a couple of familiar voices that he couldn't quite place, discussing how nervous they were. Somehow knowing that veteran comics still had to deal with nerves made Oliver feel a little better. But that all ended when he stepped back into his cubicle and found the guy with the headset on.

"There you are. There's been a change of schedule."

Oliver said a silent prayer, prematurely thanking God for answering his former request to get bumped out of the lineup. He even tried to look disappointed.

"Good news, bad news," the guy said. "There's been a couple of last-minute cancellations. So we're adding five minutes to everyone's set."

The guy smiled and clapped Oliver on the shoulder, leaving him to wonder which was the good news and which was the bad.

Alone again, he sat and tried not to panic. He pulled his notes from the bottom of his hanging bag and read through them. His material really was pretty funny. But he wasn't sure he was man enough to pull it off. He folded his arms on the folding table, rested his head on his arms, and tried to pray for his set. But that felt selfish and pointless, so he prayed for Mattie and his mother and Roscoe until he eventually nodded off.

. . .

The dream ended with applause—loud and bountiful and lingering applause. He'd been doing his act on the stage at Downers and the crowd had adored him. But of course in the elastic reality of dreams, the crowd numbered into the thousands, maybe even tens of thousands. As far as he could recall, the audience consisted of only his mother, Roscoe, and Mattie. Yet, there were hundreds of variations of each of them, all different ages and sizes and all dressed in different outfits.

It was the knocking that finally woke him all the way up, sweeping away the last few delightfully dreamy tendrils.

The guy with the headset held up a handful of fingers and simply said, "You're on in five minutes." He paused on his way out the door and said, "Unless it's part of your act, better wipe that drool off your chin."

Moments later he heard a distantly familiar voice introducing him to a raucous crowd. The master of ceremonies was Tim Something, or maybe Tom? Either way, Oliver recognized his voice from the commercials for *Dancing with the Stars*.

When Oliver took the stage he didn't see a single version of his mother. No Mattie either. Although he didn't see Barry, he assumed he was there somewhere. Joey was leaning against a pinball machine, introducing himself to everyone that passed. Roscoe sat in his customary seat near the back. Oliver's old friend beamed at him, offered him a thumbs-up, then clapped his encouragement along with everyone else in the room.

If Mattie was right, if the truth really was funnier than fabricated premises and contrived punch lines, then he hoped the crowd on hand tonight had the refined comedic sensibilities to find the funny in abject terror.

Oliver stared at the microphone. This is what he'd always wanted. And if he allowed a little stage fright to derail it, he'd never forgive himself. So he feigned enough confidence to walk across the stage, snatch the microphone off the stand, and say, "Let us pray."

He thought he heard Simon laugh the loudest. Or maybe it was Barry.

"Dear God, you know I usually ask you to help me be funny. Well, tonight I'm kind of begging." Oliver heard a smattering of chuckles metastasize into full-blown laughs. "Actually, I'd settle for you not letting me die up here. But if my heart does finally give out up here, please make *that* funny."

His prayer was as earnest as ever, and twice as sincere. He just hoped it would help. He closed his eyes again and added, "Oh, and it would be really cool if you'd heal Roscoe ... and my mom too."

Someone in the back shouted *Amen*, which by itself wasn't that funny. But since it was Roscoe, everyone laughed.

When Oliver finally opened his eyes, he tried to ignore the cameras and focus on the friendlier faces in the crowd. He took a sip of water, careful to leave it closer to half-full than the alternative. Then, he did his set.

It took a minute or two to calm down enough to get the shakes out of his voice. Of course, the laughter helped. He navigated his way through his now familiar material, most of it self-deprecating, all of it true. He'd worked up a few friendly barbs about Roscoe's smelly old car and his burger platters that went over much better than he expected. In fact, there was a gaggle of famous comedians in the back who actually elbowed each other and pointed at the stage.

Oliver wasn't killing, but he was performing respectable stand-up comedy at Downers and garnering genuine laughter from the most intimidating crowd he might ever face.

The problem came when he hit the fifteen-minute mark. That's when he ran out of material. He'd already worked up to his climactic series of jokes about the adorable kleptomaniac at the hotel. As his set began to fizzle, he realized he was searching the crowd—rather frantically—for any sign of Mattie.

When his final joke ended, what Oliver should have done was launch into an enthusiastic, *Thank you … You guys have been great … And let's give it up one more time for this awesome lineup of talent tonight … and one more round for our esteemed host, Roscoe Downs …* What he did instead was glance toward the dressing room and wish in vain for the emcee—either Tim or Tom—to magically appear and take over.

It grew quiet. And the longer he stood there staring, the harder it was to breathe.

Finally, he turned to the crowd and said, "Thanks, you guys are a great crowd. And I hope you'll indulge me for a minute or two. I have some unfinished business I need to tend to. There was a smattering of tentative laughter. First, an admission. I only prepared fifteen minutes of material. I thought when they told me to do twenty, I could fake my way through it … just talk slower or something. But that obviously didn't work."

This time he was sure it was Simon he heard laughing. He followed the sound and said, "Thanks, Simon." Then he used his hand to shield his eyes and said, "By the way, I'm looking for my manager. Anybody here seen Barry?"

There was some rustling near the back until Barry stood up and offered sheepish waves at everyone and no one at the same time.

"Barry, you've done a really nice job for me, better than I expected. So, thank you for that." The silence from the crowd thickened. But you could never tell with comedians. Maybe this was part of the act? Oliver then cleared his throat and said, "But you're fired."

It didn't break the room up, but it was funny enough to embolden Oliver. He began scanning the crowd again. "What about Mattie? Are you here?"

There was no response, no rustling, no nothing.

"Well, maybe you'll see this on TV or YouTube or something. What I wanted to say is, 'I'm sorry.' I know I say that a lot, and it's always been true. But I don't think I've been sorry for the right stuff. I should have been a better friend. And I promise I will be from now on. No matter what ..."

The crowd had gone restless again. Oliver was being sincere, but not funny. And they were there to see a show, not a confessional.

"Anyway, I just wanted to say ..." Oliver kept moving his mouth but no sound was coming out. For a moment he thought Roscoe had killed his microphone, which would preserve his perfect record of never completing a set at Downers. But then he realized the technical difficulties were with his own windpipe. "Sorry, I promised myself I wasn't going to do this ..."

His last few words were garbled by the familiar, but inconvenient, lump in his throat. And the tears sprang quickly and started trailing down his cheeks.

At least they were laughing again. Not hard, but it was enough.

"I should have told you this a long time ago. But I'm pretty sure I love you. And I really wish you wouldn't move away."

There was a smattering of applause, followed by more contagious laughter. Then a familiar voice yelled, "I love you too!" That's when the room really did break up.

It was Roscoe again, giving Oliver a one-man standing ovation.

Oliver paused to savor the moment. Then he wiped his eyes, waved at his crowd, and left.

. . .

Backstage, Oliver humbly received a handful of pats on the back from guys he idolized as a kid. Robert Klein said, "Nice work up there." Then, in his thick Bostonian monotone, Steven Wright offered a "Good set, kid."

Oliver stepped into his cubicle and was prepared to collapse in his chair and just sit there for a very long time.

But Barry was there, grinning like an idiot.

"Did I tell you? Or did I tell you? That was one tough crowd. And although you didn't kill 'em, you did make them laugh."

"Thanks, Barry."

"Cheer up, man. It was a shaky start, but the next ten minutes were solid. And that's all that matters. Although I must say, that end part fizzled out a little. And that bit about firing me wasn't really funny at all."

"It wasn't supposed to be."

"What? You telling me you were serious?"

"You and Chuck robbed innocent people at the hotel. And you let Sherman think it was Mattie."

"You're right, Oliver. You're right. And I do feel bad about it. Tell you what, I promise I'll apologize to Mattie, come clean with General Sherman. I'll even get Chuck to call the cops tomorrow and drop the charges, tell them it was a big misunderstanding. I mean, it's not like she actually stole anything. In the meantime, we need to get busy launching your career into comedy space."

"I don't think so, Barry. I need to figure out what's going on with my mom. And with Mattie."

"Why can't you do that and be funny at the same time?"

"I plan to."

"Without my help?"

"At least until we get our respective acts together."

"So, what?" Barry said. "You think you're my conscience now?"

"I'm trying to be your friend."

"Well, I don't think you're doing it right."

"You're probably right," Oliver said. "But it's kind of a learn-on-the-job thing."

"You're serious, aren't you?"

"Afraid so," Oliver said. "Now if you'll excuse me, I need to go find Mattie."

Barry looked at Oliver for a long time, then finally said, "She's already gone."

"What?" Oliver said. "You mean Mattie was here?"

"She sat in the back, in a pair of sunglasses and a bright green baseball cap."

• • •

Oliver didn't bother to change out of his stupid uniform. Instead he bolted for the back of the tent, feeling like the dopiest star of the world's most predictable romantic comedy. But the gig's promoter intercepted him before he made it out of the giant tent.

"Hey, Oliver, just wanted to thank you for doing the gig. It really meant a lot to Roscoe, I can tell."

The fact that he didn't mention Oliver's performance was not lost on him. "I appreciate the opportunity. And I'm sorry I sort of fell apart at the end there."

The promoter shrugged, and Oliver wished again he could remember the man's name. "Just thought it was part of the act. I didn't really get it, but it got some laughs. And everything up to that point was good stuff."

"Really?" Oliver said, a little too quickly. "You liked it?"

"Don't sound so surprised. Anyway, Roscoe sent me to get you. He's reserved a spot at the table and wants you to watch the rest of the show with him. As his guest of honor."

Oliver was flattered. He was also tempted, confused, and conflicted. Finally he said, "Tell him I'm really sorry. But I have something I just have to take care of. Like now."

"Are you sure? I mean, no offense kid, but Roscoe really had to lobby hard to get you in the lineup tonight. Seems like the least you could do is go out and sit with him."

"Roscoe got me this gig? I thought this whole thing was some big surprise."

"You're kidding, right?" he said. "No, I guess you're not. Let me put it this way. At the very first preproduction meeting, Roscoe told us to add your name to the bill. We reminded him that the point was to honor him with really famous comedians that he'd helped along the way, that it was going to be filmed by at least two networks. He pretty much said if Oliver Miles wasn't in the lineup, there was not going to be a show. And he meant it."

"Did he say why?"

"Yeah, he was pretty adamant. He seems to think that you're the funniest comic on the list."

Then the promoter shook his head, ambled out the door, and lit a cigarette.

Chapter Forty-Five

IF OLIVER'S CALCULATIONS WERE CORRECT—and he highly doubted they were—then Mattie had left the club fifteen minutes before he burst onto the street looking for her. So he was more than a little surprised to see her Honda idling by the curb across the street. He hadn't taken more than two steps in her direction when Mattie put the car in gear and pulled away. Oliver would have sworn they shared an instant of meaningful eye contact in the tiny sideview mirror.

He sprinted the full two blocks to Roscoe's car and managed to catch up with her at a four-way stop. She turned left at the traffic light, toward Vanderbilt and away from I–65. The light was red when Oliver got to the intersection. So he applied his left blinker and craned his neck forward to try and keep an eye on her taillights.

When the light turned green, Oliver nearly flattened a pedestrian and his yapping Pomeranian. He waved his apology, then sped off in the direction Mattie had gone. He thought he saw her crossing 21st and heading toward West End, but he couldn't be sure. As he idled away at yet another red light, he thought he saw Mattie's car slowing down. Then as he got closer, she sped away again.

Did she want him to follow her?

He hoped so. But if she was heading all the way to New York City tonight, he was going to need gas pretty soon.

By the time Oliver closed the gap to a few car lengths, he thought he knew where she was going. They were less than a mile from Shady Grove. Still, Mattie took the most circuitous route to get there.

Nearly ten minutes later she eased to the curb by the back gate. She was already working on the lock when Oliver got out. When he entered the courtyard, Mattie was sitting on the wrought iron park bench, her face illuminated by the moon and a few distant street lamps. She was using the index finger on her left hand to stir the water of a nearby birdbath.

Oliver sat by her on the bench. Then, without turning, she said, "I'm still really mad at you."

"Can I ask why?"

"That whole *falling in love* business," she said. "Didn't I tell you not to do that?"

"I don't think so. I mean, I don't remember if you did."

"Maybe I was talking to myself. Anyway, the fact you're *in* love with me—or think you are—isn't what bothers me."

"Can I ask what does bother you then?"

"Yes, but only if you quit asking permission to ask things."

"Sorry."

"And stop apologizing so much." Oliver thought he saw the merest hint of a grin. Then she said, "What really bothers me is that you said it to a whole roomful of people before you said it to me."

Oliver considered his answer, wanting to make sure it was both accurate and true. He turned on the bench until he was facing Mattie. Then to her profile he said, "But I was saying it to you. I'm saying it to you now, in fact. That big crowd just happened to be there."

"Well ..." she said. "You haven't actually said it directly to me yet."

"I thought you didn't want to hear it."

"I don't," Mattie said. "But maybe you should tell me anyway."

"Okay, here goes ..." The lump had crawled back into Oliver's throat. But his voice came out strong, and much louder than he'd intended. "I love you, Mattie Holmgren."

She released a long, pent-up breath, as if she'd been holding it for months. A smile appeared, then faded before realizing its full potential. Under the circumstances, Oliver could live with a half smile.

She stirred the birdbath some more and finally said, "So you knew I was there?"

"I was hoping a lot."

"Your mother was right, you know."

"About what?"

"You really were born to be funny."

"That's not *exactly* what she said."

Mattie shrugged. "It's exactly what she said to me."

Still facing forward, Mattie scooted a bit closer to Oliver. She leaned into him, then seemed to melt, resting her head on his shoulder. She even pulled his arm down off the back of the bench, allowing it to drape over her shoulder. She laced her fingers between his and said, "What did you think of my disguise?"

"Very convincing. I never really pictured you in a John Deere cap before."

"My dad was a big fan," Mattie said as she nestled into him and sighed, her fingers gripping his a little tighter, then relaxing again. He rested his chin on the top of her head, trying to memorize the smell of her hair, the feel of her body pressed willingly into his, the way her hand molded perfectly into his. They sat quietly for a long time. Oliver thought he could sit there forever. Without thinking about it, he gently kissed the top of her forehead.

"I felt that," she said.

He couldn't see it, but that time he was certain she finished her smile. They sat, mostly motionless, for a few minutes longer. Then Mattie began to grow restless. She sat up then, facing Oliver, staring at him hard.

Finally he said, "Aren't we going upstairs?"

"I've already said my goodbyes."

"So that's it then? You're really leaving?"

He already knew the answer. But then Mattie blinked and a tear sprang free and bobbed down her cheek.

"What about the band?"

"Reese quit."

"You're kidding."

"He *said* he was tired of all the bickering, that he needed to think about becoming a father and providing for his family. But he told me last night he was checking himself into rehab. He may actually be growing up."

"I should do that," Oliver said.

"Check into rehab?"

"Grow up," he said. "So where will you stay? New York City is expensive. And probably dangerous too."

"My dad is taking over my lease and moving into my apartment, at least until things settle down between him and Mom. And he loaned me enough money for the plane ticket and to pay the first few months' rent. I'm sure it's just his conscience overreacting. And one day I'll probably feel bad about it. Anyhow, Betsy has a cousin that lives up there. He's a dancer on Broadway."

"And you're just going to move in with some guy you don't know?

Mattie actually giggled. "Are you jealous?"

"Yes, very much."

"I have to admit," she said, "I kind of like you jealous."

"If you stay, I promise I'll be insanely jealous of every guy in Nashville and half the guys on TV."

"I'm sorry, Oliver. This is just something I have to do. I don't want to look back and wonder what might have been. Besides, I've heard they have a couple of comedy clubs in New York."

When Oliver didn't respond, she said, "What are you thinking, Oliver?"

"You moved on too fast. I'm still stuck in jealousy."

She laughed at him again and said, "He's not just some guy, Oliver. He's married. To an actual woman. They have a spare bedroom that they plan to rent to Betsy and me until we can get on our feet."

"Okay, so Betsy's going too? That makes me feel a little bit better, but not much. What happened to her fiancé?"

"I think she thinks he was in cahoots with Strahan. Anyhow, speaking of Betsy, we have a plane to catch. So I'm afraid I need to get going, Oliver. And you need to go see your mother."

"How am I supposed to do that if you won't help me?"

Mattie put her hand in his. When she opened her fingers, there was a pair of mismatched keys. "Betsy had a spare made before she left. It opens the kitchen door out back." She motioned toward the gate and added, "So you'll either have to learn to pick locks or jump the fence."

"What's the other one for?"

"It belongs to Ida." It took Oliver a moment to conjure the sweet widower with moldy mints. "She might need your help someday. Besides, I didn't want you wondering whether I'd be tempted to sneak in and watch her sleep."

Oliver nodded his thanks, then Mattie stood. It took more willpower than he thought he possessed to stand and face her. "So this is really it then?"

"For now, yeah." Then Mattie leveled her most penetrating stare and said, "You do realize, that if this was a movie, this would be the part where you'd be trying to figure out whether to kiss me or not."

"Well, I was wondering ..."

"Please don't, Oliver."

"Don't wonder, or don't kiss you?"

"Wonder."

And so he didn't. And he would never have to wonder again what it was like to kiss Mattie Holmgren.

With foreheads still touching, he said, "Man, I hope I get to do that again sometime."

"Me too." Then she said, "Here."

She handed him a folded piece of notebook paper. Across the top of the page, she'd written in bold letters: *Rain Check—redeemable for dinner, pretty much any time, any place.*

Then she said, "So long, Oliver."

He watched her turn and walk a few steps. Then she started to run. She slammed the gate behind her and pulled away so fast her tires actually squealed on the pavement. Oliver didn't move. He stood, watching and waiting to see if she would circle the block.

She didn't.

He said, "See you soon, Mattie."

• • •

Oliver looked at the key in his hand, then looked at the back door. He put the key in his pocket, locked the rusty gate behind him, and walked around to the front entrance. He banged on the glass until the security guard appeared. The guy blinked at Oliver, then reached for his keys and opened the door.

"Are you here to relieve me?" the security guard said.

Oliver glanced down at his own uniform and understood the confused look on the other man's face. "No, sorry. I'm here to see my mother."

"She a nurse?"

"Sort of, yeah."

"What floor?"

"Three," Oliver said. This was going to be much easier than he thought. The sleepy guard escorted Oliver to the security door and unlocked it. Oliver paused on the threshold, thinking. He wasn't sure if it was professional courtesy, a guilty conscience, or simply the fact that he was done with selective truths. He looked the security guard in the eye and said, "Look, my mother is a patient. Her name is Delores Miles and she's in Room 349. And to be honest, I was considering trying to sneak in here after hours to see her. It's totally against Shady Grove policy. And I really don't want to get you in trouble. But no matter what you say, I plan on heading upstairs."

The guard listened to Oliver's confession, then shrugged and said, "If you're looking for your girlfriend, she already left."

"I know," Oliver said. He didn't feel like correcting him. Mainly because he didn't feel like admitting that, despite what everyone else seemed to think, Mattie was still not his girlfriend.

"I caught her in your mother's room once. She's nice, real pretty. I didn't have the heart to break up their little party. Plus, she made my wife a really nice shawl."

"How did your wife like the shawl?"

"She smiled, real polite, and said it was nice. But then I heard her tell my sister later that it was hideous."

His mother was asleep when he found her. His tape recorder was on the nightstand, along with wads of balled-up tissues and *A Prayer for Owen Meany*, bookmarked near the end.

Supposedly, Daniel Laramy had already filed the paperwork to make Joey his mother's legal guardian. In return, Oliver promised to actually enroll in a few classes the following semester. And the good professor kept assuring him that there was no legal reason he couldn't bring his mother home soon. Oliver tried not to get his hopes up.

He sat in her only chair, propped his feet on the edge of the bed, and watched his mother sleep. Then he told her everything. He told her about Mattie, about the gig at Downers, and about how he was going to get her out of there soon. He told her they would live in her house together, where she belonged, just like old times (except for Joey). He told her she would get well. He told her he was eventually going to let Barry book a few gigs in New York City, that he was going to take her with him, that they were going to visit Mattie and he would eventually convince her to love him back.

He only believed about half of everything he said, but it felt good to tell her anyway. She was his mother, after all.

When he was finished telling her things, he covered her feet with the ugly shawl that Mattie had made for her. He stood quietly, used tap water to fill her glass to the half-full mark, and placed it on her nightstand. Then he sat back down, took one of his mother's hands, and said, "Let us pray ..."

He told God all the things he just told his mother until he fell into a deep, dream-filled sleep.

Acknowledgments

IT'S TIME ONCE AGAIN to offer some heartfelt thank yous. So here goes ...

Alicia ... my very best friend and the love of my life (not to mention an amazing editor and the prettiest girl in the whole wide world.)

Aubrey, Jesse, Luke, and Isaac ... still the best kids ever.

Andy Meisenheimer ... for believing in me, taking a chance on my stories, for making me a much better writer ... but mostly for being my friend.

Steve Parolini ... for helping make this a much better book.

Becky Philpott ... for your time, your attention to detail, and for always going the extra mile-and-a-half to make my stories the best they can be.

Alicia Mey & Curt Diepenhorst ... for my best cover yet.

Steve Laube ... for doing all the hard parts with copious amounts of grace and professionalism.

Keith Alberstadt and Chad Riden ... for the valuable insights into the world of comedy. Just don't blame those guys for the stuff I invented or simply got wrong.

And finally, but certainly not least ... any reader out there—past, present, or future—who has chosen to spend a few precious moments with my characters ... you guys rock!

My Name Is Russell Fink

Michael Snyder

Russell Fink is twenty-six years old and determined to salvage a job he hates so he can finally move out of his parents' house for good. He's convinced he gave his twin sister cancer when they were nine years old. And his crazy fiancée refuses to accept the fact that their engagement really is over.

Then Sonny, his allegedly clairvoyant basset hound, is found murdered.

The ensuing amateur investigation forces Russell to confront several things at once—the enormity of his family's dysfunction, the guy stalking his family, and his long-buried feelings for a most peculiar love interest.

At its heart, *My Name Is Russell Fink* is a comedy, with sharp dialogue, characters steeped in authenticity, romance, suspense, and fresh humor. With a postmodern style similar to Nick Hornby and Douglas Coupland, the author explores reconciliation, forgiveness, and faith in the midst of tragedy. No amount of neurosis or dysfunction can derail God's redemptive purposes.

Return Policy

Michael Snyder

In his second book, novelist Michael Snyder introduces us to three very unusual and distinct voices all torn by tragedy:

Willy Finneran, washed-up genre novelist with an espresso maker that just won't die and a habit of avoiding conflict even if it means putting the truth on a sliding scale.

Ozena Webb, single mother and Javatek's top customer service representative. She spends every evening playing board games with her twelve-year-old son who is mentally crippled from an early childhood accident.

Shaq, a small and scraggy homeless man with trauma-induced blank spots on his memory, trying to piece together the story of his life while assisting Father Joe at the Mercy Mission.

As their stories intersect, the narrative vacillates between hope and naïveté, comic relief and postmodern ennui. Startling in its authenticity, this unforgettable novel reveals that no matter how far one has strayed from hope, there is always a way to return.

Available in stores and online!

Share Your Thoughts

With the Author: Your comments will be forwarded to the author when you send them to *zauthor@zondervan.com*.

With Zondervan: Submit your review of this book by writing to *zreview@zondervan.com*.

Free Online Resources at www.zondervan.com

Zondervan AuthorTracker: Be notified whenever your favorite authors publish new books, go on tour, or post an update about what's happening in their lives at www.zondervan.com/authortracker.

Daily Bible Verses and Devotions: Enrich your life with daily Bible verses or devotions that help you start every morning focused on God. Visit www.zondervan.com/newsletters.

Free Email Publications: Sign up for newsletters on Christian living, academic resources, church ministry, fiction, children's resources, and more. Visit www.zondervan.com/newsletters.

Zondervan Bible Search: Find and compare Bible passages in a variety of translations at www.zondervanbiblesearch.com.

Other Benefits: Register to receive online benefits like coupons and special offers, or to participate in research.